A NEST OF SERPENTS

by

KATE CHRISTOPHER

LONDON
VICTOR GOLLANCZ LTD
1977

ISBN 0 575 02330 9

MADE AND PRINTED IN GREAT BRITAIN BY
THE GARDEN CITY PRESS LIMITED
LETCHWORTH, HERTFORDSHIRE
SG6 1JS

CONTENTS

ACKNOWLEDGEMENTS

This book leans very heavily on *The Murder of Sir Thomas Overbury* by William McElwee (Faber, London, 1952). Although I did not find it until too late, another modern source is *Cast of Ravens* by Beatrice White (Murray, London, 1965). Despite being half fiction and half fact, *The Overbury Mystery* by Judge Parry (Fisher Unwin, London, 1925) is quite interesting; and William Roughead's essay, "The Fatal Countess" (W. Green, 1924) condenses the plot. The starting point for me was a copy of *The Life and Reign of King James* by Arthur Wilson, published in 1653, which is in the Pepys Library, Magdalen College, Cambridge.

PREFACE

1606

S H E W A S A little girl; imprisoned by her white dress sewn with gold and padded at the breasts to make her appear a lady. Her mouth had been painted red and her face was white, so carefully delineated she could have been a queen in a card game. In the looking glass she was smokey, diffused, her apprehension misting her eyesight. "So young, so young," said the countess but with triumph.

Her daughter's marriage was by special favour of the new king who sat in a red velvet chair at the wedding and wept loudly, snorting into the shoulder of a pretty young page at the sight of two great families in his kingdom so determinedly bound together. He had approached the girl's father: "I would like to ... No. We will arrange," in time James had corrected himself, he was cautious of these English nobles, who were so tremendously shadowed by their own history, and a little scathing of the Scots king who spoke indifferent English. He had accustomed himself to penury in the past, and now, in the rich harbour of the English court, James was so overwhelmed by the wealth and splendour of his position, that he was like a small boy with sweets, picking first one, then another, eyes big with greed. What was his own past but that of superior servants? Stewarts, stewards indeed! The Howards considered their king an upstart, and let him understand that when the Howard child was married off to the Devereux boy. While James gabbled and sozzled and fondled his young men they had stood at the back of the hall, sombre faced, a little aghast at their king and his ramshackle court, so different from that of Elizabeth.

The boy was an orphan, his father was dead, topped by the old queen; was not James's eagerness to find him a good match paying off her ghost as well as furthering his own desires? "I mun ha' peace," he said. "Good fellowship amang all o' ye," and the august English nobility had slipped glances at each other in council. So she was married to please the king's whim for friendship among the great families. It was in winter, soon after Twelfth night, so that the same cake did for both celebrations. It was the only economy. The king had herons' feathers brought for the heads of the court ladies. A poet wrote a dull masque full of allegories, and Mr Jones, a Welshman, designed machinery for moving scenes when Reason despatched the figures of Perverse Affections. The men wore red and the ladies were in white so that the dancing figures looked like a flag to salute the children when they performed together. They would be put together in a great bed while the court watched them, whispering bawdily behind their hands, and then they would be removed again, having made a token of good faith for the future, each to a further education. The boy would go abroad, and for Frances Howard perhaps a place found at court, attending the queen or the princess until her young husband's return.

James sighed pleasurably and settled for a little sleep, none would notice that he had taken too much sweet wine, and he did not dance himself, his weak legs gave him enough excuse to sit and watch, and applaud those who could preen and prance about the floor. He beckoned to his boy and had another cup brought to him. What pleasure would he have in kingship if he could not do as he pleased?

PART ONE

Tom and Robin: 1607–1613

I

B ECAUSE IT WAS so warm Tom had stripped to his shirt
and sprawled on his chair, occasionally lifting one buttock or
another as the prickly heat of his velvet breeches crept through
to his skin. It was March, and Tom Overbury had hustled into
his newest warm clothes, but by midday the young men of Mr
Secretary's office were sending out for beer and pickled onions
and mopping sweat from their necks. And then they had lingered
out of the door except for Tom, even those who were avaricious
for advancement had made excuses and left for the bowling alley,
not to pitch balls but to relish green gloomy aisles of trees down
by the Thames where they could saunter in a lapping breeze which
had replaced the gusts of morning. They had all crept away on
some pretext or another and left Tom Overbury, smug as a fat
whore's cat, to sit out the noonday sun in a stuffy office overfed
with velvet hangings, Turkey carpets and the ripe smell of
Monday's pork and beans.

He sat there in case he were called for; he tilted paper-knives
and gouged them into an upholstered stool, he yawned and rustled
papers, added and subtracted accounts, picked his nose with a
quill, then discarded the same quill with disgust and cut a new one,
pulled wax from his ears, smelt Hungary water inside his wrists,
tried a new hair-style, peering into the back of the pewter plate
to see a clouded reflection, and all on the off-chance that little
Lord Salisbury might poke his head through the door, see him
working there, and decide that Overbury was slaving for the
good of England. And so I am, thought Tom, nodding like a man
of 40. He lifted one leg and laid it over the other, which was not
easy in padded hose, his codpiece, God rot it, fanned out triumphantly, its embroidery of white feathers leering up at him from
under the table. From the waist down Tom Overbury was re-
splendent, but his shirt, although clean on yesterday, smelt of
sweat. He stretched, expanding his waist muscles languorously, and
walked over to the cupboard where ink, spare pens and clean
paper were stored. On the back shelf was another flask of toilet
water—God, he got through so much!—which he splashed about

his body like a man taking a bath, slapping luxuriously as the cold sour smell flicked over his hot skin. Hush—a tap—hush—a knock—and the door had opened before he could withdraw his hand from within his shirt—a page, grinning with delight, certain that proud Tom Overbury, who would never be seen ruffled or uncurled, had been searching for lice under his linen in the secrecy of the room used by gentlemen of his majesty's foreign service. The boy had gone, slamming the door before Tom could shout at him. He heard the droning flies battering at the closed window, and far off, the sound of traffic, that perpetual rumble of wheels on woodblocks or cobbles. Tom almost left. He would have done in three minutes, he gave himself about that time, pacing out the pause by walking up and down the small dark room——

The door exploded like a little mortar, slammed back on its own hinges and then clashed to again, then re-opened and there was a young man as bright, buzzing and golden as a bee, laughing and slapping at Tom's arms and turning him round and round and all the while pelting out ridiculous expressions of delight which, for all that Tom had tried to learn the Scots accent so necessary in King Jamie's court, made no sense to him at all. Reeling under the assault, he hesitated then sat down at the table, the date of his recently completed letter glaring up at him, "Twenty third day of March 1607".

"Hold on," he said.

The golden gadfly sat down too, and hooted at Tom, then composed his face and his voice, to produce decent English. His precise tutored accent said, "Why for 'Hold on' Tom Overbury? Do you not recognize me?"

"A Scot, I presume?"

"Of course, man."

"There are so many about the palace," ventured Tom consideringly, for the youth was so well dressed that he may be worth a touch of flattery, "And so friendly withall."

"Do you not remember Robbie Carr?"

Robin Carr. Who else? That pretty boy who had been visiting with the Bruce family six years before and who had made eternal friendship with Tom, he had been turned topsey turvy by Tom's elegant English manners, never seen so far north of the Border; they had hunted together, they had read dirty stories by candlelight, and they had plotted great futures for each other. Young Robin had botched his hopes while still a schoolboy, by reading

16

a Latin grace to the king so badly that pedantic James had risen up at the royal table and ordered the lad from court, and Robin, ears flaming, heart sinking, had gone to the country, to become a Scots farmer.

"What are you doing in London, Robin? And so well set up too?"

The boy was like a torch, now flaring, now smouldering but all the time lively, his eyes were chestnut, his hair that golden auburn most appreciated about the court where red-haired Scotsmen thronged round the king like a hundred marigolds in one border. His mouth was still a boy's: petulant and small but showing remarkable white teeth. Robert Carr whirled and jigged to show off his red-heeled shoes, his white-stockinged legs and his puffed-out hose, striped like a rose. He must be 21, and he was glorious.

"You did well after all," said Tom almost enviously.

"It's all borrowed," cried Carr, "from James Hay. Who else?"

Who else indeed? Hay had been the king's best-kept minion, a beautiful youth, who, as his charms had languished, learned that promoting favourites was a better game than pleasing the king himself.

"So you're to take young Philip Herbert's place, he is Jamie's jessie now."

"That lout. Hay cannot understand why the king has kept him so long."

Herbert was not a success; he had, as they said, shot his bolt. There had been speculation about his successor, and the odds were on a Scot with red hair but gossip had prophesied a lad of around sixteen, for rough cheeks annoyed the king.

"So you are to be it," said Tom.

"We hope so," agreed Robin.

Tom pulled out his silver jug and horn cups and offered Robin a pull at Rhenish. They drank silently. Robin glanced into the cup and then at Tom; he walked about, he played with a pearl ear-ring.

"What do you think?" he asked.

"You fit the mould. Scots, a shade old perhaps, can you sustain it?"

He meant: how would Robin bear it when alone with Jamie, a slobber-chopped man, his shuffling gait spilling him over by-standers, his tongue lolling and retreating as he spoke? Could

17

Robin allow intimacies of wine-stinking breath and groping hands, and the final indignity of that royal bed?

"I can sustain it with help," agreed Robin. "I'm not bright as you well know, but they say the king enjoys teaching. He should have been a schoolmaster, eh? I'll be an apt pupil."

"There's more to being a minion than parsing Latin."

"That? That doesna' worrit me," but the lapse into tough Lowland Scots suggested some disquiet. "Youse a scholar, Tom. Wud ye' gi' me a wee bit help?"

"If I can."

"I'll see you're rewarded," patronizing English had taken over.

"What's a reward between friends?"

"Oh, come away, Tom. If I win through you know what it will be like, money in monopolies, money in silk purses, money in taxes . . ."

"Money is not everything," said Tom, thinking it went a good halfway.

"No, power is what you want, Tom. It always was when you were a lad. You've done well, one of Lord Salisbury's young men," Robin was not gibing, his round reddish eye suggested awe. "An embassy one day perhaps?"

"I hope so," Tom played with the lid of the jug, flipping it up and down with a steady metallic thud.

"I know so," Robin replied, whirling again so that his cloak caught in the letters and spilled them to the floor. Tom knelt and scrabbled for them, then paused and stood up, annoyed that the boy should have seen him sprawling on the floor.

"You still write," suggested Carr, glancing at the tightly-worded sheets.

"When I can. I'm very busy on official work just now."

"Oh, that came pat! The man of affairs, eh Tom? I might need a bit help as I said."

"How can I help you? One of many in the office?"

Robin did not dispute this, he bit his knuckle as he used to when a boy and said: "I might need letters writ."

"I'm not a secretary."

"I do not mean a scribe. I mean a man of composition. I'm not learned."

The dunce. Robin leaned aganst the desk with his head lowered, his ear-ring swaying like a dewdrop on a twig. For all his silk stockings and buckled shoes he reminded Tom of his own hopeful youth when he had ridden so bravely to Scotland, puffed up with delight at being one of Mr Secretary Cecil's secret envoys to the court at Edinburgh. He had expected at least a post in Paris by now, not to be one of a herd, the most menial of a dozen young men with powerful family connections who were all waiting for success as keenly as Tom Overbury.

"Will you instruct Tom how he can aid you for old time's sake?" he asked.

"Oh I will that," Robin had a knack as contrived as a ballet step of exhaling his perfumed breath with just that exactitude of wonder and delight. King James would find him irresistible.

The meeting was well contrived, Robert Carr rode out to tilt the next day. He wore a plain saffron cloak, for Hay had finally decided that his protegé should be simple—"and that's true enough", mumbled some commentators—yet Robin's sudden spin to earth was dramatic enough to have the front row of boxes arising like corpses at Judgement Day. As they all hopped up, white-faced and popping-eyed, Hay felt a surge of pride: he had stage-managed the best act of the show. The king gulped down the nearest tankard (which was not his own) and demanded that his own doctor should visit the lad. "A Scots lad is he? Puir wean," he murmured again and again. He would have scuttled off to see to Carr's well-being at once if Mayerne had not insisted that a broken leg might be an unpleasant sight for the royal eye, and James, always afraid of blood, also envisaged splintered bone and, heedful of his doctor, subsided in his chair.

Meanwhile Carr had been taken to the home of Master Rider at Charing Cross, admirably chosen, as it was away from court yet two minutes' walk from Whitehall. A modest house, it had a well-swept upper room, the simplicity of which would encourage the king to consider himself a benefactor. "But my best bed," mourned Master Rider as it was carried from the chamber, "the king cannot come here with the place so plain." However, Hay had organized a clean room, small enough to suggest intimacy but approached by a broad staircase (the king was mortally afeared of winding dark places) and rudely furnished, yet not that rude, for the chair was well plumped with cushions and a few bottles were laid in for the invalid.

The king arrived as soon as the jousting had finished. He came on foot, a raggle tail of chattering courtiers behind him. Only Philip Herbert kept away, retiring with relief to his true ambience of the stables.

"None but 'is majesty," said Mayerne at the entrance of Rider's house, waving his silver-topped staff at the gossips.

"E'en so, e'en so," agreed the king and ran up the stairs as if his legs were whole and straight. What happened in that calm white-washed room could only be guessed. Tom had a better report than most men.

"Och, he mumbled awa' like an old crow," insisted Robin later. "Forbye he's the weird one isn' he, Tom? Like an old nurse he rocked and moaned awa' beside the bed, and I in splints up to my thigh. I could hardly forbear laughing but kept a straight face, God knows. 'Ma puir wee laddie,' he went on and on like a bubbling pot pattering away at my hand meantime, then Mayerne comes up the stair, 'Time to leave, your majesty,' he says as smooth as cream. Eh, isn't he the grand one, more like a king than Jamie? 'I won't answer for his health unless he has sleep,' Mayerne says and the old man jerks away down the stairs so sadly I almost sat up and called him back. But Tom, it's a trial, he's back every day with a Latin grammar saying he will teach me himself and bringing a pile of books like you never saw. I didn't know there were so many books in the whole world. He don't talk clever. He hasn't even learnt to speak like an Englishman, sometimes I can't understand what he says he's so broad, and he tells the dirtiest tales, Tom, I never heard the like, not in stables or among tinkers. Then out comes another great volume on Cicero, and all this," touching a pile of grubby paper on the bed-cover, "his thoughts on being a king. Is he touched, Tom?"

Tom should not have been there. He owed his visit to Master Rider who had been sent secretly by Robin, pacified with a silver piece and talk of later patronage. Robin must be promising the world and his wife a living, for sweet-meats were thrown to the floor and jewellers' knick-knacks littered the bed; a new-fangled lute with French stringing was in one corner and a familiar but well-forgotten besom of light twigs in another.

"What's this Robin, has the king been explaining about witches to you? He's an expert on them you know, and this looks like a broomstick."

"Lord save us," replied Robin, "I fear it's only by my game leg I'm rescued from that. Do you not recall a birch when you see one? I know he'll lift it to me one day if I cannot conjugate amo." He lifted an anguished eye.

"I know well he has quaint tastes, but I never heard of this one. It may only be a threat, man."

"Buggery," said Robin firmly, "I can expect, but if his majesty turns a birch on me I'll break it over his head. I swear it."

Tom flexed the birch. "He has a mortal fear of violence. I doubt it's more than a playful game, Robin. Kings don't woo like other men."

"I'd like a bit of sport, Tom. It's lonely here with only that mad old bird visiting each day and Mayerne scowling and mouthing French over my leg. There's not even a serving girl to pinch, for they say the king will not have a woman near him. How he fathered three children is past my reckoning."

"For the good of the succession," replied Tom. "But you can hardly like wenches, Robin. Here you are set up to be a royal lover and chatting of birds. I thought you were as bent as this twig." He tore at the birch and split it.

"Now see what you've done," cried Carr. "What, Tom, you know me! I love to lift skirts."

Tom gaped at him, astounded that with such a drive for women Carr could have been chosen for the king's favourite; but even while they talked Robin was holding lengths of silk and woollen cloth to his cheek and gazing in a silver-framed glass at his own lovely image.

"So you're a facing-both-ways?"

"If need be."

Tom said weakly: "Don't let the king know."

"Och, he knows well. When I came to and saw him pouting at me the first thing I said was 'I would you were fifteen with bosoms like a pigeon'. I thought he was the doctor you see, and old Jamie just nodded away. 'That's my laddie,' he says, 'that's my braw laddie'—faugh."

Robin was right. James forgave him his love of women providing it came second to his love for the king. He fussed over the youth like a mother launching a beautiful maiden into the world. Day after day tailors and jewellers left their goods at Master Rider's house, and they lay about the little room as carelessly as dung in a stable. When Carr began to rise he plodded through lengths of fabric ripping them with his heels as he essayed to walk. With Mayerne on one side and his shuffling king on the other he staggered from bed to chair and back again. Although James thought washing bad for his own complexion he would pass wet facecloths to Robin and hold a silver bowl of soapy water. Sometimes the king sat on the young man's pillow and coaxed his hair with a comb so that it waved more luxuriantly round his pale face.

"I need to be away from here," said Robin looking at his own pallor. "I need the sun."

He finally faced it for a moment only when he was passed like a handsome-wrapped gift from the Rider house into a litter which carried him to Whitehall. James exclaimed as if it were indeed Christmas. "My lovely laddie," he cried, holding Robin closer to him by a pearl and amethyst necklet, "hame at last," and Carr was not seen for a week.

II

THE RIVER NYMPHS were turning to do homage to their queen. Anne of Denmark, pale, tall and intent on her steps, was rising, dipping, leading the way towards another devious and stately dance. Before the players, sat the court ostensibly involved with the masque and concealing their boredom with grimaces and covert smiles across the hall. Carr sat at the king's right hand, and Tom stood close behind him.

"It's a great occasion," whispered Robin.

"Aye, it is that." Pressure came from Jamie's fingers on the muscle of his upper arm, a painful and intimate gesture which made Robin turn back to look at the king again.

"Not only their occasion, but ours as well," whispered James; "four years we've been together Rabbie, and here's to many more," he picked up his beaker of sweet wine. A roguish expression, only comprehensible to initiates, flitted across that red, drooping face, unendowed by any suggestion of his real intelligence; he reminded Tom Overbury of the local carter back in Gloucestershire, a man as sad and intemperate as the king, whose eyes had blasted through so much vicious weather that they had the scoured relentless expression of a perpetual need for sleep. The king's unfortunate mouth, a tiny box to hold his outsize tongue, was almost hidden by his greying beard.

Robin must love that face, Tom thought. So many nights it has pressed so close to his own, so often it has lightened when he has come into a room; given such affection who could not feel some reciprocal heat? But Robin remained cool, passionless as a virgin, answering the king's frenzies with apathy, distant towards everybody but Tom himself. Robin Carr had become Viscount Rochester with no more quiver of surprise or pleasure than a stone. His wealth, sometimes in the form of monopolies but often as jewels or boxes of gold coins, seemed to be bribes to laughter exerted for a melancholic.

"Show some pleasure, give some thanks," Overbury had exhorted him, and yet he had to admit that in this sole disobedience to Tom's commands, Carr had been correct. The king had never loved anybody more, and presumably would never need anybody more. Jamie even seemed to enjoy Carr's ingratitude; upbraiding the boy, he would feel self-pity receiving him like a bath of hot water, cleaning away his fears and doubts. It was as near as James came to washing his body.

Overbury watched his friend's admiring eyes rather than the circling dancers and realized that they were fixed on one of the tallest river nymphs, the Lea. What was the Lea? By considering it geographically Tom concluded that she was Frances Devereux, Countess of Essex. When she next spun in their direction, her grey diaphanous cape trembling in the motion of her steps, he saw that her appearance was eccentric rather than conventionally handsome. Her fair hair, made silver by the light of myriads of candles, shimmered under a net like scales of fish under water; her eyebrows were aggressively black. Apart from these distinguishing features she had a pale face, eyes of no-colour and yet, in some lights, dark, and a mouth too tiny for her long pointed jaw.

"I admire that wench," whispered Robin, reducing her immediately by a lecherous glance.

Tom lifted his perfumed cuff to answer behind it: "I thought you had nae time for the lasses," his imitation of James was amusing enough to Robin to whimper out a laugh, immediately corrected to a cough.

"But this one is unusual," he pleaded a moment later.

"She's not one I'd care to bestraddle," replied Tom.

"And why not?" asked Robin as the music faltered, then stopped, while praise crescendoed round the ceiling, and the king's company rose and walked about the great hall.

"Why, look at her family, man. There's danger for you, a nest of serpents."

"She's married to the dullest man in England, that might have taken the venom out of her."

"Essex? He was abroad getting his education, so he was probably also the dullest man in the Low Countries."

"The dullest dog in Europe."

There, by spinning the topic out of reach with a joke, he may have distracted Robin from the River Lea. But no, here she was, coming full flood, Tom thought unkindly, as she whirled into the noisy courtiers, who were gathered about the Prince of Wales and who immediately took flight, leaving the two young people alone on the wide floor.

"She'll none of him," said Robin.

"Why not so? The next to greatest in the land, she would be a fool not to; what a captive, eh Robin? He's never looked at another woman. My God, he wears purity like a hair shirt, that boy. Of course she will make the most of him!"

"Not so. *Imprimis*, I am the next to greatest in the land . . ."

Tom laughed. "Robin, what delusions! You are not the heir to the throne."

"Come now, Tom, it will be a good 20 years before that boy has any other power than a groom at court. The king is jealous of him and he will make sure Harry never does more than decorate masques and the like."

"The prince has a mind of his own. He may demand more power."

"He won't get it. *Secundus*—see how good my Latin is since Jamie taught me—*secundus* he is the same age as she. The Countess of Essex needs an older man. She will hardly take Harry seriously."

Tom grunted but knew Robin was right; compared with the girl, the Prince of Wales was a child, still circumscribed by tutors. "And *Tertius*?"

"Oh, as to that," Robin looked down at his own long handsome body, "the final factor is myself. I'm used to having my own way, Thomas. And I need not even do my own wooing. All those pretty documents you have written for me to present to the privy council, all those quaint conceits of verse which make Jamie think I'm a man of letters, all that practice you have in writing love letters to Lady Rich on your own account—no, don't interrupt, Tom; between us we will have this bird snared, bound and popped in the pot for supper."

Overbury fidgeted, glancing back at the two young people in the centre of the floor; they were parading an interest as contrived as the masque in which she had just danced, she curtseying, he bowing, touching finger-tips and parting, now and again circling, more like stags about to engage than two lovers. There was another movement in a far window as a thin, black figure cut itself away from politely uninterested courtiers and walked towards Frances and Henry.

"There's your real problem," he told Robin, nudging him emphatically.

The man was Henry Howard, Earl of Northampton, who was called the most dangerous man in England; he was the great-uncle of Frances. His "danger" had seemed unreal until a few years before; during the reign of Elizabeth he had been lucky to keep his head as he had been an ardent plotter for catholicism and by many accounts an open traitor. That Elizabeth had spared him might be owing to his nephew, Frances's father, who had been a famous sailor and was now Lord Chamberlain; or perhaps the queen had felt some need to make recompense as Henry's own father had been executed for political treason; or after all, and this must claw at the old man like a canker, she had considered him too ineffectual to sentence and had allowed him to continue his scheming way. His present eminence seemed as much due to her disparagement as to his long dead adherence to Mary, Queen of Scots. James had said loudly that Old Howard was being rewarded for loyalty to his late mother, but most observers calculated that his patronage was owing to Elizabeth's dislike of the man, and that the king was thumbing his nose at the shade of the late queen. Northampton's strength was not only because of his position at the top of an awesomely sturdy family tree. While he had been out in the cold Henry Howard had managed to make money through buying property; he had once been so poor that he had walked about bookshops while his fellow students had eaten their dinners, unable to raise the price of ale, bread and cheese. Now he had a house fronting the Thames and facing the Strand which covered more land than Whitehall Palace, and he owned many small streets between Charing Cross and the City. He had probably supplied the pearls which cascaded so becomingly down Frances's gown.

As Henry Howard walked smoothly towards the couple, they started, separated, and smiled at the old man. He managed to say affectionate words to both, holding Frances's disengaged hand on which her wedding ring glimmered as profoundly as her hair, touching the prince on the shoulder in a manner which showed both respect and comradeship.

"Here's an embroilment," said Tom. "Who can better that old fox? He sees himself great-uncle to a king."

"Not he," replied Robin, "how can the Prince of Wales marry her, and she wed already? And her family is too powerful for her to be his leman. That's why the old man came over; to show the prince that she couldn't be had for the asking."

"Then how can you approach her?"

"Ah, but they are all playing chess you see, and move her willy nilly how they wish it. That old man leads his side, but I can take her away from the game; I would woo her by making her realize that she has a will too, and can give her favours where she wants."

"She will always do as Northampton tells her."

"Ho ho, Tom, how can you be so callow? She is longing to rebel against them all."

"It would cause a scandal if she bedded with you."

"Who need know of it?" asked Robin. He walked past Tom and out on to the terrace which led down to the pier. The sky was deep violet on the Surrey side of the river, smoothly stretched above the wide waters; oarsmen called continually like night birds as the courtiers manoeuvred their way to their boats.

"I must go."

"No," said Robin, "no, stay the night here. The king will not want me again tonight. He is playing the fond family man, chucking his little girl under the chin. I want to talk to you."

They looked back into the great hall. The candles were guttering and the pages must be loath to replace them as one in three sputtered out, and the room became as twilight as the terrace, the playground of pale moths which fluttered in from the warm night. They agreed to meet in Robin's rooms in half an hour, time enough for him to make a formal good-night to the king. Tom circuited the great hall, anxious to avoid the glance of old Northampton who would note his presence like a cat who hears the patter of mice. He walked across the terrace and into the palace by a side door. The passage was full of rubble and thin curling lathes of wood. James's palaces were always in the hands of builders; and a few boys crouched in straw beside their work, ready to rise at dawn and continue hammering and painting.

He found a door opening on to a broad corridor and walked briskly along it, hoping it would lead into the oldest part of White-hall, shrugged into dilapidated buildings behind the façade, where a warren of tailors, jewellers and laundresses lived close to their patrons. He rounded to a court and hesitated, for women's voices came clamouring to him. A stone screen concealed the ladies but he heard a few words behind it.

"Women's ailments only," said a hushed genteel voice. "I do understand, my lady, and I sympathize as well, no man could ever know how we suffer at a certain age——"

"It's as well she had a lusty youth," said an older woman, quite hoarse, a drunken dominating voice, "at least she knows what she's missing now."

"So—a potion to still his desires, a lotion for the hands and more yellow ruffs, if you please, Mrs Turner," a whimpering fadeaway voice, punctuated with sniffs at a pomander.

"Ha, yes indeed," called the strident lady. "We cannot have enough of your yellow starch. It's quite in fashion. They say the queen will wear it on her birthday."

"I am much beholden to my customers," sighed the soft voice; "without ladies such as you I could hardly make ends meet."

"Now Mrs Turner," the loud lady again. "We all know you have a fortune tucked in the toe of your stocking, what with lotions and potions and babes stopped up to five months——"

"Oh!"

"Oh!" cried both listeners but it was an indulgent sound as if a spate of giggles might follow.

Overbury cleared his throat and came upon them, two court ladies as he had imagined, bedizened for the evening, with feathered head-dresses which exaggerated them to six feet tall and wide skirts which resolutely blocked his passage. Their confidante was a little yellow-haired creature, more of a lady than he had imagined, dressed demurely but with a pleasant display of breast. Her only fashionable feature was a high lace collar which circled behind her head like a halo, and which was dyed bright yellow. He bowed as they stared at him. He asked for directions to the rooms of Viscount Rochester; as he bowed, they curtsied, he retreated, they walked away from him, the little fair lady glanced back at him, he looked back at her, he turned another corner, still shooting a glance at her, and so walked into a gathering of women at the base of a new board staircase. Looking upwards in confusion Tom was startled to see that the staircase had no top, it was directed into nothing, like architecture in a nightmare. The women he had scattered by his approach were very different from those he had met a moment before. Their eminent hair and mittened hands suggested the hauteur of ladies-in-waiting, and in the middle was the Danish maypole herself, Anne, whose blonde hair had been covered with a red wig for the masque and who looked as imposing and raddled as the old queen as she held on to the newel post of that dream staircase.

One elderly witch said: "You have an impudence young man, you should look where you are going when the royal family are about. Heh, sir? Who are you, sir?"

Tom had enough presence to bow as low as he could and say his name.

"Overbury, Overbury, thet es the name of the frunt of mein husbant's frunt," said the queen. She looked at him with some horror, as most women look at a newt or other loathsome creature brought into the house.

"I am indeed the friend of Viscount Rochester," he replied.

She continued to look at him, her mouth dropping lopsidedly, her wig tipping off the back of her head like a parody of a hunting cap. He could hardly apologize for being Robin's friend, she must know about him. He tried to bow again, deserted by any charming phrase or compliment which might make her easier with him. Her pale blue eyes swivelled about before she closed them.

"Go away, Overbury," she said quite distinctly.

He bowed, bowed, and bowed again, retreating continually until he had turned another corner. The ladies-in-waiting, there must be at least four and all were aged and respectable, looked at him disdainfully. The queen kept her eyes closed. None of them moved. He escaped from the incongruous group arranged about the disappearing staircase and ran like a frightened boy to Robin's rooms.

III

"YOU ARE BECOMING one of your own Characters," suggested Robin, "The Man of Affairs." It was so acute that Tom glanced sideways wondering if another adviser could have mentioned this to Robin. For he was right: paunchy about the waist, with an over-abundance of rings, an eye for ladies, and an attentive audience for his essays, Tom had burgeoned out with the pomposity of a city merchant; his moustachios curled up as handsomely as his personality.

They had been playing golf on Blackheath and were returning to Greenwich by cutting over the brow of the hill; below them spread the panoramic palace ornamented by the river, a strand of silver, wavering in the heat of late afternoon.

"We should play more often," said Robin, adding, "if we had time."

He stood waist-high in low bushes and bracken, his club steadied on the earth like a cane. Both men were sweating slightly for the day was unnaturally still; a few insects exploring the leaves seemed intrusive; the horizon shook in the east as a party of ladies rode across it; Tom looked down at the palace trying to spy out his own window. Lines of white tapes fluttered from poles to show where the new building would stand, and already broken lanes of rubble marked demolition that had begun before plans were laid to paper.

"I am dining the envoy," said Robin.

"You have the notes." Tom spoke unnecessarily, for Robin was well primed for the Spanish ambassador.

"I have," he patted a silk pocket which swung from his belt on a string punctuated with small garnets which sweated in the sunlight like drops of blood.

Tom felt a second's resentment; Robin hardly bothered to thank him now for small favours written on snatches of paper which expired so swiftly in candleflames, once used. Tom's irritation had caused him to return to writing his "Characters", determined that he would be remembered for his essays, as nobody bothered to recollect those *bons mots* bequeathed to Robin which would cause a gust of royal breath in sudden laughter and were then forgotten.

"You know my feeling on the Spanish marriage," he said crisply, regretting immediately his tone, as dry and deliberate as that of Cecil.

"I don't agree with it," replied Robin shortly.

"The king wants a Spanish marriage," said Tom.

"The people don't and neither does the prince. He says that two religions cannot lie in one bed."

"Since when did Harry have a voice at council?"

"I would have thought he should be considered this time. It is his marriage."

"You were not so hot for Harry when he wanted Frances."

An uneasy silence. When Robin's interest had been declared the prince had rejected her. One day a courtier anxious for his favour had chased after Henry to the tennis court; he held Frances's glove of pale grey kid, sewn with her monogram. A group of gentlemen had watched Henry sieze it; the prince had looked about the courtiers until he riveted Robin with his hazel eyes. "I care not for a glove stretched by another man," he had said, throwing it on to the jaded summer grass. It had uncurled revealing an F and E spangled with silver thread. A murmur rose into a giggle at the first sign of bawdy in the prince but the boy had glared at them and walked away disdainfully. The glove had lain on the tennis court all night; at dawn a ballboy had picked it up sodden and darkened by dew, and returned it to Frances's maid for twopence.

"Northampton and Suffolk would be delighted with a Spanish marriage," said Tom. "They long for an *entente* with Spain. It would repay all the pensions the Howards have received from thence."

"How can you say they are traitors?" asked Robin, angry at the insult to Frances's family. His hand went down to his hilt as quickly as a bird drops to a worm, he held it self-consciously, it was a useless pretty sword, inlaid with silver along the blade.

"Forget Frances. She is married," hazarded Tom, watching Robin's hand with curiosity.

He flung it away from the hilt and dangled his golf club over one shoulder like an imaginary lute. "How shall I forget her?" he sang to the latest popular tune as he descended the path, his boots slipping on obtrusive stones so that, as he leaned back, Robin was encompassed to the waist with deep-green and brown fronds of bracken, from which his velvet jerkin rose like a gigantic heath-flower, its silk-fringed shoulder knots swinging as he walked.

Tom glowered down at that well-kept auburn head, smoothed with lavender pomade. "You won't forget my advice," he called out. Robin annoyed him by continuing to walk downwards, picking his path; Tom was determined that his pupil should make some sign of gratitude. "Don't forget, d'you hear!" he shouted.

Robin lifted one hand and waved but did not turn again before he disappeared into a copse lower down the hill.

Tom moved into stillness and heat, the warm air seemed to congeal about his mouth and a pulse in his cheek, or his head, or his neck, began to beat like an insistent drum.

Tom recovered from the summer sickness in his rooms at Greenwich, where Robin came dutifully every day and sat playing with his cap, waiting for a word to release him into the world again.

"Is this all our friendship is worth, Robin?" asked Tom. "A scant half hour a day from you! Where is your love now?"

"Love?" cried Robin. "Love! Dinna use those words you cannot understand, Tom. Comradeship, aye, friendship, yes, but love from you! I've seen you about the court, kissing the correct hands, making sonnets to well-connected ladies, but what's the truth of it? All you love is Tom Overbury and your own advance. Have you ever sighed for a maiden outside her window? Could you ever be heart-wrung for a page boy? Dinna answer wi' lies. We have a bond which suits us, Tom, to be friends, to each seek good for the other. Like twa' men in a three-leggit race we aye run taegither. But only while it suits both, Tom. Love, you say, love!"

"You are right," said Tom. "I have never been in love. But it will come. It must come."

"Aye, it'll come, right enough, when a well-born heiress sails across your bows."

Tom smiled, pressing his head back to the pillows; he considered himself fortunate that he did not have passions like other men, lacking their needs for a mistress or a wife, or even another man. Was he cold? Why no, he was a poet, and yet every emotion in his life was fancied, conjured up as if he were a play actor. He knew he would never fall in love. Robin was right. He would only mouth the words if the most eligible partner appeared and she must be easily won too; for he had no time for arduous courtships. Meanwhile he was heartfree and so able to pursue his own ambitions. And lying in bed with a sweating skin kept him from those ploys. He frowned as he caught Robin's glance, knowing the boy wished to be away.

"You are running off to see Frances Devereux," he said savagely.

Robin paused halfway from the room: "What if I am? It's none of your business."

"You haven't forgotten who writes your love letters to give her in your name?"

"That!" he smiled. "Forbye we're past the letter-writing stage."

"You're a fool, Robin. What happens when you want to cast her off? Or when her husband returns?"

Essex was expected from the country any day. Robin did not answer, a slammed door was his farewell. A few minutes later Tom saw him on the broad walk that ran by the river; his elegant body parted the crowds like the prow of a ship cleaving water.

A flicker in Tom's southern window enticed him to look towards the king's apartments. James and his retinue walked through the garden; they were flattened and distorted by the glass, their bodies and legs oddly separated and waving. The older men moved stiffly after hours in the hard chairs of the council room. Tom recognized the Howards even at that distance: Suffolk as spare and ravaged as one might expect of an old sailor who would be tempest tossed into his grave; and decorous Northampton, his hand on his elderly nephew's shoulder, the two of them making obeisance to James, bowing and backing off, their heads almost turned towards the fluctuating crowd round Robin. They were perturbed by it, Tom could see that, for they laid their faces together then marched resolutely towards the river while the king half stepped the same way, then glanced uncertainly at his master builder who hovered with another plan. Like dogs released from leashes, the Howards strolled towards Robin, met him and turned his face back to Tom's room. Would he call again on his way back across the broad walk? Perhaps to apologize, to send for wine and suggest one of their old convivial evenings together in which Tom told Robin how to comport himself and Robin was suitably thankful for his advice?

The three men, Robin swaggering slightly for he had never engaged the attention of the Howards before, halted and turned towards the windows of Tom's room. But, disconcertingly, they pitched their eyes lower and by standing close to the glass, half concealed by a curtain, Tom watched Frances emerge from a door below him. Her head was covered with a veil which tremulously fell about her shoulders, she wore a gown of olive green opened at

33

the front to show a bodice of white satin, sewn with flowers; he could see this as she faltered on the pathway until, encouraged forward by her mother, who came out after her, Frances drifted rather than walked towards her father, her great-uncle and her would-be lover, her arms half raised in a gesture Tom thought theatrical but which conveyed pleasure and greetings. Behind Frances and her mother strode a tall young man, dressed in a curiously old-fashioned coat, his beard untrimmed, and his hat, which dangled down towards the pavement, dusty and faded. The Countess of Suffolk had a penetrating voice which sounded upwards through the ivy to Tom's window.

"Why here, sirs," she cried out after curtseying in turn to Northampton and Robin, "here is our Frances's lord, new arrived from Chartley and would come to see her before he had a moment to wash, or brush his hair."

Frances seemed annoyed by such lack of gentility, she moved her head from side to side imperiously and did not glance at her young husband who had been away from her so long. Suffolk seemed pleased to see his son-in-law, he held Essex by his forearms and his mouth moved swiftly under his beard, smiling, congratulating. Northampton was more restrained, his white old hand extended then dropped back, and so did he, as if anxious not to intrude on the young married people. Robin stared at one and then the other, gave Essex his hand, seemed grim, half turned, remembered his manners and bowed to the ladies who fluttered back at him, then his excuses were made and he walked away across the green lawn; old Howard, Northampton himself, went quickly after him and held his arm and then the two, rivals in council, and hitherto with no grace towards each other, sauntered to the king's garden, drowned in conversation. Tom sighed, as if he had seen a puppet show. He resolved to be on his feet and about the palace next day.

S HE WAS RUNNING through Whitehall palace like a
mouse, admitting no obstacles, with her skirts held up to show
her scarlet stockings, and heels which shimmered with glass. Ann
Turner knew that the girl was coming towards her; only she, the
purveyor of potions and voider of wombs could occasion such
fervour in her own sex. A thunderous sky was lowering on to the
grass like a curtain, and a few drops of rain fell as the demented
figure ran into the archway. It was the Countess of Essex. Mrs
Turner was rarely discomposed; her confidence had become un-
paralleled, yet she was disturbed by the flushed young face, already
blemished by white paint, and an elaborate hairpiece which was
toppling from the arrogant head, very slowly and deliberately as if
a great cake were falling apart, eaten from within.

"You are Mrs Turner?" said the countess. She was recovering
her breath and Ann instinctively moved backwards from her
darkened eyes.

"My lady," she said, curtseying, hoping to keep her glances
downwards.

"Mrs Ann Turner—the laundress?"

"That and other things . . ."

"I have heard of you," said Frances Howard. Then, "Walk with
me."

They trod on to the spongy grass. Mrs Turner pulled up her
collar against the rain; she would not find time to starch her lace
before the next day when she was attending several valued customers. Apprehension felt like indigestion, it made her belch, it
seemed to flutter under her ribs.

"What. . .?"

"Sir Thomas Monson. He speaks of you."

"Yes," said Ann. She had arranged some festivities at the Tower
where Monson was Keeper of the Armoury. Mrs Turner had
designed some nasty amusements—children, dwarves, animals. . . .
The countess was sixteen, would she wish for such depravity?

"I am a pastry cook also, my lady. I make suppers, send
servants, supply plate. I have a good name in the trade."

"I have a pastry cook," said Frances. She was walking as if in a dance, one step forward, then to the side, and then back, snapping her fingers in memory of a piece of music.

Mrs Turner said: "I have some skill as a laundress. My yellow starch is famous."

"Indeed?" She did not look at Mrs Turner.

The rain was becoming more heavy and made the laundress irresolute; could she suggest that they return to the archway where grooms were gathered, watching them from shelter?

"You are an aborter?"

"I am." She added "My lady." She even glanced at the girl's body but the heavy canvas about Frances's waist supported a layer of silk, and then an embroidered pattern of vine leaves raised another half inch from the fabric.

"I have no need of you on that score," said the countess. "I know you are a necromancer."

"Not I, my lady."

"That you are the disciple and solicitor for a wizard."

"I know a man who might deal in magic. I can only say that he knows herbs and poisons and has some skill with them. He is not an evil man, my lady. I would say he is a Christian." She had to speak carefully. "There is no harm in him."

"Will you fetch him to me, Mrs Turner?"

"I doubt that he would come."

The Countess of Essex stared her incomprehension.

"He practises in his own house, at Lambeth. He would not be able to bring his charms across the river to work in any other place."

"I would pay well."

"I am in need of money and yet I would not ask him to come to you. Many ladies of the court go to his house. There is a back door, you would not be seen."

The countess made a delicious face, a suggestion of duplicity and mischief which reminded Mrs Turner that she was speaking to a young girl who perhaps wished for no more than a good fortune told in cards or for a lotion to make her face even more white.

"It is easy," she encouraged. "You might have some sport of it, my lady, dressed in a cloak and travelling in a skiff, who would know what—what you are." She was whispering although nobody would hear them standing in the centre of the green court, with rain falling about them, and occasionally the sound of water gurgling in a conduit pipe, which was overflowing with the sudden swell of flood.

"I will meet you," said Frances Howard. "On a dry day. On Wednesday at noon, at the watergate of Northumberland House."

"I will be there," Mrs Turner said and curtseyed again, still avoiding the girl's eyes. She watched Frances shimmer away in the rain, her extravagant dress slopping against the mud of the path before she went into the palace. The laundress did not move.

Mrs Turner had been a nothing in the beginning; the daughter of a failed shopkeeper, she had won an ancient doctor of medicine and learned from him the way about a herbal, and even more, the way to trick patients and customers into parting with their money. Doctor Turner had been no romance, he had himself admitted that he was like King David and had wished for a young woman to warm his bed. When he died she was left a good house in the city, some tenements near by and a list of gulls: rich, silly men and women who would buy a lotion or a potion. Among them was Arthur Mainwaring, a foolish knight but well connected who now shared her bed and spent her money. Mrs Turner would have said that she saved and cheated and deployed for a comfortable home and retirement. But she did it all for Arthur, who needed her money to drink and gamble.

She knew that the countess would be pleased by Father Forman, a wizard who frightened Mrs Turner as well as his clients. If she could gain Frances Howard's custom she would become purveyor to the court. Of what? Yellow starch, mince pies, abortions? There would be no necessity. This one girl, if she were to patronize Mrs Turner's friends, could make her fortune. There would be no more ironing or baking, and as the confidante of the countess there would be allowances from other providers of silks, jewels and scents for an introduction to such a fat and satisfying trade. Careless of the giggling grooms, Ann Turner threw her hands upwards, her wrists and cuffs were drenched and water flowed down to her elbows, as she lifted her exulting face towards the roofs of Northumberland House which advanced beyond the palace wall like a phalanx of a conquering army. Even in her excitement she felt again that twitch under her bodice, was it more than apprehension? Could it be fear?

They said that Essex was sick and that no doctors could imagine what disease he might have brought back from the country, lying all day in a dream, his head half turned from visitors to whom he spoke in whispers, and with little interest. Frances had run away one night, darting out of his mansion by Covent Garden in her slippered feet and running down the Strand in the rain, only a scarf over her jewelled dress, and with no maid, so that the late-night revellers had chased her, laughing at her as if she were a harlot. Frances had confounded them all by sprawling full length on the steps of Northampton's house, weeping and wringing her hands and when the steward and his men had opened the gate, half armed against a mob or some madwoman escaped from an asylum, she had screamed the length of the street, "I will never go back to him, never! I would die rather!" and the Howards' men had almost dragged her into the gatehouse, gazing angrily at the stragglers who were watching, and had shut the door swiftly. After a week at Northumberland's house Frances had been taken to Audley End by her mother, but she was now back in London.

They said: at least Lawrence Davies said—and he should know as he was Overbury's bodyservant—that when a letter from a foreign country was sent to the king Sir Thomas had first opening of it, and would make notes of the contents, then re-seal the letter and send it on to the king. Davies supposed Overbury did this so that he could warn Carr what to say and how to react to news from other countries, but it looked suspicious all the same. Did the king know? Did Cecil know? The former probably did not care as long as his Rabbie shone in council meetings even if he spoke Overbury's policies. And Cecil? He said nothing, a tired old man, he should have retired before now. They said: Frances Howard, now Devereux, and Countess of Essex, was in love with Robert Carr, that she followed him everywhere shamelessly, as well she could with her husband sick. They did not say she kept him sick with powders bought from an old man called Forman who lived in Lambeth and who had been debarred from practising medicine some years before. They said—but with no notion of Frances's involvement—that Forman dabbled in necromancy for the entertainment of gentle ladies who visited him on Friday afternoons. They gathered in a small parlour, with the shutters closed. Lizard skins and dried bats were hung on the wall and the old man drew pentangles on the floor with chalk while his audience whispered over glasses of mulled wine. Forman would abracadabra his way through some spells and raise a puff of yellow smoke behind which a voice would chant strange words which he said were Greek or

Hebrew. When the smoke had cleared and the coughing had ceased Forman asked the prettier ladies to sit on his knee while Mrs Forman washed their glasses, her lips pressed close together; Trunco Forman herself was prettier than many of the visitors.

Frances went to Forman's house on Wednesdays accompanied by her close friend Mrs Turner; she did not sit on the old man's knee but she did call him Father Forman. At Northumberland's house her parents remained strangely unsympathetic to her entreaties to remain with them, even her great-uncle had begun to sniff and puff when she demanded that she need not return to Essex. Carr remained pleasantly aloof, although he had squeezed her hand several times and had made an assignation in a friend's house in Hammersmith. But what could she hope from in Carr? Dazed with longing for him she was even more anxious to confide in these unlikely friends.

"I dream of him," she told Ann Turner. "I imagine his voice when he isn't there. He is the most beautiful man you ever saw."

Ann tossed back that all men were the same between the sheets. "And that's where you will get him in the end, never fear, with Father Forman and myself working for you."

Forman made wax images of Essex and Carr. The first was stabbed through in the gut with a cruel long pin. Carr was wrapped in white-linen bandages like a baby; these concealed a monstrous male member which had made Frances blush and which smelled of a hot spicy ointment which was supposed to be an aphrodisiac. The scent made Frances so dizzy she had to lie down. It was pleasant to drowse in that closed warm room, listening to the distant humming sounds of summer outside the dark shutters. She could see Ann and Father Forman moving about the room, playing with the dolls, saying meaningless things to each other. Once she opened her eyes wide, amazed at the sight of her friend naked and looking very like a doll herself, with her golden hair falling down to her waist; it was fine spun and frizzled so that it shone like pollen against the dim light. "What, what?" cried Frances. "Don't thee be afeared," said Ann Turner, coming over to the couch, "it's all dreaming, lass," and so she had dropped into sleep once more. Afterwards, when the two ladies were rowed back to the north shore Mrs Turner offered to teach Frances to cook, suggesting recipes which would cover the taste of powders and love philtres. They agreed to meet at her small house in Blackfriars. Both ladies wore velvet masks when they shopped in the city and were dressed so simply they could have been the wives of grocers; Frances loved the game of being a commoner.

They said: the countess goes to the City to buy perfume.

After a summer spent picking petals off daisies she could at last say "He loves me!" Frances had lost her maidenhead to the most beautiful man in the kingdom. They had met in secret at Hammersmith, in a house rented from Overbury's friend, who did very well out of the arrangement. They walked to it through a vegetable garden; their horses were tethered in an orchard and occasionally put their long heads over the wall to watch Frances and Robin. Nobody else saw them, or cared to look for them: Lady Suffolk thought her daughter was at some game in the queen's apartments; Essex was to ill to care where she was; and the only creature who knew Robin's whereabouts was his dearest friend Tom Overbury.

"Why did he have to know?" she asked before they had gone through the wicket gate.

"I had to tell him," replied Robin, "he can be a bit of an old nurse, always at me, but it's for my own good, and I tell him everything. He is closer to me than any in the world."

"Closer than the king?"

"Closer than Jamie."

Frances waited to say "Closer than me?" but did not dare yet, she could ask that question at the end of the afternoon. Meanwhile they walked about the soft herbal lawn, and pulled early blackberries off their bushes. Robin ate near a pint of peas, gobble, gobble, spilling a whole podful into his mouth at once.

They went into the house. It was like playing at being married; he lifted her over the doorway into a tiny room, smaller than any she had seen before. It had a plain round table and two straightback chairs. Nothing more than would be found in a farmhouse; behind it was a kitchen with the fire already lit.

"It must have been done by the fairies," said Robin at her back while she touched the new pots and pans beside the grate. She knew servants must have been sent down before, but there was no sign of them. Upstairs were two more rooms; one with a fourpost bed which looked enormous in that little chamber where the roof sloped down almost to the floor at one end. The stairs came right up into the room and the ceiling had not been boarded so that the thatch was bared, long clean reeds shutting out the light and the cold.

"I love this place," she said to Robin. She was spinning about like a child of ten, feeling the goosedown pillows which were heaped up on the bed as if left for six couples. There were no sheets but a long shaggy pelt, lined with silk, which slithered about the bed. She exclaimed over this, feeling the tough grey hair which almost cut her fingers.

"It's from wolves," said Robin, "it came from Russia," and she knew some forgotten ambassador must have bribed him with it.

Finally she was frightened, she delayed returning to the bedroom as long as possible, dreading that he should think she was too easy, and they sat in the kitchen, drinking milk as innocently as babies. Suddenly Robin stood up and said in a hoarse voice, "Your hair is like milk," and pulled out the pins holding it in its tight spindle so that it spilled down. She looked at it, lying across her breasts which were partly exposed to flaunt her virginity as was the mode. Her tight bodice seemed to burst, she was breathing so hard. Robin laughed at her. "Wha' for d'come here then?" he asked in quite a Scots accent so that it took a second to understand him. "Aye, you're the bonnie one," and he unloosened the clips of her bodice and pulled it away so that she was left naked to the waist, the bindings of her busk had left thin red lines over her ribs and back, but her breasts, plumped up by the corset, sprang out freely like a couple of birds which had been cooped. He picked her up then, leaving the bodice lying on the kitchen floor and carried her up to the bed.

After the first shock Frances revelled in Robin's love-making. She did not realize that he was not proficient, having no experience herself. As he blundered about on the bed, now leaning on her hair so that she squealed with pain, now lowering himself on to her narrow belly so that she groaned with his weight, she secretly delighted. She had never imagined that she could retain her supremacy after a man had first made love to her, and yet half an hour after the disappointing collision of their first joining, Robin was crawling around her, kissing her finger-tips, her feet, her dimpled navel, her nipples which he said were like mulberries, and that pale hair which had first attracted him and which was already darkening at the roots. He avoided her face. Robin did not care for her famous beauty and found it banal compared with the splendour of her body. He preferred not to look at it, secretly fearful of her distinct appearance of the Howards, with black eyes lidded so heavily that they sometimes appeared like shellfish, closed in white hard hasps. He objected to Frances's arrogant chin which suggested to him her superior English birth.

She adored him. Frances would never crawl, she could not lower herself to tell him how enchanting he appeared to her. But she watched him surreptitiously with her sidelong glance taking in his pale body—why had she imagined that men's bodies would be as ruddy and tough as their faces?—the faintest sprinkle of down on his chest had an extraordinarily golden quality, sprung from his auburn hair which was echoed palely lower down his body; she shuddered at his private parts, not because she was not lascivious, she would lick him and play with him, but only if she did not have to see him, because they reminded her of Father Forman's parlour and the ugly doll with its erect penis in swaddling bands.

"When did you want me—like this?" she asked, curious about Forman's influence.

"Why, I thought you pretty enough at that first masque where you entrapped Prince Henry. I had hopes of you since. You received my letters so kindly."

"But, but——"

"Och, I first thought that this might come o't last Wednesday e'en——"

And so it had worked, while Forman and her best friend Mrs Turner had cavorted about with the dolls, Robin Carr had imagined her in his bed.

"How did it come? This need for me?"

"Oh, the need was there. It was last Wednesday that I met the man who owns this house and thought it far enough from town to suit us and yet easily reached in an hour."

This disturbed her, it suggested only that Forman's incantations had somehow coincided with a purely commercial plot, in which money had changed hands for use of a bedroom; and yet magic worked mysteriously. She insisted that she would make a supper for them and trailed down the shabby bare wooden staircase with the wolfskin wrapped round her body and flopping heavily on every step. In the kitchen she worked fast and cleanly, remembering Mrs Turner's instructions, so that she produced a passable mess of scrambled eggs and beer while Robin doused his golden head in a bowl of warm water and came to the table with tendrils sleeked round his face and neck, totally disarming. The king had already noted his favourite's extra grace which unerringly enabled him to make the right gesture at a crucial moment. Frances might have been demanding, supercilious or cruel when he appeared after their love-making, but by washing his hair, Carr had reverted to a creature needing her solace and protection. He ate the eggs, which were liberally sprinkled with the love philtre, as if they were a feast. Now she was sure he would not discard her as other lovers did their ladies once they had known them carnally. She wanted to ask him how his liaison with the king was carried out. Did they share a bed? Were they as united as she and Robin? Who played the lady? And yet as he sat warming himself after the wash, now and again looking up at her from under his long dark chestnut eyelashes, she felt shy, and even considered that he was sacred enough by his intimacy with the king to be immune from crude questions. She carried the dishes to the stone sink and looked at them with apprehension, but Robin came up behind her and held her raised arm.

"There are others will do the common acts for us," he said.

"The servants will know who we are!" It was her first sign of fear.

"Tom Overbury has well primed them."

"That man," she returned, shocked by the friends' complicity. "Do you truly tell him everything?"

"Aye."

"So will you give him a full account of this meeting?"

Robin was almost surprised as he answered: "Well of this, no."

V

"FATHER FORMAN IS dead! Two weeks since."

Frances was being dressed and three maids attended her. She had just returned from the country.

"Go," she said to them and they hardly lingered, knowing her rages too well. As the door shut behind their pattering feet, Frances sat down suddenly, closing her eyes. Mrs Turner thought she might be about to faint and looked for wine.

"There is none," said Frances as if she could read the laundress's mind. "No, do not call anybody. Let us think alone. Let us be alone," she pulled her knees up towards her chin and her blue and gold gown fell limply about her legs; for an instant her handsome eyes flared towards Ann: "Tell me," she said. "How?" Then, "So soon?"

"He foretold his own death early in the autumn of 1611," said Mrs Turner shivering. "He told his wife on Sunday. He said he would go before Thursday night and so he did. He spent the day with other doctors, for though he was barred from practice they remained friends and so he was at Doctors' Commons all the day, then in the evening he came down to the water's edge for a wherry to carry him over to Lambeth. While they came into the pier he stood up in the boat, and the boatman cried to him to sit down or he would have them all over but he called out something and fell down dead in the bottom of the boat."

"What did he say?"

"The others with him said he called out 'An Impost' or 'An Import' or something of that kind. Poor man, poor man, all his black arts could not save him, madam. Dead as a last week's duck and to be buried tomorrow."

"What shall I do?" cried Frances.

"Do? Why, my lady, you have all you wished for: your lover, your secret's safe enough now, God knows, with that conjurer dead."

"I want more magic done."

"God save us, for what?"

44

Frances said: "I will pay you well if you will find another wizard".

Ann Turner did not answer at once. She realized that she might profit by Forman's death; as a go-between she had made more from Frances in one month than in two years' laundering. She saw her country house come nearer. And being with the countess had given her a taste for riches too, other court ladies had treated her as a shopkeeper, but Frances, anxious for conspiracy, had made her a friend and in that intimacy Ann had learned discrimination. She wanted better gowns and better plate, wine for every meal instead of beer, and a few more jewels than those she had won by saving so arduously for so long.

"I will find someone," she said, thinking of her dead husband's medical books, why should she not produce pills and powders as well as any magician? Yet she realized, watching Frances's pale vicious face, that a man was needed too, a flamboyant man to persuade Frances that she was in touch with witchcraft, a man who had the gift of the gob like Forman, perhaps an actor, or another disbarred doctor.

"There is a Doctor Savory," she suggested. "He treats the lawyers at Lincoln's Inn."

"Does he make up potions?"

"As well as any man living," prevaricated Ann who had suspected that Father Forman's love philtres had been made of chalk, sugar and white wine. She thought, what the eye does not see the heart does not grieve over, and she could do as well as any wizard.

The pang of Forman's death had passed by late autumn and Mrs Turner kept Frances's head spinning with tales of the Black Mass and the unborn babies used in their ceremonies. She found enough gossip going about the city to keep the countess supplied with those stories of orgies which most entertained her. It might have been her magic which despatched Tom Overbury from court, she hinted, for James had sent him to the Low Countries after he had queried too closely into the queen's accounts.

Jamie would not listen to his favourite: "The man's a main blaggart," he said to Robin. "And it wud d'ye well to be rid o'him for a while." He made it clear that this was not a final severance, and that when the queen had calmed and the court had ceased

45

gossiping Tom might slip back into England surreptitiously, so Tom went to France and Flanders for a few months, but beguiled his exile by writing shrewdly on both countries to Robin who shone in conference with the freshness and quality of his news from overseas. "Ecod," said Jamie in council, "it was a braw thought o'yours to set that man a-rovin' for the guid o' the realm," and Robin had blushed and explained how brilliant Overbury was at playing politics, with the aid of Robin Carr of course. And Jamie had tweaked his ribboned lovelock and called Robin "my dainty dearie" while Suffolk had counted flies on the window, and Northampton had smiled that black sneering smile of his, and old Cecil had said little. He had held the king to a promise that he might take the waters at Bath, and was making plans for the journey.

"Ah weel, the royal marriage," said the king sonorously, exhibiting a scroll which was the delight of his prime, the contract by which he would establish everlasting peace in Europe and by which he would become the grand-daddy of the continent. He used his children like a farmer using twin fattened pigs for market and was not ashamed of it. A tear slipped down his nose like melting sugar and landed plumply on the paper where it exploded into a hundred rivulets of royal syrup. The Howards looked at each other. They had won: Princess Elizabeth may be promised in marriage to an unknown German elector, but Prince Henry would wed the princess of Spain and in doing so bind the two great enemies of Europe together.

While the Howards smiled and looked down at their knuckles, where moles of old age spread darkly across their skin, Carr beseeched the king to think again about a contract with Spain: "The people would not care for it, sir." But the mention of the people had set James off on one of his tangents about the divinity of kings and the impertinence of commons. Carr mumbled back into his seat, alarmed at his first setback in council. The drone of Jamie's voice hovered on like an amiable bumble bee playing about in the velvet curtains.

The day was warm, Robin longed for Frances and her ferocity, those long limber legs which gripped him with such force he felt humiliated, like a horse being brought under control; and yet, he thought, he could not exist without her wildness, her hauteur, and her remarkable jealousies which ripped her face apart like lightning blasting a tree whenever she gave words to them. He smiled and looked at the painted ceiling, half finished like so many of the king's great projects, and yet the Italians had been at it: a plump benign goddess was already forming under some painter's hand, her rounded arm and tulip-pink breast rising from the plaster like a housewife stepping from a bathtub. Across the ceiling were two cherubs, gazing blankly at her, unaware of the splendid scenes designed to come between them and the naked lady, which were still haphazard pencillings in charcoal on the plaster. In lowering his head Carr caught an eye which looked at him as shrewdly as a weasel scans a rabbit. It was old Northampton. And by turning his head just a fraction Robin saw another eye, an old one too, but as red-rimmed as a bloodhound's with overwork. Cecil was pleading with him, and Carr knew that the old statesman, who had abhorred him for so many years, was mutely asking for his aid in turning the king against Spain. Antique Cecil lived in the past in which all Spaniards had worn devil's tails and raped young maidens and were set to gobble up England for dinner daily, and Robin Carr almost imperceptibly shook his head. He was opposed to Spain but not to the extent of annoying Jamie; Tom Overbury was not in England to advise him, but even if he were, Carr was resolute for one policy only, his own future as the most applauded, envied and favoured man in England. He moved his hand and touched James's wrist, very lightly.

"Forgive me, sir," he said. "I am promised to a hawking party."

James stared one second, his blotched face wondering. "Nay, nay, Rabbie," he replied. "If you are promised you must e'en go," and he watched the young man saunter like a deer from the room.

Robin reached Aston's house a half hour after he had promised himself to her, and found Frances naked at the window, her wool-white hair undone and slipping over the sill like that of a princess in a story. He hallooed as he entered the garden before the house, and was surprised when she drew back, an expression of doubt creasing her face like a screwed handkerchief. When he bounded into the bedroom she was lying on the bed, dangling her bodice by its strings.

He explained the council meeting, brushing her face with the chin kept so smooth for Jamie, and exclaiming over her body, comparing it with the goddess on the ceiling at Whitehall. She did not laugh but looked determinedly at the wall, her eyes as black as plums.

"Come now sweet love, brave love," he said to her, raising her chin with his forefinger. "Am I not ashamed? Punish me if you will, but speak to me."

Frances moved her eyes and stared at Robin with her sidelong glance which repelled him. "I wish to have a divorce from Essex," she said.

VI

WATCH AND WAIT. And old Cecil was dead at last.

James heard of his death in the garden. It was May 1612, the lively hawthorn flowers were showering his suite with scarlet kisses, each one, wind-borne, hesitated as it fell, scurrying round and about in the gusty wind until it caught haphazardly onto held hats and shoulders, the scented hair of the courtiers, and their rose-adorned shoes, each stepping blithely towards the king. James looked down at all those pointing toes, not one turned away from him. "At Bath, or rather by the road on his return." The old man had hardly hesitated to take the waters which were to invigorate him; tears came easily to James but these were unshed, he fought them back and smiled sourly. "Eh laddies," he said, "we'll see which of ye is the topdog now awhile" and he turned away from them and began to walk as briskly as was possible for his ricketty legs towards the gate where halberdiers stared at each other.

Like all sentries they had heard the news first, heard it before their monarch and were in their small way unravelling the events of the kingdom just as the great ones, pushing behind the king, anxious to keep pace and place, were consulting together in whispers so that James would not hear their plotting. Northampton was not there. How that serpentine creature would regret his absence! But sick of an ague he kept a fire going in his rooms in his great house, and crowded close to it, his knees covered with furs which singed and smelt rusty in the fetid air.

Who would take the dead man's place? James had denied Cecil often, but had been content to allow him to run the country. He had likened his kingdom to a shop and Cecil to the senior apprentice and yet the man was no apprentice, he was a master craftsman. James paused, his wambling knees buckling as they often did and put out his right hand, and, of course, Carr was there, his favourite boy, and yet a man. Thomas Howard was at hand even if his uncle were away; and James looked at Lord Suffolk, crusty with age like a ship which needed to be cleansed of barnacles, a stubble broke through his cheek by noon, his body was covered with a robe befitting a Lord Chamberlain, blackberry colour, velvet, and hemmed with silver laurel leaves. Thomas Howard would have looked finer in a leather jerkin and worsted hose, tramping his quarter-deck and spying out for a new armada. Carr on one side, firm under his hand, was his human walking stick who could presage his needs and bend to them, and Thomas Howard on the other, was standing in for his uncle, representative of the great families of England, the old hoary catholic nobility which had survived Henry, had survived his daughter the great Eliza, and would outlast James too. Glances like mirrored messages passed about behind the king, considering those two poles, Carr and the Howards, in some equality of power. What hope did the professional statesmen have against them? Lake, Winwood, Bacon and Neville were common little men who would only serve as messengers and implements for the great ones. They stepped back involuntarily but definitely as if to a command.

"We will not yet choose a successor," said James. More furtive advances; his prim mouth tightened yet saliva emerged from the edges, owed to his accursed kingly tongue which was uncontrollable when he was emotional. James gulped and said: "I need no Secretary of State awhile, we rest with the good offices of our Lord Chamberlain," a nod at Suffolk, "our absent Lord Privy Seal," a grimace for distant Northampton, "and our dear, dear Keeper of the Signet," a half embrace for Robin Carr who stood under his arm as sturdy as one of the hawthorn trees, "to whom I give my confidence justly."

When he went they spoke all together. Was confidence restricted to Carr or had it been apportioned to the two Howards also? "Jamie can never speak straightly," they mumbled to each other kicking through the long spring grass towards the gate.

James and Robin were in the king's bedchamber which was littered with all the appurtenances of the man. There were books piled haphazardly upon the floor and table, and papers covered with James's hand, some tight lines of prose, squeezed up together with insertions of Greek and Latin as regular and separate as lace sewn in a border; and a bitch, his favourite, was laid out like an effigy but suckling four pups on a silk cushion stained with the blood left from their birth; and wine was left about the room in silver ewers so that it would be to the royal hand whenever James stretched out, just as Robin was, waiting for an indication of need. There was a dish of crystallized violets from which both men helped themselves, James eating them one after another but with some precision, breaking off the petals then chewing the marchpane stem, like a spider thoughtfully dismembering a fly.

"What would you?" asked Robin a little breathlessly.

Cecil's death made the king seem more powerful for the Secretary of State had encouraged royal avarice and had even persuaded James against gifts of money to his favourites. It had rankled that Cecil had, by a sleight of hand, managed to save the king from intemperance with gold.

He would have a successor, however the king pretended he could do without a Secretary of State; the most important job in government, accruing bribes, taxes and emoluments like water drawing reflected light. Robin Carr knew that he could do the work. With help.

"The post of Keeper of the Signet is ae difficult," said Jamie slowly, watching him.

The Keeper of the Signet! A scribe's job, reading the king's letters, answering them carefully, he fretted at the lowliness of the work, listening to the Howards formulating the policies he would have to put into hand.

"Your friend, Tom Overbury," said the king.

"Sire," a touch of servility, for this was no ordinary meeting in the king's room; in the unsettled air, Robin could sniff a sense of fitness, a time to listen this was, to allow the old man to haver on, and yet James seemed a little less of a buffoon facing his quandary of state. Carr wondered if this worried grey-haired man with large dark eyes played a part when he jested and salivated in his private rooms, piling obscenity upon obscenity as if they were animal turds. And who was the scholar whom Carr never knew, a secretive learned man who talked logic and religion with a few austere churchmen? It disturbed Carr when he was suddenly minimized by events. James looked at him as if he pleaded. For what? Wise words? A bawdy jest? Or silence?

"If you are tae take great office Rabbie, ye must be more circumspect," came that hesitant fumbling Scots voice.

"You mean me to be Mr Secretary?" Excitement bubbled up like blood in his body.

"I didna say so," James replied severely. "It's like I'll find no man to take place of ma little Cecil, puir auld man. He was a gem, Rabbie, a man with no thocht o' self. Which of us can say the same?"

Robin was about to ask if Cecil's palace at Hatfield was built with no thought of self but it seemed unnecessary to demean the dead man and so he asked: "Tom Overbury?"

"That was main thochtless o' the pair o' ye," James said severely, "that play in the queen's garden."

"What play, sir? I swear I——"

James put up his hand, and Carr looked down at his own, clenched on his knees.

He understood the king. Anne and James would have accepted Tom's complaint on expenditure. No, Tom's expulsion had not been due to his querying of Anne's accounts, for that he might even have been respected. Carr remembered how he and Tom had walked in the queen's garden at Greenwich six months before. He had been hot with lustful thoughts of Frances and, like a tiger, he had feared nobody and nothing. Tom had been his usual self, conceited enough to give tongue to the first thing that came into his head.

"That old besom," he had said, jerking his head at the queen's bedchamber window, "thinks she can gull me with promises of meanness next year, I will make her purse strings tight this one too."

"Her purse strings are not all that are tight," crowed Robin, and bent his head down to whisper his dirty thought, and that moment the window above them had opened impulsively and she had been standing there, suddenly regal, not a lonely fattening fair woman any more but with a real majesty about her, so that they blanched before her and retreated, their uneasy laughter shivering away into the distant hedges.

"You laugh at me?" she had cried out, her voice choked with rage. "Aye, he unt you, king's frunt and his catamite!"

A face had appeared by her shoulder, one of her Danish ladies-in-waiting, as aged and wan as an autumn leaf.

"Your majesty," said the face, "it is Robert Carr, Viscount Rochester."

"Whut af thet?" asked Anne, still rigid with anger.

"Why, Overbury rules Carr and Carr rules the king," mouthed the face, big with apprehension.

"Who says thet?" cried Anne throwing up her arms so that her gold embroidered hanging sleeves danced about like sunlight in the grey day. "Who says thet is a traitor!"

The long Danish face had disappeared, jerked out of sight like a puppet on an invisible string, and an English lady-in-waiting had taken its place, pink and white, all "ohs" and "ahs" as she looked out at the two handsome men beneath.

"Your grace," said the girl, and the queen crumpled down like a piece of old paper thrown into a fire, her face darkened as if by flames. She had stooped like that behind the window, then the girl had stared at Overbury and Carr with some perplexity before she drew the shutter and blotted out the spent figure of Anne.

The queen must have flitted to Jamie, and he, though he might not love her, would not allow her to be so derided and in public, too. Now Carr understood all.

"I . . ." he said.

"You . . ." replied the king. "I couldnae do wi'out ye, Rabbie, but I promised my guid wife as Tam wud have to go."

"And now?"

"Why, now he must return to you. If you are to be a man of state it's like ye'll need an adviser like yon Overbury. Forbye, he's a dangerous critter. I dread his dark looks, Rabbie, I fear he wud mak ye' rue that friendship ye' hae wi' him, but he's a canny lad, he kens his craft."

"His craft, sir?"

"Statecraft, ye loon. He cud be a great man o' state, given the opportunity."

"I thought I was to have that honour," said Robin sulkily.

"Exactly so. You will, my love, you will, but it'll be Tam Overbury's plots you thicken. Those letters he has sent from Flanders, there's a real guile in them. He is like Cecil in that. He sees all Europe like porridge in a bowl and wud ken just how tae stir it."

"He is only a carpet knight, a lawyer," Robin said derisively.

"Withall that he cud make ye' well repectit syne ye take his advice in council. No real power for him, Robin, I mislike the laddie and wud nae set him up for council masel' but as the voice behind the arras he'd do verra weel for us. Listen tae what he suggests, just that, and mouth it out yoursel' Rabbie, and e'en the Howards'll think you have more sense than common."

Robin felt a little chill. It sounded as if he were bound forever to Tom Overbury, dependent on him for every thought and expression. He comprehended all too well; he would be a bed-and-board lover for the king, but must rely on Tom for any wisdom he might offer forth.

"He writes sonnets for me now," he said. "I feel like a parrot, only saying what he teaches me."

"What's that? What's that?" said Jamie. "Why, mon, think you how I have lived these last years. Old Cecil gae me the ideas. He knew the way tae gang. What's differing 'twixt you and me? Kingship, aye, but at the most we are tools in another's hand."

Robin knew that the king might very easily begin to talk of God, the only superior he ever truly acknowledged. "Almighty-given thoughts" James had called his own advice in council while old Cecil had huffed over his papers privately.

"Be advised by me," said Jamie, leaning over to him and picking up one well-kept hand. "I wud hae ye appear most wise, Rabbie, and no man cud say ye' are so by nature. Thank God you have an intelligent and discreet friend in Tam Overbury but never let me know how needful he is to ye'. Let him slip into England secretly and I trow that at the next court meeting Annie'll smile on both o' youse."

Robin met Tom at the butts in Finsbury Fields where young poets vied for attention from the favourite's favourite by gibing at the archers; they were all left disconsolate when their patron left abruptly, following the tall youth who covered his face as well as his body with a black cloak and it suggested several pretty conceits to them, of death or retribution.

"Frances would divorce Essex," blurted Robin.

Tom was aghast. He could see no reason in it. Both lovers had what they wished, and the few who knew of their liaison would not wish to compromise it. He asked: "To marry you?"

"To marry me. Why for not, Tom? I am a good catch as they go." His reddish eyes were jumping with excitement.

"Never!" cried Tom. It was not only a warning it was an intuition of danger, for an instant he had no real reasons before they came flooding on to his tongue thickly: James would be jealous; the Howard family would never allow such a match even if they allowed the divorce; and divorce itself was almost unknown excepting royalty; Essex would arouse the court and the populace against Robin; and so on and on. Forever and ever. Amen. And after he had said them all Tom was left to add again: "Never, never. When did she think of this?" he asked finally.

"He considered it first. Essex—there is an irony! His friends have been at him this past year to put her away, and marry again and to choose a lady that will give him children."

"Frances is barren?"

"It has never been tested," said Robin.

"I have heard, Robin, that she refuses him her bed. That she stays with her father and mother or that wily old uncle. Or at her house at Hounslow which you know too well, Robin. She is a jealous scheming bitch, Robin. She will bring both of us down."

Robin's hand dropped, his cloak parted, showing how his sword blade shimmered like the small mirrors sewn into his coat. "Say you so, then have no more of me," he shouted and ran like a boy down the black tunnel of the Strand.

VII

Before next morning each man had written a contrite letter to the other. Tom's note, arrogant yet intimate, had said that friendship between men was like a magnet so that each cleaved to the other. He had hoped that by suggesting such a fond relationship he could draw Robin's attention to his proximity to James which might be threatened by an affair with Frances. If this still concerned Carr he made no remark on it, but seeing Tom in the king's outer closet, he had drawn him to a window, his arm fixed round Overbury's neck like a silk sling.

"We must nae quarrel, Tom," he said, a tear standing in one eye.

"We never have," replied Tom smoothly, glancing about the room. "Beware the Howards," he added fretfully.

"All but one—my paragon," whispered Robin. If he had no second thoughts about Frances at least he was wary of her family, for now they sought him out. An invitation from the old man sent Carr hurriedly to Suffolk's house, carried in a litter so that none of the court would see him swing out under the gates of Whitehall and in again at the nearby portico of Northumberland House. There, in a room which seemed to spread to infinity, both Thomas and old Henry Howard waited for him. They seemed of the same age, reverend men in gowns so encrusted with embroidery and small jewels that it looked as if they were wooden religious figures made inert by the great weight of their clothes. They had intended to impress young Carr and did so very easily. Everything about them was sumptuous, even their wine cups were golden, ruddy by firelight. Each had a great chair with its attendant footstool negligently kicked to one side; Robin's chair was somewhat more low, with no stool. Their servants were richly dressed in Howard livery, and they came and went in great numbers. After a while, they left, closing the doors silently, and the men were joined by a lady with a square chin and shrewd eyes. Robin recognized Lady Suffolk, she looked at him carefully, Robin thought, and said pleasant expected things, then went to the end of the room where another fire spluttered faintly on the hearth. As she settled to sew Robin realized that she would also play some part in this conference; it increased his apprehension that this meeting was more than a gesture, it was an invitation to join the Howards' faction.

He was right. Old Northampton had realized that Frances might have brought them the richest political prize of them all in pulling in Robin Carr, the only man influential with the king. Suffolk remonstrated feebly; he was honest in his concern for young Essex.

"I mislike this, I say," he began but both his uncle and his wife silenced the sailor by staring at him like basilisks, their twin frowns reflecting down the room.

"You want what is best for Frances, do you not?" asked his wife impatiently and how could Thomas deny that?

"I would do aught for my Frances," he said complying with the smile of his uncle which he translated as doing aught for the grandeur of the Howards.

"Then where is the countess now?" asked Robin uneasily looking at the three faces about him which looked back like a trio of effigies. Lady Suffolk folded her embroidery and crossed the room, her feet moving invisibly so that she approached with the sinister momentum of a ball on a bowling green.

"She is but a girl," replied Thomas. "It is best for her loving family to decide for her."

"Decide?"

"Whether she will divorce or no," answered Northampton. "You would have her?"

It was out. Robin wondered what their reaction might be if he denied Frances, repudiated their love, or said that it had merely been a frivolity of the summer. Frances Devereux was more than a mistress, she was the symbol of ultimate power and he could not refuse her. At the back of his shallow blonde skull a chirping went on and on like some light headed chicken, "this is me, me, me, a country squire's son and from Scotland to boot, and these are the Howards and we will make an alliance". He could go no higher, being the king's favourite seemed less auspicious than being related by marriage to these imperturbable Englishmen.

"Then you will cast your lot with us," declared old Henry, "and follow our advice in council."

"I cannot make promises——"

"Perhaps you will be guided by my lord and his uncle," interrupted Lady Suffolk.

"Perhaps simple consultations before we meet the king in council," added Suffolk.

"And for Frances, she will give up much," continued her mother; "she has costly tastes, Lord Rochester, but you of all men should be able to supply them."

"I am not poor," replied Robin stiffly thinking that his personal wealth had gone beyond his own calculation which should be enough even for the Howards. He watched Northampton, apprehensive of any untoward movement. He remembered a tale: that Henry Howard once had a circle of male paramours, but his passion now was politics. Northampton said nothing but looked at Robin as if Robin were his creature. This must be how foolish old women were captivated by men who claimed to be the devil, thought Robin.

"We gang aye fast," he said. "The divorce is to be jumped."

"With the power of church and state vested in the king there will be no problems there," promised Northampton. "The lady is purported to be a virgin, so Essex is judged impotent. In that we rest our case. You must stay clear of Frances until the judgement be given. You comprehend that if any thought you and she are already——"

"We have been most discreet," said Robin.

"So, so, with my daughter hotfooting to buy houses in Hounslow," said Lady Suffolk caustically, "but as well as two eminent people may be, you have been discreet. Who knows of your trysts with her? Servants?"

"No servants. It has all been arranged most secretly." He thought of Tom Overbury for one cold moment, then turned his mind away. Tom knew all, he had composed those letters and sonnets which Frances still received, some bawdy in their desire for her. He had arranged their first meeting place. Every notch upon their affair had been cut by him; even now, with Robin's passion for Frances fulfilled once a week, he went boasting to Tom about it. The man even knew of her demand for a divorce.

"Does that wretch Overbury know of it?" asked Suffolk, shrewdly.

"Some things, my lord."

"He knows where his good health lies," said his wife. "He needs the patronage of my lord Rochester here, and will keep quiet."

"Aye, or else he could be quieted," said Northampton consideringly. "Mark you, tell of your love to the king. Swoon, pine, show all those pallid casts of mind known to lovers in the plays, but do not let any man know that she and you are carnal lovers. Or if the truth be out, a divorce is impossible."

"I understand," said Robin, although he did not.

"Frances will go to Audley End," said her father, "while a brief is prepared. But doubt not, young Robin, we will dance at your wedding in a twelve-month." He clapped Carr on the back, a blow as rough as if given by a club, but Robin exulted in it, as he left looking back at those still faces he felt privileged to be patronized by them.

"You have been with the Howards," said Overbury accusingly, as if Robin had been caught in the pantry, rather than in entering Tom's room with a whistle and a jaunty step.

"What if I have? I love their daughter—great-niece—Frances, I should be polite to her family I hope?"

"Does the king know?"

"The king is not like yourself, Thomas, he does not set spies on me."

"Poor spies indeed, if two grooms and a kitchen boy had not run to my man Davies with their tales——"

"And you listened to them!"

"I do when the safety of the realm depends upon them."

"What, Tom! Cry stinking fish in another market! Does my visit to old Northampton's house bring the King of Spain in by the front door?"

"No, by the bedroom window, but it lets him in. You will be their puppet, Robin. With them to advise you, you will have no need of me."

"So that's the truth, Tom; you fear I may be unfaithful!"

"Not that, Robin, for you'd be a poor thing without me."

"But mine own. Not your blabber mouth."

"On your own you are a fool, Robin."

"Go to, go to, there are other men who can tell me what Flanders thinks of this, or the German princes would say to that."

"But not one man, Robin, who can do it all and claims no reward——"

"No reward, that's rich—when the whole court talks of flaunting over-rich Overbury, fattened with monopolies and gold like a Michaelmas goose, just a goose—gobble gobble gobble."

"Robin, I'm warning you . . ."

"Warn away, my friend."

"That woman will be the death of you—a whore, a trull, a bawd."

"Not so, not so, for in court it will be proved she is *virgo intacto*."

"How will that be stated unless by a trick? It's all trickery, Robin. She has so beguiled you with her moonlight stories, her fakery—will she take in the king and council too, and the commission?"

"What commission?"

"Did you not know that, Robin? A divorce demands a royal commission with the Archbishop of Canterbury, no less. Will you trick that also?"

Robin, who had been pacing about the room showing his white teeth, threw himself back at a chair which tottered from his assault.

"Tell me about a divorce," he said.

Tom told him. A decree of nullity would be sought of a commission that would be set up by the king, for a divorce could only be passed by act of parliament. The commission would include no doubt, the Archbishop of Canterbury, George Abbot, and several famous lawyers as well as a posse of bishops.

"We need have no fear," said Robin directly, "Old Howard is right. They will all be in Jamie's pocket and do as he tells them. I have but to convince the king that we are in love and need each other."

"But," said Tom, "if your argument is that she is a virgin, as Essex is impotent, how will you explain those days at Hammersmith or Hounslow, and the bawdy letters writ your Frances which leave no suggestion that she is chaste?"

"Those? Who need know of those? We have been secret. None know of them."

"I do."

Robin gaped at him, his jaw dropping like an axe. "Why Tom!" he cried, "d'ye threaten me, man? Without me you would have been nothing—a hanger-on in Cecil's office."

"Ah, but I am not. I am a power, the man who tells the king what to do, even if it be through your voice, Robin. Enough know who I am to listen to me. I know you have been playing four legs in a bed for a year with the Countess of Essex, and I know that if such adultery were suspected the commission would determine that divorce is not possible. Adultery alters the picture, Robin, it would make a divorce a condonation of vice. No churchman, or lawyer either, would free your whore to marry you, especially when she is leaving a young man like Essex, who has tried his damnedst to woo her and who seeks children from his marriage. One word from me and Frances would be stuck with her lord until death do them part, and you would be reviled, even if you are the king's minion, for seeking to split those two asunder—and legally too."

"Tom, it sounds as if you threaten me."

"I threaten you, my dearest friend and patron?" but said sourly with a tight mouth. "Further," said Overbury, expanding his well-kept hands to prove his points, "now is not the time to start the hare of her divorce. With Cecil dead and a clamour arising for his successor to be named, there are too many other interests in the game. Think of the factions, Robin. There is Sir Thomas Lake, the Howards favour him as secretary do they not?"

Robin stared at Tom, clutching the brooch which held a heron's feather to his cap. He said nothing, but twisted the silk about his fingers.

"You may not know so, but it will be so. A likely choice. Lake would have been high in old Cecil's recommendations too but for one thing—or two things—he favours the Spanish marriage and with it a kinder face towards catholics here in England. Neither are popular with the people. Then there is Winwood, you remember Sir Ralph? Puritan and trained in foreign service, he is a candidate too, I feel. Neville, he's a dark horse. A parliamentary man and an old hand at conspiracy—why he backed Essex, this young man's father, in his revolt against Elizabeth. He's lucky to have kept his head, and his ability to have done so suggests to me a ready tongue, a quick wit, a clear-sighted view of policies—not a man to underestimate. And Wotton——"

"Wotton?"

"Sir Henry Wotton, Ambassador to Venice. They have all hastened back to these shores like homing birds, Robin, Winwood from the Hague, Wotton from his Venice posting, and Neville from Paris. Why do you think this is so, Robin, all these wise men of a sudden spurring to London? Can it be that each feels he will be Secretary of State in Cecil's place?"

Robin pivoted in his chair, still silent, his amber eyes disquieted as Tom continued.

"It will be a great commoner of this style I say. The king would not make a nobleman his first statesman. They are too righteous in seeking out their own rewards, but all these men are skilled craftsmen at foreign policies. They know how the cat will jump. They have noblemen to back them of course, just as great lords back racehorses but with more advantages. So Lake has old Northampton behind him and would seem to be the favourite, because Henry Howard is wily, more cunning than a poacher in laying snares. Do you not think he may have laid one for you Robin?—that neither you nor Frances have acted of free will but danced to the old man's playing from that first sight at the masque?"

Robin looked shocked. He had not thought so and said it vehemently, "We love quite simply, it needed no trickery to make us love."

"But you are encouraged by your own ideas of how you stand in the world. She wanted the most beautiful man in the court, and being the king's jessie made you more attractive I dare say, for no other woman would think of you carnally, and you—well what of you, Robin? You are a little pleased at having the heiress of the Howards and the legal wife of Essex under you, are you not?" Robin did not speak so Tom went on implacably: "Let us consider the other figures behind the real contestants then. Both Howards back Lake. Winwood, the Puritan, has the authority of the Archbishop of Canterbury and the Lord Chancellor, old Ellesmere, behind him: the church and the law, a formidable grouping that one! And Neville is promoted by the Earl of Southampton and other survivors of the rebellion by Essex's father. Then there is Wotton, we must not forget Wotton, for he is the outsider in the race. They say the queen and Prince Henry favour him."

"You have been studying well," said Robin hoarsely, his scattered gaze suggested that he had not realized how important the power struggle had become. While he had been mentally absent, playing kissing games with Frances, the court had formed into parties as various and determined as partners for a dance. His fond dream, that Jamie would confidentially ask Robin for his choice and that he would hand over the name of whoever would bribe him most, turned to paper, then to grey ash, ready to be blown away. "Do I have any say?" he asked sullenly.

"I doubt it," replied Overbury; "Northampton will no doubt ask you to favour Lake. Whether the king will be guided by you I cannot say, but if you run away each day to make love to Frances you will not be here for him to ask, will you?"

"Who do you favour, Tom?"

"Neville."

"Why so?"

"He is an ambassador and understands our policies abroad. He was trained by old Cecil until his mind tick-tocks the same way. He could be a bridge betwixt the king and the commons—no, don't hinder me, for howsoever James refuses to countenance parliament now, one day he will have need of the commons, if only to raise money. And Neville has an idea, which James delights in, to bring the trade of Persia to England by way of the Caspian Sea."

Robin pouted, both Persia and the Caspian sea could have been in the Americas for all he knew or cared. "Is it a good idea?" he asked, wondering if he could make some money by promoting it.

Overbury shrugged: "Wild, impossible, but it *is* an idea and none of the other candidates has offered anything except their faces at council since their return from overseas. At least James talks to Neville, asks him questions, walks with him in the garden and consults figures of spice prices and anchorage at Archangel. He notices Neville, which is enough at this moment."

"Perchance I should favour Neville," suggested Robin tapping his brooch against his teeth.

"As to that, you will be opposing the Howards if you do so. They are for Lake."

"I may choose my own man I hope," retorted Robin. "Neville it will be."

He hummed out into the sparkling morning air, his cap clapped on to his wine-red hair, his doublet flaring about him, its ribbons looped about his shoulders like the spangles of chestnut blossom on a tree. At the corner he turned about and waved back to Tom, his smile flaming out warmly. Tom sighed as he withdrew to his opulent room. "All's well," he said to himself and eyed his own sardonic dark face in the speckled glaze of a Venetian looking-glass. I have won, he thought, Robin is still mine own. He felt a spasm of victory over that doll with the white hair and pale face who gleamed about the court so fleetingly. "A pox on you, Frances Devereux," he added.

At the year's end Lake was asked to make a speech of welcome when the Elector Palatine came to collect Princess Elizabeth. James was sometimes weeping, sometimes laughing; and Carr was kept out of the way, for this was a family celebration. Was Lake's speech perhaps a sign that he might be the next secretary?—but he slipped over it so painfully that James ordered him off the rostrum, as he had ordered young Carr from court so many years before for faltering in a public speech. Yet Carr had bounced back, perhaps Lake would too once the excitement of the royal wedding was past? And then—and then—a few weeks before the ceremony, while music sounded in the streets all night and London seemed on perpetual holiday, Prince Henry was taken ill. He lingered for a week, then died.

Whispers rustled like ears of corn. An immediate thought was murder. Had the king put his own son out of the way because the boy opposed him? A suggestion swiftly concealed when James's red eyes were seen, and his voice, hoarse with weeping, was unable to make itself heard at council meetings. Had the Howards had it done? Henry had not wanted to comply with their plans for a Spanish marriage but without the prince there would be no marriage at all. And Overbury? There were even murmurs that he had hired a groom to poison the lad, because he had disapproved of Overbury's patron, the beautiful immoral Carr, Lord Rochester.

But all these suppositions sighed away in a few days when the pale royal couple were married in mourning and left England while the country returned to considering who would succeed Cecil; although this prevailing interest was extinguished by the news that first Essex had demanded a divorce and thought better of it, but that now his wife would have one, and that her grounds were his impotency. A further rumour had been put about that Essex was only impotent with regard to this one woman which made many gossips whisper "witchcraft" and others wonder what flaw that white beautiful face might conceal—Was the countess hideously deformed so that men could only look at her with disgust? Was that the reason for the late and blessed prince's rejection of her? Had she three breasts? No breasts? Was her belly scaly like a fish? Did her breath smell vile—not that that would put most men off for there are other ways to have a lady than face to face, said the judicious ones. It provided the most tantalizing conversation since the Gunpowder Plot, and the Howards, who were already embroiled with plans to bring Lake to power were also entreating for a divorce commission swiftly so that their child's name would be cleared.

In the agony following their son's death, courtiers moved warily about the king and queen, anxious to placate them and disturbed for the future. Prince Charles, a retiring grave boy, seemingly more predestined to be an antiquarian than a king, was suddenly the only royal sprig and was hustled into all the state occasions his brother or absent sister might have graced. He walked awkwardly, his under lip pulled in with anxiety. He stammered so that citizens had to crane and whisper back the contents of his speeches. A ripple of disquiet permeated the court, enlarging and spreading in widening circles.

VIII

"Y ES, YES, YES,'' whispered Frances. Her eyes were like a blind man's, the lids almost closed over spinning white balls. As her thighs squirmed on a red silk cushion Mrs Turner and Cunning Mary glanced at each other, and both women withdrew to the little clothes cupboard by the stairhead, sure that they might snatch a few words together while Frances writhed alone.

"I mislike this," admitted Cunning Mary. "Is she often taken this way? It looks like sorcery to me."

Mrs Turner almost laughed, it would be an interesting plot if Essex were putting spells on his wife while she was working so hard at bewitching him. "It's her hot blood," she replied soothingly, patting Cunning Mary's hand but recoiling from the greasy skin immediately. "She is as wrought as if a man were in her."

They stared curiously at Frances, and Cunning Mary relaxed, for masturbation was a common human failing while necromancy was not.

"She'll be herself in a second," said Ann.

"They say she has Lord Rochester by the tail."

"By the tail, no, I'd say another part of him——" began Ann but was interrupted by Frances turning towards them.

"What do you there, women?" she said. "I asked you to attend on me."

"Why, you seemed asleep, my lady," replied Ann nimbly, "so I stole a moment to give Mistress Mary my receipt for mulled sack. My man is making some below. That'll warm her for outdoors."

"Oh that, I had forgot," said Frances gazing at the window where snow piled along the sill; some had seeped in, Mrs Turner wiped at it with a clout and called "Richard" at the stairhead. Outside, Paternoster Row was sinking into the snow, familiar cobbles and booths were obliterated by white. Several stalls had shutters up and passers-by did not linger but hurried, slipping, down narrow lanes.

"I like the winter," said Frances meditatively. "I always feel safe in winter."

"So do not I," retorted Ann, calling again at the stairs, "Richard, what would you . . .? It makes me wish I could dig a hole and crawl into it like animals do. I love the spring, the heat, the flowers, all a-bustle in the streets, and knowing that if Arthur is from home he isn't lying in a ditch freezing and drunk together. Richard!"

Richard came trudging up the stairs, Frances had expected her friend's servant to be a boy and was surprised at the old man who carried the mugs. His hair was speckled white as if he had been out in the snow. When he had climbed carefully downstairs again she said: "I had not seen your man before."

"Whish," said Ann Turner, winking, "he's been a six month in the Newgate for uttering false coinage. It's a sad tale, for Richard Weston has been my porter for many years, but he has a streak in him which comes out now and again, when he must play the fool, become a footpad or a forger or what have you? Something in him that cannot be denied." She sighed thinking that there were pickings rich enough in blackmail without her servant breaking into excesses of petty discernable crime. "He's a good man for all that," she said, "and would do anything for me and mine. His son's apprenticed to an apothecary and can fetch any potion you've a mind to," this was directed at Cunning Mary who had been selling philtres to the countess. Mrs Turner did not approve of the witch from Norwich.

Cunning Mary dressed like a figure in the Italian comedy, her black cloak was daubed with symbols, her staff carved with serpents' heads and her hair looked as if it had not been washed these three years. Cunning Mary believed that dirt aided Satan. Mrs Turner had made a good living out of necromancy but had never found it necessary to let one cobweb remain in a corner.

"Well then," said Ann Turner, unnecessarily pinning her immaculate fair hair, "is your business done?"—this to Cunning Mary.

"Indeed and indeed."

"And you will begone," Mrs Turner had to say this, even though Mary Woods was there by Frances's invitation.

Cunning Mary eyed the fire, the snow-filled window and the steaming sack, she wondered if she should curse Mrs Turner but one glance at that indomitable lady warned her that London witches, even if they masqueraded as laundresses and dressmakers, might have more powerful magic than her Norfolk spells. Mrs Turner's mouth was as prim and straight as one of her own seams.

"You will be on your way," she said again.

"Haven't been paid yet," mumbled Mary.

Frances seemed to waken from her half dream, was it of her lover lusty in her arms or of her husband withering in his bed? Both were equally attractive to her.

"Oh!" she cried, "I have none. I have no money with me. Have you any, Mistress Turner?"

"No," replied Ann shortly, thinking that she would not let this hag receive one rose noble under her roof.

"Syne I have no pay the spell wint work," muttered Cunning Mary taking advantage of Frances's abstracted glance to wipe her eye on a corner of her cloak and take away her nose snot at the same time.

"Oh, she must have something," cried Frances impatiently.

"You have nothing to give my lady, and neither have I," said Mrs Turner flatly.

Cunning Mary took a long pull at her sack and settled back into her rags like a frog settling into mud. "No pay, no magic," she said.

"Here then, here," cried Frances, "there's naught else for it." She was pulling at her finger where a black pearl set in diamonds was hanging.

"No, not that," cried Mrs Turner. "I would rather your ladyship sent out to a goldsmith and had the ring valued first. Surely it is worth more than this creature could ever do for you?" She looked into the street. The goldsmith's shop was bolted and dark.

"Worth more than getting rid of my lord Essex?" said Mary. "Is that not worth a whole pile of gold and rings together?"

Mrs Turner turned on Frances. "You want to kill him now? Divorce is not enough for your ladyship! First a spell to put him out of sorts so that he would not make love to you, then a spell to make Carr love you, and now the last spell, to kill your husband!"

"Mrs Turner, I would have confided in you if I thought you and yours could do me this service," answered Frances. "But as Father Forman is dead and you have only produced this mild Doctor Savory I have to resort to other means to rid myself of Essex, for divorce is not certain after all. I must have some other tool to hand."

"Tool! You mean a weapon," said Ann.

"And £1,000 you promised me, when your lord dies," said Cunning Mary.

"A thousand pounds! What for?"

"A potion," replied Frances, evenly, her marble face not moving at all as she released her revelations. "A slow poison, warranted not to kill for at least four days, so I will be well away from his lordship when it takes effect——"

"What nonsense is this? How you have been taken in by this creature!" cried Mrs Turner. "Why, for a few nobles my man Richard could find you the same poison I declare, and without the hocus pocus this creature sells with it. I had thought her a harmless old wanderer, half mad with her own magic, but she seems in her right mind if she gets £1,000 on demand. Your ladyship must be——" she paused, even if she had come to regard Frances as an intimate she was still too powerful to be called crazy. "Tell this beldame to be gone, my lady," she said curtly and went to the stairhead. "Mind," she added to Mary, "if you are not out of the house in two minutes you will be thrown out, snowing it may be, but lunatic I am not."

She went down the stairs furiously and was more enraged when Mary followed her to the street door in the promised two minutes, her ragged black cloak trailing in the snow on the step, and her high hat tipped sideways like a lightning-struck steeple, but the black pearl clenched audaciously in her bloodless mouth so that Mrs Turner could not help but see it.

"Out of my house, old witch," said Ann between her teeth, seizing the broom and signalling to Richard, but Cunning Mary was away, her tottering feet taking her with amazing speed down the lane towards St Paul's, and leaving haphazard tracks in the snow like the scratched footprints of a rook.

"I'm main glad she's out of the way," muttered Richard Weston staring after her.

Up in the parlour Frances watched the firelight flickering behind her fingers. "I love it here," she said, "I wish I did not have to go back to Northumberland House."

"You could have been betrayed by a madwoman like that," Mrs Turner told the countess. "Come all the way from Norwich too, when you have good friends at hand to do all necessary for your ladyship."

"But would you do—that?" asked Frances, looking at her with a sly expression.

"That? What is that?" Mrs Turner dismissed murder with a shrug as it were a momentary nuisance. "I can do most things if I set my mind to them, and if I am asked—and remember, you have never asked me for poison, my lady. Poison is not magic, my lady, it is not made by Satan but by men who grind it in mortars and sell it in packets, for a price. My lady, promise you will never consort assassination, which is man-made, with spells, which come from the devil. And, my lady, do not employ creatures like that one again. For that price and for that promise of reward I could have a better job done and no hocus pocus of magic brought into it."

Frances smiled. "I like the magic," she said.

Tom Overbury had stopped watching himself in looking glasses. Apart from his manipulations of policies at home and abroad he made more immediate plots which he had not written down but which were as neatly tabulated in his mind as if they had been printed. Sir Thomas Lake must be dismissed as a candidate for the secretaryship. As he had told Robin, he had nothing against the man except his sponsorship by the Howards and to eliminate him he would favour any other candidate at all, but preferably Neville, because he enjoyed the eccentric movements of Neville's mind and realized that in spite of his civil-servant's creed, Neville had a touch of originality lacking in the others. Then he must break any contact between Carr and the Howards, by managing affairs so that they were hostile to each other. If Carr backed Neville he would antagonize them. Otherwise the Howards could easily supplant Overbury as advisors to Carr, which was obviously their plan, and if they did become too intimate with Robin it would be "farewell Tom Overbury!" His enemies were numerous and he could hardly return to being another foreign service youth hoping for an ambassadorship. Therefore, and this was the difficult task, he must work harder than ever to separate Robin and Frances. Instead of wearying of each other the lovers became more infatuated monthly. Overbury had shut off the supply of proxy love-letters weeks before and Robin had merely laughed, saying that with a divorce in view it would probably be better there were no pieces of paper left about. Tom had put all his own drafts of the love letters and sonnets into a locked wooden box and left it at a friend's house, saying darkly "If anything should happen . . ." What could happen? Even if James had no intention of making Carr more powerful by creating him Secretary of State he had to rely on his advice as Keeper of the Signet in the discreet work which would have been done by James and Cecil in the past, and which was often too secret even for the council room. In one case Tom was omnipotent but in the other ready to fall if the Howards supplanted him with Carr.

Tom was often in a frenzy; one part of his mind suggested that he was not acting best by threatening Carr and yet, in the face of his friend's obstinate determination on self destruction (for a permanent alliance with Frances would be that, Tom thought), he shouted at Robin daily and their discussions on state policy ended with curses and quarrelling.

Tom could only threaten to reveal his letters "hidden and obviously intended for your whore". When Robin feebly said that drafts of letters were no proof the letters were ever used Tom replied that "they say things about your countess no man but yourself would know, you and your closest friend", and he also had another arrow for his bow: columns of figures which proved conclusively that Robin had been corrupt these last five years, using official money for his own purse, selling monopolies to city merchants, then selling titles to those same merchants when they, and he, had made their money. They look black, those trim tight lines of figures in ledgers, but they worried Robin far less than Tom's threat to expose his long-standing affair with Frances.

Overbury had even, in a sort of cunning madness, begun to write a vicious poem on her called "The Wife" which was intended to warn Robin against life with Frances. While he sanded the ink at night Tom wondered at his own passion. He realized that his determination to stop the marriage had more in it than political expediency and self interest although that was real enough. He hated the thought of his Robin domesticated and setting up house with that bare-faced beauty. Had he loved Robin in the same way as the king all these years and never known it, or at least never acknowledged it? His own love affairs were slack-moving businesses, soon lost in the torrential flow of his exciting packed life. Had Robin been his secret love all these years? He waited for his friend to turn on him with the obvious sneer "You do not wish Frances to have me as you want me for yourself"; if Robin thought of such a thing he never said it. Perhaps they were both aware of this suspicion of the root of their friendship and resolved, both, to ignore it.

And yet if Tom were jealous how much more honourable was the pitiful king! While Tom Overbury spat out calumnies against Frances, James had shaken his greying head over the love story. Although a bawdy man himself, he had not suspected for a moment that Robin and Frances had been making love for over a year; to him the whole fairytale was as romantic as May morning.

"Aye, aye," he said slowly one evening, dismissing his gentlemen and sitting down half-hosed on a fauteuil. "So be it, my bairn, so be it."

Robin had poured out the story as if his love were new, his eyes softening when he spoke of "The Countess of Essex" suggesting she was not merely a virgin but the holy one as well.

James pulled at his stockings himself and as he removed them, flexed his nubbly feet. His shirt lapped round him in crisp white folds, "Aye," he said, "it had to be, ye had tae fall for love like any lad, and with the countess too. The fairest flower o' the court, Robbie. Twa beautiful young things ye be."

"She is married," said Robin.

"D'ye think I dinna ken that when I rushed the two o' them into it? It was a foolish deed. I tak a' the blame for't. If I hadnae made them marry this tragedy would nae be."

He sighed thinking of his famous plan to marry the Devereux and Howard clans and gain lasting peace at the English court. He wondered if his scheme to marry one of his own children into protestant Germany and one into catholic Spain might be as unwise, but then he dismissed it. His Grand Design was too advanced for retreat. It was different for little Frances, who had carried a doll until the hour of her wedding; and the boy, young Essex, who was not endowed with his father's charm or beauty. Those plaintive children, married in haste, and repenting over five years in which they had been too young, and then too ill assorted to go to bed together!

"It's a' my fault, Rabbie," James said. "I made them marry and I will undo this marriage. If he canna bed her, there must be an end to 't," he sighed again and looked for a slipper. "Aye, Rabbie, Rabbie," he added, "ye ken your old man must do everything for ye."

Robin fell about his neck and the two of them clung close in the candlelit room, their tears falling on the bedcover, while outside the gentlemen waited in the gloom, until James called them in for the great undressing.

IX

THE CLOCK STRUCK one, and those who waited for their betters were weary. Tom Overbury's second man, a slouching fellow called Harry Payton, was half asleep as he listened for his master. The halberdiers occasionally crossed the floor, or glanced from the narrow thickpaned windows at the turbulent night. A January hoarfrost had set in like icing on a cake. Other windows were dark.

"Will they never be done?" said one guard to another.

"Affairs of state," said the second but with some jocularity.

They found the spectacle of Overbury and Carr amusing. When the king had gone to bed Overbury crept down the stairs like a lovelorn gallant and set to with Robin on the grave events of the nation. They would rustle papers and talk so low that the scratch-scratch of pens was louder than their voices. At midnight Tom usually left his patron. But this evening had drained another hour. Time seemingly stood still for great ones, it only mattered to the humble who had to wear the night away waiting for them. Then Carr left his friend, and wandered about in the court under the cold stars like a man in a maze, watched from those lancet windows by the surprised guards who were uncertain whether to leave their post or not for the light still flickered in the room where Overbury worked. At half after two Rochester returned and came swiftly down the corridor, pausing to tell the guards goodnight and bid them to bed, for with all his faults of conceit and ambition Robin was considerate of servants, and then he paused at the halfshut door and looked inside.

"What Tom, how now?" he said. "Are you yet up?"

"Nay," replied Overbury looking at his friend's cloak where the frost lay laced on the shoulders. "Why are you up at this time of night? Can you not leave the company of that filthy base woman?"

Harry Payton, whose cloak was half gathered to leave, stopped, and the two guards, who had been yawning farewells a second before, also stood still.

"I tell you once again," cried Overbury and he sounded half-choked with rage, "she will be the undoing of you and of this kingdom." His voice dropped but went on and on.

The men outside, afraid to move in case their bones cracked, hardly dared to creep nearer. They exchanged excited glances, communing delightedly at this late-night adventure. Already they were also looking at the doors at the end of the gallery, ready to sprint for them if Carr made a move to back out of the room where his best friend continued on and on, his voice so charged with phlegm that they could not understand a word. Finally Overbury paused and gathered breath, forgetting secrecy his voice boomed out with the old, often repeated, grievances.

"If you do intend to marry that filthy woman you will ruin your honour and yourself. You shall never do it by my advice or consent; and if you do you had best look to stand fast to me." Robin must have made no reply except for a sigh. "So," said Tom Overbury loudly, "we should part and you should give me that portion of your fortune which is due to me and then I'll leave you to stand on your own two legs."

"This is a treasonable matter," whispered one guard, recklessly, "if they knew we were here we would be clapped in gaol."

"Sh," said the other guard and Harry Payton. They could hear sounds of footsteps in the room but they were walking away from the door and then back to the table. They guessed that Carr was pacing the room. He reached the door again but fortunately with his back to the gallery, his long-fingered hand held the doorpost, the frost on his cloak had hardly melted but shone in the candlelight which glimmered from the room. The three listeners began a slow retreat, backs bowed, towards the shadows. If the floor squeaked Carr could not hear it for he burst out shouting, loud enough to be heard across the courtyard:

"My own legs are straight and strong enough to bear me up," then in a low sour voice, "I'll be even with you for this, Tom Overbury."

Tom gave a little hard bark like a dog fox far off. Carr stormed from the room, blessedly in the other direction from the listeners.

Two days later Harry Payton saw his master and Carr reconciled and walking in the garden amicably, occasionally singing a phrase or two from a new song. He could not understand the great ones, and he was intrigued by the notion that their loud argument was part of a sequence of quarrels. He told his friend who worked for the Earl of Northampton, wicked Howard as they called him; and he could not have been so wicked either, for he sent Harry a purse by way of his friend and asked for the names of the guards, which

Harry did not know, but he promised to send the earl any other titbits which came his way. A man had to watch out for his own interests at Whitehall.

Northampton was enraged by his great-niece but was too wise to show it. He had her at his house, where she made a great commotion about living far out at Hounslow and missing the court. After he had told her to continue being discreet, secretly appalled that she so obviously lusted after Carr (her nervous pleating fingers on her skirt, her hectic colour and her bitten lips all warned him that she was filled with anguish), he produced a ring from his purse.

"Why, that's——" Frances stopped and stared at him. The ring, a black pearl set in diamonds, lay on a table between them.

"It is your ring?"

"Yes. That is——"

"You sent a messenger after this ring to Norfolk with orders to put the case to the Norwich constables if it were not returned to you."

"Yes, I——" she faltered, secretly shocked at her own inadequacy. Frances had always been sure she could face any exposure, tell any lie, but looking at that sinister dark pearl, its diamonds reflecting the cold light outside the windows, she felt petrified. She stared at old Uncle Henry, the one man she feared.

"Where did you——?" she began again.

"You asked the constables to arrest a Mrs Mary Woods if she did not return it peacefully."

"She did nothing for it. It was part payment for a—a deed she did, but she could not deliver the goods I wanted so I asked for the ring back."

"Do you know what this ring is worth, Frances?"

"I don't know. My father gave it me."

"It is quite valuable," said Henry drily. He turned it about so that it quivered against his hard thin hands. He couched it between his fingers so that they looked like a parody of Cunning Mary's pale old lips. Frances shivered.

"A poor old woman, a necromancer, she says, but the Norwich magistrates tell me she is but a palmist, not a very good one, either. However they had wanted to apprehend her for some time on another charge than stealing your ring. She did not steal it, did she?"

"No. I gave it to her."

"I thought so. They are sure she is an extortionist. Do you know what that means, Frances?"

"Somebody who—a person who makes money by——"

"By the crimes of others. An old woman who is as much a witch as I am," —and that's not far off, thought Frances rebelliously— "but who promises to kill unwanted wives, murder old fathers with fortunes and so on. She cannot do any of these things, of course, but she then tells her customers that she will inform on them to the magistrates unless they pay her off handsomely."

"Well?"

"When the Norwich constable took her up she had a strange tale to tell of this ring. She admitted it had belonged to the Countess of Essex and said it had been given her as a reward for a potion to kill the earl. Oh she made very clear that she had no intention of providing a poison, 'what, hurt that poor dear young man,' she said of your husband, but also said you were out of your mind at the time for fear the magic might not work, and that you gave her the ring to bribe her. . . ."

Frances looked at the ring again, midnight colour, its diamonds mobile as stars.

"You had best have it back," said her great-uncle, dropping it into her lap.

"What else did the Norwich magistrates say?"

"Very little. They are inclined not to believe Cunning Mary. She tells these stories of great courtiers who patronize her but nobody listens. Who would be foolish enough to employ Cunning Mary as a witch even if they were unprincipled enough to murder their husband? And who would murder a husband when a divorce was imminent? They dismissed it as nonsense and she went into their Bridewell as a thief."

"But she is not."

"Better serve a term as a thief than die as a poisoner, I think, Frances. I thanked them and said you had lost the ring a twelve-month ago, on a hawking party at Audley End where it might have been picked up. They may even let her go on such a story."

"Thank you, sir."

A servant brought in Henry's late breakfast of herb beer and coddled eggs. She shook her head when he offered her some, yawning at the long journey she had just made "up at five" and the similar ride back again.

Henry nodded but was not listening. When his plate was clean he said: "Forget Essex, he is not a problem."

"He will be if I cannot have a divorce."

"The boy has no ill will towards you. His whole place in this story is an accident. It's not only unwise to consider killing him, it is unjust."

"Unjust!" she cried. "What is justice then? I will not spend the rest of my life in love with a man I cannot marry."

"One word," said Henry. He called for oysters and a manservant brought them in a basket wrapped round with seaweed and smelling of brine.

Henry picked at them meditatively. "Are you with child by Carr?" he asked.

"What? Never. I am more wise than that, Uncle Henry."

"You know those tricks, the ball of cotton, the days of the month?"

She did not blush. Her cool eyes looked back at his with as much resistance as onyx. "I am no foolish virgin," she said.

"You must pretend to be one these next months, Frances. Beware the midwives."

He leaned forward, pointing one long finger at her mount of Venus. "Have answers pat. Be modest. Remember you must reply to their questions and they will not all have been subborned by me."

"What of the search?"

"That?" He flicked his fingers fastidiously. "A nothing, we find a virgin like you in colour, we can bleach her hair to your shade. I believe," he pulled a tendril down from her high brow, "your own is darker, is it not?"

She was angry. Her colour flew up although it had stayed dormant at more trying questions, "I do dye it—a little," she said.

"Give the receipt of the dye, or the bottle, to your mother," said Henry. He looked at her feet. "They are over large," he added consideringly, "we must tell the girl to keep her own hid under her skirt."

"Am I here to be calumnied, uncle?" she asked.

"Why, not so," he smiled. He patted her knee, enjoying her indignant face. "Your fury at being called a murderess is rather less than that with which you respond to being clump footed," he said. "You will be a formidable woman, Frances. At sixteen a blade between my ribs for a casual word."

"May I go—sir?" She stood up but he waved her back towards

her seat with the cruel gold-hilted knife with which he opened oysters.

"No," he told her. "Your husband is a poor thing pulled into this damnable affair through no fault of his own. No man is to blame for any part of it. You cannot blame the king for match-making, or us for agreeing to it, or young Carr for being so hand-some and for being the king's lover. There is only one man who should suffer, because only one man can imperil the divorce," he hooked out an oyster and looked at it speculatively before it van-ished into his mouth. "You know the man——" She pondered. "Overbury," said Henry quickly. "He wants to keep Carr dancing attendance on him so he is working us out of power as fast as he can. And he must stop the marriage, for with it he will lose his friendship with Carr and his position at court. He knows full well we will not brook him in a high place when we are the king's secret advisors."

"Do you mean the king will allow you and my father to be his— advisors?"

"He will have no choice if he wants to keep Robin Carr, and if Robin is wed to you"—briskly—"Overbury should be put out of the way."

"Put out of the way," she repeated.

"And there is another threat from him. I warrant he knows all your dealings with Carr and would use them profitably. Even as Cunning Mary does, but he is more danger than that old crone, being more powerful. He could spoil your chance of a divorce with a few words dropped—about you and your Robin and your hiding place at Hammersmith or Hounslow. And he has another hold over Carr." She held her breath. "He could tear him from the king if Jamie knew of all your Robin's dabblings in corruption. Yes," quietly, "he should be removed for a while."

"How?"

"Not by Cunning Mary. I think you have enough hold over Carr to get him to dance to your tune."

"I know I have," she smiled, that slippery profiled smile which irritated both her uncle and her lover.

"Then use it. Get him to send Overbury abroad again on some excuse until this divorce be over."

"Is that all?"

"It may be more difficult than you think. Whatever way, he must be silenced for the next few months."

"By going abroad?"

Henry resolutely ignored his great-niece's urgent face. "That would be best," he said. "That would be most expedient."

She accepted that her meeting with him was at an end and went without asking permission, dropping a curtsey that was almost a mockery. The old man crept nearer his fire and continued to husk his oysters. He did not look up when the servant came to gather the shells, but studied the flames as if they were title deeds or mortgages or any of the other documents which had charted his life. He feared that his great-niece had a passion for murder akin to her passion for Carr's body.

X

"TOM IS LIKE a madman," confided Robin.

He was on the river with Northampton whose barge billowed across the water, its velvet hangings caught up in a breeze which whirled them against the sides like panniered skirts.

"Is he?" murmured Northampton. It was cold and he had hoped that the pull down to Greenwich would have been accomplished before the snap of evening air. Behind them, other boats dipped and eddied with the current as oarsmen clapped to their work of taking the king and his court downstream.

James's barge headed the procession, its lamps already blinking in a five o'clock dusk. The dark shapes of the palace appeared behind the river mist and the royal barge began to turn inland. They could see that Greenwich was flooded, water meres lay across the lawns and wildfowl tittered in reeds along the bank.

"We will be some time getting into land," said Northampton, gauging the disturbance which would be caused by the king's landing. He tapped his head waterman with his ebony stick and the man ordered the oarsmen to rest, so that Robin and Henry Howard lay midstream, surrounded by silence, for the men were tired and half asleep at their places. They could hear occasional sorties of laughter from other barges but all were pulled well behind them. The two men might have been marooned on an island.

"Tell me more," commanded Northampton.

"He says he has given up his own future in order to aid me in mine," muttered Robin.

"The man's a fool."

"You think so?"

"What future would Overbury have had as one of Cecil's men? The most he could have hoped for would have been an embassy in some Godforsaken spot. And many ambitious diplomats fall by the way, he might have ended as a lickpenny lawyer skivvying about the closes of the inns of court picking up groats for defending cress sellers and waggoners. If he says he gave up aught for you, my lord Rochester, he is seeking your sympathy. You say he makes out bills?"

"Accounts, my lord. He says I owe him much and has it all writ up on reams of paper."

"And yet he is one of the richest men at court, and by his friendship with you!"

"He says I would have been a Scots squireen without his help."

Northampton laughed. "The only man who aided your lordship was James Hay."

"I believe that also."

They were both silent thinking of Hay who had settled to a minor position at court, remaining a friend of James, if not his familiar.

"And of course yourself," added Northampton courteously; "it is by your own talents that you occupy so high a place in his majesty's affections."

"Tom would have it that I would be nobody without him."

"As he is your advisor. There are other men who could lend you a little of their wisdom, Lord Rochester."

"Yourself, my lord, I know."

The water paddled against the sides of the barge, emitting a thick yeasty smell like fruit a long time squashed in the sun.

"How can I rid me of him?" asked Carr, "for a few weeks only."

Northampton pointed his fingers together like a knight praying on a tomb.

"Your first act should be to discredit him with the king," he said. "Give lame advice to James, and excuse it as Overbury's."

"Yet his majesty insisted that I retain Tom to aid me in foreign letters," said Carr.

"There are many reasons why Overbury's work should—go off," said Northampton: "the man is tired, he needs a rest from those everlasting counsels. A few months abroad——"

"I had thought of that," replied Carr pleased that his own perspicacity should be echoed by Howard.

"You thought rightly," said the old man. His fur-girt wrist rested for a moment on his companion's arm. "We two together could make up one Cecil, think you?"

"Perchance," said Carr, "but the king will not make me secretary. He wishes me to stay as Keeper of the Signet."

"A worthy post. It is the keeper who sees all the royal letters, which is a position of great trust, my lord. You are honoured by it."

Robin looked at him doubtfully. "Think you so?"

"Indeed, the secretary should be a man subservient to us, who is known to hold our policies before he takes office, so that we cannot be accused of seducing him with bribes afterwards."

"I had thought on Neville," said Carr carelessly, "he is a diplomat and was well thought of by Cecil."

"And runs to the whistle of the commons," added Northampton. "Lake is my man."

"I have spoke against Lake to the king."

"You should change your mind."

"The king may not heed me."

"He has always listened in the past."

Carr did not say that nothing as important as the secretaryship had arisen in the past. He asked Northampton how he might make James critical of Overbury.

"There is no need to deny the man," said Howard, happy in his machinations. "James would be suspicious if you affected to hate Overbury——"

"And I do not," interposed Carr. "I would only have him let me alone while this divorce is on us."

"So. Tell the king that Tom Overbury irks you, no more. You would not be without him, insist on that, for if the king believes you are casting old friends overboard he may begin to look into *his* intimacy with you. Say that Tom longs for overseas and is down-hearted in London, that he is building up a fury against the court which might lead him to incur the queen's anger once again; say that Tom Overbury yawns over the foreign letters and has no patience to read half of them. Tell the king the man is tired and would return renewed after a few months in an embassy——"

"I will do all these things."

"But," said Northampton calmly, "all gently, all with discretion, begin by a few sighs, a few complaints of aching heads in the morning from arguments with Overbury at night. Tell James that Tom Overbury chides you like a naughty boy and you do not wish to quarrel with your oldest friend at court. Tell James you owe so much to Overbury that you must treat him favourably in his time of sickness, by offering him a post abroad until the divorce is over. Perhaps," he smiled, "you might suggest jealousy on Overbury's part, that you are to be married to the Countess of Essex, and the king, so conscious of his own magnanimity in arranging that very marriage when he stands e'en closer to your lordship than friend Overbury, will be generous to the wilful boy and send him overseas."

"I like it all," said Carr. He had a picture of himself playacting for the king, a drooping lip, a sudden tear, a youthful unwillingness to "tell on" Overbury to the royal master.

"We may enter now, my lord," said the waterman, glancing behind. The oarsmen methodically groaned as they set to once more.

Sir Dudley Digges was waiting for Tom by the Whitehall watergate. He had known Overbury in his humble days but seemed unlikely to claim close friendship by it. "I am come as an emissary only," he said, "from the Archbishop of Canterbury".

Overbury looked at him with surprise, wondering why the archbishop should wish to see him and also why Digges should have been sent to escort him. He was chagrined that he should be summoned to the archbishop. George Abbot was no recluse. He pottered in matters of state until the council were weary of him, for he pestered ambassadors with long liturgical questions about religious observance in the countries in which they served, and he would impede council meetings by conducting religious arguments with the king in which both became red faced and acrimonious but mutually delighted. It had been some time since Tom had been asked to move his autocratic backside, suppliants came to him for advice; and he was sulky at the thought of a morning meeting at Lambeth.

Tom affected friendship "for old times' sake" with Digges and had been remarkably affable as they were rowed over the river. When Digges was later asked if he had appreciated Overbury's egalitarianism he said, "No, he was damnably proud, as ever."

At ten o'clock George Abbot was waiting for them, chirping like a thrush about his library. Then all three talked of Sir Dudley's maggot of the mind which was the North-West Passage until that young man bowed himself out on the excuse that he had friends in Lambeth whom he would visit, but "I will return at noon to conduct Sir Thomas across the river once more."

"I am surprised, sir," Tom said to the archbishop, "that what you would want of me could not wait until you visit the other side." He nodded at the river which was still pink with morning sunlight. On the opposite shore the ricketty turrets of Westminster were in shrouds of mist from which a window or a weathervane shone out occasionally like masthead beacons.

"It would not wait for my coming," answered Abbot. He invited Tom to look at his books and complimented him on his writings—"which pass about from hand to hand and gain praise from all who read them"—but he did not say if he had read any of Tom's works himself. Politely, Overbury looked at the square-cut spines of dark leather. As he had supposed, the king's works were prominent. He watched Abbot warily while the old man picked up one book after another. His long pale face could have been handsome above more frivolous dress. Abbot would have been a great statesman if he were not a great churchman.

"I hope you do not play at politics," said Tom as lightly as he he could, at which Abbot frowned and suggested a chair facing the windows. These were so small and square in the wall of dark panelling that Tom's view of the river became unreal, as if he faced three small paintings of river life in which people plied boats, carried vegetables on barges or walked along the towpath as removed from the room as if they were enamelled. Although it was a warm morning Abbot had a fire which was still twitching unwillingly to life. As he spoke, his propositions were punctuated with noises of cracking twigs and falling coals while little claws of flame or smoke darted in and out of the hearth.

"Prince Charles is a likely lad," asserted Abbot; "it is said his majesty will replace the late lamented Prince Henry with him as suitor for the Princess of Spain."

Overbury could tell by the way Abbot's hands wandered about the books that this had nothing to do with his visit. He made noncommittal answers, not wishing to be exposed as a plotter for or against the marriage at some future time. When the archbishop's hands sat still, holding a copy of the psalms, he knew the nub had been reached.

Abbot was silent and looked at Tom with a worried smile. He folded his hands and apparently decided he appeared too consciously benign, for he uncrossed them again and rubbed his palms once. Overbury enjoyed this nervousness in the archbishop. He smiled back, waiting for the purpose of the meeting.

"Sir Thomas, your friends fear for you," began the old man unhappily. "They think you run where you should walk."

"What may that mean?" asked Overbury. "There are always envious men, my lord, who would prefer to see their acquaintance brought low and humbled rather than soar above them. As sparrows watch the hawk, my lord, and fear it."

Abbot sighed. "Sir Thomas," he said, "I am empowered to offer you the embassy in Russia."

"To Russia?" cried Tom, his handsome dark face reddening while Abbot explained that this was a special mission, connected with the hopes of his friend Neville to establish anchorages at Archangel.

"They would have me out of their way," said Tom. He stood up and looked at the peaceful river.

"Not so, not so," replied the archbishop. He tugged awkwardly at Tom's sleeve hoping to distract him. "This is only for a month or so. It is a worthy enterprise."

Tom looked at him sideways and smiled, "Why, my lord, it sounds an extraordinary venture, tell me more on't." And Abbot told Tom about the northern lights, and the bears of the steppes, and how the people of the far north could become wolves at will, and of the Lapland witches who eat baby fat in winter and survive to spring, and of the court of the Russian tsar where wild men roamed among the polite Westerners, their cutlasses naked as their black-haired breasts. They were travellers' tales which Tom had heard before, but he listened politely. Abbot also said that if he attempted this journey Overbury would be made Lord Treasurer of the Household on his return.

"Which I am now in all but name," he said discontentedly to Dudley Digges as they returned across the river.

Digges knew of the offer, which further irritated Tom as it suggested the members of the foreign service must have been consulted on it. He did not rail against Abbot.

"Pho, that old man the archbishop, he is but their mouthpiece." Neither did Overbury say who "they" were. "It is a plot to be rid of me," he tapped the side of his nose meaningfully, "I am too powerful and some would have me out of the way. They have tried before."

Digges had heard how Overbury had once magnified a summer ague into an attempted poisoning and he only nodded. "In all honesty, Sir Thomas," he replied, "the work you are asked to do in Russia would be thought matchless by any man. Why, it is an enterprise such as Elizabeth might have entrusted to Drake or Raleigh."

"And where are they now?"

"But there have to be men of adventure in every reign, Sir Thomas. This will be a noble mission, taking the goodwill of our king to a country of which we know so little yet. I would I might accompany you, to write down what we see——"

"Out of sight, out of mind," returned Tom. "Each man must look to himself in this world, Digges, and if I am in Muscovy I may as well be dead for all that his majesty or Carr will care for me."

When they landed at Whitehall steps he was away across the yard, his black cloak swirling as he ran to Carr's apartments.

Digges had arranged to meet Tom by the tiltyard in the afternoon to take his considered reply to Abbot. He wondered if Abbot himself knew who was offering Tom the embassy to Russia. If it were the king, surely James would have sent a messenger straight to Overbury?

"You must do something," said Tom decisively after telling Carr about Abbot's offer.

"What can I do?" asked Robin, he spread his hands and smiled unhappily, "a refusal to accept a post as king's envoy is contempt, and is punishable with prison and with loss of office, Tom. If you go to Russia you will be well regarded when you return. If you do not go you are likely to lose what you have. Would you throw up your career on a whim?"

"On a whim!" shouted Tom. "On a whim! Can you not see this is some devilish trick by the Howard faction and the archbishop combining, in order to remove me at a point in your life when you need my advice as never before? I doubt the king had aught to do with this offer except to agree with it when old Northampton broached it. With me away they can attack you."

"Why should the Howards attack me?"

"Why does anyone attack the king's favourite, Robin? You feel safe with them as the suitor for their Frances but there is many a slip—the divorce may not go through, they are covering themselves all ways, Robin, and one way is to take away your right hand: me. They know you are helpless without me."

"I have told——" began Robin, anxious to prove independence.

"Tell me not again—that you protect me with the king's great love—I know it all and yet, Robin, no man is safe in this shark-infested sea we call the court. They would drag you down too, Robin, whatever their love for Frances. Do they say they would uphold you? Not so. Can you think Howard would have any man share his power? They want you to be their dolly, Robin, and dance

86

on their ribbons. They must remove me to accomplish that."

Robin looked at him keenly but Tom was away on a tangent about safety and daggers in the night, wandering about the room, picking up pieces and throwing them down: a book, a dog's collar, a hat, a glove, they all fell discarded from his unfeeling fingers as he passed them by.

"You would be back ere winter," said Robin weakly.

"And find you retreated to the country and me exiled to oblivion," said Tom. "Russia is like death, men are forgotten there."

This was so true that Robin did not argue but said that the king would be angry if he were told that Overbury refused the embassy.

"Ah, but do you not see the cunning of it all?" asked Tom. "They made the offer under the blanket, not coming from the king but coming from Archbishop Abbot so that it is all tentative and infirm. It can be refused in the same way. I hate these oblique men," he added, "but for this one time I am happy they are so circuitous that their indirect offer can gain an indirect refusal and none are hurt. And yet they are like to repeat it, Robin, and that is why you must hie to James with all speed and tell him you cannot continue without me and that by sending me away you would be deprived of your eyes, your ears, your hands in all state matters. He will see the reasons why I must stay here. James will do anything you ask, Robin. Ask him this."

"He will not make Neville Secretary of State," answered Robin, "I doubt the king loves me as a member of council e'en if his love for me as a companion is as strong as ever it was."

"Beg him to keep me here," said Tom. "I told Abbot the king cannot in law or justice force me to forsake my country at a crucial time like this."

"The Russian embassy is an honourable position," pleaded Robin.

"Is it? Is it? Aye, for petty men, for the Wottons and Winwoods of the world it is an honourable position. But I have outsoared them all, Robin. You know that I am the king's chief advisor, even if by proxy, and cannot take the left-overs of the foreign service. What do they think I am?"

"I cannot tell the king you have refused outright, you would end in the Tower."

"Aye, we will be careful in our disobedience. So I will accept the post. With pleasure and profound thanks."

"You will?"

"Even so. I will ask Sir Dudley Digges—a self-appointed nursemaid to the plot—to tell the archbishop I am well pleased and that I will be packed and ready by the week's end. Meanwhile you must weep and tell the king you cannot persuade me to stay here when his majesty commands me to foreign service but that you would be desolate without me, and would retire to the country and live as a hermit if I go to Russia. James will be so affrighted by your sadness he will revoke the order."

Robin sighed. "I would indeed be woeful at your going away," he said, looking beyond Tom to the tapestry of Agamemnon on the wall.

"I will make haste and tell Sir Dudley that I accept the post," said Tom.

He met Digges by the tiltyard within the hour and told him he would be pleased to go to Russia.

"I am glad of this, Sir Thomas," Digges said, "but surprised. You were so bitter when we were on the water, declaring you may as well be dead as in Russia."

"Tell the archbishop I am ready on the instant," replied Tom.

"This is a change of face indeed," continued Digges as they began to walk across the green.

"Not completely," said Overbury.

"Ha," replied Digges encouragingly.

"My Lord Rochester will never let me go."

Digges stopped walking and forced Overbury to stand still. "You think not?"

"I know not," answered Tom. "Life without me would be meat without salt for Robin. Besides, he has a place to keep in the king's council and needs constant help to maintain it. Robin is not strong in the intellect."

"He is not an absolute fool," countered Digges. "I think you do not estimate him fairly, Sir Thomas."

"I know his abilities. He would be lost without me."

Digges allowed Tom to walk on but stood still himself.

Tom turned and waved. "I know I am right," he answered. "My precious Robin knows the king's mind better than any, and I the mind of my precious Robin."

They met by a stream at Hounslow Heath. Alders twisted out of the muddy banks, their ankle-turning roots forming cover for water rats which had run pell-mell to their holes as Robin rode up. He wore a grey wool cloak and a slouch hat as if he were a wandering preacher. Even his horse was a disguise, its rangy neck hung downwards as they talked, defeated by the few miles from London.

"Why do this, Frances?" he asked angrily. "You know we have promised your uncle not to meet. If the commissioners found that you knew me more than by sight your divorce would be invalid. You are supposedly seeking a separation because you cannot bear to live with Essex, not because you are embroiled with another man."

"Have no fear," said Frances. "If you were frightened of my uncle you would not be here now."

"How could I let you come here alone?"

He looked at her with some exasperation, for she had made no attempt to conceal herself. Her crimson riding habit was embroidered so that any peasant would turn to stare at her twice. Behind a rise of ground he could see the white-feathered hats of her attendants.

"So you are come with company too," he said. "Are you mad, Frances?"

"I had to see you," she replied.

"You cannot take chances like this——"

"I had to see you." Her mouth had been painted and its redness repeated the red of her dress; standing in that drab landscape of early spring where the brightest colour was a soft grey-green, she looked like a fire lit on a frozen lake.

"What of the divorce?" whispered Robin anxiously.

"They have not chosen the commissioners yet. My uncle Northampton thinks it may be nigh on a year before anything comes of it. How can I be without you for a year?"

Carr wanted to tell her not to be foolish, that a year was nothing compared with the rest of their lives, but she looked so resolute that he said nothing. She stood watching him and smiling, her teeth breaking through her red lips now and then like those of a hungry animal.

"Do you want me?"

"What nonsense is this? Of course I want you all the time, Frances. These weeks have been——"

"Do you want me now?" she said, stamping at him. Her voice was cracking so that she appeared her real age for a moment, a young girl who wanted to test her lover.

"Frances——" he began but she grabbed his arm and was pulling him towards the alders.

"By God you are mad," he said half laughing, and then stopping as she clawed at the ivory tags on his hose, wrenching them on to the ground in her fury. When he tried to stop her she slapped at his face with her flat hands, her rings cutting into his jaw. She retreated, but pulled him after her until they were enclosed by the ominous trees. There were too few leaves to make an adequate screen against onlookers or the weather but Frances started to pull at her own clothes, scattering hair pins into the soft sucking mud in which she swayed, her heels sinking as she moved.

"No," said Robin.

"Why not?" she asked, biting her under lip as she pulled at the strings of her bodice. He shivered as her shoulders emerged into the cold hair, they looked as blue as his breath which hovered between them.

"Cover yourself," he said roughly. He pulled off his cloak and tried to hold her in it but she slithered like a fish in its folds, discarding her skirt and hose until they lay puddled between her legs. he undressed almost resentfully, her prim arrogant face determined against the grey sky and the dingy mudbanks behind her.

"And you? And you?" she said finally, pulling the cloak close to her. Robin could see by her discarded dress that she must be naked under the rough wool but he could not strip to the waist. He recoiled against the cold like a parlour cat. Hesitantly he let down his hose, feeling slightly ridiculous and looking all the time at the crest of the land where her grooms were waiting.

"Do you not see, Frances?" he said. "If one of those lads is untrue to you——"

She silenced him by attacking his mouth, so suddenly that he thought she had slashed him with a knife; and then saw from the blood on her teeth that she had in fact bitten him. It had been so quick he had not realized that she had raised her head. Then she pulled him down on top of her, her bare shoulders squelching into the muddy grass.

He wriggled, almost in protest, as he entered her, disturbed by her continual movements, like an eel emerging from its home in the stream. As she pummelled him and whispered at him, Robin gained enough strength to make love in a short sharp fashion, so that he was spent within a minute. But Frances was satisfied. She immediately started to dress again, using his cloak as a tent, while he stood by, feeling useless as he trembled with cold. All her movements were as brisk as her sudden lovemaking.

"By God," he said, "you would make any man impotent."

She smiled at him, briefly, her little teeth were still stained with his blood. "You like it not?" she asked.

"Like? There is no liking it, Frances, it is like a play performed in a madhouse. I am numb."

She looked as if this were a compliment and even hummed as she piled up her hair and shuffled in the mud for her pins. Reluctantly he bent down beside her, retrieving them from the ground where they were only identifiable by their round gold heads.

"Help me," she said. Robin pulled at the tangles, which were daubed with mud like a swallow's nest.

"What will you say to your maids?" he asked.

"That I slipped and fell in the stream," she answered. "What of Tom Overbury?"

"What of him?"

"Have you sent him abroad yet?"

"It is in train."

"I hate that man," said Frances, "I want you to have no part of him. I would like him to vanish as if he had never been."

"He is my dearest friend," replied Carr.

"Not dearer than I, not dearer than I," she answered.

"Never, never," returned Robin. "None are as dear as you."

Frances was satisfied with that and rode back to Hounslow at a gallop, so that her attendants could not keep up with her and cursed their mistress as her horse legged it smartly out of sight. "Why does she not get up on a broomstick?" said one and the others laughed uneasily, even in these enlightened times one did not joke about witches.

XI

By the third week of April 1613 the story of the offered embassy to Russia had come out, but Overbury showed no sign of apprehension, he sauntered as proudly, and was as unbearable in conversation to many whom he thought his inferiors; he bought hugely for spring: pleated ruffs with gold thread insertions, carnation-coloured hose, a doublet of green silk so pale it appeared white in daylight, and several rings which he piled on to his knuckles. He said to Sir Henry Wotton that he was never better "than at present in my fortunes and ends".

Robin began to play his double game. It was as tentative as a man learning a dangerous sport; ever fearful of Tom's brimstone fury and of the sly manoeuvres of Northampton, Robin wished only that he could honestly retire from court for a few weeks, but the plot depended on him so that he had to smile at Tom and declare he could not understand why the king was so far adamant on the Russian journey, while to James he continued to complain that Tom was burdening him with care and nagging him as "if he were an auld wife wi' a ne'er do well man".

James laid his hand on Robin's in sympathy. "He must gi' ye a bit peace."

"I wouldna like the scandal of an outright quarrel," replied Robin dolorously, "but I canna go on like this, no sleep this twa three nights wi' that man haverin' at me. Forbye, Overbury has been a guid friend tae me. I wouldnae put him down before the court."

The 21st of April was the first warm day of the year and after the chill winter women sallied out in soft gowns and light cloaks. Their gallants walked beside them, strutting like pigeons on the broad walks about Whitehall. Overbury watched the parade from his windows; Harry Payton came in with a woollen robe against the chance of a cold evening and laid it on the bed, the smell of orris came with it, for it had been laid away all winter. Harry was leaving but came quickly back into the room, his agitated eyes signalling a warning. Before Tom could question him, Harry blurted out "The Lord Chancellor, Sir Thomas, coming up the stairs and with him the Earl of Pembroke".

Overbury had no time to collect his wits; both men were too eminent to come as anything but emmissaries from the king. He felt a pain under his heart which he immediately blamed on his cold pork dinner but he did not move. "Ask their lordships to enter," he said and took up a stance beside the window.

"Sir Thomas," said Ellesmere immediately, "we will have no beatings about the bush."

"I should hope not, my lord."

"Lord Pembroke has come with me to add weight to my offer." Pembroke looked about abstractedly, wishing he were elsewhere. "We have authority to offer you two alternatives," said Ellesmere, "the embassy at Paris or the embassy in the Low Countries."

"What, is Russia out?" asked Tom raising his elegant eyebrows. Pembroke looked somewhat abashed at this and began to draw back into the shadows.

"No games, Sir Thomas," continued Ellesmere, "which will you have?"

"My lord," returned Tom, "you intrigue me, you offer these two embassies like a card sharp proffering two aces with three up his sleeve."

"You must make a choice."

Tom turned and looked out of the window so that the two lords could only see his lounging back. His face was puckered with dismay and he bit his knuckle until his teeth closed harshly over his rings. It was minutes before Ellesmere, who was gouty and tired of standing but who had not been offered a seat, broke out: "Well, Sir Thomas, what is your answer?"

Tom, who had made a sudden decision to openly refuse, turned to them almost joyfully.

"Neither," he said.

"Neither?" cried Pembroke from the dark, while Ellesmere silenced his younger colleague with a short backward jab of his hand. He bent towards Tom sternly.

"You must have one," he said briskly.

"What," said Tom jeeringly, "you would have a poor fish like myself represent England? Why, my French is so meagre I would have the Parisians rolling about with laughter which is not a good augury for a country's ambassador, and my Low German is even worse 'Ja mein herren'," he essayed. "What an oaf I would appear!

Beside that, my lords, I have not the grace or the manner to become an ambassador. I am not like Neville or Wotton or Sir Ralph Winwood, I have none of those special talents which make an ambassador, I would hesitate to do my country ill service and so I must graciously decline his majesty's offer."

Pembroke was for bolting from the room at once, but Ellesmere stood firm and so he was compelled to listen as Tom turned back to the window where he affected to be playing with his necklace.

"We will give you secretaries enough," said Ellesmere, "that you need not consider if your talents would support your office; and I feel you are young enough, Sir Thomas, to make a study of languages."

"Not so, my lord," replied Tom rapidly, "my health would not permit me to cross the sea. I have been sick of a spleen this winter, you may ask Sir Theodore Mayerne on that, I was very chilled and like to spend some time abed. I would not journey abroad, it would kill me."

"So be it," said Pembroke in a low voice.

"I am too weak to write my own private letters," continued Tom.

"Methinks," said Ellesmere cruelly, "that a change of air would do you good, Sir Thomas, and some doctors recommend long voyages for the spleen."

Tom rounded on them then, his face contorted so that Ellesmere stepped back towards the door. "Do as you will, my lord," he said sibilantly, "run back to your masters, whosoever they be, and say that Sir Thomas Overbury is not fit. I will outface you all, even the king. There is no reason under the law for me to leave this country, and you, as Lord Chancellor, know that well. Can the king make me run? Can he harry me like a hare? I am a man with rights, my lords, I have taken enough of your jeers and open disdain. I know that many men want me out of the way," he advanced on them so that old Ellesmere retreated on Lord Pembroke who was hastily opening the door, almost upon Harry Payton.

"You are talking arrant nonsense," said Pembroke roundly.

"You may be puppets also," said Tom, "the king is but a tool in their hands."

"Enough of this," replied Ellesmere.

"Oh, you may pretend that this offer is for my good," said Overbury, "but I will not leave London now for any preferment in the world. I know that as soon as I go I will be so hounded that I will never return alive. But see here," he held Ellesmere by the cuff so that unfortunate Pembroke realized he could not leave the Lord Chancellor alone with Overbury and he had to pause again in his escape. "Tell the serpents that I have an antidote to their venom. You name the great of this land, it is not James or his queen or even my lovely Robin. It is that fiend Northampton, who would have the inquisition here in London if he had his way, and his nephew, silly Suffolk, manipulated by his uncle and his vicious wife, for you know that Lady Suffolk seduces young men for money; and what a gem they have in Frances! What a paragon of virtue! She would part her legs for anything which offered her a new sensation, my lords, until she reaches the final sensation which will be pain for all those about her. She is a whore, my lords, a Jezebel, whose body, waxen as a candle, melts before any man who points his flame at her. Think you she loves brave Robin, think you——?" he paused, spit foaming on his chin, and both lords hurried from him.

"We are sage men," Ellesmere called back as they went, "and will tell no man of your ravings, but I beseech you, Sir Thomas, speak not like this to any others."

"Is he mad?" asked Pembroke as they crossed the courtyard.

"No," said Ellesmere, "there is some sense in what he says but he hath distorted all."

"Is he in danger?"

"He will be if he speaks like that."

They tripped up the steps and along the corridor to the room in which the council was in session. Looking at those grave faces, well lit by the candles although it was still light outside, Pembroke felt relieved. All the men about the table were sane and plain spoken, and thought before they acted. The archbishop and the king had been wrangling some Biblical point and both were breathless and content. The rest of the council sat about attempting to show interest but wishing that they could direct the king to speak of the defences of the Kent coast which was the next item on their lists.

"We are come from Sir Thomas Overbury, your grace," said Ellesmere, regaining his self importance as Pembroke dropped into a chair beside the archbishop.

"What says he?" asked James.

Both envoys hesitated, for although neither liked Overbury they had both been distressed by his outburst and had some pity for him.

"Say you, my lord," suggested James to Pembroke, as Ellesmere was massaging his gouty knee.

"He refuses the offered posts," said Pembroke, thinking that a bald statement would allay the king's temper.

James looked disconcerted. None knew what to say, for nobody had ever defied the king so blatantly before.

Ellesmere spoke up. "He's tainted in his wits, your majesty," he said.

"Am I so despised?" asked James, spreading his arms as if he would embrace the council. "Am I so tyrannical a master that I cannot obtain this service from one of my servants—that this gentleman will not accept honourable employment from me?"

It was more mild than most councillors had expected and many of them looked at Rochester who had bent forward in his seat. While they watched he leant his head on his hands.

"So be it: order Sir Thomas here," said James to Pembroke who had hoped another man would be sent.

Nothing was discussed in the council room. The men were silent and pretended to study the papers before them, James sat like Judgement, his arms laid straight on the table before him, his pawky hat perched back on his greying hair. His melancholy drooplidded eyes stared down the board at Carr who could not look back at him but remained with his elbows on the table and his head bent downwards so that none of the councillors could see his face.

"Lord Rochester may leave us," suggested James and Carr immediately leaped up, then hesitated, looking at the great door through which his best friend might come at any moment. The king made a gesture to the wall behind his own chair where a small door communicated with his private rooms. Robin gratefully backed towards this while the other members of the council deliberately continued to look away from him. As the latch shuddered into place after he had gone, one or two covertly glanced at each other across the table. Was this the end of Robin Carr?

It was nearly ten minutes before footsteps were heard at the entrance to the council room. The Clerk of the Council opened the door and Overbury entered, his exquisite dress affronting the room. His colour was high and his eyes were overbright. Some of the councillors thought he looked like a man playing a part, and his furled cloak and opalescent chain emphasized his splendid, nonchalant strutting figure. Behind him, Pembroke was a lost dog trailing dispiritedly after a stranger. Overbury stood before the seated council; James looked at him like a father considering a recalcitrant son.

"Sir Thomas," he said gently, "you have been offered three positions of honour, to represent your country in Russia, the Low Countries or Paris and I am told you refused all of them."

"That is so, sire."

"You would tell me the same?"

"Neither you, nor any man," flared Tom, glaring at Northampton who sat at the far end of the table, "can make me leave the country in such a perilous state."

James sighed and beckoned to the Clerk of the Council who dropped his quill so that ink spattered over his papers as he moved towards the king. "Take Sir Thomas to the Tower," said James, "he will remain there under our custody."

A breath was taken in all over the room like a sail filling with wind. Overbury stood still. "It is not possible," he cried, at which James looked so surprised that Tom faltered and glanced around him.

Although this punishment had seemed likely none of the council had admitted it would occur and they now looked at each other silently. Northampton sat with his head bowed as two Yeoman of the Guard walked to Overbury and stood on either side of him. The Clerk of the Council seemed unwilling to take him to the Tower. He shuffled and said, "Who will ...?" pointing at his notes.

"The council is dismissed," said James.

Overbury stared about the room, even at the unfinished ceiling, and finally gave a half bow as he turned for the door and said, "Your majesty"; he did not seem to be aware of what was happening to him as he was hustled across the yard and down to the watergate.

It was only when he was in the boat and the men had taken up their oars that Overbury realized where he was going. He gave a wild, white-eyed stare at the brick court of Whitehall. As the boat pulled into midstream the distant Tower leered at him through early evening light. It was six o'clock, less than an hour since the two lords had come to proposition him.

"Where are we bound?" he asked the Clerk of the Council in a muted disbelieving voice and that unhappy man replied literally, "The Traitor's Gate, Sir Thomas."

Overbury groaned and buried his face between his fingers.

XII

O V E R B U R Y H A D A window overlooking a garden in the
Tower, and when he looked from it he saw children playing in the
dusk, a cookboy carrying a tray, and several gentlemen strolling and
talking on the lawn. It was like an inn of court rather than a prison.
Daffodils scattered like butterflies about the longer grass. His cell
was a room leading into an inner chamber where a bed was piled
high with a goosefeather mattress and a quilt sprigged with unlikely mythical flowers opening golden eyes between pink, blue and
purple petals. He had a desk, its slanting cover was deeply carved
with a heron and the date 1604, so it had been made for another
inmate some time before; and with a constriction of his throat Tom
wondered if it were here because the owner had been beheaded or
if he had gladly returned to freedom and left his pretty bedcover
and expensive desk because he did not wish to be reminded of the
Tower.

The floor was dry and clean and sprinkled with herbs. He opened
the desk and peered into its gloomy box. A sander, ink and quills
were arranged in its pigeonholes as neatly as a housewife's pre-
serves. He drew them out, unrolled several sheets of paper, and
laid them on the table. At least he could write. Tom pulled at the
paper to flatten it and set one candlestick at his shoulder; it threw
rapid shadows over the tapestry on the wall so that Diana writhed
in voluptuous wool. Tom poked his head into his bedroom where
a cool smell of lavender gave out on the chill April air. He flinched,
for he was cold, and wished he had more warning of his imprisonment, to have worn a more substantial coat than his pretty pale
green one. He lifted the flowered quilt and wrapped it round his
shoulders, then returned to the outer room where he pulled paper
towards him and began a long epistle of advice and endearment:
"Dear Robin . . ."

Robin Carr did not appear at the council meeting next morning.
His attendants said that "Lord Rochester had taken sick during the
night," and inquisitive courtiers who made the journey to Carr's

apartments found two halberdiers standing guard, their pikes at the ready and calculated to deter visitors. After the meeting between James and his ministers, the council gathered at one end of the room, their agitated puffed sleeves working like bellows with the strength of their arguments. If a vote had been taken, the majority would have said that Carr had fallen from the king's grace, and these articulate and elbowing gentlemen were already parcelling up his possessions. Only Northhampton stayed aloof, whether from lack of interest or superior knowledge his colleagues would never know. While his nephew played his proxy in the crowd the old man sat still in his chair, his thin black stockinged legs crossed neatly and his whitening head bent down to study too solicitously the latest chapter of royal decrees.

Outside a storm was blowing up the river, sending the relics of last autumn's leaves into savage fandangoes up and down the paths, their brittle skeletons breaking under buffets from the gale. The noon sky was livid, and gradually sails were furled on the waterside and prudent boatmen shouted to each other as they pulled up their craft, away from the path of the river. The agitation of these workmen reflected distantly the excitement of the councillors, closeted in artificial light, loath to go out into the oncoming storm, and away from the busy gossip of their friends. It was well they had waited. Half an hour after he had left the council chamber, the sharp rap of the Gentleman Usher upon the door signalled the king's return, and flustered men made their way back to their seats like naughty boys when the schoolmaster comes to take a class.

James looked as pale and hectic as the sky. His normally pouting red lips were sucked in, he did not come into the room but stood with unusual dignity at the door to the chamber. His council rose to greet him, two lines of sombre men, dark as an avenue of trees.

"My lords and gentlemen," said King James, leaning heavily on his thick ebony cane in the absence of Carr. He paused and looked at Northampton who was supporting himself on the back of his chair. "Pray be seated, my lord," said the king, "I know well the condition of your leg," so the old man subsided on to his chair, breaking the ranks of councillors. "We would speak of my Lord Rochester," said James ponderously, "who is not with us this day. I would have you know that I mean him daily more grace and favour, as will be seen in a short time. For myself I take more delight and contentment with his company and conversation than in any man's living," and with an inclined head James left them, having aroused more speculation and conversation.

Pembroke and Neville were asked to accompany the king, and a moment later were seen walking swiftly past the windows, their faces set towards Carr's rooms so that all guessed they were acting once more as the king's emissaries, no doubt to assure Rochester of James's unchanged feelings towards him. This so deflated several councillors that they sat heavily on either side of Northampton; none of Carr's opponents daring to remember their suggestion that he was out of favour, but looking secretly at the old earl, hoping to gain some indication of what was happening behind the scenes, but also trying to restore themselves to his goodwill seeing that he was an unexpected close friend of Robert Carr, and not an opponent.

Only old Abbot rose with a flurry which was not proper in a clergyman and beckoned Winwood to him. Those who had hoped to hear more news were disappointed, for the archbishop drew Sir Ralph into a window embrasure where their voices were muffled.

"What would you?" asked Winwood somewhat abruptly.

"Sir Ralph, I know well that like myself you wish for the good of England." Winwood nodded. "We must find a young man to supplant Carr," murmured Abbot, smiling meanwhile so that on-lookers would not guess what he said. "I had hoped that we might have good government without resorting to using the king's favour-ites, but since his majesty is so besotted with Rochester, our only hope is to find a similar young man who would be under our thumbs."

"In opposition to the Howards?"

"Aye, seemingly the Howards are playing Carr as their creature at the moment. Know you more of this?"

Winwood knew nothing of the liaison between Frances and Robin and only appeared bewildered while the equally ignorant arch-bishop continued: "If we cannot fight the favourite by ourselves we must have a favourite of our own. I had hoped that Overbury's behaviour would have toppled Carr as the two are so closely allied, but it seems nothing will turn James against that foolish young man except another young man."

Winwood shook his head. His puritan character revolted against such a plot. He was surprised that this immoral plan had come from Abbot.

"We must act carefully until the new secretary be appointed," temporized Winwood.

"Pah, the king will maunder with that for a twelve-month yet. I had hoped that if Carr fell from grace James might discover a more sage and honest advisor, but it seems it is not to be." He looked keenly at Sir Ralph. "If a supplanter to Carr were discovered, who might be manipulated by older, wiser men, would you be for us?"

"Oh as to that," said Winwood, "I am certain that any man who became the king's minion would only too soon forget his political supporters and prove as corrupt and foolish as Carr."

"Better the devil we know ...?"

"Indeed and indeed. Howsoever," added Winwood as Abbot sighed and turned away, "being unwilling to act as pander to the king's perverse tastes does not mean I would not wish to use those same tastes for the good of the state."

"So, man, if others found a pretty boy and forwarded him, and if at the same time Carr fell from favour, you would be with us?"

"There are too many ifs ..." replied Winwood smiling. "I know that Carr will never lose the king's love."

"Harkee," returned the archbishop, "Carr's intimacy is not through his winning smile alone, although I will say that is most of it, it lies also in his conversation and his advice. If these be lost James might think him pretty still, but dull and even tedious. Now Carr is the mouthpiece for Overbury, a man I mislike, as do we all, I think?" Winwood nodded enthusiastically. "Yet with Overbury in the Tower, Carr will soon lag behind as a jester, a good companion, and a councillor, with all this and the fact that he mopes and sighs these days, and behaves like a man in love with a lady, he will soon be less attractive to the king."

"It is a thought," said Winwood, trained by his foreign service to smile but remain uncommitted.

"If he continues without Overbury's aid, and in this green sickness of mind, Carr will be obnoxious to the king in a month! Then we must replace him with our man."

Winwood nodded yet again and both returned to their companions.

"What, are you a churchman now?" asked Lake of Winwood, jealous of his friend's long conversation with the archbishop.

"We but argue a point of theology," said Winwood, who could lie smoothly when necessary. He was wondering where they might find a beautiful jessie for the king. The whole plan seemed futile, and thinking of the king's public enforcement of his love for Carr,

Winwood decided that matters would never right themselves until James died and was replaced by stammering, inadequate Charles. I will be an old man then, thought Winwood who knew his rigid religion would not stomach a Spanish marriage and leniency towards catholics. He looked out at the sobbing trees, and the early scattering rain which would soon swell to a fast downpour, and sighed. What political future could he hope for, or any honest councillor?

"Buss your old gossip," insisted James, drawing Robin close to him and firmly placing a mottled cheek against his neck, "for all is what you would wish."

Rather than showing pleasure Robin seemed distressed, he broke away from the king and began to walk about his bedroom, his scarlet heels rapping on the floor like the steady beat of a kettledrum.

"I had no notion that Tom would be sent to the Tower," he replied sulkily.

"Whisht laddie, what else could I do? He defied me on three accounts, not one, and was such an o'erweening factious rogue when he came to the council room I would ha' lost my own authority had he been let to get awa' wi't. The man has a main conceit o' himsel', Rabbie. But grieve not for your friend, he can cool his heels in the Tower a week or so and come out as blithe as a lark. Better to have your friend there and awa' from court at a time like this, you told me yourself that he causes you grief and rails at you like a fish wife and is withall so arrogant, rude and violent that you are afeared o' him."

"That's all true," agreed Carr miserably.

"Then his absence will be like a holiday and we had best make the most o't. Let's awa'tae Theobalds." James joined Robin at the window and they both stared at the tossing trees.

"I have other plans," said Robin.

James looked at him coolly, his grey eyebrows went up a little and he contrived a smile with a frown hovering behind it. "I would wish ye at Theobalds," he said, "and if ye want yon lady I would tell you now laddie, that seeing her before the divorce is unwise. I may be king, but e'en I cannae stop gossip, and ye are in no position for unkind talk. Syne ye visit Lady Frances now there will be no divorce betimes."

"You can contrive anything," replied Carr, "and are like to fright me with bogies."

"Nay lad, I am not so unkind," replied James, "or so selfseeking. Some things I cannot order and one is the public voice. If you make a fool o' yoursel' wi' Frances the commissioners will ha' to decide against ye or put aside the law."

"The law, the law," retorted Robin, spinning about the room like a windmill, knocking aside books, bowls and his feathered hat, " 'Tis you make the law."

"Not entirely," said James calmly, "I cannot set aside the Chief Justice or the Attorney General, or if I did I would be afeared o' the mob."

"You afeared! That's rich! A company of soldiers would put paid to them I would say, and as for the lawyers, you made them what they are and could unmake them."

"Ha," replied the king, "I would not wish to set aside the law on a whim."

"A whim?" an echo started in his mind, ceaseless as a clock.

"Divorce is not a matter worth setting the country aflame. I would reserve my company of soldiers and my royal prerogative to use on more urgent matters. This divorce is a matter of time and discretion, Rabbie. I guess you have seen the lady since it was set in motion."

"I have and she is not afraid of being seen with me!"

"Then she is foolish indeed. I am sure her great-uncle warned ye both against meeting."

Robin nodded, but said: "She will think I am a coward."

"Then she is not worth plucking," replied James looking hard at him with his great dark eyes. "Think laddie, afore it is too late. Are ye set on this lady?"

"I cannot live without her," answered Robin, flinging himself against the panelling and clutching at it with his hands.

"Aye so," said James a little disgusted at such play-acting. "Then keep your distance till the divorce be passed."

"Why does it take so long?"

"Why! Divorces are not made every day, Rabbie. We must find commissioners who will agree to serve."

"But if you order them——"

" 'Tis not so simple, many honest men do not wish to be involved in a murky business and howsoever a divorce goes it is still murky, Rabbie. Rest your soul in patience. A month or so will see it out."

"A month or so!" he fluttered again. James patted him on the head, but dispassionately as if Robin were a passing dog, then he went towards the door without the customary kiss at parting.

"Hold," said Robin brusquely, "what of Overbury?"

"What of him?" asked James and paused. "Does he know aught of your love for Frances?" he asked grimly.

"Oh, of that—nothing—hardly anything. He knows I admired her, a year or so ago. He has no notion that I wish to marry her," Robin sat down abruptly then rose as James frowned once more.

"Good," said the king, "I would not like to feel a man were unjustly sent to the Tower because he had been worked upon by his so-called friend."

"He was sent to the Tower because of his rudeness to the crown."

"Aye, that. Even so it is like a spider's web, Robin, and we must beware to 'scape its meshes."

James did not linger, he went from the room slowly, leaning heavily on his cane, and left Robin to bite his knuckles and beat upon the wall in the unbearable silence of his rooms.

XIII

"So we must be rid of Wade," said Northampton and closed his eyes so that he would not have to look at his fellow conspirators.

"You may be sure we cannot get near Overbury while Wade is Lord Lieutenant of the Tower," said Monson for the third time. The Keeper of the Tower Armoury was half fearful, half boastful, looking at every one of them lustfully, being so near to power and yet not having it.

"Belike you wish to be governor yourself?" said Thomas Suffolk.

"Not so, my lord. I would not do that job for £1,000."

"How do we make the king replace Wade?" asked Frances.

Her face was painted white and shone luminously. On either side of her head her hair stood out on gold wire like the skirts of an infanta. Monson could hardly forbear staring at her uncovered breasts, for every time she became excited her nipples rose out of her bodice. Northampton thought she was not too old to be whipped.

"We must be sure what we want," said Suffolk, "I would not have any harm come to the man. What we must ensure is that no report of his misery reaches the king and makes James lenient. I think that is enough to hope for, that Overbury is kept out of the way only until the divorce commissioners have met."

"I would wish to go further," said Northampton slowly. Aware that both Monson and Frances were sighing with relief, he carefully looked past their excited faces, one so white and one so red. "I would hope that when he does come out of the Tower Overbury's power is completely gone, that Carr will have become used to living without him and will be aided by us rather than by his erstwhile friend. This may take some time."

"What!" cried Suffolk, "I had thought we would keep Overbury imprisoned for a week or so."

"I think it will be longer, at least a month," corrected Northampton.

Suffolk was confused and unhappy: "I had not meant that."

"Dear nephew, you are not the only man in this plot," said

Northampton while Frances shrugged impatiently, again revealing her lower breasts.

"Frances," said her father shortly, "be more modest for pity's sake."

But she ignored him, turning towards Monson and then Northampton with a pout: "I do not see why Sir Thomas Overbury need live," she said in her deliberate childish voice, "I am sure men are put out of the way in the Tower."

"Not now," said her father.

Monson interrupted: "If the means are to hand."

They sat moodily considering Wade, for the conspirators had ensured that Overbury had the tools for writing to hand, intending that he and Carr should enter into a correspondence in which one would arrogantly advise and the other placate. Wade had taken his authority as governor to stop any letters going in to Overbury and had told his prisoner that he would make sure none left the Tower. Under his pleasant manner and civilized attitude to the inmates of his prison, Wade was as disciplined as a foot soldier. Meanwhile, Overbury might become a danger during his imprisonment, for if he were cut off from his dearest Robin and hope of release, he would surely begin to blab to Wade about being a marked man and further, of the relationship of Robin and Frances and how it had landed him in jail. Overbury might be perceptive enough to consider further his own refusal of the embassies, even to guess that he had been manipulated into prison by the Howards. They had intended that he should condemn himself out of his own mouth before the king; for the Howards knew how Tom Overbury would act if prodded.

"We must work through Carr, he has the king's ear," mumbled Monson.

"How?" asked Frances.

Northampton had to admire her, although he still wished she would cover her bosom. She was a young girl with no knowledge of statesmanship and yet she unerringly made for the point. "The Lady Arabella," he said aloud.

They turned to him like flowers facing the sun; considering the king's cousin Arabella Stuart, who had confined in the Tower for marrying against James's wishes. She was thought a perpetual threat to the crown as she was an alternative heir to the throne. The king was constantly fearful that she might become the figurehead of rebellion, and therefore, had her jealously guarded. "She is in the Tower and the king has said he knows that Wade is too gentle with her, allowing her privileges such as walking in the garden and being visited by her friends," Northampton speculated.

They looked at each other and Suffolk stood up. "I'll none of it," he said, "and Frances should not be privy to this either. I am all for putting a man in prison for a few days while the law takes its course outside but this smacks of more criminal stuff: removing the Lieutenant of the Tower, making mischief with the king and Carr, directing Carr to keep his friend—what friendship?—Overbury happy by writing lying letters of pity telling the man that he is working for his release when all the time he is plotting to keep Overbury longer in the Tower! I cannot stand this double dealing. If Carr and Overbury are friends Carr shows it in a despicable way, and if they are not, let Carr be honest and declare against his so-called friend, so that at least Overbury knows the dice are loaded against him."

"No," replied his daughter, "we must make sure that Overbury thinks Carr is on his side or when he is allowed to write letters he will appeal to other people about the court who may not have been friendly to him in the past, but who would not see him linger in prison needlessly. As long as Robin and Overbury write only to each other nobody else will know the secrets of the divorce, but if the truth be out and Tom Overbury knows that my Robin is faithless to him and conspiring behind his back, why he will tell every blabbermouth at court and half the king's council."

Northampton silently clapped his hands, "Your daughter is a clever creature," he said to Thomas Suffolk, "she has it all off pat."

"I will none of it," said Suffolk again and walked straight out of the room without looking at them. They heard his voice from the lower hall calling for a horse before any of them spoke again.

"We must have one of our men in Wade's place," said Northampton, and Monson slapped the table.

"I have it," he cried.

"I trust you have a man with no scruples," said the earl with a smile at Frances. When they were truly scheming he could feel excitements pulsing in him. This was the way to keep young, to plan great conspiracies in which two or three gathered together and moved men about the court like chequers. "Aha," he said to Monson with relish. "Tell me more."

Monson smirked and fiddled with his shoulder knots, "I have

something better than any assassin, my lord," he said, "an honest man but a foolish one who will do what he is told."

"Out of fear?" asked Northampton. He was nervous of frightened men.

"Nay, nay, he is a simple country man and would do what we would have him do if it be presented as customary."

A gurgle rose in Frances's throat, "Customary to poison his prisoners?" she asked, and Northampton frowned.

"You are indiscreet," he said but continued to look at Monson, wishing to hear more.

"Let us say, if he knew of a plot against Overbury and it were put to him that the great ones desired it, he would be too timid to thwart us," said Monson.

"How could such a rabbit become governor?" asked Frances contemptuously.

Monson fumbled with his dress again, refusing to raise his eyes to the darkly-panelled room or their eager faces. "This creature is Sir Jervis Elwes, he is a Lincolnshire man, as I am, and has been wild in a little way, as country gentlemen can be, spending all on hunting and dicing; but, being turned 50, he finds himself with a wife and children and no money," he paused.

"A common tale," said Northampton to speed Monson in telling it.

"Indeed, my lord, but, being an adventurous soul, when times are hard he takes himself to court with the remains of his wealth and his hungry family, believing, in his simplicity, that if he opens his beak wide enough, the king, of his bounty, will drop something into it. He seeks some post about the court, something with honour and reward."

"But why should the king make this poor fool governor?" asked Frances.

"I will manage that," replied her great-uncle. "I am Lord Privy Seal and the king owes me some favours. But say you this Sir George or Sir Jervis can be bent?"

"Like a leaf of tobacco," replied Monson, "he is so unknowing in London fashions he will believe all prisoners are put out of the way so easy on your lordship's say-so. Eh, he's willing tool. Why, he offered me his all—a matter of £1,000 or so, to find him a position that would keep him comfortable for the rest of his life and provide enough for his children!"

"Take it," said Northampton.

"Why?" asked Frances. "We want him to do this work."

"Aye, but if he thinks he has to buy his way into it he will be assured there is no underhandedness and that he is an independent man. Why, if he pays friend Monson £1,000 to be Governor of the Tower he will be as puffed as a peacock and sure of his own importance. Mark you, Frances, it is your little vain men, being a mite nervous of their own futures, who are anxious to double deal if they are told that is the way all wise ones get on. If all his wealth is spent on this job as governor he will not imperil it."

"Even so, my lord," agreed Monson.

"No. Go further. Tell Elwes the position of governor of the Tower is worth £2,000."

"He has no such sum."

"Aye, but then reduce it, and tell him that by your kindness in speaking to so-and-so or winning the backing of such-and-such, he can buy himself into office. Let it stick at £1,200."

"And if he can only raise £1,000?"

"Why, Monson, lend him the odd 200 as proof of your friendship and be sure to charge low interest on it."

It was Frances's turn to applaud, her wide stiff collar swayed about behind her head and collided with her extravagant hair. "I like it, I like it," she said.

Northampton smiled too. He liked it. This plot against Overbury had become tired, a mere matter of keeping Carr two-faced, and the boy was so stupid that he would agree with any suggestion from Frances's great-uncle. This further episode, removing the governor and replacing him with a puppet who was too innocent to realize he was one, appealed to Henry Howard. He would have laughed if laughter had not become as strange to him as making love, a far-off memory of youth. It delighted him that he may never see Elwes and would only communicate with him through Thomas Monson, but that the new governor would be so awed by Northampton's reputation that he would succumb to the plot. And then the old man frowned. In the pleasure of plotting it was easy to forget what the outcome might be. He remembered that Frances had mentioned poison and he turned to her sternly.

"This is only intended to give us the whip hand over Sir Thomas Overbury's keeper," he said, "so that we can direct who may write to him or visit him." Frances looked at him blankly. "You understand that," he said firmly, hoping he understood it himself.

"I do, my lord," she said and Monson gaped at Northampton

for he was already envisaging illegal tortures in the Tower, and of extorting small fortunes from other prisoners through Sir Jervis Elwes's position.

"I thought——" he began.

"Never think," said the old man, "I do the thinking."

But Northampton felt alarmed as he gathered his fur-lined robe and wandered along the passages of his elaborate, regal house. His dark-eyed niece with the narrow mouth seemed to be directing his needle as he darned the plot.

Monson sent a long message within the week saying that he had told Elwes that "if he succeeded Wade he must bleed for it" and Elwes had understood that this was the way of the world; by resorting to his friends of the merchant class and borrowing from Monson he raised £1,400, which Monson kept.

Wade had gone and Overbury wondered how he had ever been incensed by fat Sir William and his honest jowls. He had summed up Elwes immediately when he came panting up the stairs and made great play with pikemen marching to and fro and banging the shafts of their weapons on the stones in unison.

"I will have order," said Sir Jervis. He glowered at Tom under shooting grey brows which gave an aspect of ferocity to a man who was no more angry than a hen flying wrathfully about a farmyard. He nodded at Cary, who had been a servant seconded to Overbury by Wade as the most suitable in the Tower household. "He is to go," said Elwes crisply.

"Upon what order?" asked Tom who had no feelings for or against Cary except that he seemed quiet and competent.

"Question not his going," said Elwes and shouted at the door, "Send in Weston," upon which a grey-haired stooping man appeared, white faced from a sedentary life, his hands as frail as eggs.

"I dislike this rogue," said Tom turning away. "Why look at him, Sir Jervis, he is puny and could hardly do more than make a bed. I need a man to cook and run errands for me."

"No errands will be run without my consent," returned Elwes. His hands linked behind his back, he turned backwards and forwards on his heels, his small belly pouted out like a pregnant lady's, and his smile was as fulsome.

"I will serve you well, sir," said Weston, inclining his body, "I have worked as a cook, and to a gentleman too, a Doctor George Turner of Paternoster Row. And as a bailiff after."

"Then how are you fallen to this?" asked Overbury. "A keeper-servant in the Tower, it is not an honest man's work."

"Sir, I was imprisoned for debt," replied old Weston, "and came out of Newgate without friends or work until hearing of this chance I came here on the run. I am not young, sir, and have to take what I can get through no fault of my own."

"What! Have you no family who could help you to a better place?" asked Tom.

"I have a son, William, who runs errands for a dressmaker. A good boy but he only makes enough to keep himself. Great ones have no knowledge of the life of the poor. This is how men turn to robbery, Sir Thomas, and would become vagrants and beggars on the highway. I am an honest man with some good labour left in me and should not be turned on the parish."

Elwes coughed a little, staring at the floor, and Overbury looked at the decayed man before him. "I will not be here long," he said; "what will you do after?"

"That will be worked out in God's good time," replied Weston, "if you only let me have a chance now."

"Do not beg from Sir Thomas," Elwes interrupted, "I will have you be his keeper and serving man and that is enough."

"Indeed," said Overbury, "I had not known before now on what slight argument a man may land in gaol and I believe debtors are assorted with common felons."

"Indeed they are, Sir Thomas," said Weston.

"It moves me that the world has been harsh with you, Weston. Sir Jervis, I am satisfied with your choice."

Elwes bowed and left Overbury, muttering on the stair: "Another little month and you will be less high-stomached, Sir Thomas, be assured of that."

That same evening, the seventh of May, lawyers and interested councillors met in Northampton's house. The Countess of Essex was represented by her father and great-uncle. Lord Knollys and long-suffering Pembroke spoke for their friend, the Earl of Essex. They determined that a plea should be made that Essex was impotent only in respect of his wife, that his chances to remarry would not be imperilled. The Howard faction accepted a divorce as their prerogative but the adherents of Essex were less assured.

Afterwards Northampton sat in a dark-red closet in his home and wrote a note for Carr. His eyesight was failing and his small-lensed spectacles slipped about on his nose, but the matter was too important to call his secretary. Only Frances came slipping through the curtains holding an extra light for him.

"Are you satisfied?" he asked her.

"Very much so," she answered, and took his left hand between her palms, kneading at it to slacken off the rheumatism.

He pulled it away: "It does no good," he said impatiently.

"You are writing to my Robin," she said, watching his quill wavering about on the paper, surrounded by shadows. She bent across to see what he had written to her lover: ". . . all is concluded about the form of the nullity . . . council on both sides is agreed and libel is approved sufficient and good in law . . ." His cuff abruptly covered the rest of the screed, but below she saw his final words: "Be still happy, Henry Northampton." Impulsively she seized the quill from him and dipped it in the ink, sending a spattering of tiny black tears across the table, but when she put her pen to paper she wrote firmly with no blots: "I am witness to this bargain—Frances Howard."

"The story of Mary Woods is out," Frances said as they left the little room and after a confidential servant had taken the note.

"Then you must go to earth like a fox," replied Northampton, "be discreet."

"But what if Overbury should tell any other prisoners the truth of the matter?"

"He will not. Elwes understands that Overbury must see no visitors. There was a bad moment when he caught him talking from his window with Killigrew, a young fool—and a friend of your Robin by the way—who was on a visit to Raleigh, but Elwes nipped that in the bud and made Overbury see that if he wished to correspond with Carr he would only do so as an especial favour."

"Does Elwes know of our conspiracy against Overbury yet?"

"He knows Overbury must be kept incommunicado, and that we will tell him how to treat his prisoner."

Frances shuddered with delight at the power given into her hands like a key.

"And *I* may order Elwes about Overbury?" she persisted.

"Do not be foolish," was all Northampton suggested, adding, "and your young man is primed, Carr must make Overbury feel that all exertions are being made to let him out, but that the king alone is obdurate."

"Suppose," she caught her lower lip between her teeth with sudden worry, "suppose that the king intervenes and lets Overbury out on his own account?"

"James has gone a-hunting, my girl, and thinks of nothing but the chase. He will have forgot Overbury the day after he imprisoned him, and if, at worst, he remembers and relents, Carr will play the unfortunate friend, so pestered by Overbury that it would be unpleasant to release him."

Frances rounded on him as they reached the brighter lights near the dining hall. "Will nobody seek to save Tom Overbury?" she asked.

Northampton smiled indulgently: "Nobody," he promised. "The man has no friends except the now traitorous Carr. You are sure of your lover?"

"As sure as I am of aught."

"In this unchancy world that says very little," grumbled Northampton; but, as he entered the hall and saw the gold plate winking like sunlight and the bowed backs of his servants arranged in obsequious lines, he felt that all his life's manipulations had some purpose in that this great-niece could treat her enemies like dolls and crush their fragile wooden bodies under her feet when she had outgrown them or had tired of their silly painted faces.

"The chaplain will say grace," he commanded.

"So please your lordship."

The ritual of dinner had begun again.

XIV

FRANCES TREMBLED AS she went into the chamber of the latest wizard, a Doctor Franklin, which was hung with cabalistic signs and which smelt of blood; but Mrs Turner, hard behind her, gave the doctor a slap which was commanding and yet skittish.

"Go to, James Franklin," she said, "I know you love to fright young girls with signs and with tales of black magic and devil worship yet every Sunday sees you safe in your pew at St Michael's. Watch these signs of Satan do not recoil on you one day."

"Am I not a warlock?" demanded Franklin. "Do you see this?" and he pulled his collar from his neck.

"I know of your lion's mane, yes, and so do all who meet you," replied Mrs Turner. "Did you say aught of this matter to any soul else?"

"My porter may guess your names."

"He may run errands, yes, but he is not to be involved," said Mrs Turner. "Why there are enough mixed up in the brew already." She began to finger them off: "Yourself and the widow of Doctor Forman, myself and my maid Meg, my man Weston and his son, and Sir Thomas Monson who speaks in his cups, and that termagant from Norwich,—and no doubt your lover," to Frances. "Does he know aught?"

Frances pouted, "He must guess most if he be not a ninny."

"Aye, and the great ones, for your family must know you consort with such as us."

"Ah, go to," said Frances, pacing up and down the room. "I am not in a schoolroom to be chid this way. I may tell whom I like of my own business I hope."

"Aye," agreed Franklin, suddenly chill and sober, "but there are so many in this, my lady, and all their necks must be kept safe."

Frances gave her shrill little laugh like a sword ripping silk. "I am discreet enough," she said, "and I am at the centre of the plot. Why should I tell anybody of my affairs?"

"You wish too many to be privy to them."

Both her accomplices stared at Frances gravely; they were

disturbed by her need to implicate all who were concerned with her machinations.

"I am the Countess of Essex," she reminded them.

"But not for long," answered Mrs Turner.

"And then I will be wife to another man, near to the king and unassailable in power. And I am a Howard."

"Does that mean you will be discreet?" persisted Franklin.

"I do what pleases me," she said, "and I have asked you for a killing powder. All you need say is if you can make it or no?"

Franklin lifted her letter again uneasily, holding it to the light so that he could read it once more.

He laid it by and said, "You wish for that which will not kill a man presently but will lie in his body a certain time wherewith he will languish away a little by little." They both agreed. "What of the Aqua Fortis?" he asked Mrs Turner. "That which I sent before?"

She spread her hands. "We tried it on a cat we caught to see if it would die slowly, but it languished and lived for two days, crying pitifully before it died."

"Is that not proof enough of its slow power?" he asked.

Frances shook her head, compressing her lips so that no red could be seen. "It is still too swift," she answered, "and too violent. I wish for something to make him slow and wistful, to give him a slackening of the appetite, a melancholy with thoughts of the hereafter, a vomiting but not too often, and so a sad decline into death."

"By God you ask for much in your poison, madam!" exclaimed Franklin, but both ladies sat and watched him with confidence, sure that some cordial could be conjured out of the cabinet behind him.

"What think you of white arsenic?" asked Frances.

"Violent also, and makes a wretched, noisy death," replied the physician.

"Come, come," continued Mrs Turner, "you are a wise man, Doctor Franklin, surely you can help us more than this?"

Franklin frowned, and began to look along his rows of jars, muttering as he passed one poison or another. "There are death dealers enough," he said, "but few which act slowly or with so little sign, if you do not want those about your victim to know he has been poisoned."

He looked at them even more keenly: "Have you the means to give the poison to him?"

"Of that, plenty," cried Frances, "in pies or tarts or medicines, or any method you can think on."

"And are none by to sound alarms and suspect foul play?"

"None," said Frances with satisfaction, "no man was ever as alone as this one. He is quite bereft of friends and in a place as safe as if he were a fly in a bottle."

"Indeed," said Franklin, "in prison, perchance?"

"Enough questions," said Ann Turner. "He is safe confined."

"I ask only as men in prison are scrutinized most carefully if they die suddenly. There may be an inquest."

"Not on this man," said Frances.

But Mrs Turner added: "Do you not see that for this very reason we must have a slow killer?"

"As I may guess your victim," said Franklin smiling, "I can fit my poison to your ends. Is his food sent in from outside?"

"It will be."

"And his attendant is in your pay?"

"He is."

"As is the Lord Lieutenant of the Tower?"

"You are too bold," said Frances. "Let us consider these potions. What do you think of powdered diamonds?"

"I have never heard of such a poison," protested Franklin, immediately looking away from his homely, well-known jars. "Would they kill a man?"

"You are a fool and do not know your trade if you have not used diamonds," retorted Frances crisply. "Will you buy some for me?"

"It sounds like an Italian method to me. But I will if you are determined on it, my lady."

"I am." She pulled out a soft leather purse and put it on the table.

"I have been given four angels by that one," said Franklin, cocking his thumb at Ann Turner.

"Then you are doing well. I will take the poison now."

"I must send out for it. I have never heard of powdered diamonds."

"Send to the goldsmiths for them. I will wait," she pulled up her fur collar as she spoke and seemed prepared to sit in Franklin's rooms all evening.

The porter went swiftly, using a horse taken from Franklin's familiar high waggon which he used on errands as a male midwife. In less than an hour the man was back, the horse was unsaddled, and there was a sad message for the countess. Franklin was not alone in being unaware of powdered diamonds, no merchant in London held any in stock and most had laughed at the porter and accused him of jesting with them. One had even kicked him into the gutter.

"So," said Frances, watching the sky darken from Franklin's window. "What should we do?"

"What should your ladyship do?" suggested Franklin smartly. "You stand as first murderer, madam."

She scowled at his impertinence but had to salvage some poison from his shelves.

"What then?" she demanded.

"I would recommend rosalgar, or red arsenic," said Franklin, unwittingly turning on his unctuous apothecary's manner. "It is well known, but has an increasing effect, some subjects even look better on it in the early stages before they die."

"What are its symptoms?"

"Those of any fever, my lady, sweating and heat, a gasping for breath, sickness and slow decay."

"So it may look as if he hath the plague?"

Franklin was shocked: "Not so, my lady, nothing as violent as the plague."

"I will have it," agreed Frances.

"Is it that with which you killed your wife?" asked Mrs Turner slyly.

Franklin smiled: "Mayhap, but I have never been hanged for a death yet, either of whore or queen."

"You are a cunning man," said Frances, as she placed the purse more firmly on his table.

"I am careful with whom I mix, that they do not tell tales of me," said Franklin, "and I have heretofore been fortunate in my customers."

"But you have never had one as great as this lady," said Mrs Turner.

As she uncurled out of the room behind the countess, Franklin dropped her commission into the dressmaker's warm hand.

"God bless you, Doctor Franklin," she said, sidling down the stairs.

"And go with you also," replied Franklin heartily.

"I am innocent of any crime," said Overbury. "What do they mean to do with me?"

"Why," replied Elwes with some attempt at humour, "they mean to refine you so that you will seem even more pure."

Tom stared at the sheep-faced elderly man disbelievingly. "Are you a simpleton? Do you not know that I am here as part of a plot laid by the Howards? They are a fine family i' faith. I say naught of Suffolk for I feel he is misled by others of his name. His daughter is vicious and unprincipled——"

"Now, now."

"His uncle is insidious and deep, and would have all England play to his tune if he had his way. Let the Howards know I care as little to die as they to be cruel."

Elwes was disturbed although he bowed away from Overbury's rooms with assurances that he would return later in the day. He had no fears for his prisoner's physical well-being, the man ranted lustily enough and threw his long body about the small chamber like a monkey in a cage. But of his mind Elwes was less sure, the demoniac shine of Overbury's eyes warned him that he might break under the strain of confinement.

Sir Jervis went to his rooms and wrote a full account of Overbury's accusation to Lord Northampton. He thought that by keeping Northampton informed he could keep his own position safe. Whom could he warn of Overbury's condition? A committee of inquiry into the matter would only be composed of the Howards or their faction, men like himself, who kept their places by keeping their mouths shout, and would not see what part Carr was playing in this game. The king's lover was still the only person who sent letters surreptitiously to Overbury and Elwes could not believe that Carr was a secret enemy of that man whom all had considered his best friend. He thought of warning Northampton that there may be double-double dealing, but then desisted. How could he advise the most esteemed councillor in the kingdom?

In the evening Elwes visited Overbury again; the stairs to the prisoner's rooms were narrow and dim, and he was surprised to nudge into some fellow who was walking before him. Elwes raised his lantern and recognized Weston, carrying a covered bowl of soup and a small glass bottle which held a greenish-yellow liquid. Weston shrank back into the turn of the stairs and looked meaningfully at the governor: "Should I give it him now?" he asked, lifting the flask and shaking it slightly so that foam ran up to its lip.

"Give him? What do you give him?" asked Elwes.

"Why, sir? Know you not what is to be done?" answered Weston, holding out the bottle so that it flickered between them in the uneasy light of the lantern.

"By God," said Elwes. He seized Weston's arm and hurried him down the stairs and out into the yard. Propping the lantern on a low wall he shook the keeper, holding him close to him. Hot soup slopped out on both their hands so that Weston gave a little cry, but held fast to the poison.

"Is it what I think?" asked Elwes, finally.

"It is that which puts down rats."

"On your knees, man, on your knees," cried the governor, and forced Weston down on to the slippery cobbles so that the soup gurgled and fell, bowl and all, into the ground where it soaked away, steaming into the evening air, and a smell of meat and vegetables rose beguilingly from the earth. "Pray to your Maker," commanded Elwes, "that ye be not urged to such wickedness more, and that if you raise a hand against one of God's creatures, be it high or low, that hand may be smitten from you. God will judge you in the hereafter for what sins you commit on earth."

After a pause, Weston knelt beside the governor and presumably prayed as Elwes did, for forgiveness. When both keeper and governor stood again, brushing the soil and thin runnels of soup from their knees, Elwes looked grimly at the intact bottle.

"What will you do with that?"

"Oh, Sir Jervis, I will throw it away."

"Do so."

Weston turned from the light with a curious reticence as if he were going to make water in the gutter, Elwes heard a slight tinkle as if glass had struck stone very lightly.

It was in Elwes's nature to be indecisive and even as he told Weston to jettison the poison, the governor had also thought of the Howards and how little he knew of their plans. Had he been too precipitate in denouncing their attempt to do away with Overbury? Or perhaps King James had ordered the poisoning as a way to rid himself of an importunate threat to himself as king and lover?

Weston turned back into the light, his normally long face even more gloomy, and pale yellow in the flare. "They will have me give it him, first or last," he said, thrusting out his hands to show that the phial was no longer in them.

Elwes said quickly, "Let it be done that I know not of it," and left Weston gaping after him at the entry to the stairs. He regretted his words immediately, for he was filled with tremulous apprehension.

In the morning, Elwes returned to see again that place where he had prayed so heartily and then turned coat. The soup bowl lay in fragments of blue and white about the flat muddy ground. On the cobbles by the gutter a few shards of glass advertised the end of the poison. While he prodded at these with his cane Weston came down the stairs whistling. "See," said Elwes to him, "how light a heart is borne by an innocent man."

On recognizing the governor, Weston looked sullen again and would have bowed and walked away if Elwes had not taken him by the arm and asked him to spare a few words.

"You collect dishes for Sir Thomas from a pastry cook?" asked Sir Jervis, seeing danger to Overbury from yet another source.

"Indeed, from the kitchens of Mrs Turner in Paternoster Row."

"That is a long way to fetch them. Are there no nearer cooks?"

"But many in the Tower buy from further afield," protested Weston. "They have the money to pay and would have the best. These gentlemen are used to dainty dishes, Sir Jervis. I warm 'em up over a fire in my pantry."

"Do dishes for Sir Thomas come from elsewhere?"

"Why yes, sometimes from the kitchen of the Countess of Essex, it is but a step further to her new house in Blackfriars. My son William oftimes collects them for me. He runs errands for a haberdasher and is always about the countess or Mrs Turner."

"Does Sir Thomas pay for these delicacies?"

"Indeed not, sir, Carr—my lord Rochester—is his banker and pays for all that is sent in. Could he do less, and he so close with Sir Thomas before his unhappy time? He also sends pies and wine from Whitehall."

"That is mighty generous in his lordship."

"He has gold to spare, Sir Jervis. Had you not heard that when the Treasury ran dry a week or so ago, Lord Rochester offered £22,000 from his own wealth to replenish it?" Sir Jervis had heard this, it was a matter of speculation all over London. "Not," continued Weston, "that I am amazed, as the king has been so generous in monopolies for his lordship in the past."

"Look you," said Elwes suddenly, "you are an uncommon serving man."

"I thank you for that, Sir Jervis," bowing. "It is a recommendation coming from such a gentleman."

"I would keep well in with what you do. Bring those dishes to me before they reach Sir Thomas."

"To you, Sir Jervis?" Weston asked with some surprise.

"God's grief! To the kitchens of the Lord Lieutenant's house. I would poke in them more closely."

"I would not do that, Sir Jervis, you know this is the way of the world and you cannot still it. Evil will not out if the great ones promote it."

"I do not understand you," claimed Elwes, who was beginning to comprehend too well. Weston bowed and was silent. "So bring those pies and puddings to my kitchens first and I will inspect them before they reach Overbury."

"What will I tell Mrs Turner? She gave me this liquid for Sir Thomas. She will wish to know how he acted on it."

"What would it do?"

Weston shrugged: "I know nothing of poisons," he admitted.

"Nor I," answered the governor. "It would give him the runs surely? Say that he had 60 stools and has vomited and is weak and in bed."

"Will she not suspect?"

"Who sees Overbury except you and me?"

"And what do I tell Sir Thomas Monson?"

"God's death," cried Elwes prodding the glass splinters again with his cane and staring at the muddy cobbles, "is he in this, too?" Weston again said nothing but nodded and spread his hands, then lifted one finger to lay it across his neck. "Up to there," interpreted Elwes, "and I suppose that all you tell Monson goes back to Mrs Turner and the Countess of Essex, and then to Northampton."

He bit his lip, wondering a little that he, a simple Lincolnshire squire with no aim apart from providing a living for his wife and family, had been pulled so quickly into such villainous affairs.

"Tell Monson that Overbury has had extreme oustings and other tokens of sickness." He thought a moment. "That should be enough. It is neither too extreme nor yet too mild. Say that, Weston."

The man had begun to lope away, his long legs moving wolfishly towards the gate when Elwes called after him, "Remember, I wish all dishes brought first to me."

The keeper turned and stood still, waiting for the governor to come up with him. "Indeed, Sir Jervis," he said with melancholy. "I cannot see how you or I can avoid this death."

"We will try," said Elwes as firmly as he had ever spoken. "We will play for time."

XV

W HAT COIL IS here, reflected Tom Overbury. He had
spent a disproportionate amount of time with his head thrust out
of the window now that April had run into May, until Elwes had
produced some faradiddle about his prisoner not being seen and had
ordered that the windows be nailed shut.

Tom broke out: "God's wounds, man, you over-reach yourself!
I am allowed no visitor, I can only send letters to Robin Carr, I
have stale food because it seems to hang about your own kitchens
all morning—and no doubt some of it disappears into the maws of
your hungry brood—and if it were not bad enough that I am confined in these two rooms, I am now told that I may not open the
window and lean out! Is this because I was rash enough to speak
to Killigrew when I was first here?"

"I beseech you, Sir Thomas," begged Elwes, "it's for your own
good."

"My own good! Do not imagine that because I am perforce here
for a week or two I will forget your manner to me when I am out
again. I am still a man of substance in the state, Sir Jervis, and the
close friend of the most powerful man in the land, as well you
know, for I have tokens of Robin's love with me daily." He pointed
at a fresh letter from Carr, its seal still unbroken, which lay like a
baton on the table. "And when I return to my glory I will ensure
that you are despatched from here. I will not have any other
prisoner suffer at your hands." Elwes stood rigid while Weston
hopped behind him, gathering Overbury's clothes and listening to
every word. "This will be your undoing," continued Overbury. "I
could have forgiven the other acts—close confinement, taking choice
foods from me, no messages to my family or friends—but I will not
allow you to bar my windows."

"I would not have others see you," muttered Elwes.

"Even from afar? Do you fear that they see me well and
smiling? Would the Howards like to think me cast down and sad?"

Elwes began to retreat from the room and Overbury shouted at
him until he saw the governor's broad back disappear down the
walk.

Messages flew plentifully between Carr and Overbury. Tom still thought Carr was his pupil and his letters continued to guide the younger man in his policies, but as the weeks wandered on, affairs of state gave way to the pressing urgency of letting Tom out of the Tower. It seemed impossible that James should continue obdurate, especially when Carr boasted that the king was as loving as ever. Tom urged many methods of release, and Robin encouraged them all, but one by one they fluttered away like dead leaves, and were supplanted with other designs for his escape.

Carr's letters were dictated by Northampton, and Tom could only wonder that they seemed more literate and cunning than he had ever thought his Robin could be. He considered that Robin had to use his own wits for once and was not making a poor show of them, except in his inability to turn James towards leniency. The most recent plan was that Overbury should become ill, so that the Tower would be unhealthy for him, Tom even considered it expedient that he might spend a week or so at home in the country, if the king let him go. This would lull James into forgetfulness, and Tom might hatch a few plots with Robin in the quiet, away from court. He asked Robin for some powders such as Carr himself had used in order to deter James when the king was amorous. These came from Sir Robert Killigrew who was an amateur chemist, and who had incurred Sir Jervis Elwes's anger by talking with Overbury at his window when he had visited the Tower a few weeks before. And the plot could not rest there. Not only would Tom be advertised as too ill to stay in prison, but an eminent doctor should visit him to attest to his sickness, and with the use of Killigrew's vomit powders Overbury thought he could convince even Sir Theodore Mayerne of his fragility.

So they set their plan in motion. But Killigrew's powders did not arrive and in each letter Carr made more excuses; that Killigrew was from town, or that he judged it impossible to worry James with tales of Overbury's sickness when his majesty was none too well himself.

Cut off from all society, Tom asked Weston about life outside the Tower: the gossip in the ordinaries, or the news conveyed by broadsheets, and he heard that the divorce commission was to be set up.

"What? That!" he cried, "I will be out of here by the end of the week and I will soon put an end to it."

But he was not out by the end of the week, and although the

divorce was a long time coming, Tom began to wonder if he would be out of the Tower in time to tell the commission about Frances and Robin, and how spurious was their attempt to call Essex impotent. Perhaps, he thought, I should not meddle after all. What does it matter if Robin marries the bitch? He will tire of her in a year and we will be back on our old footing. But by then the Howards would have grabbed all and he and Robin would be reduced to ciphers.

He returned to scribbling on the paper, secretly dismayed by how his handwriting had declined by a few weeks in prison, soon he would be unable to read it himself. He asked Robin to send Killigrew's vomit powder so that he might keep it secretly by him to use *in extremis*, meanwhile, Tom said, he would display his damaged leg to Elwes, saying his boils were better than they had been, but that a doctor should be called, ". . . and then I will use the powder two days after, which will be a new occasion for you to be importunate to send me into the country to save my life, for 'tis not the close air, but the apprehension of the place that hurts me . . ." He paused and gnawed his new quill and thought that he would need witnesses to his sickness and that Mayerne may be in the country himself. What other doctors were about the court? "I have now sent by the lieutenant to desire you (Mayerne being absent) to send young Craig hither and Nesmith. If Nesmith be away, send I pray Craig and Allen, two such as when they go back may go unto the king and relate how my body is wasted with thought of the king's displeasure and this place." Tom added that when the two doctors returned with accounts of his illness they should go into James alone, but that Carr must, as if by accident, wander into the royal apartments afterwards and urge for Tom's release.

He chewed at the feather, wondering if there were any other minute instructions to be given to Robin, who had so far been so bungling in his efforts. He thought again that he should write direct to the king. Could Elwes refuse to allow such an important letter out? But Robin had discouraged such a suggestion, and Robin must know how James felt towards Tom Overbury.

" 'Tis all worked out as neat as a play," said Carr, warming his hands round a cup of mulled wine. "I have been out of London, and yet he pursues me with these letters."

"And you send many back to him," remarked Northampton smiling. There was something touchingly intimate about the three men gathered in his little red room where each wall was painted with a different view of the seasons. He was pleased that neither Monson nor Frances jarred their gathering with their impetuous demands for violent deeds. No, thought the old man, half sleeping before the fire, this was better, a family of three men, close, secret, understanding one another. Suffolk and Carr looked at each other across Northampton's drowsing face. They were conscious, as he was not, of a sudden diminution of his spirit. Northampton was as eager as ever to turn a plot like a woman turning the heel of a stocking; all Carr's letters had passed through his hands; but he was sometimes distant, and his abstraction could not completely be explained by his ulcerated leg which was swathed in bandages and stretched on a footstool.

"Who else has he pestered?"

"Why none, to his face, for do you not remember that I am the only one he can correspond with," Robin frowned, wondering how the old man could forget this when he had arranged it himself with Elwes. "But he asks me to implore Ellesmere and Pembroke to intercede on his behalf—and Abbot. He suggests that Pembroke and Ellesmere revoke their account of their meeting with him, or say he was ill or too surprised when the king's message came to him."

"It is not like Overbury to make excuses," muttered Northampton.

"And lastly he asks that you, my lord, speak for him."

Northampton jerked upright in his chair, cursing his leg as he made the sudden movement. His pale eyes were wide open. "I?" he said incredulously.

"Believing that coming from you, a noted opponent of Overbury, the plea might have more worth."

"Why should I speak for him?"

"In fear of losing my favour if you do not," answered Carr, and attempted his boyish smile.

"That is the strangest reason yet," said Suffolk, smacking his thigh so that his uncle winced with envy.

"Not so," said Carr, fluttering letters on to the table like playing cards. "One even more strange has come. The letter which gives us our lines to say."

"The devil!" exclaimed Suffolk.

"Most ascribed for you, Lord Suffolk," continued Carr with his halting half-smile. "He hath a scheme whereby you visit the king at Greenwich, and has worked out a long speech you will have in secret with James, allowing the king many choices to answer but giving details of how you will reply to all his arguments. None are to know of this—especially not your wife or daughter—for you must give credence to the idea that you act of your own good heart, and have not spoken with anybody about Overbury."

"He must be mad!" cried Suffolk. "Why, he has not exchanged more than six words with me and has always spoken as if I were a foolish sailor unfit for office."

"Howsoever he considers you," said Carr, "he says you should begin by telling the king that Overbury is sick and will not live an hour, but being haughty he hath concealed his great malady from all, even from physicians, but he is ashamed that he should be taken sick in the Tower, for fear men might think he seeks deliverance from it."

"I like that touch," said Northampton. His eyes were closed again and he smiled.

"You are to be amazed that the king hath not heard of his malady," said Carr, "and have this speech to deliver to his majesty."

He passed Suffolk a remnant of paper and all three waited patiently as Thomas Howard brought out his eyeglasses and carefully donned them before looking at Overbury's instructions and reading them to himself soundlessly, with moving lips.

"Say it aloud," commanded Northampton, "God's death, man, we want to hear it as Overbury intended, as you are meant to tell it to James."

"I do not read so very well," begged Suffolk, but he read the speech written for him by the prisoner in a toneless voice. " 'Sir, hearing this'—that is of his illness," explained Suffolk, squinting up higher in the letter, " 'Sir, hearing this, I thought myself bound in honesty to tell you, for fear he die in the night . . . ' "

"I like that. It has a mark of urgency," commented Northampton, and Carr made an impatient gesture. He was somewhat sickened by this repetition of Overbury's secret instructions and wished Suffolk to deliver them as quickly as possible.

" 'It might cost my lord Rochester his life too, when you see how passionately he loves him.' "

"Maudlin," commented Northampton, "as if one man would die from sympathy of another!"

"Overbury believes," said Carr, taking the letter from Suffolk and adding it to the pile on the table, "that James is trying to prevaricate on his delivery from prison, hoping I will learn to live without Tom meanwhile, but that I can thwart the king by feigning sickness myself and keeping away from James, denying feasts and games and refusing to hunt while Overbury is in the Tower."

Carr watched to see by their faces how they felt towards his friend. He was almost anxious that they would bid him follow Overbury's plans and so have him released. In spite of his belief that he would not have Frances if Overbury were free and able to hinder the divorce, he hated the thought of that proud, intelligent man wasting every day concocting designs which would never come to fruition. He had a suspicion that Overbury's mind should be put back to foreign affairs and not to confused plots and subplots, and imaginary conversations.

"Is that all?" asked Northampton.

"Aye, except that Tom believes that Neville should be appointed secretary by now and that I should take care to show pleasure in the choice to the king, saying he is Overbury's man. I am also to say that I cannot rejoice in Neville's success considering my friend in the Tower."

"One thing is clear," said Northampton, "the mind of the man runs as devious as ever. If you did but a quarter of that which Overbury tells you James would have pulled him out of the Bloody Tower long since."

"That is my burden. How can I continue to pretend that Overbury's plots to please the king have no effect? He is sure to know sometime that none has been used."

"It would do no harm to send him the vomit powder from Killigrew," advised Northampton, "and we might let his own attendants visit him."

"If his attendants visit him, how can I not do so?" asked Carr uneasily.

"If Overbury feigns disease he should not be waited upon by his friends for fear of contagion," replied Northampton logically, "but we will not make it too pleasant yet. Allow one of his men to visit him with Killigrew's powder and report their result back to you. I would like some attention paid to Overbury's malady, real or unreal."

"He is the strongest man I know," retorted Carr, "that affair of the spleen was but an excuse for the king."

"I find myself amazed at his fancies," said Suffolk. "The man turns them out like a housewife baking buns."

"It would seem strange to those of puny intellect," said Northampton unkindly, "but we never made the mistake of believing Overbury a fool."

Carr swallowed loudly, and asked: "Is he safe confined and secret? My only fear is that he will send a letter to one of the others—Pembroke, Ellesmere or Abbot—saying he has asked me to intercede for him, and they would reply I have done no such thing, and belike take up cudgels on his behalf."

Northampton placed his hand upon Carr's arm: "Have no fear," he said, "none will hear from him except yourself. Elwes is our man, and is fast bound to us, as you are yourself, kinsman."

He stressed the last word which would have made Carr happy a few months before, but, although he enjoyed his intimacy with the Howards and the conferences in the rich room and the pleasant dangled offer of Frances as a wife, which spurred him on to greater schemes against Overbury, sometimes Robin remembered with regret those early days when he had nodded in agreement with all Tom had said, and when he danced nightly before Jamie, with no thought of pretence or cruelty. For was it not cruel to keep Overbury in the Tower until the divorce be out? Northampton was speaking of the divorce commission which was at last appointed. He dismayed Robin by stating that only a few of the commissioners were in the pockets of the king or the Howards. "The pesky bishops led by George Abbot!" he exclaimed, but Robin did not wish to speak about the divorce, and he left hurriedly, apprehensive of how Northampton's plots would be resolved.

XVI

"I HAVE NO communication with the outside" declared Overbury.

Elwes turned to look at him closely, and decided to reassure his prisoner that he too, was privy to Carr's subterfuges. "Nay, Sir Thomas," he said, winking. "I know what you have in wine jars, and pies . . ."

Overbury whitened, which turned his pasty indoor skin a strange phantasmic colour. He strode to his side table and produced his gilt clasped Bible, dramatically laying it on the desk before Elwes.

"Those things were innocent," he said hoarsely. "Do you doubt me, Sir Jervis?" His elegant hand straddled the book meaningfully, and Elwes hastily placed his own plump fingers on the other end of the Bible.

"Not I, on my honour, Sir Thomas." Neither face quivered as they lied to one another.

Slowly Elwes walked back towards his own house. He was alarmed by his predicament: "I would not believe it if I saw it in a play," he said to his wife almost daily. Dishes for Overbury arrived hourly. One set came from Carr, and Elwes knew that every dish and wine jar contained flasks of secret letters which he had been advised to allow through to his prisoner. Overbury returned correspondence the same way so that a table in the Elwes's kitchen was thronged with half-consumed stews and pies from which the heads of the secret flasks often protruded, for neither Overbury nor Carr attempted to be more than superficially secretive. On another sideboard rested dishes from the Countess of Essex or Mrs Turner which were ostensibly sent to the prisoner as an act of compassion, and which Elwes continually determined to dispose of in the ditch. However Frances complicated her plot by also sending innocent recipes which could be safely eaten by either Overbury or the Elwes family. She understood that the welter of food could more than satisfy one man and that Overbury would almost certainly return some dishes to the governor's kitchens.

As he walked Sir Jervis conned over her latest letter which had been brought to him by the countess's maid only a few minutes before he had left to visit Overbury: "... at four o'clock I will send you jelly, one pot, for I had one sent to me ... if he should send this tart and jelly to your wife, then you must take the tart from her, and the jelly ... but the wine she may drink it if she will, for in that there are no letters"—(Frances's euphemism for poison) —"but in the tart and jelly I know there is ..." and so on, interminably complicating the passage of food to Overbury's rooms. She added that her maid would collect any left-over food for fear it may fall into the wrong hands. The girl brought baskets for the relics of Overbury's meals and as he had determined that those which were poisoned would never reach his prisoner, Elwes made much ado about scraping away portions of the poisoned dishes so that the countess would believe that Overbury had truly tasted them. He burnt the offensive pieces as quickly as possible, for he had seen that any food from the countess turned black and furred if it were left to stand a couple of hours.

As he approached his back door it opened and two maids came running out, their white aprons flapping against their firm bodies as they first ran, and then trotted, across the grass towards the Armoury. Elwes felt foreboding hold his heart like a clamp. He walked even more slowly but irresistibly towards the kitchens where he could hear a sound of sobbing and his wife's voice, calming and yet with a touch of hysteria in it, like a blush on a perfectly composed face. Elwes deliberately turned back from the sound and walked about in the sunlight for a full ten minutes. Finally he threw his shoulders backwards, adjusting his sword belt and shoulder knots like a bird fluffing feathers against sudden cold, then he resolutely walked into his kitchen in which all movement immediately stopped.

Monson was sitting astride the corner of a table, with a dark purple cloak hunched at his shoulder so that he looked like a Tower raven waiting for a crust. When Elwes entered he clapped him on his back and turned him back to the lawn outside. In the outer air they could not be heard, and glancing back at his own door Elwes saw the cook standing with her mouth open, her onion chopper poised like a headsman's axe while onions rolled away from her feet. He said: "My wife——"

"She is afeared," said Monson. "It is nothing. A boy of mine," his fingers made implication that he was more than a page, "a lute player called Simon Merston has been poisoned——"

"Dead?"

"It were better so, Sir Jervis, the noise he makes. No, he was carrying a pie from Mrs Turner's house to your own kitchen seemingly when he stumbled and the crust broke. On which the juice oozes out and young Merston from greed or vanity that it might spill on his hose, dips his finger and saves the juice. Upon which he sucks the same finger and falls to vomiting in your kitchen. our maids ran for me, thank God, as you saw, and in a trice I had the lad bundled out on a plea of the falling sickness."

"This business cannot last," said Elwes. "What do you think my cooks and maids think, seeing every table and stool and chair is covered with pies and jellies? When Carr openly sends letters, when Mrs Turner's goods are sometimes poisoned and sometimes not!" His voice creaked with agony. "I would I were back a squire with debts in Lincolnshire."

Monson said suddenly: "What said Craig, the doctor who visited Overbury?"

"He? He was a cipher sent by the Howards."

"But he said something, what was it?"

"A consumption!" Monson gave his little fancy laugh and pulled on his glove. "A wise man, that young doctor, to find a disease which can be turned every which way and means so little. He said nothing of poison?"

Elwes compressed his lips and shook his head.

"That puzzles me," admitted Monson as they parted. He cheered immediately, "I warrant Overbury's filled with arsenic now and is too stubborn to die".

After the doctor's visit Elwes had felt an antipathy for the man confirmed. Dr Craig's knowledgeable smile, cocked head and elaborate cane all suggested a man engrossed only in establishing his own worth. No. He would call in Mayerne as soon as the great man was in London, and failing Mayerne, de Loubell, the brother-in-law of the court doctor, who rarely left the city, and who was considered a reliable apothecary. 'Please God,' thought Elwes, looking up at Overbury's window, 'I may yet save him. I do not like the man but I would save him.' He wished he might go to the king and confess his misdeeds like a penitent of the old religion. But it was too late. Sir Jervis was too deeply implicated.

Weston walked across the yard, his blue-coated body bent by sunlight as if summer were a cross he had to bear.

"Hold, you fellow!" Elwes cried. Weston obediently halted and bowed.

"What know you of poisons now?" asked Sir Jervis, coming up close to the man so that he could lower his voice. His own whisper disturbed him, it sounded so conspiratorial.

"Poisons?" replied Weston, bending even lower in a supplicating bow. "Oh, sir, we spoke on this once and I swore I would never use such magic again. Must we speak of it?"

"What poisons are easily procured?" asked Sir Jervis.

"I know not. I know not," replied the servant, his whole body writhing in embarrassment. As Elwes walked away, Weston turned towards Overbury's rooms and repeated under his breath, as if it were a Litany: "Why, what poisons? Arsenic, both red and white, Lapis Costitus, Mercury Sublimate, Cantharides and Great Spiders."

At Lambeth the divorce commissioners met, and witnesses came across the river to testify in a lamentable lack of order. The curious confiding Lady Katherine Fiennes had produced a tale which confirmed only that the Earl and Countess of Essex had lain with each other on visits to other houses where their innocent hosts had not thought to offer them separate rooms, and once or twice on these occasions she had seen the earl unlaced or in his nightgown. Servants repeated stories with licked lips and rubbed hands: that the couple had left a ridge down the centre of the bed after they had lain in it, that they had spoken unkindly to each other, or that they had never been seen to kiss. There seemed to have been a continual coming and going in the Essex house as the gossips had entered the bedroom on some pretext or another: to search for lost earrings in the bed, to present a Valentine, or to carry a hot brick, and they had been inquisitive enough to notice how Essex and his wife dressed and behaved on every occasion. Abbot felt such repugnance at the thought of these little people, crawling about the noble household like maggots in meat that he was thankful when the earl was called at last.

"It will put paid to these rumours," he whispered to his neighbour.

"We have had no real evidence yet," protested Sir Julius Caesar in return. His lawyer's sense of propriety was being buffeted by this case.

The commissioners dealt gently with Essex who said of his wife,

"She was a virgin when I came from Flanders. I loved her. I do not now. Neither shall I, ever."

They knew that they were being duped by the Howards, but how could they prove it? And many members of the commission, being pensioners of Northampton, had promised to let the divorce through easily. The qualms of Archbishop Abbot were as irritating as sand in their shoes—and his objections were all based on theology.

In the evening when the other commissioners had left, Abbot would read through the evidence. Sometimes he sat until the eastern sky had opened to the next day. He knew that the commission was being gulled, and he hoped that the Howards would not get away with it. After a sleepless night he asked if Sir Dudley Digges might call for breakfast. That busy young man arrived while the archbishop was being shaved but Abbot dismissed the barber and talked to Digges over ale and the remains of a broiled rib of beef.

"I wished to speak with you privily, and our conversation is to go no further," he stressed the last words staring at Digges and hoping that awe of the church would compel him to vow secrecy. Digges's value to Abbot lay in his ability to pick up gobbets of information like a bird picking crumbs. With his dark eyes bright in early morning light, Digges looked very like a jackdaw.

"I never spoke to any of your visit from Overbury," he replied, wounded.

"And yet I am asking much," continued Abbot, determined that all should be clear to Digges before he answered questions. "I wish to hear what others may have told you in confidence."

Digges was not abashed. "I owe more loyalty to the head of the church than any common friends," he answered readily enough.

"Sir Dudley, you are ever about the city, raising funds for your scheme of the North-West Passage," began Abbot, hoping that Digges would not begin to appeal for a contribution. He had more sense, and only sat smiling at the archibishop.

"I supped with several city merchants last evening," he said.

"What do they say of this divorce?" asked Abbot.

"That as for the plea of impotence on the part of the Earl of Essex, all know it is false and the lady herself would admit it in private, for she hath never put young Essex to the test but kept him away from her bed. Howsoever she sees that the impotency plea makes the most sense in gaining a quick divorce, and in finding sympathy for herself. She will, they say, make no bones about getting a divorce any way she can, for she has already been provided with a second husband——" He paused, relishing the effect of this on Abbot who had begun to pull at his fingers agitatedly so that the joints cracked. "It is common gossip that Lady Essex and Lord Rochester are more than ordinary friends and he sees her every day, supposedly in secret, but there are no secrets in a large house. Servants will talk. Never have great ones so lacked in scruples to gain their own ends."

"Thank you, Sir Dudley," said the archbishop and would have dismissed him, but Digges stood still in the centre of the room, eyeing the scrolls of paper on the divorce, and remorselessly continued:

"And there is gossip about your lordship too."

"What!" cried Abbot, sure that nothing in his rigid life could be turned to scandal.

"It is said that even the Archbishop of Canterbury has his price."

Digges was disappointed that this did not provoke an outcry. Abbot merely stopped pulling at his hands and tucked them beneath his full sleeves.

"Tell me, Digges, what is my bribe to be?" he asked.

"It is offered by Lord Suffolk. Know you, he has ever been a fond father and as far as Frances is concerned he is alarmed at the treatment she may have from the commissioners in the matter of the divorce. It is thought that all the commissioners may be bribed in one way or another—by lands, or preferment or even as base a thing as money. You, my lord archbishop, have been judged incorruptible—except in one matter." He swallowed and continued. "Lord Suffolk controls the allocation of apartments in the royal palaces and it is said you have complained several times that your rooms at Greenwich are cramped and dark and look out upon an alley. You will be offered fair rooms, enough for an entourage, and they will be rebuilt and decorated."

"Pish," said Abbot and closed his eyes. How well Suffolk knew him! He did not wish Digges to see how affected he was by this story. Opening his eyes he said severely: "As for your city friends who claim that all the commissioners have their price——"

"I am sure it is exaggerated, my lord," said Digges smoothly and bowed himself out.

The other commissioners gathered in the room as the clock struck ten. Abbot looked at them as if they had just met. Had Sir Julius

135

Caesar a rapacious mouth? Was Dunne seeking for more ballast for the treasury which could cling to his own ink-stained fingers? Was the little bevy of bishops capable of bribery—perhaps with more elevated sees, or more comfortable palaces?

"My lords and gentlemen," he said. "I will not allow this divorce to go through."

They hastily got to their feet as he walked from the chamber, his silk robe slithering on the stone stair. As the door half closed Abbot almost smiled at the furtive conversation which trickled down the steps behind him. The consternation of the commissioners suggested that some at least had been bribed to allow the divorce. Abbot realized that he had aided some of his colleagues who could now still accept their portions, saying to the Howards or the king—whoever had offered them bribes— "We would if we could, but Archbishop Abbot stopped us". He called for a skiff to go to Greenwich.

James was helping two pages bathe a hound which had been gored by a stag. Blood smeared his doublet and he was watching patterns that reddened the water in the bowl. Carr sat beside his king, a prim youth compared with James, whose undone doublet and stockinged feet offended his favourite. He hardly looked at Abbot but only watched James, although with a forbidding mouth which reminded the archbishop of the expression of dead Prince Henry when his father had made a fool of himself. Abbot bent to ask for a private audience.

"Why so? I've no secrets from Rabbie Carr here."

"Your majesty, I wish to give my reasons for this projected divorce being against the laws of church and state."

"Wha' mean ye?" his flaccid mouth open, James passed a towel to the pages, yet he waved away the attendants and led Abbot into an inner room. Carr came with them.

"Nay, Rabbie, nay," said James, "there are sic things unco' delicate for your young ears." He giggled into Abbot's severe face, but the archbishop saw that his large eyes were steady. James was playacting with some intent. Playfully, he seized his favourite's elbows and propelled him from the room. Above James's curled feathered cap Abbot noticed Carr's furious, rolling, red-brown gaze. The king did not see the grimace which threatened Abbot; he turned back into the room and closed the double door behind him. His puffed body, disproportionately swollen above his meagre legs, looked almost dignified.

"We ha' peace and are alone," he told Abbot.

"Did you know the Countess of Essex is having an intrigue with Lord Rochester?" He towered over the king who waved him towards a chair and sat down himself, looking at his dirty hands and broken nails.

"Forbye I thought both parties had agreed on't," he said weakly, "and I do ken that Robbie and her leddyship ha' an understanding. Is all the evidence in?"

"Not yet your majesty, but enough has been offered for the commissioners to realize they are being fooled by the countess."

James's mouth curved slily. "You are sure young Essex is not gulling you?"

"He means well. He has no desire for anything but to be left in peace. He had been humiliated by the stories about his manhood and would have done anything to prevent this disgrace."

"I had heard from other men that you were not over eager for this divorce," admitted the king. He sat limply, his ornate hat downcast, his feeble legs dangling from velvet cushions to turned-in toes, incapable of firming on the floor. From where he sat, Abbot could see that James's eyes were bloodshot, and that thin red veins wandered over his face, his hands trembled; for a moment the archbishop felt a pang of pity for the king. "This is gey sad news," said James at last. "Suffolk and Northampton have already come to me with their stories, my lord archbishop. They say you are hair-splitting and would throw out the divorce." While he watched a fly crawl up the wall, James also covertly watched Abbot. He had always respected him but would not let him stand in the way of Robin's happiness. He moved his hands placatingly. "My lord archbishop," he said, "can you not allow this divorce? It means little enough to yourself and a deal to those two young bairns."

"I cannot see a mockery made of church and law," replied Abbot.

James wriggled a little in his place; he noticed that the gold thread on the arm of his chair was loose and began to rip it away from the fabric. It gave him the same satisfaction as taking a scab off a cut, swiftly unpeeling to reveal cleanliness beneath.

"As for the law," he said heavily, "leave defending that to the lawyers. Sir Julius Caesar should be its knight champion but he doesnae come to me to say that he will not have the divorce."

"Some commissioners are to be bribed," said Abbot evenly. "I do not know the details but it is common knowledge——"

"Common knowledge," muttered James distastefully, holding common knowledge up by its ears and then dropping it. "I would nae gi' a penny for 't."

"Nor I," agreed Abbot stiffly, "if I had not been told my own price."

"And what's that?" James leaned forward.

"A fine set of rooms here in Greenwich, decorated regardless of cost, and promised by Lord Suffolk."

James slapped his knee and laughed: "Aye, they ha' your measure then, my lord archibishop. That's what you are always whittling for. D'ye think we do not know you ha' had your eye on those apartments on the west side for the last year? It's ill suited you to be pushed back where the smell o' the midden comes in the window on a hot day. Aye, ye must agree its a bonny bribe for the likes o' yoursel', a man like you is incorruptible, my lord archbishop, excepting, just perhaps excepting, a favour like yon set o' rooms." He laughed on, but his eye was fixed on Abbot's face, anxious for his archibishop's reaction.

"I would I did not have to complain to your majesty of this bribery, but I must," continued Abbot calmly.

"Ah weel, we maun hope aye for the best," replied James vaguely, his laughter stopping as abruptly as if a door had been closed. He plucked at this lower lip, staring absently at Abbot's great episcopal ring which drew light from the sun. Abbot attacked again.

"Your majesty, I cannot believe that you would desire the divorce contrived in this fashion yourself, seeing that you are so obscure in your true feelings on it." A belch rose to James's mouth and fell between them, smelling of Rhenish and shellfish. "Your Majesty hath always been an upholder of law and religion."

James slid from his chair so that Abbot had to stand too, his black gowned figure upright and sombre as a cypress in a coloured garden.

"We must aye spin it out," replied James obliquely. "The commission will not reach a decision soon and there is no immediate argument." He walked towards the door.

"Your majesty" began Abbot. "What if these tales of bribery be true——?"

"Whisht," said James, flapping backwards with his hand. "I've no time for niceties, my lord archbishop." He strutted out, leaving Abbot undecided on what the king intended.

In the outer room he brushed past Carr who did not move out of his way. In spite of James's renewed affection, the young man looked sickly and indecisive. He had always been quick to salute the church in the past and Abbot wondered unkindly if news of his complaint could have reached the young man so soon. Had somebody been listening at the door?

XVII

AMAZING OVERPOWERING AMBITION. Like Icarus. He had admired that youth, launching himself at the sun like a paper dart then frizzling away down to the sea. He even talked of Icarus to brave Robin, dainty Robin, his delight and deario. O'ervaunting nine year love, but he had written it all down and sealed a packet to be given to Robin if anything were to happen, and at that thought Tom Overbury wryly crooked his neck about to see the autumn sunlight through the barred window. Nobody could scald their wings on that puny London sun, as white and thin as watered milk, which hung like a china bowl in the pewter sky. Had he been too proud? He mouthed some of the snatches of conversation he had heard dropped when walking among the courtiers: "That peacock Overbury"; "Overbury the dancing master, the puppeteer"; and, like a refrain, one phrase repeated over and over like the dying cadence of a courtly dance—"Overbury rules Carr and Carr rules the king"; at which he groaned and shut his eyes so that white and gold rings swung up and down aganst his swollen exhausted eyelids. The pain in his stomach lurched up again. He opened his eyes, horrified to see a wingspan spread across his vision of sunlight; was he seeing hobgoblins after all his thoughts of flying Icarus? But no, the raven, another inhabitant of the Tower, dropped down from his window to join its fellows squawking on the lawn. And Tom Overbury fell back also, his head hot and heavy on the immaculate linen pillow, and fell to his dreams again, the memories which he held on to tenaciously, afraid that they might be dragged out of him like his pride, his position and his ambitions.

Overbury would not die. His mind seemed to have the consistency of gruel or mud, yes, mud was right. His groping thoughts still wavered towards those terms which would look best on paper and this pleased him. Thoughts were like objects flung into mud also, they would hover on the surface for a moment and then sink, never to rise again. Tom wanted to write down how he felt but it would be too arduous. How could he get to the desk, let alone lift up a quill? He did not move his head but allowed his eyes to shift away from the window to the other side of the room. He saw Weston, his back turned towards him, fiddling with something made of glass. The sun caught at it, tempered it to a green pomander swinging between the man's fingers, and then turned it again to a large jewel giving and receiving light. He wanted to ask Weston "What have you there?", and even opened his mouth to speak but some lack of initiative in his own voice stopped him. He closed his lips again, feeling how hot and cracked they were. Had Killigrew's powders had this effect on Robin? He tried to remember. Surely not, or he would not have persisted in taking them, and yet they had been compelling enough to stop James from molesting his catamite. How Robin must hate the king's urgent caresses if he could subdue himself to this fever in order to escape them! He realized that he must speak and whetted his lips for the attempt: "Weston," he said. His manservant came over at once. At least he had a friend in this one! He felt Weston raise his arm and place his fingers under his wrist. He lifted Overbury and propped a cushion under his head, then brought a small bowl filled with rosewater and began to stroke his master's face with calm cooling movements like those of a lover. Tom closed his eyes, pleased that his lids pricked less with fever, and grateful for such a small but necessary mercy. And now Weston had placed a beaker at his mouth and was inclining his head to drink; liquid fell into his mouth like dew on parched earth, milk and honey, and perhaps egg beaten in it, and even a spoonful of brandy, even in his illness Overbury had remembered to distinguish each flavour, for he was afraid of poison and yet impatient of his own fears. He was in the safest place in the world from murderers. He managed a smile at Weston which the man did not see for he was placing the beaker back on the table and wiping droplets from Tom's chin, all with the same concentrated care. Overbury's voice came out feebly, "Who brought that last powder to the gate?"

"Why, Lawrence Davies, your own man," replied Weston.

"He is faithful then?" asked Tom. He had never spared much thought for Payton and Davies when he was riding high. Why did they still serve him now he was brought so low?

"Why," said Weston, "had you forgot they are paid until the end of June? And Lord Rochester himself has cautioned them to stay in your service for you will out of this place ere autumn, when the king comes back to Whitehall once more."

"That's so," murmured Tom and lay back, enjoying the luxury

of his feather bed and the cool fondling sheets which had been changed an hour before. He thought angrily of Robin. What was the lad playing at, that he had not had him released after the last letter which had been stronger than any sent before by Overbury? He had said: "Is this the fruit of my care and love to you? Be these the fruits of common secrets, common dangers? As a man you cannot suffer me to lie in this misery, yet your behaviour betrays you. All I entreat of you is that you free me from this place, that we may part friends. Drive me not to extremities, lest I say something that you and I both repent..." How could Robin have ignored such a blatant threat? But no answer had come except this white powder, pinched up in a packet and sealed with Killigrew's crest.

"Is Lord Rochester truly returned to London?" he asked, irritated that all his news had to come and go through Weston when Robin did not answer letters. He remembered that he had hopes of a pie the day before, but when he had broken the crust there had been nothing in it except some sodden strawberries and this packet from Killigrew, wrapped in oiled silk for fear the juice might permeate the paper. "This silence is unbearable," he said, pushing the coverlet away with his thin hands. Weston covered him again. "You can write, man?" Tom asked Weston impatiently.

"I tell you, sir, I am an educated man," replied Weston, "I was at one of those grammar schools set up by the brother of the old queen, God bless her, for my father was a worthy man of Kent and had a house of his own and others working for him beside..." Tom groaned but Weston continued as remorselessly as water bubbling in a cistern "... and would have me be a lawyer, God save us, but I was naughty and ran away and would travel and see the world, but look where such wickedness has brought me—a dismissed felon relying on your kindness to exist, Sir Thomas, and so I tell my son William to remember you in his prayers for without you I would be quite undone."

"Silence," said Overbury but the command came out as a whisper so that Weston had to bend to hear him. "Give me some more of that posset so that I may slake my throat while I dictate a letter to you."

"Oh, as to that, Sir Thomas, I am not a scrivener. I doubt if I could keep it up for anything as long as a letter, and knowing the letter must be to my Lord Rochester, sir, I would be afeared..."

He passed the beaker to Tom who managed to struggle upwards so that he could sit quite straight while he clasped it and drank.

"Weston, I am better now but would have this letter despatched before noon so you will have to write it. This is a parlous time, man, you must not be concerned with the manner of writing but the message."

Muttering, but so that Tom could not hear him clearly, Weston pulled a chair to the table and opened the desk, fetching out paper and ink. He composed himself to write like a schoolboy, the quire aslant, his leg curled round the chair leg, his tongue poking from his mouth, and an elbow awkwardly gripped on the carved heron to steady his hand.

"You are ready?" asked Overbury. His vision seemed better now that he was upright and there was no doubt that the drink was doing him good. The roof of his mouth was moist, and his lips were more flexible. He could even think with his usual alacrity. " 'This morning'—notwithstanding my fasting till yesterday—'I find a great heat continues in all my body, and the same desire of drink and loathing of meat, and my water is strangely high, which I keep till Mayerne comes,' " he glanced sharply at Weston: "You have retained my water in a wine jar?"

"Indeed, sir, as you said."

"A washed wine jar? It would not do for the doctor to think I were a drunkard."

"Washed o'er and o'er, Sir Thomas, and dried and left in the sun before I put your water in it."

Tom relaxed and returned to the letter. He repeated: 'which I will keep till Mayerne comes. The distemper of heat, contrary to my constitution, makes me fear some fever at the last, and such a one, meeting with so weak a body, will quickly, I doubt not, end it.' " He smiled while Weston struggled to finish the sentence. Surely Robin would relent now that his friend feared for his life?

"It is done," said the servant and picked up the sander.

"Not yet, not yet. It must be finished. Write this: 'And in truth I never liked myself worse for I can endure no clothes on, and do nothing but drink. This is the story.' "

He thought for a few minutes longer about a scheme he had conjured to secrete himself in Elwes's coach and ride, disguised, to Carr's apartments at Whitehall. In his weakened condition even this fantasy seemed impossible. He added a final sentence: " 'My head is weak and I write this in much pain.' "

"Can you sign it, Sir Thomas?" asked Weston, and somehow Tom managed a scrawled signature which was the most concrete sign of his own illness. It was so unlike his customary bold name that he gazed at it aghast until Weston took it away to dry it. He watched silently while the manoeuvres of smuggling were carried out, the letter wrapped small and placed in a lead flask which was lowered into a pie dish and the stale crust replaced on it. Over all Weston placed a white cloth.

"Is Davies to be trusted?" Tom asked. "Are we sure these letters reach Lord Rochester?"

"Sir Thomas, I ha' ne'er seen a more devoted servant than yon Davies," said Weston solemnly. "Why this morning, while you yet slept, he came around and I told him of your sickness in the night and ever since you had the last powder from his lordship. He was amazed and even asked me for a bowl of your vomit, Sir Thomas, for it was so putrid that it stank the air, but I told him I sluiced it away as quick as possible and that Lord Rochester should not be annoyed by such horrible messes. It was unfit to show him."

Even Overbury's self pity had not reached such notions. What, carry his vomit through the city streets and present it like a gift to Robin! He would have laughed at the thought if his shallow breathing could allow him.

He waited for Mayerne to return to London but it was de Loubell who came at last, a workaday apothecary but highly thought of. The doctor was introduced by Elwes who hovered at the door, disliking the pervasive smell of sickness in the room but reluctant to neglect his prisoner. He stood and watched as the doctor undid his box, producing little jars of curiously smelling medicines which encouraged the lieutenant to believe that at last Overbury would have proper treatment.

"What said Craig?" asked de Loubell, tilting his head at Elwes as if Overbury could not answer for himself.

"A consumption," said Elwes flatly.

De Loubell shrugged and dismissed Craig with that gesture. He pounced on Overbury and tipped his head back to explore under his eyelids, pulling them about firmly with his splayed clean thumbs.

"Hm," he said and walked to the window where he seemed to gain heart from the roses he could see across the lawn. Decisively he came across to the table and said: "Blood letting, Sir Thomas, you choler is too high."

"Indeed," said Elwes, "I would have thought he was enfeebled."

"Are you a doctor, sir?" asked de Loubell.

"I? Nay, you know—"

"Then, Sir Jervis, contain yourself with your own business. Know that I wrote my renowned good-brother, Sir Theodore Mayerne himself, of this man and he replies that he has rarely heard of a worse case of fever. I think it is your gaol that causes it."

"My gaol!" But it is well kept, clean and the flags washed monthly. This is the Tower, Mownser de Loubell, not a felons' prison."

"It is not the state of your prison which weakens him but the fact that he is restrained," said de Loubell, "at least that is the opinion of Sir Theodore. The man imagines he is in some dank cell, subjected to torture and famine——"

"Nonsense! There is nothing of that."

"It is in his mind, you see, it is his humour. If I let blood he will be less fanciful, less inclined to melancholy, and will soon see his surroundings for what they are, well appointed chambers such as any gentleman would be pleased to occupy."

Elwes was mollified by this description of Overbury's apartment. "I'll be on my way then," he said briskly, "for I cannot abide blood-letting. It quite turns me. Now Sir Thomas," he continued coming closer to the prisoner so that Tom opened his hazel eyes and looked at him keenly. Is the man playacting, thought Elwes, he looks so spry in this fever? "Your servant Harry Payton will be passing in an hour or so," he said, "and will no doubt bring a dish for you."

He turned back towards de Loubell who was fussing with pewter cupping dishes and little twinkling knives, as dainty and polished as a lady's needles. Elwes felt a spasm of sickness himself but put it down to the smell of vomit which hovered about the room persistently in spite of Weston's scouring and strewing of sweet herbs.

"If you have any messages for the outside world, it would be well you thought on them," he said meaningfully to Overbury touching the man's hand, to help him realize he was not alone in his hour of need. But de Loubell was calling for his apprentice, Reeve, to hold the cups and the boy came pellmell into the room, a slyboots lad with a flopping lock of greasy gold hair and a bloody apron.

The sight of this last was too much for Sir Jervis. He pressed Overbury's wrist once and was away.

"Is he in a faint, sir?" asked the apprentice, seeing Tom's pale face and drawn mouth.

"Nay, nay. He feels a little sorry for himself, that is all," said de Loubell in his carefully accented voice which never slurred or gave undue weight to a word.

Overbury opened his eyes. "Am I dying?" he asked.

De Loubell stepped back, shocked. "How can you suggest so unworthy a thought?"

His doctor's patter came quick and easy, he renewed his assurances that Sir Theodore had recommended bloodletting in fever as he bound a tight wad of white cloth round Overbury's lower arm, clenching it to the skin with a twisted silver skewer so that all blood pressed back, leaving the hand limp and white. He carefully chose a knife from his little collection and opened a vein under Overbury's arm as neatly and firmly as a housewife filleting fish. Both men watched the blood emerge and run in a gentle dribble into the cupping bowl. Occasionally de Loubell pressed the skin more firmly, his nails leaving ghost-white crescents on the blue flesh. When the bowl was half full he sighed and relaxed his hold. The blood ran more tremulously, sobbing discreetly on to the rim of the dish. Overbury stared with fascination at the dish.

"That is that," said de Loubell finally and stopped the cut with a wad of linen from his box.

Overbury saw how it gradually reddened. "Can you stop the bleeding?" he asked.

De Loubell smiled at him. "Why, keep that band tight," he said, "and it will stop of its own accord in a few minutes. When a clot forms on the wound you may bandage it, but not until then. D'you understand me?"

He said this to Weston who had come in as unobtrusively as all good servants. Weston did not answer, he walked forward suddenly, knocking the basin as he passed the boy.

"Why, watch what you do!" said de Loubell, "I will look closer at that blood afterwards."

"Sir Thomas," said Weston and was down by his master's bedside, feeling at him, and pulling the bedcovers over his face.

"Why, d'ye seek to smother him?" said de Loubell crossly, jerking the sheets down again. "Are you a fool or knave?"

"Why? Is he not dead—" asked Weston softly.

146

The three looked at Overbury, whose black beard turned upwards, as stiff as a scimitar. Each bone in his grey face stood out under the skin like those of a plucked bird, his neck stretched gauntly beneath his shirt. His hair, plastered with sweat, fell about his ears which were each as white as alabaster.

"Dead? Not he," said de Loubell. He lifted Overbury's head and they saw a pulse, moving insistently against taut skin.

"You say he cannot eat?" he asked Weston.

"He should be tempted, sir. For his close friend, Viscount Rochester sends dainties to him daily, as you heard from Sir Jervis, and besides that, he hath more than enough sent by the Countess of Essex who has an interest in him as she is a friend to all unfortunates."

"I would not rank him unfortunate," said de Loubell, "for soon he will be back in his place once more."

"Think you so?"

"Why, his brother-in-law, Sir John Lidcote, is busying himself about the court, and they say both his parents are in London."

"I had heard so," admitted Weston; "but surely they are powerless when the king wills Sir Thomas should stay in the Tower?"

"The king can be lenient at times," said de Loubell shortly, irritated that he should discuss the affair with Overbury's warder, however tricked out as a confidential servant.

"He has not eaten what could be called a meal for nigh on a week."

"If he has eggs and milk and wine he will not take harm," replied de Loubell. "Keep him warm, even if he be fevered, do not open windows, and build up a great fire, as hot as he can bear. Does he have many stools?"

"Why, he is on the run all the time. I never saw the like, and is sick even when there is no reason as he has not taken food; but it seems all he has, he brings up again. It is a mort of trouble keeping these rooms clean and decent."

"Well, well, I am sure you will be rewarded for your pains when he comes to his own again," de Loubell nodded at the sick man. "He will not die this time."

The doctor was determined to see Lord Rochester; he would beseech him to deliver his friend from the Tower, for the sickness of Overbury might be boredom, or it might be caused by persistent small doses of arsenic. De Loubell was asked to visit Rochester within a week. Before his arrival, Payton had come to Robin with a piteous letter from Overbury in which was a list of his ailments.

"Why, what makes him so sick?" he had asked the manservant.

"It seems," said Payton roundly, "that it is the powder sent from your lordship by the hand of Lawrence Davies nigh on five days ago."

Carr looked at the man dubiously. He had been told that here was another in Northampton's pay and yet Payton seemed genuinely indignant at the straits of his master, so much that he had lingered outside Carr's apartments hoping to say more, and now he was inside. He stared straightly at Carr.

"Tell me, honestly, how does Sir Thomas?" asked Carr as if he might begin the conversation again and erase the stark words.

"He is sick."

"How sick?"

"Very sick."

"What means that?" asked Robin foolishly, as if he could gain some comfort from every nuance of the information: "Very sick indeed?"

Payton had enough of this fencing: "Yes, my lord, in great danger of death, for he hath three score purges and vomits in one day."

Robin Carr's eyebrows, which had been described as twin moons by a court poet who wished to please James, went up towards his perfumed hair. He was amused. The man's description was so overdrawn that he could almost believe that Overbury had paid him to exaggerate. "Pish," he said lightly, "here's for you, my good fellow," and he gave Payton a crown, tossing it as easily as he would toss a tidbit to a begging dog.

Payton flushed but held on to the crown. "It is the truth, my lord," he said as he bowed and left Carr's rooms.

When de Loubell also told him of Tom's sickness, Carr called in Rawlins, his most intimate equerry. He asked him if Killigrew had himself delivered the powder which had been sent on to Overbury.

"It was brought by the countess's maid," Rawlins told him, "and she lays it where your lordship found it, on the window seat. And after she had gone and would not see me again—the jade—I looked at it and it had the seal of the Killigrews on it so I knew it was intended for your lordship to send in to the Tower. I swear I didn't touch it but to raise it a little when I moved the cushion to the chair, but I put it down again in the same place, knowing that you set great store by Sir Robert's powders." Carr nodded, thinking that a seal could be copied by any jeweller.

Mr and Mrs Overbury were a little fearful of London and entrusted all their business to their son-in-law, bluff Sir John Lidcote, who went to Rochester and said firmly that he was not doing enough for Overbury. They had, said Lidcote, even asked for a servant of his family to be sent in to the prisoner and had that request refused. He showed the refusal to Carr who noticed with a faint heart that it had come from Northampton. However the old statesman had allowed that Doctor Craig might attend Overbury while Mayerne was on a royal progress with the king.

"He may be dying," said Lidcote "and I would like to visit him to help him make his will. If you can achieve nothing else, my lord, perchance you can gain me admission for that purpose?"

Carr was disquieted. He longed to follow the king, to escape from London where all his trials seemed to be coming together. He could not sleep at night from worry about what trickery Frances and her family may be promoting.

"I think we can manage that," he said to Lidcote.

The fellow was everything Carr hated in a man; enormously large, with straddling bold legs which seemed about to burst from his sober brown hose; his face was deliberate in its honesty and stupidity. Robin sighed, he had not even known that Overbury had a brother-in-law, and now this forceful man could make a load of trouble for him.

After Lidcote had gone he wrote a note for his friend's mother, it was better to have her from the town before James returned, for a prostrate, raving woman would remind the king forcibly of his prisoner.

"Mistress Overbury," he began in his rounded hand, and bit his nails for inspiration, then resolved to keep his news short—"Your stay here in town can nothing avail your son's delivery, therefore I advise you to retire into the country, and doubt not before your coming home, you will hear he is a free man." What else could he say?

XVIII

T HE YOUNGEST MONSON child served in the charade by
which Frances's virginity was sworn. She had been dressed in a
shroud of white linen which completely covered her head and she
was arranged on the countess's bed, her knees up and apart and her
plump feet splayed to either side. The four illustrious ladies who
had been chosen to attest to her did not enter the room. They sat
next door by a table spread with sweet cakes and wine which had
been supplied by Ann Turner. Frances had ridden to Whitehall,
sure that she could enjoy her lover as the court was at Windsor
and her presence at home was confirmed by the girl on the bed.
Four working midwives acted as proxies for the noble ladies; they
refused to look at the girl, their shrewd eyes shifted about the room
but they stayed away from the bed, standing in a line as crisp as a
female regiment, their white kerchiefs and aprons shining in the
darkened room. After a moment they retired to the outer chamber
and the leading midwife bent to whisper to the most imposing
matron, Lady Alice Carew, who said in her clear West Country
voice "It seems the lady is a virgin" and, satisfied that their duty
had been done, all the women flitted from the Blackfriars house like
a bevy of full-bodied ghosts.

George Abbot could not be moved. The other commissioners cursed
him under their breath. They all disliked meeting at Windsor,
having been ordered there when they had hoped for a summer
recess. The Howards were growing indignant at the delay in the
divorce and had urged the king to hasten the councillors to a judgement by having them meet near him. James had agreed that the
commission could meet at the castle but had excused himself from
it. He was too enraptured of his daily hunting. Abbot had one
firm ally: John King, the Bishop of London who was as indignant
as his archbishop at the sly way in which the countess's lawyers had
tried to hurry through false evidence. He and Abbot had even had
a new form of oath drawn up for Frances, for when she came to
swear her virginity "her oath was as leaky as an old tub" said King.

Seven maids, as near to Frances in rank as possible, had also sworn that she was a virgin but how they knew this was not explained. Sir Daniel Dunne and Sir Julius Caesar wished to speed the commission and the archbishop would have it delayed while he sought more real evidence that there was a physical reason for a divorce. Against the wishes of his colleagues, he had the Earl of Essex brought before them once more. He would only say again that as far as he was concerned his wife was a virgin—for he had none of her.

"We must not make a precedent," pleaded Abbot, "surely you of all men, being lawyers," he appealed to the opposition, "can understand me?"

"I am sorry for the Howards that this is taking so long," answered Dunne, "and wish to end it."

James met Abbot on one of the wide walks about the parapet. He was shivering in a summer breeze and was loath to stay so exposed, but as the archbishop looked resolved the king could do little except pull a fur about his neck and accompany him. He would not appear more feeble than the older man.

"Has Sir Daniel spoken wi' ye?'" he asked.

"He feels it would be a disgrace if the divorce is not brought forward, your majesty. I say it be a disgrace if it is not thrown out, the grounds for it being untrue and precarious but no, Dunne is in sympathy with the Lord Chamberlain and his daughter."

James let Abbot's scorn fan him like the wind. He turned to gain some shelter from a buttress. "What say you, my lord archbishop?" he asked mildly.

"If the Howards are disgraced they should have looked to that before they began it. We were not the men who set the matter afoot. If it is a disgrace they have brought it on themselves." He glared at James, his white hair riven by the wind so that it fell on either side of his long handsome face like waves parting over a sea wall. "Why must I, to save another from disgrace, send my own soul to hell, as I would do if I gave a decision with no grounds for it? I will never do it."

James lifted his hands imploringly, his face puckered against the cold. "Why mon. I hae heard tittle-tattle about the couple which may be e'en gossip but gies me doubts that it 'ud be wise for the marriage to continue. Ye canna mak some beasts lie doon taegither, my lord archbishop. Nay, it wud be agin the Lord, being as it is agin nature, to mak them do so."

"Your majesty talks of beasts, not men," countered Abbot, "and wedlock is holy and cannot be sundered simply. I would to God I could believe the evidence of the countess. I would it were true and all proved, but I fear it will ne'er be so."

"Aweel," said James taking a brief walk to try and rouse the cold blood in his feet. "It is aye your monarch's faut, my lord archbishop. It was I told Suffolk to try for a divorce syne his dochter wud gie him nae peace wi'out it. If it gangs awry can ye no see I wud blame masel'——?"

He paused, shocked, for Abbot was slowly lowering his long stiff body to the ground. He knelt before James as if he faced an altar, tears creeping out of the sides of his eyes.

"Your majesty," he said but his voice was fierce although his demeanour was humble. "I would wish to be out of this business. Think on't. I am not married and tho' I cannot but know that the testimony we are given is useless I have not wit or words with which to ask questions on the condition of the countess's body. And I am not a lawyer, your majesty. I had thought that being the head of the church, under yourself, would make me fit to judge on this case but I find myself harassed and sleepless. I am determined that I can never bring in a case for the countess. I believe, your majesty, that her lawyers are lying—as she is herself. I do not believe that Lord Essex is impotent. I am sure she has never allowed the boy near her bed, and whyfor not? Does it not seem possible to your majesty that she has been longtime enamoured of another, and this case is brought in desperation to release her from a marriage which is right and proper in the eyes of God, but a mockery for the countess?"

"Return to Lambeth, my lord, and tak your commission wi' ye," answered James. 'Belike the air of Windsor is unco cauld for decisions to be made." He held on to Abbot's hands as the old man rose, first on one foot and then on the other, taking his weight off the ground. "Sakes mon," said James, throwing his arm about the archbishop's neck in the fond gesture he usually reserved for his paramours. 'Ye ken I would hae this divorce done properly."

The verdict brought in by the divorce commission in two days' time was a deadlock, five declared for a divorce and five against. As Carr and Suffolk belaboured him with their pleas for a speedy end to the commission James agreed to appoint two more members who would be sympathetic to the Howards. He also postponed the next hearing until the middle of September by which time he hoped that the opposition would be so weary of sitting on the commission that they would declare for a divorce as soon as they had the opportunity.

A letter fell from Tom Overbury's hand and lay on the floor. Weston picked it up and placed it on the table. He knew without feeling them that Overbury's hands were dry and hot, that his tongue was swollen in his mouth, and his body aching and tired. Weston tiptoed from the room as a Tower raven flew across the bars of the little window. Tom opened his eyes and snatched at the vision nervously then fell to looking at something more familiar and near to hand, his coverlet, its gaudy flowers softened by repeated spongings after he had been sick. He had hopes of Lidcote. He had never liked his brother-in-law who had been left far behind during Tom's success at court. And yet it was Sir John Lidcote who had persuaded Carr or the privy council—Tom was not sure which but then were they not the same?—that Overbury must be visited, if only to make that accursed will. And Lidcote had brought with him as witness the same Robert Killigrew who was so attentive in making powders. Lidcote had wished to discover if Overbury's sickness might be traced entirely to those drugs he had from Killigrew. The amateur apothecary had been startled by Overbury's dull eyes and feverish face. He had gaped while the will was drawn up, half afraid that his powder might have caused this dissolution; but then he had been quick enough on the uptake to accompany Elwes to the door of Tom's room so that Lidcote could have a private word with his brother-in-law. Tom had looked up at that wide honest face, with a beard too long and straggling, and an ancient hat above it. He seized Lidcote's hand, pressing it between his fingers like a flower so that the man gave a little yelp of pain, not supposing a sick man would have such strength.

"What of Rochester?" asked Overbury, "does he juggle with me or no?"

Lidcote hesitated, his face was sweating, his blue glance moved towards the door: "As I believe, I think not," he whispered, knowing he must be discreet.

Tom followed his gaze and saw that Elwes was listening to them. The governor came back into the room and said:

"You are to have no private conversation with the prisoner, the council is firm on that."

He pulled Lidcote by the arm so that he dawdled after Sir Jervis, anxiously watching Overbury's closed eyes, but he said nothing more, for Sir John hoped to return another day. He did not.

Although the first warrant for his visit had implied that Lidcote would have access to Overbury again, he was presented with another paper when he called at the Tower gate next day. It came from Elwes and said that the privy council had warned that the prisoner was to be kept close, and that no man should see him. Lidcote swore and went directly to the nearest tavern. He wrote white-hot, a letter which Overbury would never have imagined his brother-in-law capable of understanding, let alone penning. He had said that the council pretended that Overbury was in prison owing to the king's anger but that it was through the machinations of Carr and others. He added that Lawrence Davies should not be admitted, for this erstwhile intimate of Overbury was too close to Carr, and carried pies and tarts from his household and from the kitchen of the Countess of Essex. He offered to pay Davies off. Lidcote continued that he thought Harry Payton was still loyal and could be trusted. Above all, he said: "Change your style if you write to Lord Roch:—for there is no honest quarter to be held with him. As you love me, burn this, and forbear writing all you can, for it was never so dangerous."

Upon this, Lidcote had stolen Carr's own trick, for he had a quince pie brought from the tavern kitchen and thrust the letter within it, wrapped only in his kerchief. Then he had called on Harry Payton and so sent his message inside the Tower.

Tom licked his lips and thought of that terrible letter. It had destroyed his hope as utterly as this fever was eating him away. Robin was more than unkind, he was Tom's gaoler. As he lay, comatose as a corpse, Overbury realized that only Robin could have arranged all things against him. He remembered the spring and summer, filled with his own urgent letters, which had been smuggled out so furtively and may as well have not been written at all. He had insolently commanded Robin in every one of them. Tom rolled upon his side, hoping the pain in his back might go. He thought again of Sir John Lidcote's letter which should be burnt. He wanted to burn it, as if sending it into flames would eliminate the truth it had told. So Robin may be his enemy! Brave Robin who had played golf with him and paid attention to his many political lessons—and all the time he had been waiting to escape from Tom, to make his own decisions, and follow his own counsel, or that of Henry Howard! He struggled his damp head on to the pillow and lay still, his eyes focused only on the rough weave of linen under his face, the creases of fabric which writhed and crept near his cheek every time he breathed.

"Vipers," he said loud, but there was nobody to hear him. "They have let poisonous snakes into my bed," and then he stopped moving and the creases ceased wriggling. Tears began to spread in a wet swab under his eye. It was humiliating. Tom had been Carr's governor, his manipulator, the most powerful man in the kingdom and now was brought so low! Was Robin killing him in secret? Or were his new friends, the Howards? Tom would put nothing past that curds-and-whey lady of Robin's. He lifted his knees up to his belly, amazed by how slight his body seemed. He had not noticed how he had shrivelled in this little room. Like an old nut in a shell. Was he dying then? Was this death? This longing to escape pain? Did Robin hope he would die forgotten in the Tower and that none outside would hear the name of Overbury again? He gritted his teeth, shocked again to feel how loose his back ones had become. All this had happened in those long weeks when he had imagined himself uppermost, writing arrogant instructions to Carr, eating those dishes which were sent to him daily and which contained he knew not what. Yes, I have been poisoned, he thought. And then, But I will survive.

He lifted his head from the damp pillow and looked about the room. He wished to burn Lidcote's letter first of all, and saw that a puny fire was still living in the grate, a relic of the cool night. Tom pushed one leg from the bed. It dangled over the edge like a dead weed, limp and white, not making contact with the floor. Slowly he pushed the other leg out to join it, then lowered both together. Lifting his weight to his feet was more than he had bargained for, his body, though wasted, was still too heavy for walking about the room. He held on to a stool and then to the table, propelling himself like a child learning its first steps. When he reached the table, he leaned both elbows on the desk. His face, which had been so dry and feverish a few minutes before, was now running with sweat which formed drops under his unkempt beard. Tom felt the carved surface, his fingers tracing out the pattern of heron and fish like a blind man learning the face of a loved one. There was nothing there. Amazed, he concentrated on the floor, it was empty except for some balls of dust which rolled about on the boards like crippled mice. Overbury was enraged. He went to the door and was then surprised by how easily he had managed this journey compared with his trials on the way from his bed to the table. "Weston," he called. He hardly spoke above a whisper so it was as well that Weston was in the outer room, eating an apple and reading what looked like a child's grammar book.

"Weston," he continued, waving aside the man's outcry and encouragement to return to his bed.

"You are a sick man, sir, I would not have you——"

"Weston," he said firmly, holding himself upright by clinging to the door, "where is the letter that was on the desk?"

"Letter, Sir Thomas?"

"Aye, from Sir John Lidcote. It came less than an hour ago." Tom's voice was coming back, prompted by his rage.

"I know of no letter," answered Weston, peering past him at the desk as if a letter should appear there. "Nor never saw one."

"Fool! Davies—no, Payton—Payton brought it in a pie. You took the pie yourself saying it would do for a bite with your beer at mid-day. You left the letter with me."

"There can be no letter," returned Weston stubbornly. "You are not allowed letters from any man except those sent in pies from Lord Rochester, and they be secret. How could you have a letter from Sir John Lidcote?"

"I read it!" replied Tom. "I had it in my hand a few minutes ago. You took it from me when my eyes were closed, and laid it on the desk there."

"You must a' been dreaming, Sir Thomas. If'n your eyes were closed, were you not dreaming?"

"I was not dreaming. The letter warned me against Robin. I had it in my hand."

"Ah, your fever is powerful bad. Lie down, Sir Thomas and sleep now."

"Where is my letter?"

"I saw no letter, Sir Thomas," said Weston, soothingly as he half carried Tom back towards the bed. "There is a fine pasty with beef and turnip in it delivered from Lord Rochester. You will want that at noon."

"No. I will not," replied Tom with some spirit. He turned his peaked face to Weston authoritatively. "I will have no more dainties sent in. I will feed as do other prisoners in the Tower. Sir Walter

Raleigh has survived on the diet, and so will I. I will have broth made in the warders' kitchens."

"Sir Thomas, that is not right for such a great man as yourself. You need more dainty food."

"Broth only," replied Overbury. "And I will only take medicine sent by Mayerne. Or from de Loubell, but not from any other meddler. I want to see no more of Lawrence Davies. He has been coming here since he was permitted in, and always with a new drug or potion. Who knows who really sends them?"

He lay back exhausted. Weston almost ran from the room, disturbed by Overbury's sudden accession of vigour. He tucked Lidcote's letter into his jerkin before he met Elwes in the court below. For the last week the governor had wandered about near Overbury's rooms without entering them more than was necessary in the course of his work. Sir Jervis was so lowered by the demands of the Howards and the health of his prisoner that he wished he might be taken ill himself and relinquish his duties to an inferior, but he knew that if he retired, even for a few days, Monson would come in with his deadly determination to put an end to Overbury. Pleading sickness would be tantamount to murdering the man. So Elwes hovered below the stairs, pretending he had plans for enlarging the Tower and talking familiarly of building to those warders who were curious at meeting him there.

"Well, well, Weston," he said with assumed surprise as the servant bolted from the Tower door like a stopper pulled from a jar. "We meet again in this place. How is Sir Thomas Overbury?" He rocked back on his heels and smiled benignly while he thought how two-faced he had become. Honest Elwes, his neighbours in Lincolnshire had called him with something like a sneer, and yet here he was, smirking at a would-be poisoner, hired for the occasion, and all done under the sunlight.

"He seems a whit better," said Weston, anxious to confide. "He has asked for broth, and says he will refuse the dishes from the Countess and my lord Rochester."

"Tell me," said Sir Jervis, "have there been any other attempts? Have you tried to kill the man directly?"

Weston looked back at him coyly. "Did I not kneel by you on the cobbles here, Sir Jervis," he asked, pointing at the stones under them, "and swear I would not be used as a tool again?"

"Yes, yes," agreed Sir Jervis, "but are you honest?"

"There was a pot," confided Weston, dropping his voice so that the governor had to bend towards him to hear, "a little white pot and in it a jelly as white as the jar, so small and sweet smelling it was, I'd 'a tried it myself. It was more like to the creams ladies put on their faces than a drug."

"What of it?"

"It was brought from the countess. I smelt it, Sir Jervis. I turned it about and then I thought on your words. I must be honest, for Sir Jervis Elwes made me swear so, I thought, and so I threw it in a homely place, along with some tarts as had mould on 'em."

"You mean they went in the jakes?"

Weston nodded.

"Have you any other news?"

"Aye, I have that. Know you Doctor Franklin, that they call the male midwife?"

"I have never heard of him," Elwes was taken aback that the man thought he knew of such low persons. But Weston went on tonelessly: "I met him in a tavern outside on Tower Hill, for, know you Sir Jervis, I must have my pleasure too, I cannot be always about Sir Thomas—and Franklin comes in and asks if I am Weston warder and servant to Overbury. 'I am he,' I said, and then he told me that some apothecary had been offered £20 if he should give a poisoned clyster to Overbury as would kill him straight."

"A clyster!" exclaimed Elwes. He had not thought that an enema might send poison into Overbury's body by another route.

"E'en so. I asked if it were Doctor de Loubell who had been paid to do this, but Franklin said it was another and by his look I would say it were himself."

"There's no way he could treat Sir Thomas," said Elwes, relieved that the Howard precautions had again proved fast in keeping Overbury alive rather than killing him. He said: "So we must be sure none but de Loubell or his assistant, Reeve, shall bring medicines to Sir Thomas. You are sure he looks better today?"

Weston shrugged. "Aside from some foolishness of a letter from his brother-in-law."

"What! No such letter could reach him."

"Indeed, Sir Jervis, he was raving like a Tom o' Bedlam of the letter which he thought he had been sent, and had read——"

"Did he say what this letter was supposed to have told him?" asked Elwes slyly.

"Not so. Or perhaps he did, something of being warned of

Robin. He was in such a taking over it I only wished him in bed again."

"So he is still feverish?"

"Aye, Sir Jervis. And if I were you—an I could not think myself so great a man——"

"Go to, what would you do?"

"Why, Sir Jervis, when Doctor Craig were here some weeks back he was ready to swear that Sir Thomas was near death with a consumption," Weston fidgeted, enjoying the attention of the governor.

"Aye."

"Sir Jervis, would it not be wise to ask Doctor Craig to put his findings down on paper? If anything untoward were to happen to Sir Thomas it might be well to have a doctor's word that he was dying of a consumption in July."

"I will think on it," Elwes admitted, and walked away, knowing that he would ask Doctor Craig for the letter to cover himself if Overbury were to succumb to one of those ointments from a little white jar.

The familiar trio met at Northumberland House where the old earl was in bed. The news that the divorce commission had been adjourned until September had sent him under the blankets like an animal burrowing to safety. Over the past few years of greatness Henry Howard had become accustomed to having his own way and the divorce commission had confounded him. And yet when he was alone and could think straight he knew that a hasty decision would very likely be one which the Howards did not want. His frustrated mind almost considered Frances an innocent, bedevilled by calumnies and spite. His nephew was more openly furious. As he had always had the means to give his daughter anything for which she cried Thomas felt he was failing her. He was not jealous of Carr, who had similarly failed her, for the boy was designed to be Frances's plaything and it was probably better if he did prove weak and foolish—Suffolk might even enjoy his little maid's anger when she discovered, as she surely would, that a bright eye did not mean a quick wit—but he was enraged that she should have a reason to complain of her old daddy and consider him lacking in love for her.

"More letters," said Carr explosively.

"Aye we ha' all had them," replied Northampton wearily. "I had thought we were shut of Overbury but he seems to attack with new vigour. Does he suspect you are betraying him, my lord Rochester?"

Robin winced. "I know not. Tom ever knew how to fight clever. He has said nothing but soft words. He hath letters going all ways at once it seems: to me, to Lidcote and now straight to your lordship and my Lord Suffolk here."

"Our's come through Elwes," explained Suffolk, "and he sends us news daily on how his prisoner goes."

"And how is he?" asked Robin.

Northampton groaned: "He seems better, but sees none but de Loubell and his man Weston."

"The last is in your pay?"

"By mysterious means, through Frances and her confidant, Mrs Turner."

Robin thought. Overbury was like a bear at a baiting, surrounded by immense mastiffs all intent on the kill, and behind the circle of dogs, another circle of excited men were all yelling for death.

"When he will be away from that place?" he asked. Did a glance pass from one Howard to another? Or was he tricked by the sombre light?

Northampton sighed: "He has sworn that he will be ever faithful to me if I gain him his liberty."

Suffolk laughed, a jolly libertine sailor's bellow which went oddly with the words that came afterwards: "He promises to patch up any quarrels betwixt Lord Rochester and myself—as a Christian and an honest man." His teeth showed—black stumps as decayed as dead treebolls. "He adds an afternote, that I should forgive the blotting, for he is very weak."

"How should we answer?" asked Robin.

"Why, Thomas and I have sent our replies this morning by way of Elwes. My nephew only thanked friend Overbury for his protestations of love, but I said he should withdraw some of the false witness he hath uttered on Frances afore he thinks of release."

"He is too proud to admit he insulted her."

"You know not your dearest friend," Northampton's voice oozed slowly from the bed, where his face was hidden by velvet hangings "He thinks on death and will do anything for release. We have seen that he knows through Elwes that the divorce commission is put off to September——"

"So he knows when he will be free?"

Neither of the older men replied, they seem immersed in other thoughts. A servant's footsteps clattered in the passage outside. Thomas rose and went to the door. They did not wish their meeting to gain gossip in the world beyond that small oak barrier. He returned with a sealed packet.

"Is it word on Scab?" asked Thomas, as his uncle read the letter. Robin was not concerned, he guessed that Scab might be a dog. He looked out of the window at the mist rising on the river, which dimmed to grey and violet; sails dipped and swayed on the close horizon.

"What says Scab?" asked Thomas, enjoying the joke hugely.

"Nay, be not so insolent, dear Thomas, let our friend Robin know that Scab is a code word among us——"

"For what?" asked Robin shortly, turning back to the gloomy room.

"For your dear friend Overbury. Elwes speaks of him so on our command."

"Whyso?" Robin frowned, he did not find the code name amusing.

"As it draws Sir Jervis further into our plot," explained Northampton. "We think, or rather know, that he has been over-scrupulous to his prisoner and even protected him from us. Aye, be not amazed, the little Lincolnshire squire had some notions of niceness in him, but day by day we sap his strength. Monson is ever at him on our orders, swearing that he must be more strict with Sir Thomas, allowing only that in——" Suffolk's hand rose once, like the white flag that waves a truce. Northampton checked himself and sank back to his pillow. "Let me say only, that Elwes is not so kind to Overbury as he was before."

Robin stood up. He had realized that there was no place for him in this meeting. The letter brought so quickly back from Elwes was something he was not meant to see or hear. He preferred to be away, he did not want to know what persecutions may be in train for Tom. He picked up his hat. "I leave this little congregation, my lords," he explained. "I have fixed to meet Sir John Lidcote at six. He wishes to confer with me on Overbury."

"You will not encourage him in his protests?"

"Not I, my lord." He bowed to Northampton, and to Suffolk who was now moodily walking about the room. The Howards hardly answered him.

161

"So," said Thomas as the young man's steps echoed away from their hearing. "What says Elwes? Is he wholly on our side now?"

"What other course has he?" asked Northampton. "He has qualms, but knows that we can advance him if he works for us, and that Overbury will suffer whatever he may do to save him. And yet it is as well he was an honest man, for if this business should ever be exposed—as pray God it be not," both men crossed themselves perfunctorily, "it will appear that all possible were done for Overbury. Sir Jervis even adds a note to the man's letter of contrition in which he admits that Overbury could no more be truly friends with either you or me than a negro could change his skin or a leopard his spots. With Elwes so wholly committed to us there is no evil may not befall friend Overbury."

He glanced quickly at Thomas in case he were shocked but his nephew was too concerned with the outcome of the divorce to worry about the fate of Overbury. Northampton sighed his relief, he had known that any man loses his scruples if they are tested over too long a time. Elwes had borne this out, so had Suffolk, and he was sure that if the dead bell tolled even Carr would be pleased by an end to Overbury's life. He nodded at the long letter from the prisoner which Elwes had enclosed, with its vows of love and communion. Would Overbury live or die? Or should he leave the decision to little Frances? Northampton knew what she wanted and also that she might wish to witness the murder herself. What a Jezebel she is, he thought fondly as his men came in to shake his pillows and prepare him for sleep.

"You are to be moved, Sir Thomas," said Elwes abruptly.

Tom stared at him. "I am to be released?"

"Not so. You are to be kept closer, by the commands of the privy council." Sir Jervis swallowed hard.

"I do not understand you, Sir Jervis. First I am allowed to eat what I please and as I recover I have doctors to see me——"

"De Loubell only," reminded Elwes. He looked past Tom and out of his barred bedroom window. It was the first week in September and betokened a cold winter. Berries were already hot in the hedges and country folk said that stoats had donned their white coats early. Overbury would never know of this, thought Elwes, and then ah well, what will be, will be.... "It is for your own protection, Sir Thomas," he said.

"Is it for my own protection that in the last week you have suddenly cut off all my connections with the outside world? That having raised my hopes by saying that the Howards would deal with me kindly, you then refuse me access to them? That I am cut off even from my dear friend Robin——" His voice broke on a tear.

Has he learned nothing, thought Sir Jervis wonderingly, have all Lidcote's proofs of betrayal and the known rapacity for revenge in the Howards meant nothing to him? Could he have believed all those false to-ings and fro-ings of love and friendship which have been playing out like a comedy these last weeks?

"The divorce commission meets next week," he said, "and you hoped to have had a part to play, did you not? Did you not seek to be a witness against the countess?"

Tom stared at him, distraught: "But I have abjured all that! I have sworn over and over that I will be a friend to the countess and all her family."

"The catopard, you called her, did you not?" continued Elwes. He was attempting to summon a rage of his own against Overbury but could not, pity came breaking in. "Come now, Sir Thomas," he said and held out his hand. Tom stood up holding to the table as he did so, he was still wasted but had grown stronger while only de Loubell and his assistant Reeve had access to him. His furred robe hung about his shoulders like a draped sail. "Come, come," said Elwes.

Overbury's eyes glared back, as wild as those of a fox. "You are my friend, are you not, Sir Jervis?"

"Why yes, and yes again, Sir Thomas. It is only a little, little way."

"You would not be untrue to me?" asked Overbury as if pleading. "I have begged forgiveness of the Howards and offered them my loyalty."

"That is enough," said Elwes, backing from the room but still holding to Tom's tall figure with prominent bones, which leant upon him as they passed under the lintel.

"How far? How far?" asked Tom.

They made a halting journey to a cell, one of those which Elwes had thought disused, and yet it had been inhabited recently as an uneaten crust of bread lay on the floor. "No rats, you see," said Weston, but Tom was horrified. He pulled at the flowered quilt which Weston had lowered to the bed and tried to see from the lancet window, but his only view was of another wall on which water dripped ceaselessly.

"How long must I stay here?" asked Tom, taking in at a glance the truckle bed and stool.

"Until the divorce commission meets," said Elwes briskly, "which is in a week. It is for your own safety, for I fear that the friends of the countess may seek to put you away." He swallowed swiftly again.

"I will not have it," said Tom suddenly. He frowned. "I will have Robin know how I am treated, Sir Jervis. This is not kind in you."

"It is a dry cell," said Weston, "and I can light a fire in the hall outside."

"May I have paper and ink?" asked Overbury.

"You may have aught you wish for," said Sir Jervis placatingly.

"Except my freedom?"

Elwes bowed. Tom bounded after him with the strength of a fit man as he retreated. "I will not have it," he shouted. "I have crawled and licked arses too much in the last few weeks in hopes that I may get out of the Tower, and all it has earned me is this——" he waved his arms at the dank small room. "I will be heard, Sir Jervis. If this is what time-serving brings, it is better to be proud and speak the truth. I will bear witness at that commission." He rattled the barred door as Elwes walked away. "I will tell all of my treatment. I will be out of here and speak to Archbishop Abbot."

Weston followed the governor as far as the staircase. He looked at the guards who obediently disbanded at a nod from Elwes, whose face was still wrinkled with distaste at his own actions. He had hoped to avoid Weston.

"Should he have pen and ink?" asked the man. "What if he does send letters to all these people, and the archbishop does deliver him from the Tower as an important witness?"

"I would believe that could happen only if King Jamie himself took up residence in one of the cells," answered Elwes with an ill-contrived jocularity. "Be not afeared, Weston. Sir Thomas will condemn himself out of his own mouth as he has before."

They could hear Tom talking to himself of revenge and release.

"Will he turn mad?" asked Weston with a touch of eager interest.

"Not he," replied Elwes, and hoped he was right.

XIX

Tom would write it all down for Robin. He did so, resolving not to spare the feelings of his lost friend. Words tumbled out like the ready tears which fell hotly on to his hands. From the outer hallway Weston watched him and smiled covertly. "I will speak to you as I used to ... And now to make so poor a pretence to say you will alter towards me for the style in my letters. Alas! This shift will not serve to cover your vow, your sacrificing me to your woman, your holding a firm friendship with those that brought me hither and keep me here, and not to make it your first act of any good terms with them to set me free and restore me to yourself again. And you bid my brother keep your intent secret that you might steal away with your wickedness." He poised his pen for a thundering threat: "But that shall not be: you and I shall come to a public trial before all the friends I have. They shall know what words have passed between us ..." He bit his lips, tasting the sour savour of salt on them. "When I heard how, notwithstanding my misery, you visited your woman ... held daily traffic of letters with my enemies without turning it to my good, sent me nineteen projects and promises for my liberty, then at the beginning of the next week sent me some frivolous account of the miscarriage of them and so slipped out of town." He did not cease his threats until the end: "... so that this wickedness may never die, I have all this vacation wrote the story betwixt you and me from the first hour to this day. When I found you at first, what I found you when I came, how I lost all the great ones of my country for studying for fortune, reputation and understanding, how many hazards I have run for you —what secrets have passed betwixt you and me."

Overbury added a narrative of how it had taken him several days to write the story of Carr's betrayal and how he had sealed it eight times before sending it out of the Tower secretly to a loyal friend who would circulate it among those men who had remained true to the prisoner. He ended vindictively: "If you deal this wickedly with me, I have provided that, whether I live or die, your shame shall never die, but remain to the world to make you the most odious man alive." He folded the letter and sent it by Payton. When

Robin read it he rode hastily to Blackfriars and broke in upon Frances as she sat at supper.

"He will tell all!" he cried, and threw himself on the floor, burying his face in her embroidered skirt. But Frances merely took the letter up, licked butter from her fingers and read it slowly.

"Think you he has truly written about us and sent the letter to a friend? Could he do such a thing?"

"He might, he might," acknowledged Robin. "In spite of Sir Jervis's renewals of strict imprisonment, he may have sent a testimony out by way of any servant—a week ago when Elwes was easy with him. He has no doubt said it should be opened when he is declared lost or dead—or something——" He faltered and sank back on his heels on the floor. A lapdog came and sniffed him curiously.

"It may all be a threat," said Frances, "of what he may do yet. What friend has he who would be used like this?"

"Lidcote is most likely. His brother-in-law, that he speaks of in his letter."

Frances read the relevant parts again. "Then we must muffle Lidcote," she said.

"Are you touched in the head?" asked Robin. "Do you think you can go putting down every man who threatens you? How do we know Lidcote would act on the story if he had it? He is a wise man, he may find it better to be silent until Tom is out of the Tower."

"Your friend Tom may die in the Tower. He has been sick, has he not?"

"They say he recovers. I thought we were finished with him, Frances, I did in faith. He has been so compliant these last few days and now—this, sudden. He is a danger, as you have always said."

Frances drummed her fingers on the edge of the table. She poured Robin a cup of wine.

"Drink that and pull yourself together, Robin," she ordered. "He must be silenced. We have been playing with him too long."

"What mean you, Frances?"

"Who visits him?"

"He has Weston, his man——"

"I know of him," she smiled.

"And Elwes himself," Robin gulped down the wine, its sour taste fighting the bile that was rising in him.

"No. He is too careful for my needs."

"What needs are those, Frances?"

"We have been too slow," hissed Frances like water tipping into a fire. She had pushed up her sleeves and was counting out a little sack of money which she had pulled from a cupboard. Her rings hovered like fireflies in the candlelight. "I have £20 with me," she said. "What have you? I mean with you, in your purse, not back at Whitehall. We have no time for such pothers."

"I have nothing," replied Robin, his eyes distending as she called for her maid and told her to go to Franklin.

"Must I, my lady?" asked the girl, showing a sign of trepidation.

"Indeed so. Send to him now. Go yourself. It is yet light. Tell him to meet his young friend Reeve, the apothecary's boy, and order him do that which has to be done. Will you remember the message?"

"To go to Franklin's house at Doctors' Commons and ask him to tell Reeve to do that which has to be done."

"That is so, and give Franklin this purse. It is all for Reeve, tell him when the deed is done, I will reward him for the goods again myself, but after all blows over."

On the next evening, Reeve arrived at the Tower as the gates were closing and by bribing a guard was let in to administer some medicine to Overbury. He paid the man sixpence in advance to allow him out again in less than an hour's time. Weston came grumbling from his bed.

"My master sends an evening clyster," the boy insisted. Weston considered him by lantern light, flopping hair covered Reeve's blemished face; he looked uneasy and chewed at his thumb. The clyster was concealed in a small box from which Weston heard the chink of glass.

"It is a poxy time to come," he said, "but if the doctor sends you —we must, we must."

He released Reeve's sleeve and led him to the cell where Overbury lay awake, reading by the light of two candles.

"Alas, you see how my condition is altered," he said to the apprentice. "For when last you met me I was in a fair apartment, and now am here."

"Indeed, Sir Thomas, there are many poor wretches without a roof," returned the boy, methodically feeling his patient's pulse.

"He has come to give a clyster, Sir Thomas," said Weston maliciously.

Overbury hated enemas, they were another humiliation to which he would not easily succumb. "Must it be this night?" he asked.

The boy looked at Weston. "Will you aid me, sir? It is the first I have given alone."

"Not I," said Weston, "but I will hold the candle up for you."

Tom frowned. "I will not be botched by such as you," he said to Reeve. "Wait until your master can give it."

"Not so," said Reeve. "He is from home, but left an order that I must give it this evening."

"Well, well," said Overbury, "I must allow it," and while the boy and Weston fetched warm water and a cloth he modestly pulled down his hose.

Sir Jervis Elwes was eating breakfast in his bedgown by the fire. He had been up all night with an aching head caused by worry over Overbury. His wife had insisted that he was an invalid although he had very little reason to be pampered with coddled eggs at eight o'clock. The repetition of the hourly cries of the guard emphasized that he was malingering. Lady Elwes was relieved that her pantry and kitchen had been cleared of dubious dishes from Mrs Turner, and she had been up at five, to scrub the boards with her scullions, determined that no grain of arsenic could lurk in a corner to be gobbled up by an inquisitive cat.

Although it was but mid-September, winter fogs were settling early on the river and even from his upper room Sir Jervis could hear the dismal cries of watermen as they fumbled about their business. He promised himself a walk by the water this morning, for he loved the secrecy of mist and river, the sudden resolving of shadows to reveal spars and masts cleeving their way through the gloom like scythes through grass. Boats with furled sails reminded him of the fens and those sinister figures on stilts who stalked through the marshes, hunting heron. His wife was at the door.

"Tell the boy to bring my boots," he said. "I should check the river gate."

"And catch an ague," said she, "be not so quick to rise, Sir Jervis, Weston is here."

Elwes leaned back against the hard wooden panels. He stared up at the ceiling where dust and cobwebs had settled in cracks between the beams. He had hoped to be away and avoid this man who had a surreptitious suggestion of evil. And no doubt the morning would bring some of those demanding, arrogant letters from Northampton, which he was flattered to receive, but which were continual nudges about the vulnerability of his prisoner.

"Tell him I will see him at noon."

She twisted her apron between her fingers. "He is in a taking."

Elwes sighed. "Then I will see him now."

He looked back at the bed wondering if he could get into it before Weston came up the stairs and so have the excuse of sickness to send the fellow away. But the man was in the room, his slippers flapping softly across the floor. He had worn them when Overbury was very ill to silence his movements but Elwes had always thought them affected for silent spying. He stood in the centre of the room, his bent body shutting out the light and his expression part shocked, part satisfied.

"What would you, fellow?" asked Elwes.

Weston licked his lips: "He is dead, Sir Jervis".

Elwes wished again that he had taken to his bed so that he could hide his face. His emotions were too clearly revealed. He was relieved. He had thought to be unhappy, disturbed by what deeds might be laid at his door, shocked, or in any other way discomfited, but his immediate reaction was relief. His burden had been taken away. He did not care what the result might be. In a moment or two, when he had thought of the implications of Weston's flat statement he might weep or start writing furiously to Northampton, or call for a jug of ale, but now he only said: "Then that is over."

"For Overbury," said Weston, his wink suggesting other puns.

"Silence, rogue," said Elwes, who had wanted to speak so plainly ever since Weston had been foisted on him. "How did it happen? This is not a matter to be glossed over. It must all be recorded carefully." Disregarding the servant, he threw off his gown and pulled his hose on, then fetched a grey cloth coat from his cupboard. "I will come with you at once to view the body."

"I would not do that, Sir Jervis."

"Would—not?"

"It is not a pretty sight and might be better seen by as few as possible."

Elwes considered, "I have seen dead men afore now."

"But none so foul, Sir Jervis. Only a doctor could view it without vomiting."

Sir Jervis sat down on the chair again. "How did it happen?"

"At four in the morning or thereabouts—it was not yet light but the birds were moving in the bushes—I heard Sir Thomas give a great groan and went to him. His body had broke out in sores like a man with the plague."

Elwes crossed himself. "Is it so—the plague?"

"It appeared to be the plague, but was not. His bed was sodden through with blood and pus and sweat and he he had dirtied himself like a babe."

"Poor man, poor man."

"So I carried him to my own bed in the outer hallway and made up the fire. He lay on his face, for his back was like a flame. He was in great pain, Sir Jervis, like a man in torture and said his back passage was filled with molten lead—or so it felt to him."

Sir Jervis held up his hand. He could only receive a little of Weston's story at a time. He looked out from his window at the fresh bright morning, sniffing up the smell of decaying leaves which was so much more pleasant than decaying flesh, a veil of morning rain was beginning to fall softly on the grass.

"Go on," he said.

"He could scarce make sense, Sir Jervis, but moaned of Robin several times—I thought he meant Lord Rochester at that—and he said he was betrayed by those he loved. He mumbled many things I could not hear."

"Why did you not send for de Loubell?"

Weston smiled pityingly: "He is away from London. His apprentice came late last evening and told me so."

"God's blood! Why did he come? Sir Thomas was much better yestere'en."

Weston shrugged. "I know not. He came."

"What did he do?"

"He gave a clyster. It did not take long."

"Hm," said Elwes, but this did not sound suspicious to him. De Loubell had been running in and out with one remedy or another for the past few weeks. He had given several clysters, seeking, he said, to purge Sir Thomas of the foulness within him. It had at first seemed nonsense to Sir Jervis that a man with the runs should be made more incontinent but de Loubell had told him that if a man had that in his gut which made him ill, it should be evacuated as soon as possible, and on reflection, Elwes had admitted to himself that this might be a good way to clear Overbury's body of poison.

"What then?" he asked Weston.

"At about six he seemed less weak and the pain abated somewhat. 'I must drink,' he said, 'I am burning up inside,' and all the water had gone. I thought to call a guard——"

"You should have done so ere then," interrupted Elwes.

"But he seized my hands and said he felt a little better. It must have been a quarter before seven. He asked me to go to the Buttery and fetch him a pint of ale to slake his thirst. I took his purse and ran there as fast as may be. I was back as the clock struck seven, Sir Jervis. I could not have run quicker with the jug, and he was dead."

As Elwes said nothing, Weston asked. "What shall I do now, Sir Jervis?"

"Do? Do? Why, prepare the body for the coroner."

"Does that have to be?"

"You must know that all deaths in prison are rigorously gone into," said Elwes.

"I will let you know more by and by."

Weston said: "How can I make it decent?"

"Clean the bed and clean the room," said Elwes severely, "straighten his limbs if they be bent and put a clean nightgown on the body. Go, go, do all as soon as possible."

He wrote a brief note for Northampton and sent it to Northumberland House, telling the boy to wait for a reply. It came before ten.

Noble Lieutenant,

If the knave's body be foul, bury it presently. I'll stand between you and harm, but if it will abide the view, send it for Lidcote and let him see to it to satisfy that damned crew. When you come to see me bring this letter again with you, or else burn it.

Elwes obeyed neither instruction about the letter. He locked it in his wife's stumpwork box. He wished to preserve any evidence that he had acted from orders, not of his own volition, and he wished to have proof that the earl had promised to stand by him if questions were asked about a hasty burial. He was turning the key when de Loubell arrived.

"I was told you were from town," said Elwes.

"But to Hampstead. I have seen the body."

"So Weston has laid it out?"

"He has placed it naked on a bed which is what I desired of him."

"What think you of this death?" asked Elwes cautiously.

"Why—it seems strange," admitted de Loubell "and yet many men of medicine see cases where the patient looks to recover, as Sir Thomas did, and rises from bed, as he did, and eats heartily, as he did, and yet it is too late to save them and they die—phoo!" He snapped his fingers. "I was surprised," he continued, "by the state of the body since I last saw it two weeks agone. It is covered with sores and ulcers and has great plasters on the back which were not put there by my orders. Yet, seeing him naked, I am not amazed at his death. He was wasted to nothing, Sir Jervis, and his belly fallen in. His legs and arms are like bare winter twigs. I have never seen so shrunken a man."

Sir Jervis dared not ask if de Loubell thought it a natural death. He said: "Your boy, Reeve, was here last night after dark, making a clyster. He said you had told him to do so."

De Loubell seemed mildly surprised: "It is carrying kindness to extremes," he said. "I had asked him to view Sir Thomas some time while I was away, only from the Friday to Monday. I said nothing of a clyster. I had thought Sir Thomas might not need one again. But then, I had been following a treatment which included purging, as you well know, Sir Jervis, having taken me to task for it, so the boy did what he thought best."

"A coroner will view the body at noon with a jury of six warders and six prisoners, to decide if death be natural or no." De Loubell nodded. "And I have asked Overbury's brother- in-law to visit the corpse."

Elwes was listing his duties as if he hoped de Loubell would reassure him that he was being correct, but the doctor only thought that Elwes was being over-particular.

"If the day changes," he offered him, looking at the window where the rain still fell, silent, and pale as a shroud, "bury him quick, for on a hot day the body will stink." He picked up his cane of office, a degree less imposing than the ebony and gold staff of the royal doctor, and he was away, explaining that he had a city merchant suffering from the pox who cried for him day and night.

Coroner Robert Bright and the jury ate before they saw the body for fear their appetites might be taken away. They were careful in their scrutiny and made notes on how they found Overbury, paying particular attention to many ulcers on him, including a remarkable pustule on the back into which, they said, they could have put two fingers. They also noticed that the belly was covered with blisters, as yellow as amber. Their chief concern was the emaciation of the body. "In effect," said the final report, "it was consumed away, having nothing but skin and bones."

The warders returned to their tramping and the prisoners to their various rooms, all pleased at having had a break from their routine lives, sad though the occasion might be. Bright was shown the letter from Doctor Craig.

"As far back as July," he said, holding it by the corner while Elwes watched him anxiously, "the poor fellow. It is amazing he lingered so long," with which the Lord Lieutenant agreed so fervently that the coroner wrote a firm 'death from natural causes' on the certificate, shook Elwes's hand, and set his horse for Tower Hill at a fast trot. Like de Loubell he was unable to linger, death called him as imperatively as disease had called the doctor.

Between twelve and one o'clock Elwes had two letters from Northampton. Although he may not have struck that final blow against Overbury the old man was alarmed lest any of his family be implicated. He had never spoken his suspicions of Frances but he recognized her fine Italian hand in the prisoner's death. The sudden demise of a man who had seemed to be improving in health, the hasty ride from Whitehall to his great niece's house by Rochester —for his spies had been out along the Strand—and the news of the corruption of the body, all made Northampton apprehensive. He intended to tie the purse strings of the plot so tightly that no rumours on Overbury's death could ever seep out. His nephew Suffolk would have the body buried hastily and Henry Howard agreed that this was necessary, but it should not be done so swiftly that it occasioned talk, for Lidcote must be silenced, and this was only possible if he were given a fair warning of his brother-in-law's death and were asked to view the body.

He sent Elwes two letters. One was to be made public, and in it Northampton spoke of the lamentations of Carr, saying that he had intended to approach the king at Theobald's and ask for his friend's release. He also said that Robin wished to attend a sumptuous funeral but that he, Northampton, had heard that the body was noisome and that keeping Overbury above ground might cause more offence than honour. This public reason for a hasty burial should placate any enquirers.

Northampton's second, secret, letter told Elwes to call Lidcote in to see the body, and then commanded him to bury it before any questions came from court, indeed he hoped that it would be some days before the king heard of Overbury's sudden death, and by that time earth should cover all. He told Elwes to have the priest ready as soon as Lidcote had been satisfied, and added that if Overbury's family did not arrive that same day the body should be interred, pleading corruption as a reason. As usual he told Elwes to destroy the second letter or return it to its writer.

Upon this, Sir Jervis sent out for a ready-made coffin and had no trouble in finding one, Overbury's body having shrunk so much that it could have fitted a woman's box. He hardly waited for Lidcote. A few hours after he had received Northampton's instructions, Elwes stood in the Tower Chapel waiting for the body to be brought in. It arrived on a bier, borne by four warders who were already squeamish at their task. Weston alone walked behind, his face concealed by a kerchief.

"It is high," he said, coming over to Elwes and nodding in the direction of the coffin. "We stayed not for a winding sheet, for his skin is dissolving like jelly in hot water, we had to put the body straight into the box for fear it would come to pieces as we handled it."

Sir Jervis bolted back the vomit that rose in his throat. "So be it," he said. "A short service, sir," he called to the Tower Chaplain.

Overbury had been dead nine hours.

At the moment when the box was being tipped into the black earth and a flagstone was poised over the hole, Northampton was writing a detailed description of Overbury's body to Robin. He spared nothing, for he wished Carr to understand what had happened to his friend. "We must not have any man in the plot crying that he did not know what went forward," he told Thomas Howard later, and added as a footnote that it were well that none of Overbury's adherents had seen the corpse, which might have made them suspicious. Northampton felt like a drover herding ponies, and drawing in a prodigal with his rope to net it to the herd. He was curious to see if Carr had enough strength of will to run to James and accuse the Howards of murder, but whether Carr were alarmed by his suggestion of foul play, or whether he were too stupid to understand what Northampton meant by insisting that Overbury should be buried immediately. The old man did not find out, for Robin Carr said nothing.

Lidcote arrived at the Tower on the next morning and admitted to Elwes that he was satisfied "for the nonce" by the explanation of his brother-in-law's death. He prayed for five minutes in the cold empty chapel then left without paying Elwes for the coffin. There was some speculation as to why a Middlesex coroner had been employed rather than one from the city, to which Elwes retorted that he had used expediency and Mr Bright was to hand. Northampton busily engaged himself with the most unkind rumour, by paying apprentices and ladies' maids through the offices of Mrs Turner, to say that Overbury had died of "the pox, or the French illness, or worse". He knew that a story that the prisoner had decayed from venereal disease would make Overbury's friends hold their tongues about his sudden death.

Robin sent a letter to Overbury's parents in which he gracefully blamed himself for not working more assiduously for their son's release, and vowed he would do any services possible for them in their time of grief. He hoped never to hear from them again.

By the end of the week the demise of the man was as smoothed over as the flagstone in the chapel. When Elwes went to Sunday service he could not take his eyes off it. He almost expected the stone to rise up, revealing the disintegrating body below; but no charnel stench eddied out of the corner where Overbury lay, and nobody except Elwes glanced in that direction. He thought, as he and his wife led the congregation from the chapel, that he saw the stooped blue-coated figure of Weston moving behind a pillar, but when he peered into the dark cavernous corner of the building he knew he was mistaken. The man had vanished, and for Sir Jervis that was a relief as great as Overbury's death.

Archbishop Abbot prepared a document of 8,000 words against the divorce and was not allowed to read it. By the end of September he was tired of arguments against James and the other divorce commissioners. The new men appointed to serve with him were promised to the king, and as the month lengthened to colder evenings and the sombre darkening of leaves, James became more obstinate on the matter of nullity. The week before the divorce hearing had been rudely broken into by the scandal of the Earl of Essex, who was finally goaded to declare himself innocent of the slanders about his potency. He had done so in a most riotous way, by challenging Frances's brother to a duel after hearing some of the tales told of him by the Howard family. Both had gone separately to the Low Countries for a few days in order to fight a duel away from English soil, but James heard the story and sent a group of gentlemen after them, who brought the young men back like naughty boys who had played truant. James had tried to mediate between them, vowing to himself that he would have the Howard and Devereux quarrels ended for good as soon as the divorce commission met. He confounded Abbot by telling the commission that none may speak on the divorce but could simply vote "yea" or "nay" and "so have an end to 't". And so Abbot was defeated, and the divorce was granted in the last week of September.

Yet the Howards would not let it rest. It was well known that the archbishop had disapproved of the divorce, and they attempted to persuade him to allow the young couple a special licence, although a date had not been fixed for the marriage. Abbot refused, and his opponents, realizing that by harassing the man for approval they might stir up some of his strong arguments against the divorce once more, contented themselves by asking the archbishop to attend the wedding of Robin and Frances but not to officiate at it. And Abbot agreed to this, for the commissioners who had assented to the decree were so criticized that he decided to act as an unguent and heal the wounds. James had been too quick to reward those who had opposed Abbot and as each new privilege, office or estate was handed over, the mobsters, and then the middle-class citizens, began to say openly that all the commissioners had been bought except the archbishop.

The lovers were rushed into marriage by the Howards and many were surprised that Frances did not bring forth a seven-month baby, so speedily were they wed. They planned on early November, at Audley End, but James wished to console the couple for their long drawn-out frustration, and suggested a "right royal wedding".

"Could I do less for ma ain braw bonnie Rabbie?" he asked, rumpling the boy's hair, as they sat in his bedchamber at Whitehall.

"Frances is gey pleased," admitted Robin. He was slitting chestnuts and pushing them into the ash with his dagger. James had sent his gentlemen away and they both crouched by the fire, with twilight hovering at the windows.

"Aye laddie," said James sighing, "I fear there'll be few cracks like this allowed us from now on. Ye'll be close wi' your Frances."

Robin lifted his face, made russet by firelight, "All married men must cleave to their goodwives," he said, "and you will see me by day."

"Aye," agreed James, allowing his parched hand to travel down Robin's neck where it hesitated over his throbbing pulse. "But it will ne'er be the same, Rabbie. It'll ne'er be the same."

"Nay," said Robin, too brightly, "you will have to make shift with the two of us about you."

"Ha' ye all ye' wish for, Rabbie?" asked James, suddenly anxious, pressing Carr's back with his knee.

Robin looked steadily into the flames, then pulled a chestnut out with his fingers. Meticulously he scored the skin, then slipped off the husk, stripping the nut of its fibre. He turned to James and held the nut provocatively before his mouth.

"It's ae for the king," he said playfully, "if your majesty gies ane favour."

"And what might that be?" asked James, laughing and holding on to Robin's wrist to steady the nut before his lips. "Ye know it'll be anything I have."

"This," said Robin and dropped the nut into his left palm, considering its charred flesh while he spoke. "Frances is gey disturbed at losing her position at court. One who has been a countess mislikes walking with the wives of viscounts."

"She wishes to be the wife of an earl?" said James. "That's small beer, my laddie, and weel ye ken so. What'll it be?"

"Oh, we would let your majesty choose," said Robin with becoming modesty, his face dropping lower so that James could see a whirl of hair on the crown of his head. The king laid his fingers over it. "Somerset," he suggested. "Earl o' Somerset."

Robin looked up, elated, "Aye, I like it fine," he said, "and Frances will like it too. The Earl and Countess of Somerset."

James leaned back in his chair smiling. "It's glad I am to gie ye so easy a gift," he said, "I hae another, especial for the bonny bride."

'And what might that be?' asked Robin coyly.

"Why, a wedding to outdo her last, and ye ken that's been the talk o' the continent since she was twelve year old. In the Chapel Royal, wi' a great dinner afore given by the merchants o' the city."

"The merchants of the city cannot abide me."

"They aye trot to their king's command, Rabbie. And more than that—what say ye to a masque by Ben Jonson?"

"Well enough," said Robin drawing aside a little, for in his enthusiasm drops of spit flew from James's lips as if he were a laboured horse.

"And more than that, much more," James bent forward, leaning his elbows heavily on his feeble padded knees, he stretched out his hands and clasped one of Robin's, squeezing it excitedly. Ashes fluttered from their joined fingers. "What say you to £10,000 in jewels, as a fatherly gift from her auld king tae the bride?"

"I like it," said Robin. He fondled the nut in his other hand, watching Jamie's big dark eyes which were rarely so expressive. "I hear you're doing fine from the wedding gifts," he said, running his fingers in and out of Robin's palm. "Lake ha' sent ye braw candlesticks I hear, that should win him the secretaryship. And Winwood ha' sent some fine horses I'm told. Well, he shall be paid for 't in kind."

"All the court has been generous," murmured Robin, gradually drawing his hand away from the king's, but James was imagining the marriage and would not release him.

"Ha, ha," he said, "and I ha' heard that Frances will be clad maist audaciously as a virgin, heh? I like that fine, Rabbie, for we will all see those paps o' her's, ye canna keep a' tae yoursel'."

He felt a tug from Robin's fingers and finally relinquished them. "And a' for the day after Christmas——" James continued, but his voice faded. "Are ye no happy, Rabbie?" he asked, bewildered by Carr's reticence. "Has your old dad not done weel by ye?"

"You have been most kind," said Robin, almost formally. He suddenly stood and faced James. "I will tell Frances she is to be a countess again," he added quickly, brushing ash from his silk hose. He walked away with no attempt at a bow, "Good night, sweet dad," Robin said as he reached the door. "Why!" he cried, "I had forgot your own reward!" He lifted his fist, enjoying the wincing crouch with which James reacted to any sudden movement, and threw the nut down the length of the room so that it bounced on the floor, and ended in white shards at the king's feet.

James stared down at it sadly and when he lifted his head to look at the door again Robin had gone, leaving his king in a sudden draught as a wind lifted the hangings.

PART TWO

Robin and Frances: 1614–1616

"Eclogue at the marriage of the Earl of Somerset, 1613, 26 December"

... At Court the spring already advanced is,
The Sunne stayes longer up; and yet not his
The glory is, farre other, other fires.

First, zeale to Prince and State; then love's desires
Burn in one brest, and like heaven's two great lights,
The first doth governe dayes, the other nights.
And then that early light, which doth appeare
Before the Sunne and Moone created were,
The Prince's favour is defus'd o'er all,
From which all Fortunes, Names and Natures fall...

John Donne

"On the fall of Carr"

Our Summer sun is set
And winter is come on,
The robin redbreast leaves to chirp
Because his voice is gone

Anon.

XX

FRONTING FRANCES ACROSS the long table, Robin felt ashamed that a few minutes before he had wished that some diversion had separated them, taking him to Jamie. She had become more beautiful in the past few months, her adolescent fat had deserted her face leaving it pale, with decisive bones on which the candlelight hovered so that she had the transparent grace of an Endymion. Robin sighed, for more and more often, since he had been divorced from Tom Overbury and the king's company he found that he longed for the languorous young boys who drifted about the court and who were denied to him by the decrees of his wife and his king. And then Frances could disturb him by looking like a lad herself, her hair looped back under a cap, her stubborn chin prodding out from her face like the prow of a boat.

"Would you pleasure me?" he asked along the expanse of table.

"In what way?"

He looked down at his plate. "By appearing as a boy," he said, "by wearing hose and a short cut coat—so."

Her laughter came fluting down the room like wind in a chimney: "And a codpiece, no doubt, my lord, to hide my sex? Is it that way your pleasure lies?"

He forced himself to look upwards once more at her malevolent eyes which shone in the light as she leaned over her plate.

"You'll none of that from me," she said, "and I will see to't you have no dirty games with the stable lads, for one thing it is to have the king and so ensure our position," she stopped to laugh consideringly, "but another to play cock and ball in your household and make me a laughing stock."

"I would not want that," he mumbled and laid his new-fangled fork aside.

"I would hope not," Frances could not leave well alone, her delight in finishing the argument made her flushed and excited.

"As to the king," began Carr, crumbling his bread around and about into grey greasy balls, "I fear he will be less of a friend if I am not more with him."

"Ho-ha to that," returned his wife. "Do you not know that you can do no wrong, sweet Robin, brave Robin, and that love quickens in the absence of the beloved? Let the old man alone. What, would you go winning favours like lickpenny courtiers? Let them all go to Cambridge—and they will. You are more potent here."

Robin wished he could believe her. It was a strange stratagem of Suffolk's, to entertain the king at Cambridge less than a month after the death of his uncle, Northampton, in June 1614. The old man had made an event of his end, arriving by road from Greenwich with such a display of force that London had sounded alarms, sure that he headed a rebellion. The old man, in striving for life, had relinquished his struggle for power; but Suffolk had continued to fight for the supremacy of his family. Was he attempting to emphasize that the power of the Howards flourished in spite of the root being lopped? Suffolk was an unchancy chancellor of the university; blatantly unacademic, he was even praised by the learned men for his lack of affectation.

"I will ride after them," said Carr. "I must not lurk like a dog in London when such entertainment is toward."

Frances lifted her shoulders, immense in puffed sleeves, so that they stood for a second on either side of her head like grotesque wings. "Go, my lord," she said, uncaring.

Next day he took horse and hurried along deserted roads in which white dust lay thickly like summer snow. It spurted behind him so that his attendants rode cloaked to their eyebrows, a sinister train of dark retainers. They entered the court at St John's like a group of soldiers come to take arms, and servants ran from them, to hide behind pillars or in the deep interstices of doorways and corridors, from where they peered out at the retinue.

"What!" cried Carr, "are men afraid of me?"

He wanted his horse to bound and caracole but the heat and pace had dejected it and so its head drooped down while Carr stared out over the dusty mane.

"Welcome, dear son," cried Suffolk, coming down the steps from the main lodging.

He was dressed in a cloth-of-silver robe trimmed with marten. Carr had to shield his eyes to see him while the older man's dress clashed with the bright sun. He slowly dismounted and his shuddering horse was led away. Suffolk put an arm about his dusty shoulders.

"Lie down, and change your dress," he advised. "You have missed some of our feasting but will see a play tonight and sup with his majesty, as do we all. As do we all."

Robin scowled, feeling that his father-in-law was emphasizing his own commanding position in this strange town, seemingly ruled by the university, and so by bluff Suffolk who had the dons running for him like rabbits.

"A thousand pound a day it costs me," whispered Howard behind his hand as they entered the welcoming dark cold passage between the dining hall and kitchen. "And worth it all to have the king my guest."

Carr buffeted his arm. "Aye, it is your terrain," he admitted. "I saw your palace as I passed, at Audley End."

"It promises well," said the old man as his pride made his chest swell like a sail. He led Carr to rooms which had been kept for him. They overlooked the river. "My good wife is across the road at Magdalen College," Suffolk told him, "where there is place for Frances."

"She did not come."

Suffolk said nothing. He straddled the window, looking away from Robin. "Is all well?" he asked, keeping his face turned towards the water.

"Aye," said Carr, but nothing more. Thomas Howard sighed and paced about, then abruptly clapped his son-in-law's shoulder and walked away.

Carr met James after they had supped, being separated from his king by a bevy of local notables. Around him ebbed his own constellation, chosen by Suffolk for their mediocrity so that nothing would be said wittier than those comments from Carr himself. But Robin did not appreciate this kindness. He sat silently while others ate, and occasionally drank from a silver goblet, presented to him before the meal by a fresh-faced undergraduate. "As a mark of the college's esteem." After the king had laid down his knife the tables were cleared away and velvet-covered chairs were brought for the great men while lesser ones sat on wooden stools or stood at the back of the hall, obliterated in the dark beyond the circle of candlelight.

The play was called *Ignoramus* and was presented by the undergraduates. As the Latin prologue uncurled, Robin disposed himself for sleep. Two seats away, James sat delighted while Suffolk bulked out the space between them, hiding Robin's defection. As Lord Chancellor he had to stay awake himself and look alert at all the Roman speeches. Suffolk had no Latin that he could remember, but being a Howard had not been ashamed of that, when made Chancellor of Cambridge he had listened to the oration which had greeted him and then said candidly that he had understood no word of it but spoke a universal language himself and hoped that in it they would dine with him, at which the academics had yelped with pleasure and forgiven him his lack of scholarship. Since then Howard had rubbed along very well and was provided with a tutor who translated for him when necessary. But this evening Thomas had waved the lad away. Why spoil the play by repeating its verses which the king understood well enough? He would enjoy the mouthings, the posturings of the undergraduates.

"D'ye see yon lad?" asked Jamie urgently, tugging at his sleeve. Suffolk checked a movement to pull his cuff "embroidered at £20 an inch" from the royal hand. He leant towards his king.

"What lad?" he asked, whispering so that Robin would not waken.

"Yon lad wi' the white satin breeks," said James. "Can ye no see him?"

Suffolk saw a myriad of legs passing about the small stage in a crowd scene.

"Wait a wee," sighed James, "when they are still again," and when they were he gripped Suffolk's knuckle, his big ruby ring clamping the sailor's hand with sudden passion.

Suffolk saw at once that only one lad could have roused James. Among the hobbledehoys—young lads from the Fens who carried Roman spears as if they were rakes—was one long youth who towered above his fellows in the row at the back, his pale face was moving this way and that while the other lads turned their eyes downwards, for they had been rehearsed not to stare. James checked himself and glanced beyond Suffolk to Robin.

Suffolk said nothing. He tried not to notice the boy, who had come forward and said some pretty phrases then walked back—unfalteringly, as if he had left the royal presence a hundred times. His expression before the king was unlike any Suffolk had noted before. The youth seemed amused and to enjoin James to complicity. His eyebrows expressed disdain of the lads surging about him. We two, his gaze suggested, have naught to do with this childish play-acting, and we two have an understanding. Suffolk, catching that hint of intimacy, which vanished as the narrator stepped forward, was almost tempted to forget the king's command and let the lad disappear into the throng of students who would run beside the royal coach, each indistinguishable from the other. But as the applause died down and men looked to the king so that they might rise with him, James held Suffolk's cuff again, smearing its hunting scene worked in gold thread and rubbing the fur with his thumb, his breath was working deeply with excitement when he tottered from the hall, his weak legs wambling from sitting so long. Before him, the lads bowed low, flushed with pleasure that their own production for his majesty had been received so well. James conversed with the master, his Latin interlarded with Scots intonations so that the dons leant towards him earnestly, their ears pricked. He changed to English as they walked into the fresh air of the court.

"We are well pleased," he said to the master who was bowing and bowing as he passed. "A fair night," he added.

Robin appeared by Suffolk's side, his face still suffused with sleep. "God rot the place," he glowered, staring up at the peaked towers, "I say we could ha' drunken and eaten wi'out this faradiddle."

"The king——" began Suffolk.

"Aye, he finds it good enow, a route of boobies wha'd send——" he swayed a little and leant against the door.

"It was not to my liking," admitted Suffolk.

He left Robin by the stair to his apartment and walked across a court which was suddenly empty, and echoing to the last lusty cries of the delighted boys, who whooped back to their rooms as if released from school.

The dean met him by the inner court, his cap and gown subdued to a denser black in the shadow. "The boy is not one of ours," he said. "He is visiting in the town and was put up for a part in the play by Sir John Graham—a Scot." His disgust caught Suffolk like a whiff of bad breath.

"Aye," he replied. "One of the gentlemen of the bedchamber."

The dean was annoyed at having to pass on gossip. "I know nothing of the lad," he complained, "by rights he should not have been in a college play."

"But was. I know well how these things are contrived," said Suffolk.

"Not by us," hissed back the dean. "He is a young sprig from Leicestershire, called George Villiers. I know not how it came about that he——"

Suffolk left the old man's words trailing in the wind. He marched towards his own rooms, resolved that George Villiers must be trounced and sent back into Leicestershire.

XXI

PEMBROKE SUMMONED HIS allies to council at his house in London; Winwood came, and Lake, and the archbishop sat at the head of the board. Wotton was in official disgrace, but arrived early, anxious to consort with powerful friends.

Wotton said: "And yet why need we plot? The king is already enamoured of young Villiers. They say his majesty met him secretly at Apthorpe in Northamptonshire before he ever arrived at Cambridge."

"Is Graham able to school him?" asked Winwood.

"I would rather," said Abbot, "have one of us take young Villiers in hand."

The conspirators applauded the choice of George Villiers as a successor to Robin Carr. He was the son of a poor squire by, it was rumoured, a waiting woman, and so he would be submissive to his superiors. Only Wotton talked of Overbury, as he and Winwood waited for their boat. He had added a poem to the preface for the dead man's poem: "A Wife".

Winwood laid a hand on his arm: "I like your verses, Sir Harry, I would they had not appeared so closely allied with reverence for the memory of Overbury."

Wotton said: "I did naught to aid him when he was alive, I can show some care now he is dead."

"We are all anxious to do that for him. Overbury never had a true friend in life and the court is full of them now, as plentiful as fleas in an old dog's carcase. No, I do not think it wrong in you to subscribe verses to the man's memory."

"Each memento of Overbury is a nail in the coffin of Robin Carr," said Wotton.

"Think you so?" asked the Secretary of State turning his heel on the slippery cobbles by the water's edge. "Think you so? That the common men cast blame for Overbury's death on Somerset?"

"I know they do. Oh, not in terms of 'murder' or 'revenge' but as he did nothing to succour Overbury when he was in the Tower—and could have done."

"The common men—no men cared for Overbury living," repeated Winwood.

Wotton grimaced like a man with a loose tooth, feeling it. "All causes have their martyrs" he answered. "You and I know well that Tom Overbury was the last to fight for any cause except his own advancement, but seeing the Howards and Carr so high, and suffering from them, the merchants of London—aye, and the more humble too—have made Overbury their dead hero, and Carr his killer by default." Exiled from councils, he could afford such plain speaking.

Winwood glanced up and down the river, as if he might be overheard. "What use is that to bring down Carr?" he asked. "We must shuffle Overbury's death off as history."

"They say he was poisoned," suggested Wotton, not looking at him.

"*They say*," retorted Winwood. "Men will say anything which enters their silly heads. Can they prove it?"

"I for one do *not* believe Carr had him killed. I do believe he allowed others to kill him and could have stopped them."

"How?"

Wotton smiled. "How easily he could have plucked Overbury from the Tower!"

"Aye, and did not." Both were silent.

Wotton came close and Winwood inclined his head. "Take not my word but that of Lake," urged Wotton, "a man of the world who knows how it trots. He says that you should ask Sir Jervis Elwes to sup with you, Sir Ralph."

"Elwes?" Winwood frowned.

"The Lord Lieutenant of the Tower."

"I know him. He is not a murderer." Winwood was definite.

"He? No. But he is a man bent by others. Bent by great ones."

Winwood seized Wotton's arm as the boat edged towards them. "What know you?" he asked quickly before the oarsmen came within hearing distance.

"I know nothing," said Wotton and spoke the truth. "I only tell you what Lake wished me to tell you, when he knew we would travel in each other's company."

"Why could he not tell me himself?" Fast and faint before the boat was moored.

"Sir Ralph, he could not see you until Friday and in this matter he would have all speed. Suffolk and Carr are away from London

190

When they return they will silence their men if they know we are asking too many questions."

"Northampton is dead. We may no longer fear the Howards," said Winwood shaking his head.

"Northampton is dead. His heirs have learned his lessons," replied Wotton.

Winwood was surprised, for Wotton was not an acute or a vindictive man, and was renowned for his honesty and innocence. They descended into the boat, which lurched away from the steps like a drunken man.

"They have done it from malice," said Robin, his voice choked.

"Now, now," said James placatingly. He was turning over some saddle ornaments of chased silver which an aspiring jeweller had sent to him. He concentrated on them, preferring not to see Carr's swollen face, hot and red with hypnotic rage.

"Listen to me," cried Carr, seizing a spur and throwing it to the corner of the room where it fell chinking against a chair leg.

James sighed and laid aside the silver. He still looked downwards, his hands stiff against his padded breeches.

"Listen to me," shouted Robin again. " 'Tis very fine to go jaunting off to Cambridge by a roundabout way, but what of me—me?"

"What indeed?" said the king. His rounded shoulders suddenly went back like the ears of a nervous animal. He slowly rose to his feet and padded towards the fire. His stockings were curled under his toes and flip-flipped as he walked. He held a tall cup towards Robin who shook his head but who had calmed his shout to a whimper. Suddenly he went down on his knees and curled against the edge of the king's chair like a frightened child.

"What means this?" asked James drily. "You enter without any ceremony, turn out my grooms as if you had the bidding of them, begin to cry aloud like some rutting beast. What means this, Rabbie?"

James had fought down his own temper so that Robin felt that he had won the argument. Contentedly he dropped his wrists forward and locked them round his clenched knees. He even smiled. At last James allowed himself to frown.

"I want them to be punished," said Carr.

"Who? And for what?"

"Those that did it. There was a gey grand meeting at Baynard's Castle, know you that?"

"I had heard."

"All those ill-disposed towards us. Us," he repeated, frowning at the king.

"Aye," said James, still affecting calm.

"And some stayed late. Not with yon Pembroke. He is not so slow in the wits, but with his brother, bawdy Philip Herbert, him you made Earl of Montgomery."

"Is he is London?"

"You ken full well he is in London. Did you not have him to sup in your privy rooms?"

"No," replied James, which thwarted Robin for a second so that he jerked back on his heels and hit his ruffled red-gold head against the seat of the chair. James motioned to one side with his hand, intending to return to his seat but as Robin continued to glare and did not move, he leaned against the lintel of the fire, but still did not look at his favourite. "The tale is long in telling," he said. If Robin's ear had been alerted he would have realized that James's Scots accent, which was the voice of jocularity, and of love towards him, had gone. His master spoke firm pedantic English, now and then softened by an intake of wine.

"They came riding down Fleet Street as if at a tilt, way past midnight and shouting and singing obscene and harmful words to me—to us. Then one must halt at a booksellers which had a picture o' me pinned against the door. A print he had sold well." He looked at James's inclined and disbelieving face. "Some like a braw lad to hang in their chambers," he asserted.

"Aye," said James, "some silly wench 'd care for a picture o' you I ha' no doubt, Rabbie."

"The one of these foolish knights must pick up a handful o' filth from out the gutter and fling it at my face."

"Your printed face," corrected the king.

"Is it not the same? The insult is the same."

"Not so."

"Are you not angry?"

"Nay. See here, Rabbie, these ill humours must arise from time to time. It would be better to forget them."

Robin's voice rose like a high-pitched flute: "Ignore them?"

James came over to him then, and lowered himself weightily into the chair, pulling Robin's head until it touched his thigh but Carr stayed rigid and even turned a little away.

"Howsoever, I am pleased you are here," said James, "for another matter. You had asked for a post about me for one of your kinsmen. I would like that post for a young man brought to my attention by the queen and I have promised her that he will have the place."

Robin said sulkily: "You cannot do so. You ha' promised it to me."

"But this cousin of yours is of no import," replied James. "Why you had not even known him a month ago. Let us please the queen and admit her gentleman."

"You promised it to me, for mine."

"Rabbie, Rabbie. Do not try me too hard."

Robin stood up, uncurling his long body like a fern unfurling after the rain. His face had become pale once more. He stood curiously still as if he were rising out of bed after a long illness which had weakened him.

"I will not let this place go," he said sullenly. "A king should not break his word."

"I hope I may have about me gentlemen of my own choosing," replied James.

Robin said: "I would not have you bring your catamounts into court to stand between us."

"I would hope that naught would stand between us unless by your own desire. I have no wish to quarrel with you, Robin."

"Aye, but you will not let me have what I wish. You sent my best friend to the Tower——"

"Upon your wish." Robin opened his mouth, then shut it firmly and locked it into a straight steel line. "You had told me that Tom Overbury was a damned incubus, pestering you or commanding you. It was you determined he should go abroad and I even believe you knew that he would spurn those proffered offices and so be committed to the Tower."

"You could have let him out again."

James shrugged and spread his hands looking like one of those Jews who stood about the city streets in dingy gabardines, their caps set on bald heads, saying more with gestures than with the voice. "I cannot be guardian of all men's morals," he said at last.

Robin flounced across the room, his short cloak of silver cloth sagging despondently from one shoulder like an unshed tear. "You will rue this day," he said at the door and went out suddenly, allowing it to bang behind him and shrilling at a page on the other side.

Robin's voice, as sharp as a raw glass edge, cut into James's head. He drank another cup of wine and felt no better. He rang his little gold bell and a page came running.

"Send me one of the gentlemen of the bedchamber, boy. No, not any one. Bring Sir John Graham." His dirty fingers chased each other round and round his cup. He would not have Robin use him so.

He said: "Have you put young Villiers into the queen's household?"

Graham did not say yes, but bent his head low, "Your majesty," he answered.

"What said her majesty?"

"Sire, your grace, she said he was yet another favourite and might prove more trouble than all who had gone before."

While Graham panted out his message he looked anxiously at the king's face. He was a noted stirrer-up of factions.

"Why did she receive him then?"

"Your majesty, upon the advice of the archbishop who seems disposed to favour young Villiers."

James smiled grimly. "He does not favour him too intimately, I hope."

"The archbishop? None have ever said he was——" Graham paused and dropped his eyes but James hit his shoulder.

"It was a jest, my friend."

"Even so, your majesty," replied Graham leering as if he had known so from the start.

"I have a commission for you, Sir John." Pause. "It is about the Earl of Somerset."

Sir John felt he must break the following silence but could only bow again and say "Your majesty".

"Afore now he had been most welcome in my bedchamber and in my most privy moments, but a king must have some time alone. I love the earl but would not have him so—importunate."

Graham bowed once more.

"He must be announced like other members of my court. He will not move one jot in my estimation," James said censoriously, half expecting to see a smile of gratification on Graham's face; but he, an old retainer, knew when to present blank features to his king. "Do not let him come upon me unannounced. Hold him at the door until I have allowed him entry."

Graham said: "I will command the men-at-arms and pages." He walked backwards from the king.

"One word," cried James, and Graham stopped.

"There is a place about me as a groom of the bedchamber. I had minded to give it to young Villiers."

"He would be filled with joy, your grace."

"But it is spoken for. I had forgot. There is one other place. I have need of a cup bearer, Sir John. It is a position which is bought, you understand——?"

"I know George Villiers would be happy to buy a place about your majesty."

"It is in the giving of the Earl of Somerset, but he knows to dispose of it to whosoever pays the price. I doubt he will ask who the fortunate man may be."

"I understand your majesty."

"Has Master Villiers a fat purse to buy this favour, Sir John?"

"He has those about him who wish him well."

"Like my Lord Archbishop of Canterbury."

Graham nodded. "I am the more pleased if the head of my church is agreeable," said James unctuously.

"He will be agreeable," asserted Graham confidently. He went from the room and James set about his jug of wine with a will. He wanted no company that evening.

Frances was cleaning her nails. They had been sharpened by her maid that morning but now she was earnestly prodding under them with a spatula of bone, ceaselessly turning its claw round and round under the white crescents. They looked clean to Robin but he knew better than to say so. They were eating in her rooms for Frances was suffering from one of her ailments which he supposed came with the moon. He never knew when it was her time of the month for she would lay any pain or headache to it, shaking her head at the frailty of women, and he would lie in his own room next to hers and listen all night as she moaned in her sleep, waiting for those screams which would be his signal to run to her and pillow her pale hair on his arm. Her anguish seemed to be increasing and he was growing less amiable. Once he had even cursed her.

"Am I never to sleep easy?" he had asked. "I would take an oath, Frances, that you do this to rouse me from my bed," and he had peered at her slate eyes but she had shut them at once so that he could not tell if she were triumphant at his coming or truly awakening from a nightmare.

He told the page to go away and Frances did not contradict him. She was off in one of her fantasies and humming her own song, a perpetual murmur as distracting as rain falling on a roof.

"You were right, my bud," he said, to divert her. "The king will do aught for me. He was set upon giving the place in his bed-chamber to one of the queen's lackeys but he has kept it for my gift."

Frances said consideringly: "I wish you had allowed him that. We may need him as our ally in a greater cause."

"Why, what would that be?"

"Mrs Turner says that the citizens are all gossiping on the Overbury death."

"I know naught of that."

"Mrs Turner says that with such a turmoil some questions must be asked."

Robin said confidently: "Only the king can ask those questions and he will not."

"Why should he not?"

"He knows well he could have delivered Overbury from the Tower before his fatal sickness."

"His fatal sickness. He would have died. He had the French disease."

"Even so," agreed Carr, unable to follow her argument. "But I had no cognisance of that, no more had his own serving men. Harry Payton would have known. He was a shrewd fellow."

Frances's hand stopped its turning. She laid down her ivory tool.

"Where is Payton?" she asked.

"Why, I delivered him to Bourton-on-the-Water. He had enough of the life of the town, and of the court. I would have ta'en him myself but that he was set upon going."

"Bourton-on-the-Water?"

"To serve old Squire Overbury."

Frances returned to her nails. "I would he were in London," she said, "Ann Turner could have used him."

"Mrs Turner, Mrs Turner," said Robin harshly. "She is like an evil spirit in this house. I would you had sent her packing, Frances."

"Why so?" asked Frances, as sweet as marzipan. "I cannot live without my Mrs Turner." She smiled at him from where she sat cross-legged on the bed, her shift open down to her belly, which was creased in the candlelight. "Do you not know that yet, my Robin?" she asked.

XXII

ROBIN REFUSED TO believe that his place was being taken by young George Villiers. He played a part in an ugly scene upon St George's Day when the youth was formally presented to the king by his wife; having done this she would have begun her next speech but Robin stepped out of his corner and out of his part to say:

"Hold, sire, hold, did we not——?"

"Go," said James firmly, "we will not have brawling in these chambers," and Robin, sure that he might indeed be cast out, retired and glared at Anne who was moved by his behaviour to say firmly:

"Be kint to Master Villiers for my sake," and she held the boy's arm firmly as if he were one of her children. The young Prince of Wales was watching with large eyes, storing up the scene to retell to his pet dogs afterwards.

"Es St Cheorge's es our patron," she said, "and es this jong man is George also——"

She could say no more but pushed the sword towards James who took it unwillingly and as Villiers knelt tapped him with it awkwardly, "Sir George," said James huskily and the boy got up in one long graceful movement and bowed to both king and queen, who jerked their heads back at him like a couple of puppets performing in a booth.

"It seems to me that the new knight will have to keep his house betimes," said James with that air of joviality with which he acted out all his contrived scenes, "and so I award him a pension of £1,000 a year". While he said this he looked at Carr unwaveringly, so that he should not cry out.

Robin turned away and walked to the back of the room. If he left without permission from James he would be emphasizing the importance of the young man. He resolved to injure Villiers irreparably. He walked with James to the dining hall, secure that they would not be overhead among the chattering courtiers who walked before and after them.

"By God, I will not have this," he said wrathfully.

"Rabbie, Rabbie," murmured James, touching his hand.

"Do you not see there is a faction against me that means to bring me down, and that they are using your new jessie for it?"

"Do not use such words," said James crisply.

"But it is true," said Robin striking at his hip with his clenched fist. "They will reduce your majesty by turning me off," and while he said this he remembered Overbury saying much the same to him in the close stuffiness of a quiet room.

James lingered by the entrance to the dining hall to wave his hand at his attendants who all fell back, and as he continued to brush them off, they had to retreat out of hearing, which considerably annoyed them.

"Hear this," said James boldly, "I know little of these factions and I will not be accused of lack of friendship towards you. I have allowed more impudence in you than I would in my own son. I have loved you long and dearly, Robin, and would that we could continue thus, but your sulks and tempers have broken me altogether. If you cannot mend your ways I will not have you at Whitehall."

Robin stepped back and stared at him.

"I will not be so cruel," said James. "Forbye I know well that you are distracted and perhaps have a sickness, but think well on this, my friend, with all my heart I would not love another if I were not driven to it."

"I cannot bear it," said Robin, sweat had broken out on his face and lay along his determined upper lip.

"Nor more can I," admitted James, "but I will promote whom I will about me and none can gainsay me. For my sake will you not befriend this young Villiers and teach him the manners of the court?"

Robin said nothing but clenched his fists more firmly so that James sighed and passed before him into the dining hall while the other men pressed close behind him now that his parley with Carr had ended. They looked with interest at Carr as they followed the king. He made no move to join them but after all were seated left the palace, his chair empty by the king's right hand. A few days later young Villiers visited him, cap in hand, and said his master, the king, had asked him to appear and present his services to the earl and be his friend.

Carr replied: "I will none of your service and you shall have none of my favour. I will, if I can, break your neck, and of that be confident." As he said this loudly in a billiard room, the news soon spread, to the delight of Carr's enemies.

He could not believe that he had lost his power even when those who turned with every kind of wind began to veer away sharply from him.

"I hear that Sir Francis Bacon is seen with young Sir George Villiers," said Mrs Turner one day when she came calling, her excuse a tisane to lift the spirits of the countess, for Frances was doleful.

"What is that to me?" asked Robin haughtily. He stared at Frances as he said it.

She was in bed, her favourite place these last months, and in one of her monthly moods. Her hair was as carefully dressed and braided as if she were a virgin about to go to court for the first time, with golden celandines and silver snowdrops plaited into it like real flowers. Her night shifts had become more elaborate, as if she had realized that they were to be her habitual dress. Her world had shrunk to her two bedchambers, the outer one filled with servants, the inner shut to all except Mrs Turner and her husband.

"Why," replied Mrs Turner, pouring the liquid into a glass and stoppering the jar purposefully. "They say Bacon always jumps like a cat to the right side of the wall."

"And what," asked Frances lazily, "is the right side of a wall?"

"Why, that with no hounds baying at it, my lady," she replied and began to put her phials and pots back into her little osier basket, the size of a small girl's plaything, which she carried about with her.

"You hear that, my lord," said Frances turning her still face towards Robin and smiling. "Those Grays Inn lawyers know what they are about."

"He took a basket of yellow plums to Sir George Villiers and with them two bottles of a white French wine and asked to be remembered—we may be sure at giving time."

"What mean you—giving time?" asked Robin, resentful at being pulled out of his silence.

"Why," said Mrs Turner, "all favourites have something to give —who would know that better than my lord Somerset?—and the wise man looks for rewards before they are about. Yes, that Bacon knows when the plums will begin to drop—into his mouth if he shakes the right tree."

"Damned women, who only speak in riddles," said Carr.

"They say riddles are a good pastime at court these days," said Mrs Turner, "the king laughs at them and at all Sir George's japes. Why he had the king to visit with his family they say, and his majesty made much of them, and most of the mother, Lady Compton as she now is, and promised her—and hers—all they might wish for in this world. Even the king cannot promise for the next—that's sure."

"Enough of this," cried Carr.

"Not so," said Frances. "Merry tales make me laugh when I am out of sorts. Tell us more, dear Ann."

"Why, they say that young Villiers invited the king to a baptism of a friend's child, aye, in the chapel of Savoy, no less, and asked the king as a favour to go along, and the king, who can refuse him nothing——"

"The devil!" cried Robin.

"As you say, my lord," continued Mrs Turner comfortably. "He went and was seated in the front when a bishop entered. I trow the king did not know him but the light was dim and truth to tell it was one of Villiers's cockaleary Alsatian knights—one Turpin."

"The scoundrel!"

"Ssh," said Frances.

"So in comes a young lady, very pale, dressed like a noblewoman and carrying her babe. She hands it to a nurse and curtsies low to his majesty and thanks him for standing godfather to her son, at which the king huffs for he likes well to be well liked as your lordship knows."

Her eyes slid round to Robin who stood behind the bedcurtain, anxious to hear the rest of the story but unwilling to have this sly creature know it.

"Then two come with prayer books and a ewer of holy water and all stand by the font. The king walks up to them when the moment comes to stand godfather to the child, a little surprised they say, for he had not known he was to play a part in the service, and when the time comes for him to hold the babe, why the young lady passes it to him, dripping silks and jewels from the christening robe they say, and his majesty takes the weight of the blessed child and——" She began to laugh, her kerchief stuffed against her mouth. "I cannot—cannot——" Helpless with laughter she lolled against the bedpost.

Frances pushed her sheets back and rolled down to the end of the bed, pressing her white painted face close to Mrs Turner's which was red with mirth. "Tell me, tell me——" she pleaded.

"It was no baby, but a pig! And it grunted!"

"Faugh!" cried Robin. "I know the king did not laugh at that——"

Mrs Turner was dabbing tears from her eyes while Frances, prone on her back on the bed, lay with arms and legs outspread, deep laughs making her body jounce up and down.

"I do not believe the king laughed," shouted Robin.

Mrs Turner wiped her cheeks and said soberly, "No, you are correct my lord, the king did not laugh. He said for shame, and that it was blasphemy."

Robin nodded and gave his own laugh, short and self conceited. "Aye. E'en for Villiers he would not laugh at an act like yon."

"I am laughing," said Frances between gasps of pleasure.

"And I," said Mrs Turner and began again to whoop against the bed end.

Robin left them but was more pleased than he had been for some months. This crude game played by Villiers might have exposed him as a country boor. Robin resolved to have him expelled from court.

He asked the king and Villiers for a quiet supper at which there were not more than twenty guests. Carr made it an excuse to hire a French cook, who produced ceremonial dishes. One was a pastry stag, filled with chopped meats, spices, and red wine. It was offered to the king, Robin and Villiers, borne by one of Carr's servants who bowed deeply each time he walked forward with the immense salver on which it rested.

"I'll none of it," said James. Carr also shook his head but Sir George, as he had imagined, was taken by the invention and asked the servant how it was made.

"Why, Sir George, we will have the cook in to tell you his secrets," cried Robin, cruelly.

Villiers was nervous of exposing his low background. He never spoke to servants, except inasmuch as they might aid him in acting his part, as this stalwart fellow was, by heaving the great dish from side to side and grinning over it, pleased that they admired his burden.

"Why not kill the beast in the accepted way?" suggested Carr.

"Wha, wha," spluttered James who was delighted that his two young men seemed at last reconciled and who had drunk their healths with abandon. "Prick it there, there——" He pointed his thumb at the animal's shoulder blade, shining with an egg glaze.

"Why—I will stick him!" cried Villiers, arising, "if I had a hunting knife."

He swayed tipsily while several about, determined to make themselves his friends, made blasting noises with their pursed lips like hunting horns, or barked liked dogs.

"First blood! First blood!" shouted James, banging the table with his beaker and Villiers seized an offered poigniard and thrust it deep into the pastry case. A spout of blood—red wine—rose out of it like a fountain. It splashed the cloth and saturated the white satin suit which Villiers wore for the first time. "Why! Why!" screamed the young man. The pastry deer fell unheeded as Villiers gripped the servant, twisting him down to the floor, a cascade of dishes and glass fell with the man who held on to the tablecloth. The king stood up, sobered by the violence.

"I will kill you for this," shouted Villiers and suddenly held the poigniard up short and close to the man's chest, twisting the point through his livery coat.

"Nay!" shouted James and all the others began to cry out, and two who were stronger and more quick-witted than the rest pulled at Villiers, dragging him off the servant who cowered on the floor, his greying hair tousled over his sweating pale face. A small star of blood appeared on his coat and began to spread greedily over it, darkening the cloth. Two men from Carr's retinue ran over to the man and propped him against the table leg, feeling at his wrist.

"Is he dead?" asked James, dropping the words slowly into the sudden silence. Carr leaned forward and lifted the lackey's eyelid. He knew not why, but had seen physicians do so with acclaim.

"Not he," he said, "remove him."

A page helped the servants carry their fellow from the room.

"It went betwixt two ribs," said one gentleman more knowledgeable than the rest.

They all looked at Villiers who hung between his companions like a bag of washing between two clothes props, his head sagging forward. His white suit was more horrific than that discreet bleeding by the servant. The whole front of his coat had exploded into a great red carnation.

"You drew a weapon," said Carr, instantly and venomously.

"We cannot say he *drew* a weapon," said Pembroke who had said nothing before. "The weapon was already drawn to pierce that beast." He looked at the stag, now in fragments upon the floor, its cooked meat tumbling out incongruously in place of guts.

"It was a noble beast," essayed one gentleman who had hoped to taste it.

"He drew a blade in the king's company," repeated Carr.

"Aye, he did that," agreed James, "but under some provocation."

"Immense," said Pembroke.

"The law is the law," said Carr firmly, "and your majesty has oft times said that you cannot change the law."

Villiers wiped the wine from his face and sat down heavily, he even managed a smile at the king, a glance of intimacy. Pembroke cleared his throat but said nothing, he allowed Robin Carr to say what all were thinking.

"Why, Sir George, you must learn the courtesies of Whitehall. If a man draws a weapon in the presence of his king, he loses that hand with which he drew it."

Villiers looked down at his right hand, sodden at the wrist by wine; it already looked half severed, it hung so limply. "Nay," he said, and his face was so white that those men who had pulled him back before leaned down to hold him if he fainted.

"Nay," said James.

Carr stuck out his chin pugnaciously. "It is the law," he said.

"My lord Somerset," said Pembroke. "Only those here know of this mischance. Sir George was holding the knife afore he was angered. He did not hurt the fellow and will recompense him so that he will not boast of his injury on the morrow. Shall we not allow the matter to lie?"

"He has drawn a knife before his king," argued Robin. He looked for an ally among the courtiers but they were irritated by his fervour. Even those who did not care for a new favourite, having ingratiated themselves with the old, were bemused by the event and none wished to see one of their kind, a gentleman who had eaten with them, condemned to lose his hand. Carr looked at Sir Francis Bacon, invited at Villiers's request. He was a lawyer and should uphold him, but Bacon gently shook his head.

"It is an ancient law and we will not allow it to be used against Sir George," said the king.

"But think, sire," pleaded Carr, "any mountebank could run at your majesty in a crowd with a drawn knife."

"It is for that we have the law," explained Bacon, determinedly gaining the king's attention, "to preserve his majesty from assassins;

but if this be made a just cause for——" he looked at the pale young Villiers, "for cutting off a hand, why any verderer who guts a deer in the company of his majesty could suffer the same fate."

"That is so," said James delightedly. "I would ha' said so myself if Sir Francis had not. This is an accident and must be forgotten."

"Will he not be punished—exiled from the court?" suggested Robin.

James's mild gaze defeated him. "Nay, Sir George has been punished enough. The man can be bought off. It was a sudden chance. Any of us could have done the same."

He looked round the company who agreed with mutterings and shuffling feet. Robin flushed, he knew that James was the only man who would never have drawn a knife, with his aversion to steel. But in this fearful accident James had remained composed.

"We had best forget this night," said James and when Robin escorted him from the room he pressed his hand. "Rabbie, Rabbie, do not try me too far," he warned again.

XXIII

Rₐₗₚₕ Wᵢₙwₒₒd wₐₛ plagued by letters from ambassadors; Trumbell in Brussels had not sent a letter but he had despatched a servant, to repeat his story to the Secretary of State. The boy was exhausted after his journey from Flushing. He told his tale between gasps as he drank deeply. He had accompanied Trumbull to the room of a young Englishman who thought he was dying and who had called for the English ambassador. It had not been the customary appeal to pay his debts or to demand a free passage home. The sick man was called Reeve, and two years before he had been apprenticed to the royal apothecary, de Loubell. He had been paid, in his master's absence, to make a clyster of mercury sublimate which he had applied to Sir Thomas Overbury. It had killed him. Reeve was admitted to a convent hospital and he said no more; Trumbull thought he would not have strength to name those who had employed him; but de Loubell had not known of the murder.

"My master said I should tell you but to commit naught to paper," added the servant fearfully.

Winwood smiled. Trumbull was well versed in the foreign service. He sent the lad away. He remembered how Lake had warned him of this plot, through Wotton. His secretary hovered by him.

"Send to the Earl of Shrewsbury," said Winwood. "I sup with him this night. Ask him if he will honour me by asking Sir Jervis Elwes to be of the company, and if he will sit him by me."

Elwes was asked, as well as Winwood and Shrewsbury's immediate family and allies. They were to meet early, an hour before suppertime and Sir Jervis arrived dressed in mulberry-coloured velvet, his soft face creased with pleasure, for he had long wished to meet the Secretary of State. Winwood did not seek him out, knowing that the table would be arranged so that they would sit side by side.

Arundel said: "So our Keeper of the Signet, or should we say Lord Chamberlain," alluding to Somerset's new position, "has made all clear before him."

"What mean you?" asked Pembroke, who was the other Shrewsbury son-in-law.

"He has obtained a general pardon for any sins committed while he was in office," replied Arundel meaningfully.

Winwood broke across their exchanged glances with his dry explanation: "It is courtesy only. Somerset would be a fool not to gain a general pardon as would all holders of high office on relinquishing their seals."

"Sir Ralph is silent on the other news," said Arundel.

"What was that?" Pembroke turned to him like a chorus in a play, indeed Winwood felt he was being drawn out to give the company recent news of Carr.

He hesitated and said, "If Lord Arundel knows the story he might tell it better than I."

A mutter like applause ran round the room. Arundel, left with the ball in his hand, looked disappointed and would have changed the game but one of the company said from the shadows: "If you know aught, my lord, give speech. We lesser mortals have no news from Whitehall."

"Know then that the king allowed the pardon to go its way, forbye that with the business of state as parlous as it be," he recollected Winwood and bowed. "Pardon me, Sir Ralph, but until you took office little was read or written and——"

"I know," said Winwood, "that in the press of duty his majesty had little time to study every letter that he passes."

"So this demand for pardon, a reasonable matter, as Sir Ralph has said, came to the Solicitor General, old Yelverton, who is a pesky fellow for looking into every part and he refused to put the seal upon Somerset's pardon, saying it had divers clauses not usual in such a request, on misdemeanours above the common."

From the shadows the muttering swelled like gathering rain. Winwood looked into the gloom, trying to identify the company, were they city merchants whom Shrewsbury had introduced to the gathering specifically to hear this story of villainy? He looked at Pembroke but could not believe him cunning enough to release news in this haphazard way. What if he, Winwood, had been cajoled to tell such a dark tale? He thanked God for his own caution, otherwise all London would have gossiped the next day about Somerset's perfidy "as told by the Secretary of State".

"Then," said Arundel unwillingly: "His majesty, who still is filled with love for Somerset, tells Ellesmere the Lord Chancellor, straight, that this open pardon is the common practice for any man relinquishing high office and that it must be signed. But Ellesmere took the pardon away and read it over as diligently as Yelverton had done, and came back to the king in an hour or so and says he cannot sign the pardon for it puts Somerset beyond the law and has been written beyond common practice to absolve Carr not only of small felonies and briberies—the which all great men commit—but of great and awesome villainies as well."

"Such as murder?" asked a frail voice nearby.

Winwood saw that it was Elwes, his beard perked up with enquiry.

Arundel hesitated: "I know not. It may be," he said.

"Is that the whole cloth?" asked another unseen man beyond the candlelight, his voice suggesting that it was not.

"No," said Arundel. "For the king insisted that Ellesmere sign the pardon. Whereupon the old man, so they say, went on his knees to James and begged to have a pardon of his own, to absolve *him* from any blame in pardoning Somerset."

"And what then?"

"Why, the king said that if he, meaning himself—the king—were to die, so many enemies would crowd upon Somerset seeking to destroy him, that he would need a pardon to escape them. Whereupon the queen, they say, begged the king to let the matter lie and so James went off and thought Ellesmere would sign the pardon."

"And did he?"

"He did not."

"What fear," asked Pembroke, "would make Carr so determined on an open pardon unless he has a crime to hide?" He spoke for all. After a silence he began again: "How doom-laden is this man, Robin Carr! He has not even the wit to please the king, but seeks to destroy himself. Why, with Villiers knocking at the door he does not stay about the king, keeping him company and pleasing him in a hundred ways——"

"The which only he could do," suggested somebody.

Pembroke ignored him and went on: "He has spent a good part of the summer with Lord Knollys in the country when he should be seen about the court."

Old Shrewsbury growled: "But are we not pleased that he seeks his own destruction? Do we not wish to humble Carr and the Howards?"

Upon which there were several coughs and conversations for

Arundel was himself a Howard, being nephew to Suffolk and cousin to Frances. He seemed not a whit disturbed by this condemnation of his family but whistled a new tune to Winwood as they walked to the table. Winwood had long thought him a foolish young man.

He sat gently by Elwes, allowing the Lord Lieutenant of the Tower to become accustomed to him before he suggested anything untoward in Overbury's death. Encouraged by the great man's affability, Elwes drank a little too much French wine and expanded on his strange office.

"Aye," he said. "The sad truth is that we like our prisoners and are quite put out when they are taken from us."

"To Tower Hill?" suggested Winwood, smiling.

"Nay, nay," said Elwes, jogging him in the ribs. "Men are not beheaded so easy in these times. Released, Sir Ralph."

"Yet some die in the Tower," said Winwood.

Elwes appeared shocked: "Men die every day, and not only in the Tower, through great age or sickness. Why, in a plague year we lose many warders, owing to close confinement and exhalations off the river, they say."

"Think you it was a fever off the river which killed Overbury?"

He was almost ashamed at the look of abhorrence Elwes gave him, his round eyes as amazed as those of a child whose ball rolls down a conduit. "Why—why?" he stuttered. "He had a fever it is true. Were you not told by de Loubell of his sickness? And Craig, a court doctor, visited him and gave out that he had a consumption."

"The Tower must be a swamp of fever, Sir Jervis. He was well enough when he went in."

Elwes leaned over and tapped the side of Winwood's goblet, his horny finger nails made the glass hum with sound. "Look you," he said, "it was the confinement. None less than Sir Theodore Mayerne said that of him. Overbury was a man made for free air. He sickened in the Tower. Aye, from a fear that he might not be let out of it. It was fear alone that made him ill. Ask the king's doctor. Ask Sir Theodore."

"And was it fear that made him die so quick, and so fearfully," said Winwood, stressing the words, "that he was buried at once in the chapel, and in lime?"

"Why—his body stank. He had the French disease—they say," asserted Sir Jervis.

Winwood held the man's cuff. "Be not afeared yourself, Sir Jervis," he said. "Look about you. These are powerful men have taken you up. Shrewsbury and Pembroke, and I am Secretary of State. With us to guide you, do you not feel that you can wave away the Howards? Their stars are falling, Sir Jervis. Carr may have become Earl of Somerset but in other ways he has not advanced any. He was ever promoted by the king's good wishes and you have heard yourself this evening how afraid he is of being accused—of what, Sir Jervis? He has been displaced in the king's love. Northampton was an awesome man. I would even say," he whispered, "an evil man—and could use honest upright fellows as if they were lackeys. But he is dead, and Suffolk has not the old man's abilities."

Elwes murmured: "There is the Countess of Somerset, she that was Frances Howard."

Winwood laughed: "When did a woman have any heart to politics?"

Elwes would have said that the old dead queen had been better able to play at politics than any man, but he said nothing, pulling down his lower lip and gazing at Winwood fearfully, his eyes wet with drink.

"I will tell you that——" he began.

"Ho, another cup for Sir Jervis," said Shrewsbury on his other side, who had not seemed to be listening. When the cup was filled Winwood placed his heavy velvet sleeves, lined with ermine, on the table before him. He nodded at Sir Jervis.

"If you have aught to tell," he said, "I am the man to tell it."

Elwes breathed deeply and said: "How to tell it, Sir Ralph? It is a tale full of strange sorceries——"

"How's that—sorcery?" Winwood did not want to hear of witchcraft, any fool could weave a story out of moonshine compounding wizards and nightmares in it. "I want only truth, Sir Jervis."

"It is all true," he said stoutly.

"Then let me have it all."

It tumbled out like water over a weir and was almost incomprehensible to Winwood. It began with a man called Weston, who was sent by Northampton, or his niece, to be Overbury's servant; Elwes had distrusted him from the start, but had wished to please the Howards and had thought the fellow was sent in only as a spy. So in spite of his doubts he had allowed Weston to become Sir Thomas's confidential servant and he admitted that at a time when

Overbury was truly sick and loathsome with it, Weston had performed his duties well. And then there was Monson.

"The Keeper of the Armoury?" said Winwood disbelievingly.

It seemed that Monson had been a go-between to gain the office for Elwes and that he had persuaded the honest Lincolnshire knight that he should do small favours for the Howards, such as ensuring that letters from Overbury should only go to Carr, and that they were to be sent in and out in pies and jellies.

"So Carr was writing to Overbury all those months?"

"And Overbury back to him," agreed Elwes, "thinking Carr was seeking to release him from the Tower, while all the time he was plotting with Northampton that Overbury should be kept strictly in prison."

Winwood was accustomed to small cruelties but he shook his head over this one and waited for Elwes to tell more alarming tales; that Frances had sent in a feast daily, all of poisoned dishes, which he, Elwes, had diverted into the Tower ditch. Suddenly relieved at confiding in another man, Sir Jervis leaned upon Winwood's shoulder and told of the phials of poison and the clyster and how he had tried to keep Overbury alive all that long summer and at last had failed. He did not tell Winwood how welcome had been Overbury's death.

"Why did you not tell the king?" asked Winwood.

Elwes lifted his damp face from his cup. "How could I? I was too far in. If I had told aught I would have been in prison myself and I had hoped for a comfortable life for my wife and my children. I am a country fellow, Sir Ralph. All I knew was from Monson, and he was sure the Howards ruled all, and could break me like an egg if I disobeyed them."

"You were right to tell me this," said Winwood. "You see how the world wags," nodding at the company. "The day of the Howards is over and we wish to dig their grave deeper by telling the truth about Overbury."

"The truth!" Sir Jervis drew back. "I could not—cannot——"

"Pish, man, you are safe. You have powerful friends, aye, more powerful than those bloodthirsty men who employed you against Overbury. Would you please me—and the king?"

"I would," said Elwes earnestly.

"Then write your story down and deliver it to me. As you have told it now. With a date here and there. If you do this you will be thought free of complicity when the true villains are brought to trial, and you will advance yourself. There are rewards for honest men now that Carr and his friends are out of office."

"But they are not," protested Elwes. "Lord Chamberlain—Lord Privy Seal——"

"Not forever," said Winwood. "Look about you, my friend. Do you not see these are our new rulers? Carr and his catamites are falling and will soon lie in the dust. If you cannot trust me, who would you trust?"

Elwes stared at him, seeing not the man but his office. Winwood was newly Secretary of State and would not lose his position soon. His personal word to advance Elwes was like a promise of an ambassador's post. He held out his puffy hand and Winwood gripped it hard. How tightly these puritans hold on, thought Elwes, but he was reassured by the man's powerful clasp. He smiled at Winwood.

"I will write it all and send it to you, Sir Ralph," he promised.

Winwood smiled back: "You have my word on it, Sir Jervis," he said. "You are a made man."

"Hey, hey, hey!" called Villiers as his animal plunged across the sward, its legs splayed with exertion. The deep confident note of a hunting horn sounded to their left as the verderers ran in the wood, their green jackets easily seen among the gold leaves and bare branches. "So-ho" cried the court behind them, "So-ho". Carr struggled with his horse, a fine deep chested beast, given to him two years before by the king. He had hoped that its chestnut coat would remind James that she had been his gift, "A lassie tae match your own e'en," James had said tenderly.

Robin caught up with Villiers and the king when the huntsmen were already cutting up the deer. Blood splashed about the leaves, staining them where they were not already red. He stood silently by his mare's neck, her reins looped about the arm of his leather coat. James looked up at him and said:

"Was it not a bonny chase?"

"Bonny enough," said Robin, and then smiled, "as bonny as ever I saw."

James, flushed, smiled back at him. Before them, young Villiers was still whooping like a lad, with his cheeks ritually smeared with blood. He carried a forefoot in his hand, clipped off by a huntsman, its fragile black hoof was smattered with gore. "Phew," said Villiers and cast it off into the fall of leaves. A dog disengaged from the press about the dead animal and snuffled for it.

James slowly got up, discarding the knife with which he had been carving the deer. Robin thought how strange it was that the king could bear no weapon, would not hear of sickness and disease, refused to have men fight with swords, and shivered if a table knife were spun too near his nervous eye, and yet he could hatchet in like a paid huntsman if a dead beast were to be butchered. He felt revolted and stepped back when James advanced on him.

"Aye, Rabbie, a grand chase," he repeated and came up close.

Robin smelt the thick fusty scent of unwashed flesh which James carried round with him like a penitent's hair shirt. The king lifted his hands. The palms were bloody. He raised them to Robin's face and clasped it. The courtiers around them were quiet, their horses fidgeting in the crisp fallen leaves. Robin could not help himself. He stared at that sad dogged face and jerked back, away from the bloodstained, unsavoury man. For a second, pain shuttered down over James's face, reducing it to a blank surface. Robin flushed and made himself come forward again, into his welcoming arms; he could feel the blood from the king's embrace running stickily down his cheeks and caking in his beard.

James said: "I loved you, Robin." Or did he say "I love you"? It was only a mutter, lost as James turned away and opened his royal smile to Villiers who was triumphant with one foot planted on the overthrown beast, its antlers breaking out of the ground like the broken boughs of the fallen trees. His olive-green jerkin was blotched and spotted with blood.

Robin had lost his chance. He knew it. He looked down at the ground; the dog came panting up and laid the loose hoof at his feet. A tear came rolling up, and he brushed it away with the back of his hand which came away red like his cheeks.

"Ho, ho," sounded a congratulatory hunting horn. Robin walked forward, his feet moving slowly through the beech leaves and looked up at that English face of Villiers, so smooth, so confident, and with an hauteur that reminded him of Overbury. He hated looking up, acknowledging that the young man was inches taller than himself and the king.

"Well now, Rabbie," said James, his bluff jocular voice warning Robin that he was being false. "Ha'ye a word of praise for our roaring boy here?"

Robin spoke unnecessarily loudly so that all the company could hear him. "One word only," he said, "that I am well pleased that Sir George enjoys blood on his person, for he was mortal feared of wine."

Villiers's eyes looked like two small diamond chips, blinking coldly in the grey light. He said nothing. James coughed and held on to the boy's arm.

"Eh, I'm gey worn by yon ride," he said diplomatically. " 'Twas a fast pace you set us, Georgie."

The others were pressing closer now, offering their chorus of congratulations. Robin walked away from them towards his chestnut and mounted her wearily. His page obediently ran behind as he set her for the castle; their upright figures were distant by the time drops of rain fell on James and George and their bloody carcase.

On the same day, 27 September 1615, a constable and his lad brought Weston to the rooms of Sir Edward Coke the Lord Chief Justice, at the Duchy House in London, and formally took him into custody, "while inquiries be made".

At the beginning of October, the king sent a letter to Sir Edward Coke in which he said: "There be but two things in this case to be tried. First: whether my lord of Somerset and my lady were the procurers of Overbury's death, or that this imputation hath been by some practised to throw aspersion on them. I would have you diligently enquire of the first, and if you find them clear, then I would have you as carefully look after the other . . ."

Robin was at Windsor with the king. He knew that James had sent a letter to Coke asking for an inquiry. His instinct was to run to London, sound out Coke and make some attempt to clear himself of any trace of complicity before the inquiry had been set afoot. And yet, by simply claiming a general pardon he had already aroused a clamour of suspicion against himself. He was advised to do nothing by his lawyer, Sir Robert Cotton, but Robin acted precipitously, and bought some letters he had sent Tom Overbury, from the dead man's servant, Davies.

XXIV

"**H**AVE YOU ALL of them?" asked Frances. In answer Mrs Turner spilled her apron upon the bedcover, scraps of paper, twists of dried herbs and thumbs of wax were scattered upon Frances, some bounding off and rolling under the valances. "Pick them up quick," said the countess. "I know what there was."

As Ann Turner stooped in the dark she felt her blood rushing swiftly up to her face and she had to crouch for a moment until she recovered herself, making scrambling motions with her fingers to convince the girl that she was still hunting for those things she had taken from Mrs Forman. All had been evidence of her own complicity as well as that of the countess, so she had been pleased to rescue them, despite the complaints of Trunco that these were all she had left of her dead goodman and that she would call a constable if anything of her own were touched.

"Did you have to pay her?"

Ann hesitated, then avoided her accustomed demands for money. "Not a jot. She was glad to see the back of 'em, I know. It's one thing to have a dead husband who was a great doctor and a white witch but quite another to have him condemned as a poisoner."

"Condemned?" Frances's voice went up like her eyebrows. "You have to be tried before you can be condemned. Forman's memory would have been safe enough under my protection."

"Protection or no, my lady, I think none are safe now."

Ann was trembling for herself. The constables had been round, she admitted, although they had done no more than warn her and since then she had been afraid of the most innocent errands, so that she had come by night to see the countess. Frances looked at the collection on the bed which had once meant so much: love potions for Carr, riddles and rhymes which were invectives against Essex, a few sad curls of hair dried out at the ends and losing lustre, even the ribbons which bound them were fading. She had an account in her mind of what should be there and she separated each item with her eyes, under the uncertain flame of a tall church candle which flickered in a draught from the window.

"Some are missing," she said decisively. "You must search for them again."

"What, my lady?" Ann felt faint, she should not have run so fast through the backstreets, or worn such a heavy cloak to conceal herself. She did not ask permission to pour a cup of wine, while she did so she could collect herself, and face this imperious child more easily. She imagined her own head which must be like a little model house with a dozen things happening in separated rooms: her business was in one, where maids were laundering and ironing while cooks produced huge pasties for her famous supper service, and seamstresses sewed as fast as fairies to finish masque costumes on time, in itself that part of her mind could have occupied the whole it was so multifarious and complex, but there was more. There was Arthur Mainwaring, half the time drunk or else beseeching her for more money to pay his card debts, his voice was always demanding or complaining. She had to care for him, any protection in her world was extended to Arthur and his frailties. There were the children, growing up and needing more and more of her. She wished to send the boy to university, the girl expected something better than work as a maid or the dull life of a shopkeeper's wife; with a good dowry she might marry well in the country and bring up grandchildren to call Ann blessed. But the largest compartment was taken up, and swollen to outsize proportions, by her crime. It had not seemed a crime at the time, running about the city after necromancers and the ingredients of their potions; dancing languidly on a sun-speckled floor with old Father Forman; it had begun as innocently as springtime for milkmaids and now here she was, shackled to evil by the countess and all for need of money. It was too late to retreat. Watching Frances make another inventory, Ann wondered if she could walk away. She could not, she was fast embroiled but might yet be saved if the countess could be found innocent. Ann knew that if Weston were taken surely Franklin would follow, and her only hope lay in the power of the Howards. She was in it to her neck, and involuntarily she clasped her little pretty neck under its yellow ruffles. Ah, thought Ann, looking at the countess's glass, I am still beautiful, I am not old even if I feel ancient as a serpent, I could make a good life for myself, but her maundering was cut off by Frances who rose in the bed like an angry sea monster, pillows and sheets falling away from her naked shoulders.

"They must be found. The mommets!" she cried and beat upon the coverlet.

"The dolls?"

"The dolls!" Ann remembered Forman moulding them so that she had blushed, the pretty little figure of Frances with a painted mouth, the long mummy of the earl, wigged with a lock of his own red hair, and his phallus rising up from a doublet made of a piece of lace torn from his pillow by a servant who had sold it for a handsome profit to Mrs Turner.

"Go back and get them! Destroy them!" said Frances.

Ann did not resent her commands, for once she was too eager to obey. She ran to the Strand and down to the watergate. In the dark she had to wait while a waterman made all ready for her passage, but he had her over to the Lambeth quay while Frances was still supping that first glass of wine. Mrs Turner was too late. As she thumped the Formans' door until the neighbours opened their shutters to shout at her she knew that Trunco had fled or had been taken into custody.

"What do you seek?" asked a passerby, more curious than the rest.

"A potion, a lotion, some pills!" panted Ann, averting her face from his lantern.

"Alas, you are too late, mistress" called a woman from across the way. "All was took an hour ago by men from the Lord Chancellor's office. You will have to win your lover some other and more honest way."

It was a tame conversation, for Coke reserved his bluster for a later meeting. This first examination was not intended to frighten Weston but to give his allies reason to run about like rabbits and to incriminate themselves by collecting together and destroying, or attempting to destroy, evidence. Coke had made sure that the whole city would hear of his actions by asking Alderman Jones to keep a room close, as a prison for a gentle lady, Coke had said.

"How now—Richard Weston, is it?" asked Coke.

"That is so, Sir Edward."

"Late a servant to Doctor Turner, now dead, and then to his wife, Mrs Ann Turner, notable as the mistress of Sir Arthur Mainwaring of Paternoster Row?"

Weston blinked. He had never associated the house in Paternoster

Row with Sir Arthur, but supposed it must be in his name. He said so. "At which address Mrs Turner makes her renowned starch," suggested Coke. Weston nodded.

He was launched into his service with Overbury. Why had he gone to the Tower? His mistress had bid him to go and work there. With what object? That he might tell her what was toward with Sir Thomas. Did he know any with evil designs toward Overbury? Weston fumbled with his cuff. There was a Doctor Franklin, he said softly. He had never liked Franklin.

"And he sent the poison to you with which Sir Thomas Overbury was killed," hinted Coke benevolently.

Weston looked up, amazed. "Poisoned? Sir Thomas?" he cried, "He was not so."

"Then," said Coke heavily, "how do you think he died?"

Weston looked confused but ingenuous. "He caught a cold. That was the start of all," he told Coke. "And I know how. He would sit in the window and talk to those who visited the Tower. I told him to put his cloak about him, but he would not listen. Sir Thomas was a proud man, Sir Edward. He would not take advice from a servant."

"And he died of this chill?" asked Coke, smiling.

"I would not say that," reasoned Weston, "but it was the beginning of it all. He would take potions sent him for the ague. I know not what was in them. He did not confide in me, sir."

"To what would you lay the cause of his death?"

Weston considered: "It was all weakness, sir, that and the corrupt indisposition of his body."

Coke frowned. They would be back to the French disease if he did not halt Weston. When he had dismissed the man, he conferred unwillingly with Bacon, who thoughtfully rubbed his hands together.

"We must have some good evidence," he said. "We cannot act until we find a point where Weston's story goes with that of Sir Jervis Elwes."

"Elwes is not lying."

"Nay, but what have we to act upon?" Bacon was earnest for the law. He added: "If we have to check all Weston's stories, and he gives us six or seven different accounts we will still be examining by Christmas."

"I will examine him until he is broken," growled Coke.

"Aye, Sir Edward, but if he hinders us too long, the big fish will have swum away."

"How mean you?"

Bacon thought. He was too pedantic in his use of language to say they would cover their tracks, so he said: "Fouled us with weed". It was a happier metaphor.

Coke hardly noticed how well Bacon had continued his fishy vision, he said, "Evidence or no, I will have Mrs Turner in Alderman Jones's chamber by the morrow."

Bacon said nothing. He had told a man to watch the apartments of the Somersets by the Cockpit, he was sure Mrs Turner would be there again to sup that evening.

Francis Bacon was right. Hardly had Robin taken off his boots from the ride back to London than Mrs Turner was tapping at the bedchamber door. He cursed, "Bid her go".

Frances looked at him. She had dressed and was painted as if she were going to a banquet. He had thought it was in his honour, for he saw that her little table in the anteroom was laid for two. "I bid her come to me," said Frances, and he understood that the table had not been laid for his return.

"Do you see none but that—witch?" he asked, hissing at her.

Frances moved her shoulder so that it shone under the candle flame. "Would you rather I had a man to sup with me—in my bedchamber?" she asked.

As he strode into his own room Robin realized that he would much rather Frances had a man, he thought her friendship with Mrs Turner dangerous and nasty. He came out to tell her so but Ann Turner was already in the room and she curtsied at him several times, pathetic as a fading jonquil with her yellow hair and yellow collar, her breast palpitating under her lace bodice. He scowled and went back to his own bed.

He remembered the end of the hunt, Sir George had been looking at James with the glance of a conqueror. How did *he* accommodate his young manhood to the king's fawning caresses? Did he enjoy them as Robin once had himself? Or had he? Was it possession of the king that had excited him, not the act of love? He shook his head and thought he would sleep. Voices crept in from outside like the soft scratching of mice in the floor boards; he could not sleep while Frances and Mrs Turner plotted beyond the door.

*   *   *

With her head cocked to hear sounds from Robin, Mrs Turner was drawing close to the countess who had her soft red mouth wide open as if a sweetmeat were to be popped in:

"Have you more secrets, Ann?" she called out softly, delighted at the thought of another scurrilous tale.

Mrs Turner was so distracted she seized those pale shoulders and shook them very slightly so that Frances pouted and then drew herself rigid, her face as long and hard as an icicle.

"Why," she said angrily, "What would you——"

"Hark ye," said Ann urgently. "Weston is taken."

It seemed more curious to her than the disappearance of the dolls. Frances looked shocked and broke away from her friend to move crabwise across her daybed; she looked once at the door to the inner room to make sure that it was shut. She was composed by the time she had pulled her fur robe over her cold shoulders.

"What is that to do with me?" she asked.

Mrs Turner made a small exasperated sound. "Do you not see? He will tell all. We are lost."

Frances seemed uncomprehending. "I am not lost."

"It is like a daisy chain," said Mrs Turner; "break one, break all. We tumble down." As Frances continued to stare at her bleakly, she added: "Do you not see? This is a hanging matter."

For the first time Frances looked alarmed and put her pretty white hands about her small neck. Too late, Mrs Turner remembered that for such as the countess there would be no hanging, her kind had the mercy of the headsman's axe on Tower Hill.

"I have sent for Franklin," said Mrs Turner.

"For him? What is it to do with him?"

Mrs Turner said: "We sink or swim together. He must be silent."

Frances said: "I have paid him enough to be discreet."

"There is no purse wide enough or deep enough to pay for a man's life," asserted Mrs Turner. "There is nothing we can offer him except a vow that we will keep him out of the story if we be taken."

"I? Taken?"

Frances Howard still could not accept that she was affected by the law. Ann realized that it was not fear which had urged the recovery of the wax dolls, but discretion; although she looked at Mrs Turner with anxious eyes her friend thought she was still apart from reality.

She said: "My lady, you are still allied with great power, can you not see that Franklin is but the purveyor of poison and acted for you. He may be let go, for they will want the great ones behind him. He will be offered a pardon as just exchange for information."

Frances seemed bewildered: "And you, Ann? They will pardon you also."

Mrs Turner shook her head: "Why, I would hope so," she admitted, "but I am fearful."

There was a flurry on the stairs like a bat in the beams and Franklin came in. As he bent over her hand Frances looked at him with pleasure, and Mrs Turner cursed under her breath. All this talk of necromancy had turned the girl's wits. At first secure through her station, Frances now felt secure through her dabbling with imagined sorceries. Mrs Turner realized that the countess did not truly believe that Nemesis had come for Ann Turner and Franklin and herself.

"What now, Franklin?" said Frances with a wry twist to her mouth and a choked laugh. "We shall all be hanged, for Weston hath been sent for by a pursuivant and he has confessed all."

Franklin's great head went up, like that of a stag who hears a hunting horn, and then lowered again. His ruddy face turned ashen, but slowly, as if it were being daubed with paint. He said nothing, then he looked at her as if to ask if he might sit. Frances nodded and he went down in a chair, lumpily, as if his muscles had been extracted from him.

"I want you to swear, Franklin," said Frances swiftly, "that you will be silent. They will come for you, for Weston is sure to toss them your name at the first. He has no love for you. When they come, be confused. Say naught of Mrs Turner or myself. Will you swear on that?"

"I will swear, as I have done before," he said heavily, "but if they offer me a pardon what will I do?"

"My husband is in the inner room," said Frances. "He is the Lord Chamberlain and he knows of the working of the law. I will speak to him of you." She walked through the door, her fur gown lapping the corners of the doorposts.

Mrs Turner said nothing, she knew that Frances's conversation with Robin would be a pretence, that the countess only sought to reassure Franklin of the power of the Somersets. Frances was back so soon that Ann guessed that she had found her lord asleep.

"The council will offer you a pardon—says my lord," she told Franklin, shutting the door behind her firmly as she spoke, "but believe them not, for when they have got out of you what they would, we will all be hanged." She smiled as she added this, almost as if she conferred a favour on Franklin.

"No," said Franklin. "You will save your own neck, madam, at the expense of ours."

Frances looked at Ann Turner questioningly. She was gathering up her osier basket, a little red stitched box, and her dark cloak; while Franklin and Frances watched her she made for the outer door. Frances said: "You will be true, Ann, will you not, and tell naught of what you know?"

Mrs Turner looked at her disdainfully. "Nay madam," she said firmly, "I will not be hanging for you both." Her glance took in Franklin, still seated like a sack. He rose unsteadily to his feet.

"Stay, the both, and have some wine," suggested Frances.

But they shook their heads and were away, one after the other down the dark back stairs, they did not speak to each other as they went.

By the next week Coke had a pile of conflicting material from Weston. It came out slowly, like extracting an old back tooth. In his anxiety to keep his son William out of the story, Weston had told them that the dishes were brought mainly by "The countess's maid, Mistress Horne". He had seen his mistake almost immediately but Coke was on to him like a falcon after a pigeon. Frances Howard was in the story and Weston might as well tell all. But he refused to do so, continually snarling the path with lies about minor events until Coke was wrathful and Bacon despairing.

"If we chase all his wild goose tales they will be out of the story," he said to Coke. By "they" he meant the Somersets, for nobody had used their names during the enquiry except the circuitous Weston.

To make all safe, Coke had Mrs Turner clapped into the upper room of Alderman Jones's house. Hardly had he done this when a roundabout tale reached them that de Loubell was decrying attempts to prove that Overbury had been poisoned. Coke sent Sir Franci to question him but the apothecary was away and would not be back that day. His landlord offered information. It was he had spoken with de Loubell on the matter.

"He said it was madness to say Overbury was killed," insisted this man. "De Loubell said he had treated Sir Thomas for a consumption which proceeded from melancholy and was owed to his imprisonment."

Bacon did not think de Loubell had been in the plot. The doctor was too august to stoop to making up poisons or administering them, yet he could have been cheated, especially if his own apprentice was a tool of the Howards. Bacon wrote down all the gossip which the landlord offered him, even that the house was actually owned by his mother, he merely collected the rents. Rider's evidence was added to the growing collection of papers.

Alderman Jones had sent round word that Weston had spoken with him when he was first taken up, but Jones, overwhelmed with the thought of his forthcoming gentle prisoner (who had but turned out to be a city wife and she the mistress of a rapscallion at that) had forgotten Weston's words before: that "Coke was setting nets for little birds while the great ones go."

Coke knew this as well as his host of advisors but he still had too little to act upon regarding the Somersets. He sent for Master Bright the coroner who had performed his office after Overbury's death, and read the post mortem report. It made him retch. Finally he sent for Elwes. Sir Jervis added nothing to his written evidence, except for his problems of conscience it contained all that had passed.

"It is medical facts we need," cried Coke. The lawyers—and by now there were several on the case, talking to witnesses and weeding statements—all shook their heads.

All the medical evidence was hearsay. What else could it be after two years? And the few doctors who had examined Overbury had attested that he was near death with melancholy, consumption, corruption of the body or some other unnamed ailment when they had seen him. Coke admitted to himself, but to nobody else, that he did not wish to speak to the doctors directly. He knew de Loubell was walking about London but did nothing to pull him in. He shrewdly guessed that James wanted Carr implicated to remove him from office; and that the story that Overbury had died of natural causes would allow the Howards to go free; more, they would triumph in the vindication of their good name. Finally he asked Bacon to serve notices on the apothecaries in the case. The purveyors of medicine would give the right evidence for Coke's case. In all those purges, vomit pills and potions there would surely be some arsenic or Spanish Fly, and on that he could pin his case for poisoning. In his haste to glean evidence of murder he had apothecaries questioned who had never heard of Overbury's poisoning until that hour. Among those seized was Dr Franklin.

XXV

Sᴏ Jᴇʀᴠɪꜱ ᴄᴀʀʀɪᴇᴅ on his lawful duties, as solitary as a spider in a corner. His wife, silenced by the fear they both had for the future, occasionally asked him to repeat word for word what the Secretary of State had promised. As time had passed and he had been drunk, Elwes's memory of the evening with the Earl of Shrewsbury and Winwood became less and less distinct and yet, to his consternation, all that had passed while Overbury was his prisoner became more clear and memorable. He lay awake at night thinking of the smallest inflection in Sir Thomas's voice when he was ill; and of that accursed passage to and fro of doctors, so eager then to declare Overbury sick unto death, and so silent now. Meanwhile, the stories of Reeve's deathbed confession fluttered round London like ashes in a wind. Gruesome tales gained credence: that Overbury's screams had awakened folk outside the Tower from sleep; that Elwes had held a candle while Weston and Reeve invented terrible tortures with which they had killed the unfortunate man; and above all, admiration for dead Overbury grew, until he was a London hero, higher than any lord mayor, a man who had laid down his life for the commons. It was said that Overbury had defied both his friend Carr and the king in opposing the Spanish marriage. He was a Protestant martyr.

In his palace at Lambeth, Archbishop Abbot had smiled over that piece of gossip. "How soon are we translated!" he exclaimed to Winwood who had visited him after the promotion of young Villiers.

"Ah yes," said the Secretary of State sourly. "I'll warrant Overbury will be better remembered than you or I, or even young Villiers."

Abbot laughed. "Why as to that, I never expect my renown to live after me."

"Write a scurrilous tale or be found dead in a ditch and you are sure of immortality."

"Is the countess taken up?" asked Abbot.

"Not she. We are amazed that Coke acts so slowly. He has Mrs

Turner safe in an alderman's house and yet messengers go to and from the countess daily. Mrs Turner is close in her answers."

"Or so says Coke."

"No, I have it on excellent authority she has admitted nothing, neither to poisoning of any sort, nor of paying the fellow Weston £180. There is nothing to convict her."

"Is it not thought strange that the countess is in communication with her?"

"Oh, as to that, the first time a servant came running from the countess the worthy alderman Jones told Coke, and that he was offered a service of silver or some such treasure if the countess were let in to see Mrs Turner. But the lady, Mrs Turner that is, plays chaste: 'What,' she says, 'would the countess have with me? I am but her dressmaker.' She is a sly bitch and could go free, if the countess were not worrying to see her all the time like a terrier at a rabbit warren, and that makes men suspect d'you see? The countess is foolish, for a Howard. In her determination to control her coven she will let all heads roll off, her own as well."

"She is distracted," suggested Abbot.

"Not she! The Lady Frances had ever a remarkable oblivion to what others might think of her actions. She believes she is above the law."

Abbot shuffled over to the window, looking at that sharply-etched picture of the north bank of the river where every spire and roof was crisp against the sky. "Is her husband mad" he asked, "that he lets her imperil them both, for none will think him innocent, as Overbury was once his intimate? Indeed, did the countess even know Sir Thomas beyond the courtesies of Whitehall?"

"It is said," replied Winwood, "that she was hungry for Carr, even as long ago as that, and that Overbury said he would impede their union, by divulging letters he had writ for Carr to send to her."

Abbot brought his venerable hands together in a smack. "So-ho," he said. "Even in his lovemaking, Carr leaned on other men."

"So it is said."

Winwood picked up an ember with the tongs and applied it to his pipe; it gave him time to consider his conversation with the archbishop. Once he would have been open but now that he was Secretary of State he had to use discretion, he respected Abbot for asking him no questions although he knew that the archbishop was waiting for more news. He decided to tell him what had happened that evening.

"So now friend Coke has found evidence of who served the countess, and, it is said, he could tell all about Mrs Turner and the poisoned pieces, and that draught from Killigrew which near sent Overbury off."

"Aye, women, women," said Abbot as if they were a species as distant as the African lion. "They ever seek their confidantes and in that they are undone."

"I doubt there were many confidantes," admitted Winwood, "for Mrs Turner played that part so excellently well no other had a look in. It was Mrs Turner, I have heard, who carried the countess to that magician Forman e'er his death, and then to a poor apologetic creature called Savory, and at last to an apothecary called Franklin."

"At last, we have a medical man——" said Abbot. "Coke must see that only a doctor's evidence is of any value in this affair."

"That is why he does not call a doctor in," said Winwood. "Any medical man who saw Overbury would swear he died of natural causes, and to make a case against the earl and countess Coke needs a murder. Why not call de Loubell, or Mayerne, or even that posturing fool, Craig? Because each would swear that Overbury's death was no surprise. Reeve, perhaps, is dead, so he is not a suitable murderer. Weston is too small to pursue too far. No, Coke must play cat's cradle with what witnesses he can find, to be sure that any called in a trial will swear Overbury was murdered, and that the Somersets had a hand in it."

"So he is sure that James wants Carr out of the way?"

Winwood said: "We must all suppose that, as James is now calling out for justice like a tomcat on the tiles."

He suddenly thought he had gone too far and glanced with apprehension at Abbot but the old man only smiled and continued: "Having set his course against Carr—Coke may over-reach himself."

"He is about to do so," agreed Winwood. "Even as I left at this late hour, he was fiddling with some depositions that Carr and Overbury had a hand in the death of the late Prince Henry." He looked fixedly at the archbishop to see if Abbot's reaction tallied with his own.

"That is unwise," said Abbot. "Think you of the dirty tales there were when the boy died—that James himself had put his son away. That he was jealous of his favour with the mob, and angry at the boy's loud complaints of the Spanish marriage—disturbed that

Harry would have been the hope of the Protestant world, a knight errant, while his old dad sat at home in his palace and played with his young men, telling filthy stories."

Why, Abbot is quite overwrought, thought Winwood, amused. "I think," he said, "that Coke has gone too far if he asks questions on the prince's death, for James will think he is being accused himself and will put Sir Edward down as hard as driving a nail into wood."

"Which will promote another of our friends."

"Bacon, aye, I do not care for that man, he was fast friends with Carr a year agone and now is as close with Villiers."

"So—he attempts to please those in power," said Abbot wearily. "Which of us does not? Bacon is perhaps more open in his dishonesty than other men. He has cunning, expected in a cousin to Cecil."

"He is aching to displace Coke."

"Coke is how old? Sixty or more. He is due for the country."

"He will be sent there fast if he goes on this way," said Winwood.

XXVI

By THE MIDDLE of October Robin could no longer bear
it. He was at Royston with the king and news filtered uncertainly
down to the country palace where the young huntsmen talked about
the earl behind their hands. Whenever he appeared in any company
they would fixedly look away from him. His decision was made
when the queen had come to him after supper. She said very little,
and all that about the day's sport and yet he realized that her action
was aggravated by pity. What! Pity me? he thought later in the
stillness of his apartment, the Danish whore dares to come and
show her pity for me! From below stairs came a thin spitting sound
of laughter. He knew that Villiers and his friends were entertaining
James, and he had not been asked to join them.

As a pale trickle of dawn ran across the sky his lumbering coach
was crossing Royston Heath. Near Hatfield his coachman called
back to him. "My lord, another coach, and coming at great speed."
It was ripping up the track towards them, its bulging sides ricochet-
ting against tufts of grass as it ploughed in the well-worn ruts; as
it passed Robin looked curiously at the dull red-leather sides,
painted with indistinguishable heraldry; but he did not need to
identify the arms for he saw the pale face of Coke illuminating the
interior, and he guessed that the Lord Chief Justice was hastening
to Royston in pursuit of Robin or Frances.

He knew that he would have no more than a few hours in
London; in spite of Frances's pregnancy—and he cursed that it was
true—he must be back with James while Coke was still persuading
him that a commission was needed.

He ran against Davies as soon as he entered the house. The man
seized his arm as if he were an equal and they went into a closet.
Robin grabbed the servant's sleeves and pummelled him, half in
relief at seeing the man and half angry that anybody, even an ally,
could make him so apprehensive.

"I stay but a moment," he said to Davies. "My countess has need
of me, and I must return to Royston at dawn."

Davies stared at him with his mouth drooping open like a zany
at a fair.

"You have the letters to Overbury?" asked Robin, afraid.

"Nay—my lord," said Davies.

"What, what!" Disregarding his cries, Robin began to beat him about the head. The closet was too small to do more than patacake at the man, who sank to his knees on the dark dusty floor. "Why not?"

"I went to the house of Overbury's friend as you directed, my lord, and found that a box of letters had indeed been there. But the varlet who owns the place said he had supposed they were to do with the Overbury murder as he called it, and he has sent the box, letters and all, to Sir Edward Coke."

Robin leaned gasping against the wainscot. He allowed Davies to open the door, the man's worried face, contorted by candlelight, looked back in at him.

"Can I fetch anything, my lord? Aquavit, or wine?"

"Nay, nay," Robin made a curious flopping movement with one hand. He wanted to sink down on the floor of the closet and weep like a baby, but he stiffened and walked gravely out into the room, clasping the closet door behind him. Davies was puzzled but no more, he still gazed at Robin with some sort of awe.

"Look you, Davies," said Robin, passing his hand familiarly across the fellow's back as he was wont to do with dear dead Tom Overbury. "Know you the gist of the letters? You carried them to that house for Sir Thomas. How many were in the box?"

"I cannot say, some 20 or so—30."

"And with them an account, a story of his dealings with me?"

"Ah, I know not of that, my lord. I had the thought as he pushed them into the box that they were all letters and scraps of poetry. Truth to tell, my lord, I had a feeling that there was nothing secret in those letters but that Sir Thomas wished to arouse your fears by saying he had sent the tale of his imprisonment to a secret place."

The thought of the letters in Coke's papery hands made Robin sick. He remembered those protestations of love, and stories of plots to make Jamie agreeable to Tom's release, coupled with promises of future honours and delights—"When you are free from that place"—; if they were brought to court they would damn Robin Carr as a false coward.

"As I deserve to be damned," he said, so low that Davies cocked his head at him in inquiry. "Naught, naught, Davies," he said hastily, and gave the man a handful of coins gripped out of his purse. He supposed there was gold among them for Davies thanked him twice before he went away. He remembered that there were further letters which Mrs Turner had removed and left at the house of William Weston. He wanted to recover those at least, but not with Davies, who would then know too many of his secrets.

Frances lay in his bed like a pearl in a shell. Her white skin glistening with oil which had been rubbed in by a maid. She yawned and stretched at Robin's entrance, writhing her beautiful body about, her swell of child was displayed as prominently as her breasts and thighs. When Robin looked away from her she exclaimed: "What have I done, my lord, to deserve this harshness?"

Obediently he put his cold mouth to her neck while she moved luxuriously against him. "I am for Royston before light," he told her.

"Robin! You are but from there. It is madness."

"Then I am mad. I passed Coke as I came."

"That fusty old man who has clapped Ann Turner into prison! I will break him." Her teeth shone momentarily.

Robin sat beside her, sinking into a profusion of silk and fur which surrounded her. "Frances," he said, "I know you killed my friend."

She did not deny it but looked at him with her sly sloe eyes.

"I have not listened to the tales before, or else been foolish," he said. "I had wished not to listen, or to believe." She opened her mouth but he continued: "Listen, lady, I am to blame as you are. Between us we pulled that proud man down. I had rather we had not. At any cost."

"What!" she cried, rearing up on her haunches like an angry animal: "If you had lost me, what then?"

"I had rather have lost you than let this happen," Robin said. "But we are fast in it now. Coke has gone to the king, no doubt with a plea for a commission——"

"Another commission," she shrugged and lay back; her body, suddenly opulent with pregnancy, seemed to unroll under his eyes like a map.

He shut them and went on: "Another commission, and that is because Coke knows—all—all—knows that more than Weston and your silly Mrs Turner have a hand in this. They are holding Weston and Mrs Turner as bait to pull the great ones in."

"Aye, maybe."

"But we—we are the great ones."

She did not seem to understand this urgency. She said: "A commission. It will sit for a year or more with disputes and arguments and then your loving king will tell it to declare we are innocent and that will be all."

"Fool," cried Robin. "That last commission, for a divorce, was formed on your family's urging. This is made by the king. It will be bent on destroying us. James is not my lover. He has a new paramour."

Frances at last looked fearful. Her surprise shifted over her face like a cloud on the sun. It cleared almost at once.

"Who can touch us?" she said. "They will hang a few rogues and I believe Weston should be hanged. He has botched one or two matters. And they will torture that creature, Cunning Mary—and that will be an end to't."

Robin said to her: "You poisoned Tom Overbury, to whom I owed much." He was choking, part in sorrow, part in rage.

"Alack," replied Frances. "You should have thought of that when you played your trick to put him in the Tower. Maybe I ate the fly, but it was you wove the web to hold him fast."

He walked out on that and ordered his coach to be ready to return to Royston.

On the way, near Baldock, he was called by his coachman: "See here, my lord. A pretty thing. Yon coach is about its business again."

Leaning wearily from the pillow on which he had hoped to find some sleep Robin saw that Coke's coach was veering down the hill towards his own. He told the man to pull to one side so that he might stop and beg Coke to drop his case against Weston and Mrs Turner. Had the man not discovered enough, that he should seek further? Anxiously Robin slipped from his coach and leaned against it. Fine rain was covering the horizon with mist, and out of it came Coke's coach, lurching like a galleon. The curtain parted and the Lord Chief Justice peered out, his hair shining against the rain which was the same colour. He did not stop. The wheels spewed up a stream of muddy water as Coke passed, and the coach creaked as it righted itself on the road. Robin was left standing against the wheel. His face was dewy with perspiration as well as rain.

"My lord", said the driver looking down at him. "You are sick. You should be in bed."

"We must drive on," said Robin, swinging back into his place again. His thighs and head ached. The man might be right. It would be fine irony if he were to be seized with a wasting sickness like that of Overbury and could not face his accusers. He wished he might be ill, grievously, so that more than the queen would pity him and he might sleep in a herb-strewn room, frequented only by quiet and obsequious doctors. Frances could retreat into the cocoon of her nobility and her pregnancy. Robin envied her. She did not feel as he did.

Robin wished to see James alone, and could not. The king had surrounded himself with a phalanx of youths who hooted about the palace like night owls, rejuvenating him, for as he approached 50 James was displaying more signs of age. He slept through many feasts and masques, his previously bony face was beginning to pad out into jowls, and his hair was becoming thin and fading in colour. In aping his dear Villiers he had discarded his plump trunk hose for new-fangled loose breeches which hung down over his slender legs like cows' udders. Robin saw him often from a distance, his jaunty cap proclaiming him among a bevy of bare-headed boys, some scarce bearded. He understood that he was not welcome near James, and that the king was either bored by his conversation or afraid of his rages. And yet Robin sometimes saw in the king's eyes a spasm of love; these emotional expressions made Robin bold; while James directed them at him could he have fallen out of favour? Was this assumed affection for young Villiers not a form of flirtation to prove to Carr that others could kiss and fondle the noisome old man too?

It was raining, and even too wet for a hunt. The palace was over-crowded with courtiers. Anne had gout and her complaints and attendants took too much attention and space. So James and his favourites were pushed together in the long gallery where a game of carpet bowls kept some happy while others tra-laed to the lute or wrote dirty verses to amuse the king.

Robin pushed his way forward, thrusting the friends of Villiers out of the way as carelessly as they threw bowls down the floor. He was before James almost at once, nearer to those doglike eyes than he had been for weeks.

"I must have speech with you," he said, cutting into another's conversation. He added for good measure: "Your majesty".

"Well, well, my lord, what is it?"

"This," he held out Coke's summons, which was muddy and creased from hard riding. "This man, this Chief Justice, so called, demands me in London, as careless as if I were a felon. There is no invitation in it, but an order, as if I were one of his constables. Well then, see," Robin tore the letter across, flaking the pieces off his fingers into the fire. "A fig for Sir Edward Coke! I will not go. Not I!"

James took his elbow, bending his face towards Robin. "Nay, man", he said. "If Coke sends for *me*, I must go."

Robin stared at him. "What is kingship if one be at the beck and call of any rogue?"

"Sir Edward Coke is the law, Robin. You cannot gainsay him."

At that Robin began to bluster and finally had his way, for James motioned off the other interested gentlemen and led him to the bedroom, where he dismissed the pages. Young George Villiers followed them to the threshold and looked on, as if he watched a raree show.

"The sky clears, sir," he said casually, "shall we go hunt?"

James looked from his eager handsome face to that of Robin, which was lined with despair. "Go now, George," he said, "and close the door. Let none disturb us."

The abrupt snapping of the door, for Villiers was angry, closed out the sound of voices and laughter. James pushed Robin towards a chair and poured a cup of wine himself, Robin accepted it silently.

James sighed, sat down by him, and looked at his pantoufles which were already grimy where he had trailed the ribbons into the slough of the stableyard; with some effort, for his arms were enclosed by a Spanish cape, he passed his hand across Robin's shoulder and pressed it gently.

"Nay, nay Rabbie," he said. "You have been warned."

"Ah, I am importunate," said Robin sourly, discarding, like his king, the familiar Scots tongue. "I should have taken my dimittis, is't not so? Gone into obscurity without a sound like James Hay who fostered me, or that buffoon young Philip Herbert? When you cast men off they are meant to stay cast off, are they not? That discreet way leads to a retirement with honour, to titles and wealth. Even as a rich man passes his mistress off with a pension against her old age and mayhap the wherewithall to open her own brothel and supply him with younger meat—so you bid your lovers goodbye. I cannot take such cruelty. Therein lies my end."

"Alas," replied James, "the temper you have will not take 'no' lightly. I would have ever cleaved to you, Rabbie. D'ye think this flippertigibbet Villiers, for all he is a delight to me, would have ever meant aught if you had not been so surly and uncivil with me? Ever since you married that lady you have treated me as if I were an elderly whore, pouted and grimaced if I demanded your company, made excuses to leave me for your countess, and in company you have derided me like an arrogant young man with a mewling old wife. Did'st expect thanks for this, Rabbie? You have become unbearable and that is your downfall."

"I will not be treated so," Robin declared.

"Treated? How? You are ever railing at me, either covertly or against my officers such as Coke or Ellesmere." Robin could not answer. "You upbraid me as if I were untrue to you, Rabbie, yet the fault lies in your own nature. You accuse me daily either to my face or behind my back. 'Fore God I have nothing on my conscience, and my reputation is whole before the world."

"You use men who are harsh in their judgements, and in this Overbury affair."

James sighed again: "I use men who are strict in the point of their examination. If a man be an honest lawyer it stands best with my conscience to employ him. It would say little for my honour, if, having appointed a judge, I were to dispose of him on the whim of another. This is not a peccadillo, Robin, it is murther. I cannot stand in the way of the inquiry, for you or any man." He set his loose lips to firmness. "In all things I go by the rule of my conscience."

"Aye," said Robin. "Your conscience veers like a weathercock. If any tax or imposition were involved your conscience would not be so nice."

James looked as if he had not heard the last but he could not resist saying: "Look you here, Rabbie. You and your father-in-law, aye, and old dead Northampton, have behaved from the beginning of this affair quite contrary to all forms of honest men."

"So you will not shield me from Coke?"

"See you not the reason for't, Rabbie? This is like to be a murther trial, and you have dabbled part in it, deny it how you like. Is it not better for all to come out? It may be a plot against you and your countess laid by your enemies. For my part I hope so, and that you will be restored to your high repute."

"Will you not believe that I am innocent of all accusations?"

"No accusations have yet been made."

"I am guilty of nothing except in letting Tom stay in the Tower."

"It will all come out," said James. His eyes were filling with tears and Robin thought he had him! That a few further pleas might make the king maudlin in spite of his highflown sentiments about the law. Yet at that crucial moment a tap came on the far door which led only to the queen's apartments and the slight figure of Prince Charles appeared, waited upon by dogs as his father was by young men.

"What is't?" asked James, annoyed that his remaining son should see his weakness.

"It is her grace, sir," said the boy. "Sends me to ask your majesty if you will play cards with her."

Robin scowled. He had expected complete privacy with Villiers sent to bar the outer door, and then this petty family demand had called James to his duty as a husband, which he would not have followed if he were not immured by rain and anxious to dismiss Carr.

He went close to Robin and whispered. "I will see you on your way to London."

Less than an hour later they met at the head of the great staircase. James was distraught but had controlled himself and sent young Villiers away. He was publicly out of love with Robin but he would not let him be humiliated by the watchful gaze of his successor. The king's tears were bolted back but still came too readily to his cheeks, coursing into his thin beard as if they were raindrops on a window pane. He greeted Robin by gripping both his hands and leaning on him as he was wont to do in the past.

"For God's sake," he muttered, "when shall I see you again? On my soul, I shall neither eat nor sleep until you come again."

Robin was encouraged by this display of grief to look about him triumphantly, noting which courtiers were abashed by this evidence of the king's love.

"Why," he said loudly, "it is but a query from the old man. I will hasten back on the morrow."

He strode downwards, James close by him, clutching at his arm with plaintive, fretting fingers. At the turn of the stairs the king leaned over the balustrade and gripped Robin's arms tightly. Then he cradled his favourite's face between his palms, looking searchingly at him, but he was weeping too much to see more than the wraith of Robin's chestnut hair and those amber eyes, now set in swollen pink lids.

"For God's sake," blurted James. "Give your lady a kiss for me." Using Frances as a pretext he pressed his mouth against Robin's, pleased that there was no withdrawal as there had been sometimes of late. Robin clung to him, drooping his cloak so that their fettered embraces should not be seen by some curious on-lookers. James was quite undone, he leaned heavily, his breath coming in short fetid gasps. Gently Robin straightened the king, propping him by the banister so that his declining figure would not be too obvious. He anxiously lifted his mouth towards James's ear.

"I love you," he whispered, knowing that this would dismay James even more. Then he hopped down the step and walked firmly towards his coach.

James leaned on the rail to watch him go, occasionally wiping his face with his cloak. None went too near him, they were awed by the misery of the king. As the outriders passed from sight James turned to go back to his rooms. Courtiers were clustered round the landing like flies on honey, they parted and allowed him through between them. One was bold enough to offer a handkerchief which was waved away. Divorced from Robin, James began to smile, a watery thin expression assumed for his gentlemen. As one bent to remove the dirty royal shoes James said, "Now, Rabbie Carr, the de'il go wi' thee, for I shall never see thy face more."

When Robin was again in London, he sent a royal messenger to find Tom's letters, who was accompanied by a city constable, Errat. The letters were found, but Errat, suspicious of the errand, reported his work to Coke.

The commissioners were already in session and received this news with surprise. None of them had thought Carr would be foolish enough to suppress evidence. Their first reaction was to order him to the Tower, but could this be done? Somerset still held seals of office and could only be deprived of them by the king, who was at Royston.

However, they sent two documents out before that evening, em-ploying that same Errat, the constable, to deliver them, perhaps feeling that he should carry his duties out to the end as he had informed against the messenger and so against Somerset. Their demands were short and explicit. Carr was to remain in his house at the Cockpit and only personal servants would be allowed to visit him. A band of halberdiers marched away to stand by his door. The other letter was to the countess who was staying in the house at Blackfriars which she had bought before her marriage. The commissioners courteously suggested that she should stay where she was, guarded, or else at the house of Lord Knollys at the Tilt Yard. In order to keep all their birds safe within cages, Coke removed Weston and Mrs Turner from the pleasant rooms in the houses of aldermen where they were imprisoned, and put them into other houses, still private, still informal, but owned by sheriffs of the City of London. Outside every house a watch was placed.

They should have been well guarded, but real seclusion proved impossible. The guards did not know who were servants of the houses and who were friends of the prisoners. Like rats scurrying in a wainscot, a passage began from one house to another in which servants carried dishes or clothes, gentlemen gained admittance dressed as scullions, or ladies in the cloaks of their own maids.

Robin could not comprehend the order telling him to stay in his home. It was signed by Coke, Ellesmere and Zouche. Thinking it merely a request, he resolved to begin again that doleful journey back to Royston. He knew James did not wish him to be imprisoned. He called Rawlins, wishing he had about him a man more privy to his deepest secrets like Davies, who had been so loyal to poor Tom. There was no reply and when he stuck his head from the door he saw a halberdier, in a confused livery as if it had been hastily thrown on.

"What d'ye here, fellow?" asked Robin.

The man made a deep bow, being unsure how to address an earl, but he came up smartly clutching his weapon close to his shoulder as if on parade. "I am sent to guard the door, my lord."

"Where is my man, Rawlins?"

"Why, he were out when the guard were set and will stay out I daresay."

Robin went back into his room. His food came to him from the kitchen so he realized that he might not even go downstairs to his dining hall. In the evening a discreet tap at the wood brought him to his feet. The head of his lawyer, Cotton, came round the door, as hesitantly as a maiden coming to his room on bridal night. He put his fingers to his lips and crept across to where Robin sat, dismayed.

"How now," he said. "I hear you have a flux, my lord."

"What foolishness is this?"

"Hush, my lord," said Cotton in a low voice. "I am your doctor.

By this means we are all able to visit each other. I will bear any message you wish to your wife."

"My wife—ha! She is like a spoiled brat in this, so accustomed to having her way she cannot see any danger. I would rather see her father."

Sir Robert shook his head. His round bewildered eyes almost amused Robin, who gave a curt laugh.

"Aye," he said. "Old Suffolk will have us out in a trice."

Again Sir Robert shook his head. "Not he. He is quite ready to cast off his son-in-law, aye, and his lovely and beloved daughter. His own affairs are to be inspected they say. He has £30,000 unaccounted for from the royal estates and talk has been revived of that pension from Spain. Aside from that he has incurred the wrath of the queen and she is in the ascendant, taking with her a train of notables, most prominent among them, the Archbishop of Canterbury. The only particular in which Great Anna is daunted is in young Villiers, for you know, he has been sponsored and set up by a cabal of Abbot, Pembroke——"

"I know it well," said Robin almost convinced that it was he who had first told Cotton of the plotting.

"So the queen dislikes young Villiers," he said after a pause, conjecturing how he might insinuate with her and contribute to downfall of his successor.

"She dislikes you more," Cotton pointed out. "She was all for the new man until it seemed he had outreached himself and that he no more dances where his masters bid him. Aye, clever plotters though they may be, those men have made a besom to beat their own backs."

"I will yet return triumphing——"

"It were better you thought of a house away from London."

Robin was annoyed by Cotton's plain speech. He said: "Now that you have crept in here we must destroy those letters taken yesterday."

"Have you not done so?" Cotton's trim legal mind was affronted.

He poked at the fire. "Best have the cupping instruments out ere we begin," he said and produced the tools of a chirurgeon, laying them exactly on a velvet cloth, that any who came in might suppose him at work.

They tumbled everything from the messenger's satchel and crammed it into the flames. Letters unfolded like living hair in the fire, displaying secrets to their anxious eyes: "Come soon, I have need of you"; "2 lengths India silk, curiously patterned with shells . . ."; "Good Mistress Turner, and you come at ten this night I will tickle . . ."; "This is the cup will bear away My sinful life and let me lay . . ."; "I would have you fetch in cheeses from Whittaker at the sign of . . ."; "Adieu, I would we had parted better . . ." Letters from Overbury entwined with those of Frances, and Robin's uncertain hand was clasped close to that of Forman. They flew like fireworks up the chimney, their ashes dropping down again to lie on the hearth. Cotton absently prodded them back to the heat and both men watched as they whitened and then crumbled completely into snow.

"That is the end of it," said Robin quite cheerfully. His companion looked at him curiously thinking that Robin was as far from facing reality as his foolish witch of a wife. What of the letters Coke held? What of the accumulated evidence from witnesses which was employing a dozen lawyers with complicated cross plots and deductions? He knew that Robin would not escape.

XXVII

"RICHARD WESTON, BEING about the age of 60 years, not having the fear of God about his eyes, but instigated and induced by the devil, devised and contrived not only to bring upon the body of Sir Thomas Overbury, knight, great sickness and disease, but also to deprive him of life." The accusation had stuck fast, for Weston would not speak a word in court; asked how he should be tried he refused to make the response "By God and my country" only staring back at his judges and swaying a little. The court was adjourned, but not before Coke had threatened to torture the prisoner into submission.

His fellow judges had shaken their heads, knowing that those few years since the Gunpowder Plot had made torture odious. There was no necessity to use it; a few days later Weston was persuaded to make the proper answers to the traditional questions of the court. He was swiftly found guilty and sentenced to be hanged.

Elwes had never attended an execution and he went to Weston's hanging secretly. It was not revenge, he thought, but a desire to see the story played to its end. Even his wife did not know where he had gone. He was relieved at being away from the Tower. Events were cramming so fast that he was almost sure that he would be arrested, if only to be released when Mr Secretary Winwood begged that he should be shown mercy.

Tyburn was as he had expected. A plaguey windy desolate place set at two crossroads, surrounded by a dull plain scattered with thickets and hovels. The few decent houses were all set well away on the horizon. Elwes was amazed at the crowd. People lined the Oxford road two or three deep and some had stood there all night.

Sir Jervis sat on his bay at the back of the crowd. His horse raised him enough to see over their heads. Two dirty children had made a fire nearby and squatted close to it. Alas, he thought, the poor are ever with us. He threw a penny to the boy who glanced at him sharply, then bit the coin.

"Buy a pie," advised Sir Jervis waving towards the pie sellers who were progressing through the crowd, their steaming trays heaped with hot pasties. The boy waved back and grinned but put the penny into his blanket. He would not buy food with it.

"That was a penny wasted," said a voice at his other side. Elwes looked round at a big bluff fellow, a gentleman, but with shabby leather clothes and a worn beaver hat. He sat a huge chestnut horse, which looked to have come from ploughing, for its fetlocks were caked with mud. The man pulled off his glove and held out his hand. "We have met before, Sir Jervis," he said.

"I cannot remember—old age, poor sight——" suggested Elwes.

"I am Sir John Lidcote, the brother-in-law of your prisoner, Overbury."

"Aye, aye," he held the man's hand absently, sure that Lidcote must also be here as an act of retribution. "This must be a good day for you," he said.

"Why so, Sir Jervis?"

"Why—it is the end of your brother's murderer."

Lidcote smiled: "Is it so, Sir Jervis? I think not, but you would know better than I."

Confused, Elwes began a farrago on how the Bible teaches us to love our enemies but how more human it is to hate them. Lidcote did not listen, his ear was attuned to a more distant sound, he rose in his stirrups, gripping Elwes's shoulder as he did so.

"Aha," he said. "D'ye hear? They come! They come!"

Far to his right, beyond the woodland and a few wooden tenements, Elwes could hear a booming like the sea heard from a mile inland. It sounded like the nagging yet subdued roar of the Wash, that odd deep water which skirted his own home county, and with it there was a persistent gurgle, as if the force of the water were being diverted at regular intervals into a dyke, to sob down a channel then erupt again by the sea's edge.

"What is it?" he asked Lidcote.

"It is the mob," he answered.

The swell was coming nearer; about Elwes the crowd stopped idle chatter, and began to draw nearer the gibbet, thrusting themselves right under the wooden platform with weather-worn steps. Elwes noticed how green and slimy they were with rain. The piemen were stacking their trays on their handcarts. They knew that few would pause to eat when Weston came in sight and they hoped to find a good lookout post themselves. Elwes allowed his horse to take two steps forward and then pulled him back. He was ashamed to be seen in such a place. Lidcote was grim, his high-bridged nose jutting out from under his hat.

"See here, who comes," said Lidcote abruptly, more to himself than Elwes.

Sir Jervis turned and was surprised to see that a bevy of well-dressed men had silently joined them, they gathered on the other side from Lidcote, separating Elwes from the road so that even if he changed his mind and decided to go back to the Tower, he would not be able. He felt a pang of distrust, although none of the men seemed armed, they were all solemn faced, and their dress was sober if rich.

"Who be they?"

Lidcote glanced at them almost savagely: "I know not all, but that man in the lead is Wentworth, and he by his side young Harry Vane, I have seen one or two others but know not their names."

Elwes continued to watch the men until Weston's cart pulled up by the scaffold. Before it stopped, the mob's music had swelled to a crescendo but as soon as the sad black horse was halted such a heavy silence fell that Elwes thought all held their breath. Far away, out of sight of the scaffold, voices chimed from the road to the city. Any who could see the execution were quiet.

Elwes was surprised that Weston seemed so small. Had his trial and that threat of torture shrunk the man? He stumbled as he came from the cart and half a dozen hands went out to save him, the rope about his arms was pulled tight, so that his coat was creased and twisted round by his bonds.

He went slowly up the scaffold steps. The hangman had leaped up before and stood on the far side, waiting for Weston, almost dispassionate, as if he were also a spectator but less interested than any of them. When Weston finally reached the top of the steps, he doddered for a second and the sheriff pulled him round to face the throng. The hangman leaned forward and slipped the noose about Weston's neck. The prisoner did not seem to notice. The sheriff was reading out the sentence while Weston teetered about on the platform, now and again pulled upright by the steady hands of the hangman.

"Is he sick?" asked Elwes who would not be surprised if the man fainted.

"Drunk," said Lidcote and snapped his mouth shut.

The sheriff's words were suddenly interrupted by a sonorous voice from Elwes's side. "Hold, hold!"

At that all stopped—even the clocks would have stopped, thought Elwes, for those words could only herald a royal pardon for Weston. The man who had cried out was one of the group beside Lidcote who were urging their horses towards the gibbet, where the prisoner looked rheumily at the foremost rider. The sheriff waited to see if a pardon were flourished in his face and as none appeared, said "I must beg you, sirs, to stand back. Do not hinder——"

"I would ask a question of your prisoner," shouted the man.

Weston murmured something. Almost against his will, Elwes edged forward. So did Lidcote; knee to knee, they forced their horses through the crowd towards the scaffold. Sir Jervis had a rambling idea that as an officer of the crown he should intervene if any mischief were toward.

As calmly as a maid passing a kerchief to her mistress, the hangman pulled a dripping napkin from a pail and applied it to the back of Weston's neck where his collar was pulled back for the noose. A shock passed through the prisoner. He swayed once more, but for the last time—quick as a butcher, the hangman held to his prone body and swabbed at his face with the water. Under its saturation Weston gasped, groaned and looked about him. Even in his anxiety and dread of the man Elwes felt a spasm of sympathy.

"I am Lord Wentworth," called the foremost rider. "I want to know the truth. Did this man poison Sir Thomas Overbury?"

"You cannot stop the hanging," said the sheriff looking about him for the constables who were all waiting fearfully for an order to attack the intruders.

Weston looked balefully at Wentworth and his tongue came running round his lips in that familiar way which had chilled Elwes once. He turned towards the sheriff. The rope would have caught and bruised his neck if the hangman had not lifted the slack from his collar.

"You promised me I would not be troubled this time," Weston said reproachfully.

"So do I," said the sheriff boldly. "Stand back, sirs, and let us allow this poor sinner a chance for a better world than this."

"Nay, nay," called several of the riders, and one said clearly: "I am Sir John Holles, you may have me under arrest if you will, Master Sheriff, but I and my fellows were at the trial and we would know if the poisons given by this man killed Sir Thomas, or if it were a clyster, applied by some other persons that carried him off."

The sheriff said: "If you will not stand back we will hang this man at once!"

"What? Without prayers?" called Wentworth, and Elwes realized that this was where the questioners had the sheriff, for the parson was standing by like a mute, astonished by the affair.

"Discharge your conscience," shouted Holles to Weston, "and satisfy the world."

Weston said nothing but looked pathetically at the sheriff who signalled the parson to begin a gabble of unheard prayers.

"Nay, nay," shouted several in the crowd, "let Weston answer them"; and a brawny man began to roll up his sleeves to defend the prisoner if the hangman looked too ready to cast him off. That stolid figure, dressed in black, seemed unwilling to do anything except keep Weston sober. Lidcote muttered under his breath:

"I would this man were guilty," so that Elwes looked at him anxiously. He stood up once more in his stirrups, his buff coat breasting the cold air.

"I am Sir John Lidcote," he announced like an antique knight entering the lists. Even the sheriff seemed shaken by this and a spasm of recognition came over Weston's face. "Did you poison Sir Thomas Overbury or no?"

Weston's voice came thin and plaintively across the muddy waste, "I have said all I know to the Chief Justice".

Wentworth leaned from his saddle and held his arm across before Elwes. He seized Lidcote's hand and shook it firmly. "Nobly said, Sir John," he commented. "Ask him again."

Lidcote hesitated. He looked at the other riders, at their rich equipment, and their avaricious, politically-aware expressions. He shook his head. "Let the poor wight go to his rest in peace," he said in a low voice.

Elwes pulled back with him, pleased that Lidcote's intervention had subdued the cavaliers, for they could not pursue arguments with Weston while a relative of the murdered man stood by. Several of them seemed thwarted for they muttered and looked angrily at Lidcote as if he were a schoolmaster who had stopped them in some boyish game. While Elwes was still considering them a great shout surged up, making his horse leap forward, and a scream came from the women. He looked at the scaffold. As the parson had ended the hangman had launched Weston's body out into space upon a hurried signal from the sheriff who wanted no more arguments with Wentworth or Holles.

The body spun in the air like a child's puppet on a string, already it was inhuman, its lank grey hair moving in the wind like weed in a stream. As Elwes turned away some of the crowd were clamouring for keepsakes from the hangman. He looked about for Lidcote but the big man had ridden away, disappearing while the crowd had clapped and yelled its delight at Weston's death.

Sir Jervis went slowly back to the Tower, savouring the frosty evening air, noticing how early the haws and rowan berries were reddening. When he rode gently into the yard before his lodgings his wife was waiting, standing on the cobbles, her cap awry, her hands —also reddened by long years of washing and dairy work—were clasped before her as if inseparably joined. "Ah, Jervis," she cried as he dismounted, "Ah, Jervis," and held on to him, sobbing.

"Well, well," he said huskily, "I went but for a jaunt towards Kensington," but she continued to weep and he saw with a pang that two gentlemen were standing by his house door, looking at him with some sorrow, he thought.

"Alas, my love," cried his wife. "They have come for you."

And he knew that he had spent his last day of freedom idly, watching another man go to his death.

XXVIII

FRANCES HEARD A voice; she thought she was under the ice, surrounded by cold, dark-green water in which bright diamonds also swam, which occasionally knocked against her, and pierced her skin. The ice lay above her like the lid of an ivory box into which she was shut. She thought she was floating up to it and pressing her fingers on it, she could feel the cold, like a thousand needles against her hands.

"Frances!" said the voice and cracked the ice into pieces which were carried off on a tide. At last she had to open her eyes. Lady Suffolk stood at the end of her bed, she wore matronly black looped with gold chains, and had a severe mouth. "So," she said. Then: "You are even more wicked than I had ever thought." She spoke quietly, thrusting out her words at her daughter.

"You had the rearing of me," said Frances.

"You tried to commit murder!"

"I succeeded." Lady Suffolk looked confused so that her daughter could continue: "Ah, you mean the baby—or myself?"

"Can you imagine anything more wicked, more scandalous than that the Countess of Essex should try to kill herself, and in such a way?"

"Ah," said Frances, "it was not in high Roman style, was it? To throw myself down the stairs, wrapped in a wet bedcover?" She stretched her arms upwards. "It was calculated to kill the baby, but not me. I would never try to find such a way out of my troubles, mother."

"I am only too pleased you failed."

"And you had the privilege to carry off the baby. What was it?"

"A girl, very weak and not like to live," and Lady Suffolk began to cry feebly like a young lamb. She recovered herself almost immediately and sat on the big oak chair.

"We have called her Anne, hoping the queen might look upon you with mercy," she said.

"I want no mercy from that cow."

"Frances, Frances, you must seek mercy somewhere, perhaps of God."

Frances kept her silence. She allowed her mind to flutter like a moth on the window for she knew that Coke was after Robin and herself, even though it made his condemnation of Weston an irony: for if Overbury were killed by a clyster the serving man had not poisoned him.

Watching over her, Lady Suffolk remembered the child she had been and could not recognize Frances. Courtly rearing had prepared her daughter for an honourable life. She blurted out: "There's talk of dolls."

"Ah, you are back with the baby once more, mother."

"Terrible, carnal dolls, used for witchcraft, found in a cupboard belonging to an old man who is now dead. His wife declares they were made for you and that the dressmaker acted for you, running messages and so forth, taking you to the Black Mass."

"Alas," said Frances, "I would it had been as merry."

Checked, her mother sat awhile saying nothing then asked: "Do you wish to have your baby? Your sister is caring for her."

"Pish," said Frances.

Lady Suffolk stood again, her face firmed with determination to advise Frances even if she could not order her. She looked at her daughter's body, almost blue white in the blatant northern light. "Cover yourself," she said automatically and pulled the wolfskin over her. Frances lay back on her silk pillows and laughed, somewhat wildly, her eyes were set deeply into purple hollows.

"D'ye sleep at nights?" asked her mother.

"Why not?"

"Without your husband, and in a strange house? Watched over by a wool merchant?"

"Oh as to that, the alderman cares not for me. As if a poxy little alderman could hurt me by his lack of care. But he has," her ever-ready tongue crept out salaciously, "a pretty son."

"Beware, Frances. In all things you must be an honest married woman. God knows you got Robin Carr by deceit and dishonour, now you must cleave to him as he were your own true love, for ever and ever."

"For ever is a long time, mother."

"At least keep your legs closed until this trial be over." She scowled at Frances's plum soft mouth. "Painted at a time like this —why you will be cried for a whore by Fleet Ditch if you go on this way."

"Who sees me excepting warders and dolts of that order? As for the alderman's son, he's the best thing in breeches I'll have for a while."

"Frances," she plumped down again, on the bedside, her thickening waist diverting her daughter to a smile.

"Why, mother, you grow old and fat, you who ever had young knights at your chamber door, and within. D'you think I cannot remember how intrigued we were—Elizabeth, Catherine and I, to count the young men visiting you o' nights when our father was at sea?"

"Enough of that, Frances," said Lady Suffolk who had never attempted to hide her infidelities from her daughters and now wondered if they had set Frances on her dissolute way. "We must be sensible of time. I am allowed to see you for you need diversion, so says Coke. But this isn't only kissing time, it's time to plan and think on the future. The past is bad, and you have been wicked but with the aid of the king you might be brought off."

"Brought off. What means the woman?" asked Frances of the air, indulgently.

"Brought off the scaffold, girl—saved from death."

"What!" She was silenced as if she had never thought of death.

"Do you not know that a whole regiment of little people are due for execution for what you did? How can they fish for tiddlers and let the big pike go?"

"You mean I might be beheaded?"

"You may."

At last Frances was alarmed. Her face turned a sickening pale grey, her painted mouth stood out like a wound on her livid skin. "Can they kill me for't?" she asked, whispering. "Why, my great-uncle had men killed——"

"Killing a dangerous man in a backstreet brawl with a knife, or using a paid assassin is somewhat different from having a prisoner in the Tower poisoned, and he a well-known man, to gain a divorce through his death. Tell me," asked Lady Suffolk bitterly, spinning a loose thread round her fingers, "was your Robin worth it?"

Frances was silent a moment, looking up at the top of her bed where feathers curved into the dusty air. "No," she said. "What man is worth a farthing dip? I should have bedded him and any other man too and outwardly lived with my other Robert, safe honest Essex."

"Why did you not?"

"I could not allow that ham-handed wretch to touch me, and as respectability meant bearing his children—a host of little Devereux —I had to be free of him."

"And catch the bravest man at court?"

"Aye, brave in finery, but a laggard in all else. What did I see in Robin? It amazes me now. Was it his body, for I like a good pair of legs, mother, as you should know, or was it his Scottish voice, or his red hair? Or think you it was because he was the king's leman? I knew that if I captured him it would be like leading a unicorn home. He was a fantasy, a man yet no man, the king's male mistress. I had to have him out of perversity."

"And only virgins capture unicorns, is that it?" Frances did not answer.

"Can you prove he alone was in the plot?" asked Lady Suffolk sharply. Like a clock her mind ticked on whatever hour her voice was striking. "Let him take the punishment."

"He has not wit for anything except cards and hunting and bawdy tales," sighed Frances. "He would blush and stammer and be so foolish in a trial that no judge or jury would believe him guilty."

"And yet it's a likely tale that he alone killed Overbury. He was the man's best friend and had turned enemy, there is nothing so implacable or so vicious as an erstwhile friend."

"No," said Frances. "There is no evidence he was ever in the plot. He hated Mrs Turner and her companions. The only wrong he did was keep Overbury in prison by double dealing."

"Your father will not stand by you, my girl. You may have run to him in the past for succour but he would be damned afore you would get it now."

Frances's voice came out strangled: "I know full well he is afraid for his own skin. We have all known where the money came from these many years—out of Spain, or out of defrauding the royal accounts. Make him lie low, mother, and keep to Audley End, and pray to God the king never sees what a magnificent mansion he built out of what ill-gotten gains."

"Your sister would repudiate you if she could," said Lady Suffolk, determined to spare Frances nothing. "Catherine swears she knew you would end on Tower Hill."

Another unnatural laugh like water gurgling down a drain: "Tell Catherine I know her too well. She married a Cecil, thinking it would bring her a rich and clever husband but she stumbled on the fool of the family. Her William will never be the man his father was. Poor wight, he must be chasing his tail with fury at being allied to me."

"He has taken your sister to the country."

Frances stared longer at the ceiling, then said: "Begone, mother. You cannot aid me. Why make me suffer? I would rather be alone."

"You will take care what you say in court?"

"I will not say aught of you or my father."

Lady Suffolk sighed with relief. It was to hear this that she had come to Frances. She said: "Elizabeth will rear your baby, be glad one sister cleaves to you."

"Bet cleaves not to me. She seeks another slave to her mother love. Let her have Anne and keep her and bring her up as a housewife who will marry some fat Berkshire squire and never ride to London."

"If that is to be your daughter's fate it will be better than your own," said Lady Suffolk hastily. She was already half-way from the room.

Frances lay still hearing the slop-slop of her mother's gown over the stairs as she left. The house was quiet, for the alderman had placed the countess on the side away from the street. Her windows looked on to a grass courtyard. The only movement in it came in early evening when the alderman's son would chirp like a bird under her window, hoping his father was engaged on the city side of the house. Until then she would be lonely, unable to read, to sew or to play music. Frances felt suspended, waiting all the time for a rap on the door when the guards would take her to Westminster Hall to stand trial. She longed for that day, yet with apprehension, like an actor preparing for a big part on an unknown stage.

XXIX

Mrs Turner was like the sun. She dazzled the court with golden light. She wore yellow cuffs and ruff, a gown sewn all over with seed pearls and pieces of mirror which danced and shimmered in the low light of candles; and on top of her hair, which rose up in a great confection like a yellow cake, was a saffron coloured hat, audaciously plumed with small yellow feathers. A murmur arose from the court like a rising wind in trees. A special rostrum had been built for high-born spectators and all in it leaned forward, pushing with elbows and knees to have a closer look at the witch of Paternoster Row.

Ann Turner looked back at the court, eating up all the excitement, her fear was so concealed by jauntiness that she almost persuaded herself of safety. She leaned very lightly on the arm of Alderman Jones who was her involuntary host. He was anxious to give up his position for his sense of propriety was shocked by her. When a warder took charge of Mrs Turner he went into the back of the court where Sir Arthur Mainwaring was wandering about, his boozy face pale instead of red. He could not comprehend what crime his mistress could have committed which would land her here. "My Nan," he repeated, "my little Nan, what is't?" and his neighbours poked at him to make him quiet.

She almost danced on her way to the bar of the court, her feathers and mirrors as splendid as those of an acrobat at Bartholomew's Fair. Hyde, who was again the prosecutor, scowled at her. He was immune to dimpled smiles and the swell of her breast.

"Prisoner at the bar, how plead ye?" asked Coke, equally impervious to her impudence.

"Not guilty," said Mrs Turner, "and it please you." She almost curtsied and was caught on one foot, her smile coming and going like that of a whore entertaining a constable.

Coke looked at her, his hooded eyes coming off the paper for one instant. "Women do well to wear hats in church," he said grimly, "but not for their arraignment."

Mrs Turner was not nonplussed. She smiled, and looked about

her as if the Chief Justice might have meant another lady, then lifted her arms in a rounded caressing motion to unpin her hat. Staring around her with wide eyes she smiled again when one of the audience passed her a folded kerchief, and murmured "It will be laundered ere you have it again," before pinning it over her edifice of hair.

Coke sighed. He knew that the evidence against Mrs Turner would be long and dramatic. Beside him, Justice Crook was shuffling his papers. After the legal criticism of Weston's trial Coke hoped to retire a little in this one by having Crook take on some of the condemnation. Even Francis Bacon could not complain of the testimony which double damned Mrs Turner; and most of all had come from pretty Trunco Forman, getting her own back for all those days when her dead husband had dallied with Mrs Turner and other light ladies.

Hyde read out that terrible prosecution which listed all Mrs Turner's wickednesses, even her witchcraft against poor Mainwaring which was supposedly exerted while Frances was casting evil spells to captivate her lover. When Hyde told the court how the knight had ridden through a stormy night for fifteen miles in order to see his Nan, Mainwaring cried out in his drink-saturated voice: "Nay, nay—they had not that from me."

The weight of evidence was that to be brought by Mrs Forman. The dolls were carried into the court and with them, and even more sinister, a brass mould which had been used to manufacture them. As the mommets were congregated at the front of the court the whispering on the rostrum where the rich sat became so loud that Coke had to intervene and threaten to clear the court if there were not silence, at which all stopped but stared bright-eyed, determined not to miss the evidence of sorcery.

Half way through his deposition Hyde accused Mrs Turner of assisting the "late Richard Weston". Until then she had preened her gauze ruff like a bird of paradise caught and netted in that shabby dark court room. Her breath came out in a little hiss at Hyde's words.

Coke silenced the prosecutor by raising one hand. He inclined towards the prisoner, almost jubilant that she was taken aback. "What is't?" he asked benevolently. She had a small square of lace out and was holding it to her mouth.

"What? Is my man Weston gone?" she asked in a whisper.

Hyde nodded. "Hanged twelve days agone," muttered a warder

close by her. Mrs Turner swayed and might have fallen if the fellow who had told her the news had not held on to her while another brought a chair for her. She seemed to hang on its edge, her face downwards, her hands ceaselessly folding lace.

"What think you?" asked Justice Crook, his beaky nose pointing at the prisoner. "Is she well enough to continue?"

"Aye, she hath the devil knocked out of her now." Coke was delighted. He might have been looking all day for a weapon to flay Mrs Turner. This pert and pretty witch would not last long, he thought, and he looked forward to quenching the Countess of Somerset in just such a way when she came before him.

Hyde's fat white hands fidgeted with the dollies. He spread out a black cloth with cabalistic signs painted on it in white. Bacon rose at that one and went to inspect it.

"What think you, Sir Francis?" Coke asked, leaning before Justice Crook, who sat beside him.

"Why," whispered Bacon, "I think they be baubles to frighten babes."

Coke scowled at him. "This is no place for you, Sir Francis," he said indicating the judges' bench and Bacon smiled and returned to his seat. As he crossed the floor, Hyde was emphasizing the presence of the devil in all the acts of Mrs Turner, carefully including the countess in his condemnation.

"They knew him privily and with their carnal bodies, yes, with lust for damnation in their hearts," he cried, at which the rostrum gave a crack like the earth opening and swayed along one side. Those who sat there jumped up, their arms and legs outspread as they tried to escape their wooden box. Leaping over the edge, the ladies fell to the floor.

"The devil is amongst us!" screamed a white-haired woman with rings up to her knuckles. "He seeks his own!" Her gaunt and trembling hand flung outwards to the downcast figure at the bar. "He seeks Ann Turner!" After which there were screams and faintings and crashing on the rostrum as the bodies tight within it tried to escape. They plunged pell-mell into the centre of the hall. Dust quivered in the hot air. A jagged edge of wood stuck up awkwardly within the box like a punt pole left in the water when the boat floats on.

In the subdued silence which held the court for an instant, a warder's voice came creaking out like the sound of the splintering wood. He walked over to the rostrum and kicked it very gently, it sighed and settled on the floor, the benches inside were still intact and sturdy. "Poor workmen," said the warder.

Coke smacked his hammer down on the bench. "I will have silence," he shouted. "You, Master Clerk, keep order in this place or all will be removed and we will hear the case *huis clos*." Even the simplest wits knew that this meant behind closed doors. The sobbing women looked at each other and at the fallen rostrum.

The clerk stood up. "The seats are sound enough," he said. "Will all return to them?" There was no sign of the devil.

In all the noise, Mrs Turner sat still, her body shrinking within her gaudy dress. For her the trial had ended when she had heard of the death of her serving-man, Weston. She knew she could not survive if he had been hanged.

"The fight is out of her," Hyde whispered to Coke under the cover of the commotion as the spectators tested the rostrum once again. "We can make a speedy end to this trial."

"Play it out, play it out," said Coke. "I want this case remembered." He nodded at the witnesses' door. "Now play your trump card," he directed the warder.

Mrs Trunco Forman was called in.

"I have a book here, kept secret until now," jabbered Mrs Forman, producing a canvas bound bundle of paper from under her arm. "It tells all my late Simon's assignations, his meetings with great ladies, those who would have love philtres from him, and moreover," her cheerful girlish voice was subdued as she leaned forward, "it tells what ladies love which men about the court, who are not their husbands."

Coke took the book from the bench. "Continue with your examination," he said.

Hyde's unctuous voice emerged again: "And after the death of Doctor Forman, did Mistress Turner and the countess not come to you, weeping, and ask for the name of another magician who could aid them in their wicked deeds?"

Coke saw Bacon's mouth curl, the Attorney General was annoyed that Hyde could so blackguard the accused, again and again, condemning her by inference. Well, let Bacon object as much as he would, he *was* but Attorney General and this was not his case. Moodily, Coke opened the shabby book and put on his spectacles, while Hyde continued his dreadful, well rehearsed tale. The list of love-lorn ladies was first. Well, that would be useful reading. "... those what would have spells to estrange them from their lawful husbands and make others love them carnally". He smiled and scrutinized the top of the list. Forman's meticulous old hand had written "Lady Coke". He did not look for her hoped-for lover. He shut the book hard and pushed it to one side. His mouth was trembling and he forced it back into firmness. Lady Coke had been a rich widow and accustomed to her own way. He shook his head, putting the book aside even more definitely. As his gaze cleared and Coke was once more in control of himself and of his court, he saw the quizzical face of Bacon in especial clarity turned towards him, intent on the Chief Justice when all else had been concentrating on Mrs Forman and Mrs Turner. Can I have no secrets from that man? Coke thought and decided to burn the book that night, in the fire at his Gray's Inn Chambers. It was destroying evidence, but Mrs Turner would be found guilty without the name of his wife being flaunted in the court as a would-be courtesan.

As the jury returned Mrs Turner looked up at him. It was so long since he had noticed her face that Coke was quite shocked. She was white, and all the captivating smiles had long since gone. Ann Turner looked stern, as if she were the judge and he the culprit. She stood up, at which the court strained forward, their buttocks squirming on the hard wooden stools for which they had paid ten shillings apiece.

"My Lord Chief Justice," she said, her soft voice quite clearly heard at the back of the hall. "I pray you have mercy on me. I am a widow with children who need my care." Mainwaring half rose as if to admit that he needed her care more than any of her family. "I was ever with the Countess of Somerset," continued Mrs Turner, "and had been long time her servant. As God is my witness, I knew not that there was poison sent to Sir Thomas Overbury." She looked at Coke steadily. She could not hope that he would believe her, indeed all the courtroom knew she lied, and yet, for an instant, some were ready to shout her innocence.

The jury looked away from the prisoner as their spokesman said "Guilty". Mrs Turner sat down abruptly and cried. Not the discreet weeping that Coke found pleasant in a woman, but a loud bawling sound like a calf led to the slaughter. Coke covered his ears.

There was a disturbance in the courtroom for the audience was distressed by this unseemly behaviour in the prisoner and people were rising, crossing the floor and talking to each other. Some were passing clouts forward to Mrs Turner and plainly did not care if she did not launder and return these offered handkerchiefs. Over it all Judge Crook tried to be heard, but his plaintive voice was quenched by the noise in the chamber. "She hath had a fair and honourable trial——"

"Pish," said Coke louder than any. Many stopped speaking, thinking he would unloose another dramatic speech. "By God let her be hanged in her own yellow starch, seeing she hath such affection for it. As she brought yellow starch into vogue, she will end in it and so bring such frippery into general detestation."

As he went from the court, Coke saw once more the sharp face of Bacon, studying him as intently as some men study insects caught in a glass.

"How went it? How was she? What wore she? Tell me all."

"Why she made a good end as they say. My goodman was enraged for both 'prentices went off at noon to see her go."

"But what of her end?"

"A good one, as I said."

"In a ribboned dress and feathered hat? That would have pleased Coke."

"Not so, not so, but very plain and comely, excepting those yellow cuffs and ruff he made her wear. She wore black as if in mourning for herself. Aye, a black velvet ribbon bound back her hair and she had a black veil fell over her face. Certes 'twas a pity, she was a pretty lady."

"And the hangman? I had heard——"

"Aye, bad 'cess to him, he wore ruff and cuffs to match Mrs Turner but his were of coloured paper. He hoped to raise a laugh on the way to Tyburn but had nothing but groane from the crowd."

"How went she?"

"Why, by coach to Newgate and from there by cart. That two-faced whoreson Doctor Whiting, the chaplain, with her all the way, supposedly to comfort her but I'll wager it was to see what stories he could wring from her at the end, to send to his master, Coke."

"Did she weep?"

"We could not tell, in part from the press. I have never seen a crowd like it at any hanging, and in part as she kept her veil over her face. She wore black gloves and kept pulling at the fingers as if uncertain if they should come off for such a ceremony."

"I was told that many were moved by her end."

"Aye, poor soul. She was so submissive, so gentle in her movements. Why, when Whiting came after her into the cart he trod on her gown and she asked his pardon for't."

"What then?"

"They went to Tyburn at a fair speed and she tossed pennies to the crowd."

"How did she pray, being a Papist?"

"Why, the Lord's prayer, like to you or I."

"How died she?"

"Why, she stayed in the cart and the rope was put over her head within it and so the horse was driven forward and she was left hanging."

"Wasn't fearful to see?"

"Nay, nay. She did not jerk or scream or toss in the air but hung as neat as a dress in a closet, only swayed a little in the motion of the air."

"Didst catch a piece of ribbon or a kerchief to say you had it off her body?"

"Nay. There was such a throng of gentry and nobility about the scaffold we common folk could not come near, but nothing was taken from her. She was left alone, with a guard about the body and it was cut down in a moment or so, and carried away."

"How, carried away?"

"Why, Coke gave orders she might be buried in a churchyard and some of the royal servants were to hand and took the body off."

"Was she quite dead?"

"Quite, quite dead, quick as that," and the housewife drew her finger across her throat as if it were a knife.

The two women went slowly under the arch from the yard. Their looped skirts swung easily above the mud. Frances crouched back behind her window, her eyes like pits. She did not move for a long time. She had not thought to hear of Ann Turner's death so baldly, the same afternoon. Presently she began to walk up and down in the chamber, rubbing her wrists and making a crooning sound as if she were mother and baby both and longed for sleep.

XXX

FRANKLIN SWAYED THROUGH the door of the Duchy House as if he had come for a good meal in a tavern. He raised his sandy eyebrows when he saw the Lord Chief Justice.

"What is your tale, fellow?" asked Coke calmly, nodding his head at the prison chaplain to remain for he valued Dr Whiting's advice.

"Nay, I will make a bargain of that. I will tell you a story if I have a glass of ale and a pasty and these removed," Franklin lifted his hands and they saw the chains which held his wrists together.

"Would you deal kindly with this villain, Whiting?" asked Coke of the parson.

Whiting could judge the man, for he saw none but prisoners from one month to another. He hurriedly said: "Doctor Franklin is a man of good sense. He could be freed."

Franklin bowed exaggeratedly as a warder was sent to collect the keys. Franklin was disposed to talk five minutes later, chewing hugely and supping his ale with great breathy gasps. "But I must tell the tale my own way," he said, "no prying questions until the end."

"You ask too much," said Coke, annoyed by Franklin's impudence.

"Then have it your own way, question and answer like a catechism. You will get less like that but it follows the habit of the court, I dare say," answered Franklin lowering his big bull's head as if to read the spines of Coke's law books on the shelves before him.

"How and when met you with the countess?"

"Oh, as to a date, that is hard. It was a few months after Forman's death and must ha' been early spring, say March, for snow lay on the ground and yet the celandines were coming through."

"That would be two and a half year agone, in 1613."

"It was not the countess I met, then, but Mrs Turner who asked me to stand firm by a promise I had made to her, to assist her with poison if she so wished."

"To murder?"

Franklin moved uneasily: "All poison is not for murder," he submitted. "Some is to rouse carnal appetite or take it away, or to make a master sick so his workers can go their own way, or to make an old father think of death and so make his will. Poison does not always kill."

"Yet you are said to have killed your own wife, aye, and boasted of it in your cups."

Franklin laughed: "Not only in my cups. I know a good tale brings custom. Would any lawyer get a brief if it were not thought he could get guilty men off? Never—and so it is with my trade, masters. I believe truly my late wife died of noxious shellfish taken in abundance. It was self destruction I daresay, for she would not stop gobbling them, try though I would to stay her. It serves my purpose if credulous men think I put her in her grave."

"Mrs Turner came to you?"

"Let us say she had heard of me—poor woman—and thought I could help her skin the countess."

"Skin!" cried Whiting remembering too well the pieces of white kid bandied at Mrs Turner's trial which were said to have been flayed off a hanged man.

"Take off her what she had; and money she had in plenty."

"So you met the Countess of Essex, as she then was?"

Franklin smiled. "I did not say so," he replied, "but that Mrs Turner came to me and suggested I should work for the countess through her—by supplying powders which were supposedly made up by Mrs Turner but which I would compound."

"So that the countess could kill Overbury?"

"I will not have words put into my mouth," replied Franklin. "I have told you why Mrs Turner came to me. That is enough. She may have wished for drugs to soothe her babe to sleep for aught I know."

"Are you a papist?" asked Coke suddenly.

Franklin laughed again. "Why sirs, you are moithered by the thought of Spain, are you not? Seeing a don under every stone and under every bed? Nay, I am no papist. I cannot say I am much of anything, being careless of religion and the squabbles of churchmen. I would not have Spain overrun England of course," he added seriously, "but 'tis unlikely is it not?"

Coke, who was so anxious to unmask a Catholic plot, said nothing. "You met the countess later?" he suggested.

"Much later. She had arsenic of me and had a great desire for powdered diamonds which is the most costly way to kill a man as ever I heard——"

"Ho, is it a tool to murder?" asked Coke who had not heard of the weapon before.

"An Italian pastime," said Franklin, "or so I supposed, for none I spoke to had ever needed diamonds in that way, having a better use for 'em. But diamonds she would have. I could ha' found other means to kill a man but none she sought."

"Did the countess say she would kill a man?"

Franklin buried his face behind his cup. "I say naught," he said. "If she had no poison of me, how can I say what she wished to do?"

"Know you of a clyster?"

Franklin said: "You are talking of the one that fetched Overbury off?"

"Did you supply it?"

"I gave her nothing which would kill a man," repeated Franklin and Coke saw he would not be got at that way.

"Heard you any tale of Lord Somerset wishing to put an end to Overbury?" he asked, tacking round into the wind with this suggestion.

Franklin looked at the window studiously, where a pearl-washed sky was opening up. "I never met Robin Carr," he said deliberately.

"But did the countess speak of him when she visited you?"

Franklin shook his handsome leonine head: "But once she said he was in a taking as things were not despatched."

"Ha, what meant she? That he would have Overbury despatched from this life?"

Franklin looked at him mockingly. "It is for you to interpret my words, not I. I tell you them with as much sense as an actor who is given lines in a play."

"So the countess confided in you?"

"Why, she confided in all of us, even those who did not wish to hear her had a bellyfull of her plotting. She showed me letters I would not have read willingly, and told me tales of the court and king I could not repeat here——"

"What did you hear of Sir Jervis Elwes?" asked Coke realizing he was not going to go far with Franklin in this meeting, but remembering that Elwes was to be tried that same day.

"Elwes?" said Franklin, wrinkling his nose with a fair attempt at lack of memory.

"The Lord Lieutenant of the Tower."

"Ah. The countess showed me a letter from Elwes to herself."

"What said it?" asked Coke, not stopping to consider why Frances should have showed her letters to Franklin.

"I will write it out for you, the better to remember it," obliged Franklin. "It was a short note."

It was no more than two lines on the paper. Coke looked at Franklin's hasty illegible apothecary's hand. "What means Scab?" he asked.

"It is the code name for Overbury, used by those who put him down, such as Northampton, Elwes——"

"It is enough for now," agreed Coke, folding the paper after he had committed it to memory. "It serves our purpose."

He stood up.

"Well, masters," said Franklin in his jaunty impudent manner, "I have served you well. Do you serve me?"

Coke looked at him disdainfully. He hated prisoners who bargained for a pardon. "Doctor Franklin," he said heavily, "you will have to offer me more than this trifle."

Franklin looked up at his old, pale face. "Odswounds," he said roughly, "would you have me make up evidence?"

Coke did not answer. He motioned to the guard to take Franklin away. They heard his bellowing voice all the way down the passage, calling back to them with a hearty echo. "Another cup of ale, so please you. By God 'tis thirsty work pleasing the Lord Chief Justice, and I deserve it."

Whiting said mildly: "I would not believe a word he says for all he is so open in his nature."

Coke said: "You are a man of the church, Doctor Whiting, and should keep to your trade. I am sure there are souls to save in Newgate even at this hour," and the ponderous man took his hint and went away, leaving Coke to con over the brief letter Franklin had said came to the countess from Elwes, as if he were a boy learning his Latin primer.

His bowels were turned to water and yet he had been to the jakes at least six times this morning. He felt there was nothing left in him to come out, from the fever in his cheeks he knew his face was white and red, like that of a painted lady. He had to lean against the wall now and again to keep from falling. Was this what men declined into when death was not met in action?

There had been so many better ways to go: on a hunting field, tossing over a horse's head while a stag pranced up the hill ahead, mocking attempts to capture him. Or in battle. That was the way knights went in the old days, wrapped in armour as closely as he was wrapped in wool cloth, their visors down so that they could hardly have seen the enemy as they charged. It would be better not to see the face of the man who killed you.

"Go on," said his guard and nudged him forwards.

Elwes saw the door was opening like a little black mouth leading into a gullet, and from deep down the throat came a roar. It was the crowd muttering as he entered the court. Elwes looked in front of him, refusing to glance to either side in case he would see old friends, whose faces would unman him. He tried to walk with dignity, and succeeded, with his elderly face fixed to the front. He was conscious of his good black suit, bought especially for his trial, and laid over with silver lace. And there was Winwood aiding him, and all those sober faced city men, and the Pembroke faction, and with them the Archbishop of Canterbury, no less; could he be condemned with such great men at his back? He looked up and saw a man equal in rank to any of them, the Lord Chief Justice, Coke, who was trying to make him, old Jervis Elwes, an honest man, lower his eyes by glaring at him. Godshooks, did he think a Lord Lieutenant of the Tower was afeared of him? Coke had planned this trial more cleverly than any. He called for a chair for Elwes, "being a man who is accustomed to such civilities", and as the knight gratefully sat down he began a careful introduction which said nothing at all about Elwes.

It might have been a fairy story told for the pleasure of the court, for it was all about the great friendship between the late Earl of Northampton and the present Earl of Somerset, when the latter was still Lord Rochester. He quoted from several letters sent by old Henry Howard to the man who would wed the paragon of the Howards, sweet Frances. Northampton had said that pain was no more than the "cracking of a nut for the sweet kernel, or my niece's pain in the silver dropping stream of your pen".

"Enough of that," said Coke folding the letter in half, "I shall not have more of this bawdiness exposed in court." He finally came to a passage which spoke of "prompting the lieutenant with cautions and considerations," and at this all looked at Elwes who had been so firmly implicated by the instructions of Northampton. Letters were then quoted which Elwes had sent to the earl. Nothing in these suggested that Elwes wished to murder his prisoner, but they told Northampton how Overbury did, and what he said of the Howards.

"And of Weston," said Coke severely, "did you not admit knowing of his endeavours? For he said in his confession, and you the same in yours, that you met him carrying a phial of poison, and Weston said 'Sir, when shall I give it?' or words to that effect. You answered him plainly 'Let it be so that I know not of it'." He rested his arms on the bench and looked at Elwes grimly.

"Indeed," said Elwes, "as I told of this myself in my confession to the crown, you know that it happened, but that I did not have a hand in the prisoner's death. My best endeavour was to stand betwixt Sir Thomas Overbury and those who would harm him. In this cause I threw away those poisoned dishes from the countess and Mrs Turner, and kept him safe for many months."

"But those letters which you sent Lord Northampton tell of divers plots to do away with the man."

"I had to please my masters and did much out of fear, and yet I would not have him die——" his voice broke off for a second. "I will say this, I am guilty of neglect in my great office at the Tower, but I have never aided Weston and had indeed a mortal distrust of the man."

"And yet he came and went about the Tower, and was admitted by you as Sir Thomas's bodyservant when you must have known it was for a foul deed—and in the end, you acquiesced to the admission of one Reeve who gave the clyster which carried the prisoner off."

Elwes looked at Coke steadily while phlegm gathered in his throat. If he were not gentle-born he would have spat upon the bench, but he was no beggar brought in on a charge of vagrancy and must behave with respect for the law. He knew that Coke would condemn him without a proper hearing. He looked at the Clerk of Court imploringly, obligingly the man came over, trailing the sleeves of his gown across the bar as he bent to Sir Jervis. "If I speak slowly will you have time to write?" asked Elwes.

"The prisoner must not confer with the officers of the court in secret," said Coke loudly.

"Sir," said the clerk, who was growing tired of Coke's behaviour. "Sir Jervis did but say he would speak more slowly and I would write down his words."

"What, does he intend making a speech to the court?" asked Coke, amazed that any accused should square up to him.

"I have the right to defend myself I think," said Elwes in his slow Lincolnshire speech. Crook nodded before Coke could answer and so the Lord Lieutenant began his defence which was not only a defence and had many in the court agog as if it contained new revelations.

"My lord," said Elwes, "before I answer the charges against me, let me remind you of a speech I once heard from your own mouth. You said that when a prisoner stands at the bar, tried for his life, and comfortless, and has no counsel himself but a strong counsel against him; when he is perchance affrighted with the fear of death, and his wife and children are to be cast out of doors and made to seek their bread, you have always pitied such a man." He paused for this plaintive prisoner seemed so like himself. He knew he must bring the situation home to Coke and the court more forcibly. "I have heard you protest, my lord, that you would willingly hang in hell for saving such a man. My lord", he said slowly and quietly, keeping an even tone so that the sympathetic clerk wrote it all down, "you have not observed your rule in my case."

Coke looked up, suddenly haggard like an animal roused in its lair. He could not stop Elwes.

The prisoner's voice strengthened as some indignation crept into his speech: "You have paraphrased upon every examination, you have aggravated every evidence and applied it to me, so that I stand clearly condemned before I am found guilty. If I were so vile a man as you have suggested I would not be worth any consideration; but I hope you do not think me so. I will deny nothing that is true evidence against me. I would not tell a lie to save my life," he added proudly, lengthening his back so that many in the audience were near applauding him. "And for that reason I hope you will judge me honestly."

He then looked down and consulted a little notebook by his hand which contrasted oddly with the sheaves of paper upon the bench for prosecution.

"As to Weston," he said, "he was forced upon me by Lord Northampton and Sir Thomas Monson. I do not deny I was weak to allow him into Overbury's service but I had no thought that anything as evil as murder was toward at that time. I conceived him to be a spy, put there to report on Overbury and for that reason it was wrong to admit him and I do not deny I should have refused him, but having my office off Monson, and being told this was in order, I let Weston in. As to the poison," he continued while the court still whispered about his disclaimer behind his back, "when I first knew of it I cried out against it and made Weston throw it away and asked him to pray for pardon that he had thought on it. You may say I was foolish to believe a prayer in the yard would turn Weston from his course, but to tell truth I thought that if he knew I was apprised of his evil intent he would not go through with it. At that point," Sir Jervis said with a sour smile, "I was on the side of the angels, my lord, and, thinking more enmity than otherwise to Lord Northampton, I had determined he would not harm my prisoner, and to that end I had bars put on his windows that none would see that his health continued well, for no poison was introduced to him. My greatest fear was that he should become sick from confinement so that I urged continually for a doctor to visit him. I ask you, would I have done so if I were poisoning Sir Thomas Overbury privily?"

There was quite a hubbub in court which, Elwes was pleased to see, did not deter the clerk from finishing writing his sentence, sanding the ink, and conscientiously dipping his quill in for another paragraph.

"As for the countess's letters," Sir Jervis continued, "I have been asked if I did not know when she referred to poison in her jellies and tarts. My lord, she wrote so curiously, using code-words for so many things, I stopped translating her missives, sure I would learn nothing of import from them." He cleared his throat. "You will say I was unwise in this, and I would say so now that I am brought to this unhappy place, but would any of us act the same knowing we would be tried for our lives upon our actions?" A warder passed him a cup of water which Elwes took gratefully. "As to those letters from Lord Northampton," he said, "if you scan them carefully you will see that I promoted nothing but the countess's marriage with Lord Rochester. I knew not murder was toward. My duty, as Northampton told me, was to keep Overbury fast and from communication with any but his so-called best friend. I did this and no more. Indeed I allowed him visits from his men, Payton and Davies, which the Howards would not have sanctioned." He took a drink and went on. "I trust that the court understands that I made a full confession of all that passed without any asking it of me. I told the Secretary of State my story and it is owing to my doing this that there is a trial at all. My mistake was to become the servant of the Howards rather than of the crown. Consider my case," he said, making the first movement of his speech—a peculiar half-raised motion of his hands, "if a man knows not of a plot to murder another, but only suspects it, and thinks perchance it be part and parcel of his own imagination, should such a man be considered guilty if his suspicions are later shown to be founded on fact? Is he a murderer? Or has he abetted the murder out of ignorance?" He faltered and the warder touched his sleeve. The court hummed with approval of Elwes's speech. Coke considered as the prisoner sat down.

In order to persuade the court that Elwes was overstating his case, Coke immediately said that the situation was not one in which the prisoner was being tried for his life but the doubting silence which greeted this made him determined to so discredit Elwes that he would be exposed as a plotter. Coke leaned back in his great chair, placing his fingers together in a gesture which the officers of the court recognized as an attacking posture.

"If you were not privy to a plot, Sir Jervis," he asked "why did you have the fine hangings removed from Sir Thomas Overbury's rooms and hung in your own lodging two days before his death?"

Elwes looked surprised at this, and did not answer immediately, thinking back to those days before Overbury had been killed. He shook his head. His wife might have an explanation, or he could have maintained that he stole them as Overbury was removed to a more meagre room, but he thought slowly after making his forceful speech and when there was silence in court he felt that his audience was less sympathetic towards him.

Coke continued to look at Elwes, allowing some coldness in his eye or thinness in his lip to suggest that he knew so much against the man that he was amazed that he attempted to refute the evidence.

Crook, who ever seized the wrong moment to interrupt, leaned towards him and said, "My lord, it *is* mighty little evidence we have against Sir Jervis when all is said and done".

Coke ignored him and said very slowly, for he had noticed how Sir Jervis's style of speech had gained attention, "Your protestations and appeals to God will not sway a jury from considering the evidence, and to that you have not made any proper answer. To leave you without excuse, and to make all as clear as can be, here is the confession of Franklin." He touched the paper. The court rippled like a ripe field of corn.

Elwes looked confused and disturbed. How could he know what the apothecary might have said? How could he guess what the countess might have told the man about the Lord Lieutenant? Elwes looked wild and guilty which was all Coke had hoped for, he unfolded the paper carefully although he knew so well what it contained. On either side of the courtroom he could see lawyers shaking their heads at each other, suggesting that all evidence should have been presented when he had accused Elwes, and that he could not drag it into court at this stage when the prisoner had already made a speech of defence. Coke did not care. He meant to have Elwes. He continued in a pleasant conversational voice, as if the two of them sat over supper. The court was captivated by him.

"Franklin," he said again so that all knew the importance of what he was saying, "this poor man, not knowing that Sir Jervis would come to his trial today, called for me last night for he was sorely troubled in his conscience and said he could not sleep until he had made a confession. He said it was such a one—and these are Franklin's own words—'emphatically that the eye of England never saw, nor the ear of Christendom ever heard'." He studied the paper, holding it closely so that none could tell how long was the message upon it. "It tells of sundry terrible acts against Sir Thomas Overbury, against the law and against the crown of this kingdom. Pardon me that I do not tell all now, but it does not appertain to this trial and Doctor Franklin must prove much of it." He nodded at his own integrity. "But among other things there is this letter, sent from the man before us, Sir Jervis Elwes—incorruptible Sir Jervis—to the Countess of Essex as she was then. I will not add all the long tale about it, of how Sir Jervis came to write it, or what deed he committed after it. I will read the letter. It says 'Madam, the scab is like the fox, who, the more he is cursed, the better he fareth.' The scab," he said into the silence which greeted this, "was the plotters' name for Overbury."

Elwes looked about him, and studied the buff jerkin of the warder next to him, then said to the man very quietly: "But this does not say I was privy to the murder." The warder's shoulders moved, no more. Elwes looked at the calm face of Coke and struck his own chest hard with his left hand, tearing at the silver lace with his hanging little finger nail. "Now Lord have mercy upon me" he said as the babble of the court overwhelmed his words.

The jury stood upon a signal from the Clerk of the Court. As they shuffled out each one looked at Elwes, most thinking that they might easily stand in his place themselves. When they were shut up in their little room which was as close and airless as a coffin, the foreman wiped his face which was sweating with anguish. "What say you, gentlemen?" he asked and each said "Guilty" although they all added riders that they felt sorrow for Elwes and would they could have said otherwise.

Coke left the court before the stupefied Elwes was removed. He was unable to look longer at that honest face, so determinedly facing destruction. "Send Whiting to sound him out," he told the clerk as he passed from the room, half shedding his robe as he went.

XXXI

T HE LODGING OF Sir Jervis Elwes was not as comfortable as those rooms he had supervised for prisoners in the Tower; and yet it was on the better side of the Fleet, where sunlight came glimmering through the barred window between twelve and two. He was allowed books, candles, writing paper and visits from his wife and children. These last he would have preferred to be without for they were spent in weeping, and after they had gone Elwes would lie awake, afraid for their future.

"Have you no regrets?" asked Dr Whiting, who came to play chess with him. "Do you not have more to tell of the plot against Overbury which would show your true sorrow and confession?"

"I? Nay," replied Elwes, moving a pawn so that Whiting could capture his queen. Whiting fidgeted, his broad backside overlapping the stool which faced Elwes's bed.

"I have not sins," continued Elwes obstinately, "excepting that of wagering all my inheritance on false cards as I told you. I would repent of that."

"But think, Sir Jervis, on your part in this dreadful plot, can you not say more of that? More of the wicked deeds of the Earl and Countess of Somerset?"

"I have said all I know, it was all writ down ere ever these trials began, in the true confession I wrote for Sir Ralph Winwood."

Whiting scratched his bald head. "There must be more you can tell," he urged "and any confession would make things happier for you in the hereafter."

"I have no more to tell," persisted Elwes and studied his game.

A warder came rattling at the door with his nightstick and Whiting went unwillingly to answer it. He was sure that in a few minutes, if wrought upon with enough emotion, Elwes would implicate Frances Howard and her husband further.

The warder said, "He is to be hanged tomorrow, Doctor Whiting," nodding at the prisoner.

"Why did you not tell him before to allow him a chance to make ready for't?" asked Whiting, genuinely shocked that he would have to hurry a man through his death-bed repentance.

"I know not of that," replied the warder, "but 'tis a favourite trick of the Lord Chief Justice, thinking that if death be sprung on 'em quick, they tell much more."

"Will the prisoner be moved?"

"Not tonight. We leave in the morning at five or thereabouts."

Whiting groaned inwardly at the thought of another early rising. He returned to Elwes and sat down pondorously on the tiny stool.

"I ha' made my move," said Sir Jervis, who played slowly and with great caution.

"Sir Jervis," said Whiting, "I have news for you."

Elwes knew what it would be. His mouth gagged open suddenly, his droop-lidded eyes beseeched Whiting as if he were a fish caught on a hook and could only gasp for air.

"It is your execution," said Whiting swallowing, for he hated this part of his duty. "It is set for the morning."

Elwes put his head down on his hands and his voice came through them, muffled: "Now thanks be to God for that. This waiting is the worst of it," he said.

Sir Jervis Elwes was taken to the Tower by coach and put in the Lord Lieutenant's lodging until the time for his execution. The captain of the guard, who had served below him so recently, was embarrassed and insisted that Sir Jervis had been brought into his old home "as it was the warmest billet". Elwes assured him several times that he was sensible of the kindness of the action, and tried to be careless, yet his watery eyes kept wandering about the familiar walls, seeing the faded patch on the panelling where his wife's portrait had been hanging, and marks on the floor from the feet of the cradle which were rough-edged. He had not asked where his household goods had been taken. He recognized the chair offered him as one which the captain must have brought from the guardroom.

"Holla," called a man outside, "is there a fire within? My hands are quite froze off."

The captain looked out from the doorway, "You cannot come in here, fellow," he said.

"And what may hap if my hands be cold?" asked the rascal, "I could drop the rope."

"What! Is it the hangman?" asked Sir Jervis starting from his chair. "Let him in, let him in, by all means. He needs a fire as much as we do."

"Is it wise," asked Whiting raising his eyebrows at his assistant, Felton, a weak young man carrying an overlarge Bible.

"Is not a dying man allowed a last request?" asked Elwes. "Then mine will be to let that fellow in to the fire."

The captain shrugged and went to fetch the hangman and his two assistants. The man had the grace to look surprised when he saw Elwes.

"Your pardon, Sir Jervis," he said, doffing his cap. "I would not have come in——"

"Enough," said the prisoner, "I had hoped for a word with you before I die."

The hangman looked disconcerted, perhaps afraid that the condemned man might preach to him on his gruesome trade.

"I will say a few words ere I am hanged. I am allowed that, am I not?" asked Elwes.

"Indeed sir, the last words on the scaffold are much cherished by the vulgar."

"And I am told sundry of my friends may be on Tower Hill to see me off," continued the prisoner. "Will I be allowed to speak with them?"

Whiting would have interposed but the hangman looked resolute.

"As you wish, Sir Jervis. We would not hasten matters if you have business with the crowd. Are your friends peaceable, sir? There was a cruel scene at the end of Weston. I was not there but I am told he was questioned by the crowd."

"I will not make this a political occasion," said Elwes firmly, thereby aggravating Whiting, who had hoped for a speech decrying the Somersets. "Now as to my suit of clothes. It is, I think, your perquisite."

The hangman looked ashamed. "As to that, Sir Jervis, I would not be so bold, having met you like this——"

"Take it, take it," said Elwes, "I have need for no more than a winding sheet. But be not cheated on it. The lace alone was 30 shillings a yard from the mercer first on the left at Cheapside. Return it to him and he will pay you handsomely." He played with the small ruff about his neck. "Shall I take this off before I go out?"

"It is a cold morning," said the hangman, "unless you have a cloak with a collar I would not remove it too soon. Belike you will shiver if you do so and the crowd will think you are afeared."

Sir Jervis smiled: "You are man after my own heart, hangman," he said. "I would we had met upon a happier occasion. You are in the right. This fire is so warming, I will feel the cold."

"If you please," said the captain of the guard, "why not wear my cloak, Sir Jervis? It is made for the night watch and is of good wool cloth, well lined, and with a collar."

"You see," said Sir Jervis, spreading his hands towards the two divines, "how all men conspire to aid me?"

He removed his ruff and handed it to one of the hangman's assistants while the captain pulled the cloak over his shoulders and lifted the collar so that the prisoner's bared neck was warm.

Whiting said: "It is six."

"Oh, as to that," said the hangman, "a minute here or there is no matter."

"Where will you be?" asked Elwes, suddenly anxious.

"At the top of the gallows-tree, sir."

"So if I lift my hands, thus——?"

"I will understand, Sir Jervis."

"Enough of this," said Whiting, "it is time for justice to be done."

Immediately he felt that he had antagonized the other men in the warm room so he led them outside into the sharp cold morning. It was quite dark; stars showed above the masts of boats on the river. Tower Hill was grey and bare except for a few horses and the scattered figures of those who would go to every execution. As the group passed out of the Tower towards the gaunt black scaffold a horseman pricked forward, looking at them keenly under the brim of his wide Spanish hat.

"What, is that you, Jervis?" he asked. " 'Tis Max Dallison here and some more of your old drinking companions."

The captain did not stop him from shaking the prisoner by the hand.

Sir Jervis smiled, "I will have word with you in yonder place," he said pointing at the scaffold.

Sir Maximilian hesitated then drew back and allowed his horse to walk slowly after them. When they reached the gibbet the animal began to crop the grass about it while his master sat looking at his old friend with tears accumulating on the fierce moustache that showed he was a soldier.

Sir Jervis looked to the top of the scaffold where the hangman was perched like a monkey. "How far shall I mount?" he asked.

"High—to the fourth or fifth rung from the top," called down the man, his voice clipped by the frosty air.

Elwes slowly climbed the ladder, and hesitated. " 'Tis too tall for me. I have no head for heights," he said plaintively. "I would be one step lower."

The hangman said: "If you be lower there will not be a long enough drop to break the neck, Sir Jervis."

"I cannot bear this height."

"Go down, Sir Jervis," said the hangman, "and let my man alter the slope of the ladder and it please you."

Muttering under his breath, the prisoner climbed down again, revealing to all who watched that he must have some rheumatism in his left leg. The hangman's assistant carefully altered the angle at which the ladder leant to the gibbet.

Whiting blew on his cold hands. He had hoped to have all over and be away to his own house by now.

"Does it always take so long?" asked Felton, the other divine.

"Nay, most are not so calm or so prudent," said Whiting crossly. "This man is like an artillery sergeant, he must have all just so."

When Elwes was satisfied with the arrangement of the ladder he mounted it and the hangman clambered down a foot or so to place the halter round his neck, then returned to the top of the gibbet again. He would throw the ladder away when the signal came, leaving Elwes swinging in the air, while his two assistants jumped up to pull the prisoner's feet and so make sure that he was killed swiftly.

Sir Jervis was speaking and the crowd had drawn near to him. It was a strange close group about the high gallows, so few that they were made intimate by gathering near against the cold. Their intense faces were illuminated by the light of tall torches carried by the guard. "It is right and just that I should die," Sir Jervis was saying firmly, "for I knew of the plot and gave way to it, and might have prevented the death of Sir Thomas Overbury. I can only pray for those others who implemented this plot and most especially for the soul of the Earl of Northampton, and the Earl and Countess of Somerset." The crowd muttered and shifted from foot to foot. Whiting waited for more confession of misdeeds but Elwes said a few words with Sir Maximilian, of their riotous youth together. "How we turned night into day in low houses on the south side of the river."

Sir Maximilian's long dark face shimmered with tears in the hesitant light of the stars.

"I wish," Elwes continued, "to deny some things which were said by Lord Coke at my trial."

Whiting withdrew his hand from inside his sleeves, hoping that Felton would have an inkhorn and paper and could see to write, but all Elwes wished to refute was an accusation that he had not been a protestant. He looked emphatically at Whiting, and bent to the sheriff who stood by him: "I ask, without offence, is it lawful for any to question me at this time?"

"It is not lawful," replied the sheriff.

"It is enough. It is enough," answered Sir Jervis and removed the good woollen cloak lent to him a few minutes before, handing it to one of the hangman's assistants who laid it on the platform. He also put a few coins into the lad's hand and said: "Here take it. Spend it. It is all I have by me."

The youth began to cry so that his master looked down from the top of the scaffold and told him to bear up, for he would be needed very soon.

"Doctor Whiting, Doctor Felton, will one of you say a prayer for me?" asked Elwes. The divines looked at each other, each loath to speak. Whiting said, "I think it were best if you were to pray yourself, Sir Jervis, that being an office for which you are most fit."

"I will do my best then," said Elwes and seemed suddenly to be aware of the silence around him, the patient soldiers, the listening crowd, and the alert hangman. "My hearers," he said "I crave your forbearance. With half words and imperfect speeches I am chattering like a crane."

He prayed in silence for a moment while the cold wind blew against the spectators and against the rope which slackened and tautened under the skilful hand of the executioner. Whiting was for ending it all more swiftly and yet there was one more sigh before a sudden movement from Elwes's hand, and his body hung free before the silent watchers.

"Was not Coke your friend once?" Villiers asked Bacon unkindly. He was still unsure of the clever lawyer who professed such sudden friendship.

"He? Never. Excepting in the civilities of court. Nay, Coke and I are old enemies."

"Aye," said Villiers. "I had forgot, did he not steal a wife from under your nose? I have heard that both of you pursued her and her fortune but that he cut you out and bore her off like a knight at the lists in olden times. That must have chastened you, Sir Francis, excepting you are said to be of our perverse kind."

Bacon said nothing. He was content to let Villiers revile him, he was sure that one day this young man would fall and he could then crush him underfoot. Meantime, he must smile and smile and take all the insults Villiers could heap upon him, for the sake of destroying Coke, if no other reason.

"I would talk to you of the case," he said. "See, the rain has held off. Let us walk a while in the gardens."

Villiers allowed himself to be led down to the lower park at Royston where a gusty wind blew other strollers off the paths towards the luxury of a warm house.

"I hope it is worth this," said George, patting at his hair which was lifted by the breeze.

"Would you have Carr downed for ever?" asked Bacon bluntly.

"What mean you?"

"I mean this. Coke is hard after him and would have his head, but as Lord Chief Justice he is laying so many false trails, and is credulous to so many tales of papist plots, and is so hot after underlings in the case, that when the trial of Carr comes up, the world will be sick and tired of Coke's vehement denunciations and are like to let the great ones off."

He watched Villiers, calculating if this extravagant reasoning would sway him or not.

Villiers said: "Hm, tell me more."

"Know then that there are two arch conspirators left, Monson and Franklin. The last is a villain and deserves to die—and die he will for Coke is firm on the gibbet being the only end for these puny rogues. Monson is another case. He was a crony of the king once, was he not?"

Villiers said: "I know that his majesty has laughed at his drolleries and many times hath been drunk with him. He speaks well of Monson."

"Then he must be our saviour," said Bacon. "Arouse the king in Monson's favour, and he will enquire more particularly into the justice of Coke's dealings. Coke will have many depositions from

Franklin who truly breathes a new confession daily, and each refutes the last. Can you ask his majesty to be more careful in reading Franklin's testimony, for half of it will be arrant nonsense, although Coke believes in it."

"How? The king would never read such depositions in the common way. He leaves that to his judges, 'tis what they are for."

"In this matter let him read all," whispered Bacon. "He must read Franklin's foolish evidence and see what a zany Coke is making of himself and of the law."

George gaped at him and pulled his cloak closer. "How will I get the testimony?"

"I will have it sent to you by a special messenger who will ride through the night back and forth. All your work is to make the king read it."

"Mayhap," said George, who looked disturbed.

"Mayhap you are not so deep in his majesty's love as I had thought," suggested Bacon, uncurling his viperish smile.

"I hate such men as Monson," confided Villiers, "those old drunkards who throng the court and puff their heavy breath at me, and talk too loud and fall under the table."

"Aye, Monson was such a one," agreed Bacon, "but if he 'scapes the noose he will not be so ready to bully it in court again. Would it not look well in you, Sir George—a new man, an exquisite—far removed from the lewd vulgarity of these fellows like Monson, if you were to plead for one of them—for the love the king once held for him?"

"Carry that song further and I would be begging for the life of Carr," said George, jaundiced by the argument.

Bacon saw that he must not pursue it further, he added simply: "The death of Elwes aroused great feeling in the populace against Coke and his conduct at these trials. If you save Monson and the others by your pleas for clemency, you will be a hero to the crowd."

"Faugh, the crowd, it stinks," said Villiers. "And I know full well that the king has sworn not to meddle in this case."

"He swore so before this madness of Coke had revealed itself."

George puffed and played with the scented curls which hung about his face in the new fashion. "I will do what seems best," he said. "Send me Franklin's depositions and I will lay them where the king will come upon them. I will instruct May to beseech a hearing for Monson. I can do no more. Nay, I *will* do no more."

"It is enough," said Bacon who had not hoped for so much. He held out his dry-skinned lawyer's hand. Villiers took it briefly, as gentle a passage as the brush of a moth's wing. He left Bacon standing on the damp grass and walked quickly to the tennis court, his tall slender body inclining against the wind as he travelled.

Large spots of rain began to fall, spattering over Bacon's boots and his cloak of fragile silvery silk. He wondered if he could meet the king that evening at supper and promote his own fortunes further. He would send his man to seek a room in town. He began to run in a ricketty elderly way as the rain increased. For myself, he thought, I will sleep on any pallet and any floor if I can reduce Coke by staying here and blackening him. In spite of his wet cloak he was humming as he reached shelter.

XXXII

Robin lay in his bed at noon. His unshaven chin pressed down on his shirt, while he watched the movement of light on the floor; the pale luminous sunlight of early winter still came creeping into the room however he might try to keep it out with heavy curtains. He abhorred the light; was it because of a pain in his head, or the effect of the startling brightness on his tired eyes, or was it because he wanted it to be forever night and being night he might sleep and all the horror of the day would pass him by? For he had heard that Robert Cotton had been taken to the Duchy House to be held there until Coke interrogated him.

The passing days reminded Robin of a game played when he was very small—so very small, not more than five and closeted with the girls and babies in some dour Scots castle. It had not been home, for he had been on his best behaviour and in his best dress, a stiffly pleated affair with a skirt which spread over his stockinged legs like the frills of a woodland mushroom. He could shut his eyes and remember how the girls had ruled over him, pulling him about, and finally allowing him to join their game. It was a terrifying one. He had been made to stand with his face to a mossy damp wall where silver rivulets might have been made by water or by slugs. Behind him he had heard giggling and muffled voices and then he was told he must turn suddenly now and again and if he saw anybody move when he turned he could change places with the girl. Every time he stared round they were standing still; sometimes on one leg, sometimes with their arms extended towards him; but silent, still as statues, he never saw them move until one came close to him while he stood, frightened and facing the dark wet wall, and seized his shoulder so that he screamed and they laughed and then his nurse had come running in to rescue him. Robin was exactly as he had been then; facing the dark and unsure of what was happening behind him but aware of movement, only seeing ominous still figures when he looked round—and his dream was of moss and stones and the secretive dripping of water. He was trying to remember happiness, either those evenings with James, or his hours of lovemaking with Frances.

*　　*　　*

"Not guilty," said Sir Thomas Monson. In a recess at the back of the hall, Francis Bacon hugged his gown close to his thin body, against the cold, but also in delight. This plea by Monson was both the end and the beginning of a tug-of-war between Coke and the king.

James, who had been prodded by Villiers after Bacon had left for London, had finally asked Coke if his interrogation of Monson, and the evidence he had against the Keeper of the Armoury, justified bringing the man to trial. If Coke had been less zealous to discover a Great Catholic Plot and thereby restore himself in the king's favour, he might have paused to consider his own position. But Coke did not. He replied that Monson had come to trial, less to be proved guilty or innocent but rather to tell his stories about the countess and her part in the plot. He also hinted that Monson could tell of other plots against James's family. The king had pished and tushed over Coke's reply. He was irate that his Lord Chief Justice flouted his royal advice and that he had harassed a man who in retrospect seemed a hearty good fellow.

Meanwhile, acting upon the secret advice of Bacon, Monson sent off two cannon shots which echoed in Coke's mind. He asked that Suffolk be brought into court and that he should be asked two questions: Was it not Northampton who chose Elwes, not Monson? And had Elwes ever been anything more than a go-between, used to make Overbury aware of the strength of the Howards? In some ways Coke was relieved at Monson's arguments, the more the prisoner expostulated the closer grew the chance of a trial and for Coke trials were meat and drink. He relished them.

And so Monson stood at the bar of the court, his puffy red face swelling like a frosty sun as he was charged with aiding and abetting Richard Weston in the poisoning of Sir Thomas Overbury: in a warm angry voice Monson was pleading "Not guilty", for all the world as if he were an innocent man.

Hyde came to the floor of the court, his gown billowing out behind him in a thin wind which blew through an opening door. He coughed—his usual preparation for an attack; but before he could speak Coke held up one of his wafer-thin hands.

"I would have a word," he said.

Hyde looked annoyed, for he summoned so much spirit for his orations that he faded quite away if thwarted, like a bladder, blown up by a child, if lips are removed. He fizzled into silence and stared at Coke.

"I would lead the trial," he reminded the Lord Chief Justice, forgetting or refusing to call Coke "my lord".

"I must remember," said Coke, among other things, "that owing to royal clemency, Sir Thomas Monson hath been used most gently." His sliver-thin smile suggested that Monson had escaped the real rigours of the law through underhand influence.

In spite of his bluff and hearty manner Monson was no fool where his own advantage was concerned, and he opened his mouth to answer both counts, but, as Coke continued, he began to write anxiously upon a piece of paper, using a quill and ink loaned to him by the recorder who willingly passed both to the prisoner.

Coke thundered: "I will not have my authority abused by the court," but it was too late. Bacon guessed that Monson was scribbling his own arguments down and sighed with pleasure. He had not needed to do more than trundle Monson into Court like a battered wooden fair-ground effigy so that Coke could hurl his useless bowls at him. Coke thundered and the hearty face of the prisoner stared back at him with distaste. Bacon heard no more, he left the court and scurried back to his chambers in Gray's Inn.

Coke stridently claimed that Overbury's death was a revenge for the murder of that Sweet Prince Henry who had died before him and a hubbub arose in court so that he had to strive to keep silence, unable to shout down the crowd or to make his arguments heard across the excited courtroom. He signalled to the Clerk of the Court and to a sergeant of the guard who banged his staff on the floor for five minutes before the audience quietened.

"Sir Thomas Monson," cried Coke, his voice unnaturally loud after grappling with the noise a moment before. "Think you that Mrs Turner and Richard Weston were filled with grace and confessed their sins, aye, so that their souls smelt sweet in heaven, and you have not shown this kindness to the court?"

Monson said nothing but looked straight at the bench. It was unnecessary for him to answer that both Ann Turner and her servant had ended on the gallows, brought there in part by their own confessions and because they had not opposed Coke's powerful accusations.

"I will not have this court played with," called Coke down the room. "But you will be sent to the Tower, where you were imprisoned at the first, and where you may be kept under greater constraint."

Monson's lips curled under his moustache. It might have been a smile, for his Yeomen of the Guard in the Tower were loyal to him and indignant at his imprisonment. Unless Coke had freed him, he could not have given Monson a greater benefit than that of sending him back to the Tower.

Coke looked down at the paper before him. On top lay a letter from Suffolk who had been questioned on Monson. The Lord Treasurer's reply had not implicated the prisoner but Coke felt constrained to read it out, as if it were proof of the keeper's guilt. He held up one hand, and the crowd, who had been silenced by his outburst before, were so quiet Coke might have sat in an empty room.

"Sir Thomas Monson," he said, as if the prisoner's name were part of his disgrace, "sent to know two things of the Lord Treasurer, the Earl of Suffolk——" He paused, as if wondering whether to point out that Suffolk was the father of the countess who had been castigated throughout the trials, but he continued: "He asked if the late Earl of Northampton had not chosen Sir Jervis Elwes to be Lord Lieutenant of the Tower. He also asked if the condemned Elwes were not used as an instrument for the Howards, bearing no part in the poisoning." Even to Coke this sounded ominous and he wondered if he would have been wiser not to read out Monson's queries, they so clearly eradicated blame from the dead Elwes. "I have an answer from the gentle and reverend Lord Suffolk," he said putting on his spectacles. Accustomed to the veneration with which audiences regarded any letter produced in court, he was not surprised by the quiet that followed. If Bacon had been there he would have realized it was the heavy silence that precedes a storm. Coke was less percipient and read out Suffolk's reply to the questions: "I have heard that Sir Thomas Monson thinks that I can clear him, but I know nothing of him to accuse or excuse him; but I hope he is not guilty of so foul a crime." He stopped, savouring the last words. "So foul a crime," he repeated looking steadily at Monson while the court also thought about Suffolk's letter. Coke was sure the indecision of the reply suggested that Monson was a murderer, the listeners considered that it absolved Monson from blame. Nothing was said. Into the silence Coke threw: "You hear that Lord Suffolk will neither excuse nor accuse you?"

He might have been alone with Monson, who answered: "I never accused Lord Suffolk of any crime because I know he is honourable, all I asked for was an answer to those two questions— who appointed Elwes? What part did Elwes play?"

Coke's pale face reddened with indignation as Monson's eyes stared him out. He said swiftly to the prisoner: "You shall hear more of that in good time. Why do you not acknowledge your sin?" He wondered if his basilisk face would encourage Monson to a full confession.

It did not. Sir Thomas looked more stubborn than before: "I would if I were guilty," he said. "But I am not, so I renounce the king's mercy, and God's, because I am innocent."

A ripple quivered across the court at this disobedience from the prisoner. Coke thought he would choke, his ruff seemed to grip his neck too tightly as he half-raised himself from his seat on the Bench and shouted at Monson: "You are popish!"

There was a crescendo of sound in the court, as many stood up and called to the bench that Monson's religion was not in question, or else shouted that the Lord Chief Justice should stamp out the papists. Elated by these few cries of encouragement, Coke held up his hand once more and when the excitement subsided, he said:

"Oh, Sir Thomas Monson, I am not superstitious, but other papists have been condemned where you stand now and you will follow them."

Judge Dodderidge tried to speak, his frail voice making little impression on the court until the sergeant banged his staff again. All the judge could drop into the ocean of silence was a word of advice, "You speak like an aetheist if you renounce God's mercy, Sir Thomas."

Monson shrugged: "Why should I fear if I am innocent?" he asked, almost nonchalantly.

Hyde jumped up, his face suffused with fury, for he had hoped to denounce Monson and have the jury swayed against him by this time. Instead he had been sitting mute while Coke had thundered out his accusations. "I protest, I protest," he shouted, his voice shrill with anger and excitement. "My Lord Chief Justice, this man Monson is as guilty as the guiltiest. I have looked into the matter, and I know."

Monson was as tenacious as a bulldog, he bent his head to look at Hyde as if the prosecutor were beneath him: "Protest away," he suggested, "there never was a man more innocent than I, and in this I will die innocent."

Coke realized that he could not continue the trial. He said: "You will return to the Tower, Sir Thomas, but not by coach as you were brought here. You will be walked through the streets that you may suffer the indignation of the crowd."

Monson half opened his mouth then shut it again, resuming his pugnacious face but the clerk of the Court came up close to the Bench so that Coke and Dodderidge had to lean to hear him.

"My lord," said the clerk, "consider that while he looks hale and hearty, Sir Thomas Monson hath an ague and rheumatism. It is snowing and he might take sick if he be sent through the streets in this inclement weather."

Coke looked suspiciously at the prisoner who wore a light velvet gown, as he had been brought by coach and expected to return to his prison, wherever it might be, in the same way. He could not believe that this ruddy faced man was ill. He did not concede.

"Nay," he said to the clerk, "let him suffer somewhat for his misdeeds."

Dodderidge looked unhappy: "Perchance we should think on his health——" he began.

"Pish," said Coke. "Look at him watching us! There is naught the matter with him. It is a trick to try our strength. Let him walk back to the Tower." He enjoyed the thought of Monson bareheaded in the snow, his light gown speckled by white and perhaps smattered with a rotten egg or two as the urchins in the streets used him unkindly.

Monson was walked to the steps of the hall. His Yeomen of the Guard handled him carefully.

"Never fear," whispered the sergeant. "We are happy to have you safe amongst us once more, Sir Thomas. Aye, there were merry times when you were Keeper of the Armoury."

"There will be merry times again," said Monson. "Eh, my lad? My purse is not empty and your thirst is as great as it ever was."

The sergeant laughed and looked from the doorway at the whitening street. Monson shivered and the cough which he had restrained so well in court began to break into his throat.

"A walk to the Tower would be the death of me," he said, "I would not need the gallows like poor Elwes."

"Aye—poor enough," agreed the sergeant turning his grizzled head this way and that to see through the snow. "And yet so foolish he deserved what came to him. We all thought so at the Tower. Well-meaning, but knew not what time of day it was." He nudged Monson's arm. "See here, sir, my lads have a litter by the corner of the street. We cannot bring it up as the Lord Chief Justice's men might see it, but if you can make your way there——"

"Will Coke not watch my progress as if it were royal?" asked Monson sardonically. "He longs to see me humbled by trudging through the streets while all the little boys pelt me with dung."

"He will not have that satisfaction," replied the sergeant, "and he will be by the fire betimes, warming his toes and never venturing out before the snow be cleared."

Monson accepted the arm of the sergeant and leaned on it as he ran. Closed in the leather box, listening to the muted sounds of footsteps, which were stilled by the snow, Monson coughed and coughed again, but as he exploded into his cupped hands he smiled, he knew his brave lads of the Tower guard would not let him suffer. He suddenly leaned towards a young soldier who was marching by the side of the litter; the right side of his doublet, which was away from Monson, was frosted over by a thick crust of snow.

"Tell me," said Monson, his voice jerking with the movement of the litter and his own hoarseness, "what became of the so-called magician—Franklin?"

The boy turned towards him, numbed by cold; he hesitated before he opened his stiff lips. "Why, Sir Thomas," he answered, "he hath been dead this week past. He went at Tyburn and cried his innocence to the crowd."

Monson nodded. "So do we all, lad, so do we all," he said.

XXXIII

"I WILL GIVE Coke a fine Christmas gift," wrote Frances, "for I will confess." She had sent the letter on 20 December and since then Robin had not heard from her. He had not believed her. It was now February 1616: "Filldyke indeed," said the guards watching the rain bounce upon the cobblestones all day and all night. Their earlier joviality was muted by the long time they had spent at the Cockpit. Some of them had been kept there for the Twelve Days of Christmas and resented Robin, although he could not see why they should be so surly when it had been so long since he had seen his own wife and family, he thought briefly of the baby Anne who had been swallowed up by the Howards.

Robin yawned, rubbing his tangled hair which had grown thickly round his ears, and allowed his page to play bawdy songs on the lute. When he heard a rumble of a coach below the window he craned out to see it, annoyed by his own pettiness that so small an incident could excite him. It stopped by the door, its heavy body unevenly distributed so that one wheel rested in the gutter. From it leapt a thin man with some air of importance. He glanced up and Robin could not retreat quickly enough to avoid his eyes. The visitor was as crisp as an autumn leaf, his coat sponged and pressed to nicety, his thigh boots glowing with care. He must be for Robin.

Suppressing his excitement, Robin went to the fire and affected a casual lounging upon his chair, then thought that looked too careless and went to the table, laying out paper and ink as if caught at his accounts; and yet this seemed too cold and too mercenary; he would be changing, and could greet the visitor with an easy "Hold there and I will be with you," as he pulled a clean shirt over his head. Yet that seemed as if he had to change his dirty clothes or as if he thought the man worthy of better dress than that he wore already. Caught in indecision, Robin was standing halfway across the room as if in flight when his page announced, "Sir George Moore," and the visitor came straight in upon him, sniffing at the musty atmosphere.

"My lord," said Sir George, bowing as if Robin were still of some consequence.

Robin waved him to a chair and called for wine: "Indeed you are too kind, my lord," remarked the man, "I call on my way to the Tower."

"To the Tower," repeated Robin foolishly.

"My lord, I am the new lieutenant, Sir George Moore."

"Forgive me, I did not know there was a new Lord Lieutenant of the Tower." He almost bit his tongue as the words came out, remembering that this man must be successor to that Elwes who had been hanged.

Moore spread his hands as if his authority were of no importance, and sat easily in Robin's own chair, where he crossed his legs and smiled faintly. "I have two messages for you, my lord," he said.

Robin realized that this was the moment for which he had waited so long. "So, so," he answered casually, determined that this man should not see how happy he was to return to court.

"The first is an answer to that message you sent to the Lords Knollys and Hay, my lord, in which you promised revelations of the Overbury plot which were for the ear of his majesty."

"That is so, for his majesty alone."

"The king hath sent his reply, my lord. He says that it is unfitting to pass by the commission and go direct to his majesty. He advises you to deal with the Lord Chief Justice if you have any information on the death of Sir Thomas."

Robin stared at him: "Have you no letter from the king—no privy communication?"

Moore smiled easily: "His majesty was in some haste when he saw me."

Robin sighed and said: "What is the other message?"

"His majesty would have you removed from these lodgings——"

"Now certes, that is welcome," cried Robin heartily. "I tell you, Sir George, I am sick of these walls and long to be about Whitehall again. What said the king—no word of having missed me?"

Moore's smile crept away like an animal going into hibernation. "My lord," he said, "I am to remove you to the Tower."

Robin looked at him again. After a moment he said: "You now to whom you speak?"

"Aye, my lord."

"I have the king's word that I will return to Whitehall."

"Sir, it was the king ordered you to the Tower."

"The traitor's gate?"

"My lord, we will not go by water. That is why I brought a closed coach with me."

"I am to go now?"

"Upon the instant my lord."

"I cannot go. I am not ready."

Moore had recovered his smile, as smooth as that of a fashionable physician.

"My clothes, my furnishings, my——"

"They will come close behind you, my lord. Indeed you will not have need of much in that place."

"My friends——"

"Sir, I find that friends know soon enough when one is taken in adversity."

Robin's mouth was like sand. He rolled his tongue round it. "I am to go at once?" he asked again as if he did not believe Moore.

"Aye, my lord." The fellow was unmoving and Robin was beginning to hate his curious ever-present smile which was as defensive and secretive as a mask.

"Am I to be tried?" asked Robin at last.

"Perchance—in good time, my lord."

"What of my wife?"

Moore did not answer but continued to smile at Robin.

"Then," he said sulkily, "since needs must I will come with you."

"It would be wise."

Robin noticed the lack of "my lord" but resolved not to comment on it. He had no alternative. He called to his page and told the boy to put a nightgown and a shirt in a bag, which would be taken at once, and then to pack any other things he might need in the Tower. He remembered how Tom had been taken directly from the council room dressed in his gaudy light summer clothes without a knife or plate to call his own. He hesitated: "Will be safe in the Tower?" he asked. Moore took his meaning at once.

"Safer than here, my lord," he said. "There are none can come near to harm you there."

"I must have all I eat tasted, and no doctors allowed."

"My lord I will be most circumspect."

Robin seized the fellow's arm, crushing the fabric and twisting his spare flesh.

"Sir George, are you honest?"

"I hope so, my lord."

He had to be content with that. He knew of none who would have him dead, and yet—had Overbury? He thought of all his expostulations to his friend, those promises of early delivery from prison, letters which had told Tom that a week, or a month would see him out of the Tower and safe from harm.

"Coke will keep me there," he said bitterly.

Moore's smile altered to an expression of surprise. "Not Coke, my lord, but Sir Francis Bacon. I think it is safe to tell you that the moon of the Lord Chief Justice is on the wane."

"Is he removed from office?"

"Not that, but if you and the countess are to be arraigned the Attorney General will act for the prosecution, which is to say Bacon. He has been appointed to the commission. He cannot supplant Coke but has overtaken him and the true reins of justice are in his hands."

"Coke is out of it?"

"He is not absolutely, my lord, but he has been diverted to hear the gossip of tailors and cooks."

Robin could not understand if this was a blessing or no. He said determinedly: "Bacon has ever been a friend to me."

"Sir Francis is the intimate of many," replied Moore thinking of the close relationship of Bacon and Villiers. It was not his duty to alarm his prisoner. He nodded at the page and led the way from the room. Robin bumped down the staircase behind him, disturbed at going to the Tower but pleased that he would leave this airless house and travel through the open streets, if only for minutes. He was to be disappointed. The coach had leather curtains which were fastened shut with clasps, and Robin made the journey in a dark as deep of that of the room he had left behind. He heard the salute of a guard as the coach went through the Tower gateway and the ominous silence of the place, divorced from the rancorous sounds of the city without its walls.

On the second day of his imprisonment Robin sent another letter to the king. In spite of his realization that he should placate James, try to win him with remembrances of their happy times together and then offer submissively to leave the court, the letter came out dictatorial and venomous. He suggested that he could damage James with tales of corruption and of old plots in foreign policy which the king had planned in the past. Like Franklin's confession, Robin's threats of "I could if I would," damaged rather than aided him, and he knew it, and yet, when he sat to compose himself and to write sensibly, he found it impossible. Well, well, if all be for the worst, so be it, he thought as he watched the relentless rain saturating the gutter.

Rawlins came into the room and hesitated before him. "The countess," he said.

"What of her?"

"She speaks of you, my lord."

Robin's eyes moved curiously, towards the window, to the roof and back to the window. He would not look at Rawlins. He finally said in a coarse Scots accent: "Say ye so, say ye so? Oot wi' it, mon!"

"On—on January the eighth," Rawlins had it off pat, he had kept the information oozing in his head for a long time.

"What said she? By God, what *did* she?"

"She confessed to Coke," his head bent low and miserable, Rawlins was regretting his admission.

"Look at me," screamed Robin, and hurled the chequers board at Rawlins, striking him on the knee, not enough to hurt, but the noise was like a falling tree in that small room, while the chequers went bounding and rolling over the floor.

"I know not—no detail—naught," said Rawlins, confusedly as he knelt down to pick up those draughts which had come his way, piling them in his hands like outsize coins. He held them out to Robin, a suppliant.

"Go to hell then," cried Robin and turned his back, his shoulders trembling as he faced the empty sodden green and the tireless walking of the warders from station to station, their voices piercing the Tower as they saluted each other.

"My lord, pardon me," said Rawlins. He did not wish to leave Robin alone in this grim place, and yet if he were dismissed what else could he do? Secretly he believed that his master might yet win back his position with the king or something very near it—that summer would come, that maids would laugh, that purses would be thrown his way as before and that he would be able to press among the minor gentry while the earl and countess rode to Whitehall in a golden coach. But now he was miserable.

Finally Robin said: "Go now and come again," grudgingly as

if Rawlins were an old dog he had not the heart to cast off. As the man bowed his way out Robin thought how much more lenient he was than James. He favoured Rawlins and did not dismiss him utterly for a momentary lapse. It might be fateful; if he, Robin, were kind to Rawlins, the king might be kind to him in his turn. Love was all links like a daisy chain. He forgot that chains snap and fall, that flowers fade, and that Tom Overbury was quite dead.

That same evening brought a message from Sir George Moore. The Lord Chief Justice had asked the Earl of Somerset to appear before the commission which was enquiring into the death of Sir Thomas Overbury. His lordship was to visit the commission on the morning of 8 February. Sir George was happy to put his coach at Robin's disposition.

"We must trap the countess first," Bacon said in a low voice so that they had the atmosphere of conspiracy about them. "If Somerset—Carr—is innocent of all but stupidity, then we must urgently have her found guilty that he might be implicated, for as I say, he is an accessory after the fact. As Weston was found guilty to bring the others to court, so she must be found guilty to bring him in."

Ellesmere said shakily: "Are we sure the king wants this?"

Bacon said: "I have correspondence with his majesty," which was news to Coke. "He knows as we do that his brave Robin is a fool but not a murderer. The king wants to keep him safe out of his way."

"Executed?" asked Ellesmere.

"Found guilty," said Bacon evasively.

"Speak not in riddles," growled Coke, but Bacon gave a half smile to silence him. "Then we are agreed, my lords," he said, rolling up those long scrolls of haphazard evidence which Coke had collected over the past months. "Bring her in, and him in, and forget the others."

"Monson," said Coke.

Bacon scowled. "My Lord Chief Justice," he said, "the king was wroth when he heard that you denied Sir Thomas Monson's coach to take him to the Tower. Did you not know that Monson is very sick? He was a close friend of the king and once delighted him by winning a match of English against French falcons. Did you know of that?"

Coke did not know, for Bacon had only heard the tale a few weeks before. He had conveyed the story to James who was lamenting Monson's imprisonment as if the Keeper of the Armoury were an old friend. Bacon enjoyed this twist to the tale of Coke. He added, "By great fortune the yeomen who attended Monson at the trial had been in his service at the Tower, and they prevailed upon Sir George Moore to lend a litter for Monson to be carried to prison. He was still grievously sick," watching Coke's shocked face. Bacon added in a low voice: "Indeed his majesty commanded his own physician to wait on him, and de Loubell visits the Tower daily."

Coke said angrily: "I am amazed that de Loubell dare take drugs into the Tower after the clyster came by way of his boy Reeve."

"Ah, did it so?" asked Bacon, almost whispering. "But you would have it was Weston or Elwes, or e'en the Earl of Somerset, and I have here your own notes, stating that the countess's maid carried a powder into the Tower from Carr, supposed to come from Killigrew, and it was that carried Overbury off."

Coke wrestled with words but before he could bring them out, Ellesmere said, as Bacon expected: "My lords and Sir Francis, let us stop these conjectures, the truth of the matter is that Overbury may even have died a natural death as the doctors say, but that several hands wished to have the killing of him and now his majesty wants some criminal intent laid to Carr's door."

"In a nutshell," said Bacon striking his hands together. "In a nutshell. How happy that our revered Lord Chancellor should be so clear and expressive!"

Coke said: "I still believe in a Spanish plot."

"Is that why you had some old women at Deptford frightened out of their wits?" asked Zouche shrewdly. "Some of your so-called confessions were oddly extracted. None would blame a barber who pulled out rotten teeth but it seems that the Lord Chief Justice pulled out good teeth too."

Coke looked round at their unsympathetic faces. "You will have Somerset here in the morning," he said. "Then you will see there was a papist plot," but his own voice sounded unconvincing. He felt ill. He longed for his bed. He wished he did not have to collect information from Robin Carr, whom he had ever despised. And yet, as he saw Bacon's swift neat movements gathering up and casting aside all the notes he had taken months to prepare, he was, despite his sense of injury, oddly consoled by the thought that even if Bacon considered a man innocent, he could somehow make him appear guilty with more guile than Coke could use himself. It seemed Bacon had the ear of the king, and that he and James conferred together on the case. Ah well, thought Coke, let them do so. I am well out of it.

XXXIV

"WHAT SHOULD I do?" Frances asked Bacon, throwing out her hands, palms upwards in a gesture of supplication. He did not fail to notice the bracelets which lay upon her wrists like deep cuffs, half hidden by the demure sleeves of her gown.

"Madam," he answered, "it is not for me to tell you. I am the prosecutor in the case. It is not my place to advise you."

"Then why am I brought here?" she asked showing her teeth at him, annoyed that she had humbled herself before a man who now seemed useless. She almost stood up, lifting up her skirts and half-rising, then sinking back immediately. "Yet as I am here there must be a purpose for it," she said consideringly.

Bacon did not tell her, as Coke had, that he had the disposition of her coming and going, he had realized that an appearance of independence was still important to the countess.

"I have a note upon the questioning of Franklin," he answered clearing his throat.

"What does Franklin matter? He is dead," she replied.

"His deposition is still to be considered, as are all the confessions of those who have—suffered in your cause."

She wrinkled her arrogant nose at him and thrust out her Howard chin. "As to that, they came to me of their own free will, brought by promises of reward."

"Some knew not the importance of what they did?" he suggested.

"Ha," she said throwing back her crest of hair which was only half concealed under a filigree cap, "that is a coward's excuse—that they knew not what they did——"

"You would not use such an excuse yourself, my lady?" he asked, curious.

"I, never!" She studied him, her eyes darting under those heavy white lids like birds in cages. "I am no fool and would never plead that as a reason to be excused punishment."

"Others have ended on the gallows," he commented.

"Others, aye, and of my family several ended at a block on Tower Hill. Little necks, ladies' necks, snap off so quick, Master Attorney General. Why," she added closing her eyes, swaying a little like a drunken whore, "like a flower stem, one blow, it falls off." She lifted her hands away from her neck and opened her eyes very wide. "An end to it," she added, briskly.

She might have been a seamstress snipping off a thread with her teeth as she clenched them together and stared at him. Her glare changed to a demure expression as she settled in her chair, the excitement past, Frances would play soft again. She might have been that twelve-year-old child first given in marriage to Essex, when she pouted even her voice was that of a little girl, lingering over long words while she shimmered her eyes at him. She was momentarily a figure in a masque, Bacon thought, called "innocence". She changed so much from one word to another he was left aghast and yet admiring. He wondered which character she would assume at a trial.

"I must tell you that your husband is being questioned also," he reminded her.

For a second she looked surprised, as if uncertain of whom he was speaking, then she laughed: "My good dog, Robin," she said. "He will not help your case, Master Bacon."

"Sir Francis," he said automatically.

She said nothing but her shrewd eyes told him he had lost a point in the game with her. There was no help for it. In half an hour he had not gained anything from Frances. She may as well return to her lodging and continue to devise her schemes until the trial. Yelverton must be aiding her, for he was the Howard's lawyer. Bacon bowed her out of the room and watched morosely from a window as her coach was brought, palpitating with rain, towards the door of York House.

While he stood there he was surprised to see a closed litter enter the courtyard, carried by Tower warders. He intended to caution the guard, and yet he knew he could not run down the stairs in time to stop Frances leaving the building as her husband entered it. Here she was, standing under the portico, a heavy travelling cloak upon her shoulders, and, as she was going by coach, no mask upon her face. Several servants were running like rabbits at harvest time, for she still commanded attention. One opened the coach door, another brought forward a little stool that her feet may not falter in the mud. A third held his own cape above her head, determined no rain would spot that white autocratic face. For all these services Frances made no effort of thanks. She accepted this treatment as if the men were her slaves. Now she put one foot forward, then hesitated. She had also seen the litter. Its bearers were panting up to the steps and halting behind the coach. Robin would have to squelch through the mud to reach his interrogation. Bacon watched Frances's lingering figure, and Robin's extended leg leave the litter before his long handsome body followed it. Ah, now they saw each other, now they would speak. Regardless of the pelting rain Bacon opened the window and leaned out hoping to hear a few words which would not be swallowed by the wind. There were none. Robin had stopped, shocked by the apparition of his wife, who was her customary self, while he was so altered by confinement. She looked back at his bloated features as if he had drowned long ago and was only a corpse dredged up before her. That movement of dismissal might have been to the foot boys or to her husband. Yet the motion of her hands, pushing all away from her, disturbed Bacon as it must have alarmed and horrified Robin, who hesitated, stepping back so that he almost collided with his own bearers who were still hang-dog in the rain, standing patiently until the coach moved and they could also leave with their burden, for a backdoor to the house.

Robin started forward as soon as his surprise had abated. Frances was moving, oh, how slowly, to the coach. One foot was on the stool, and one within the dark interior. Then Robin was by her, his eager face staring into the gloom. Bacon saw his lips move as he said "Frances" and again—imploringly—for his tone caught his ear even if he heard all imperfectly, "Frances," but she had knocked upon the front of the coach and it was away, leaving the Earl of Somerset abandoned on the door step, his hands still stretched towards his departing wife, his mouth still gaping anxiety and chagrin.

Bacon sighed. He almost felt sorry for the man, ingenuous Robin Carr who had once had faith in his king, his wife and his friends. After such a shock he would be easy to question, Coke could have played cat's cradle with the man's senses. Bacon sighed again with satisfaction and prepared to join his fellow commissioners in the room below.

"I will not have him hounded like an animal," James had said to Bacon. "He must understand that owing to his part in this affair he will not have my support for him at a trial. When I read these," tossing the confessions of Franklin and Weston at the Attorney General, "I am sickened."

Bacon was not sickened but he had said nothing to the king. And now he must face Somerset, knowing that James would not aid and abet the man, and that he was innocent of anything except stupidity and a desire to have his own way. He is like his wife in that, thought Bacon watching the ceremony with which Robin took his seat before the commission into Overbury's death.

He could still pathetically assume the air of Lord Chamberlain and king's favourite. He sent the servant off with a lordly hand, then smiled at the commissioners as if they were menials and gazed somewhere above their heads, at the flyblown ceiling or the tattered hangings of the Siege of Troy where moth had bitten through Achilles's head, and Helen's beauty was ravaged into rags.

"Before you speak, my lord, I must warn you," said Coke, "that your wife, the countess, hath confessed all."

This ominous opening did not seem to discompose their prisoner. He smiled and crossed his elegant legs. He wore gold silk which was shot through with rose. The audacious colour gripped their eyes in every movement. Over all, Robin had a chain set with stones which matched his clothes, on his left hand, which was under Bacon's eyes, a ring sprouted like a flower from every finger. In spite of his lethargy and coarsening features Somerset was still handsome, and Bacon was pleased the king had so determinedly refused to see the prisoner; Robin's conceit was part of his beauty, it burgeoned about him like a lady's perfume. It pervaded the council room. Ellesmere coughed again and again.

"I had heard you were unwell, my lord," said Robin condescendingly. "You should take physic, and keep from cold. Old bones do not fare well in winter."

Ellesmere was affronted. He knew that all his legal colleagues hoped he would soon shuffle off to the country and that Bacon hoped for the Lord Chancellorship, and yet he would not submit to age. "I am well enough to head the bench at your arraignment," he said to Robin between coughs.

If Bacon and Robin had been in complicity it could not have been decided better. James and Bacon had both realized that Coke must not preside at the two trials to come; although he had expected that he would sit on the bench, as Ellesmere was thought too ill to take his rightful place. Yet in one phrase, Robin Carr had ensured that Coke's place as judge would be taken by the indignant Ellesmere. No rantings and false condemnations at this trial then, considered Bacon. He must now eliminate that posturing idiot Hyde, and the next court scene would be less farcical and more expeditious. Concealing his smile Bacon bent over his papers, rustling them in some semblance of order.

"Indeed you seem so sick——" began Robin to Ellesmere again.

The old Lord Chancellor flushed with anger: "If I am sick at your interrogation my lord, you may be sure I will be hale and hearty at your trial, let who will hinder me ... and however long you may have to wait for a day."

A double knot tied. Ellesmere's innocent fury had not only ensured that he would himself be presiding judge, it had also put off the trial, for even the old man would have to admit that he could not sit in a court while his cough racked him. Robin smiled, to Bacon's surprise, until he realized that Somerset hoped that by delaying this trial he may escape it altogether.

"What know you of Franklin?" asked Zouche who opened the proceedings. He became bored swiftly and would be less skilful towards the end of the interrogation.

"I knew my wife knew him—nothing more."

"Know you that he claimed to be advised by you, when the murder of Overbury had been discovered and he came to your house for succour."

Robin held up one hand: "A moment—Did he come with Mrs Turner?"

"That is so," replied Zouche with satisfaction.

"Of an evening, and they supped with my wife, just afore they were arrested?"

"Aye, my lord."

"Did he say he saw me there?"

Zouche was confused and looked at Franklin's deposition but before he could find the place Robin continued easily. "He did not see me. I had come in haste from Royston and slept at once, while I could. The countess had them visit with her in an outer room. She may have told Mrs Turner and this mountebank Franklin that I had advised them but, my lords, would she ever ask my advice? She gave some of her own, and said it came from me maybe. I never met Franklin. Mrs Turner I knew, to my own unhappiness. She cajoled my wife to deeds she would never have done if they were not portrayed to her as easy and permissible. That woman squandered my wife's money, and by her various plots brought her into evil ways, even to the thought—the thought, I say, of murder." At their murmurs he went on: "But thoughts are not deeds, and if every man were hanged for wishing his wife dead, or his father in the grave—would we be here, my lords?"

It was an unexpectedly firm defence from the man and confounded Zouche, who had discovered by searching through Franklin's confession that the doctor had never claimed to have met Robin, any more than he had said he had read any of those letters of which Frances had evidently told him, about Carr's plans to put away his friend.

Bacon shook his head, warningly. Franklin's testimony was purely circumstantial and had been denied so often and then retracted with different names and dates that it could be eliminated in any court of law. The youngest student in the Inns of Court could have demolished Franklin's confessions. Only Coke looked hungrily at them, determined to keep his prize hugged close, for he had believed in Franklin. Bacon thrust the pieces of paper, with their many dates at the top, towards Coke. If the Lord Chief Justice were so gullible he might keep them, to the rest of the commissioners his gesture indicated that Franklin's testimony was gossamer, fit to be blown away. Robin, Earl of Somerset smiled with relief and settled more comfortably in his chair.

"If you will not admit Franklin, will you admit that a phial of poison passed through your hands which supposedly came from Killigrew?" asked Coke.

"Who said it had poison, my lords? I am sure you have asked questions of Killigrew. He gave me those drugs which make men vomit or so affect their bowels they will lie groaning two days together. If you have asked so many questions you will also have discovered from Overbury's servants that he asked these medicines of me himself, so that he might feign sickness and so be released. Indeed my lords I know," he gulped a little, "that you have some of my letters and so have an explanation of these potions in them."

"I believe you knew of attempts to poison Overbury," pressed Bacon.

Robin looked at him sadly. "You were once my friend, Sir Francis," he said.

"And am so still," Bacon's voice rang out heartily.

Robin smiled and slowly shook his head: "In these straits all men fight for themselves. I did not know this a year or so ago."

"Did you know it when Tom Overbury was dead ere he had a chance to reach his prime?" asked Coke.

"Tush," said Bacon, "my lord Somerset hath just now admitted he was more unfeeling then."

He and Robin smiled at each other like confederates.

Coke made a smothered sound and came quickly back to the attack: "If you did not intend his death, why were you so ready to keep Overbury in the Tower, my lord? That, at least, you must admit. He was not kept there by chance."

"I admit that, aye," agreed Robin which seemed to confound Coke, who was silent while Ellesmere took up the questioning.

"We have information on bribes given you for offices——"

"They are not in question," said Bacon smoothly, afraid of what might ensue. He had promised James that no mention of pensions or the selling of offices should be brought in, for the crown could not bear close queries on corruption. Ellesmere looked amazed then took Bacon's point and huffed at the floor, his eyes rheumily filling with unshed tears as his cold became more persistent.

"We have a letter from Sir Thomas," said the Lord Chancellor when his unintentional weeping had abated. "It was sent to you only a few weeks before his death." He opened it reverently as Robin stared at him.

"How did you come by that?" he asked rudely.

Coke smiled. "You thought to have it safe at the house of Master Holland I believe, but you sent a relative of Mrs Turner to collect it—only at Christmas. Aye, you thought, my lord, that we would not watch the movements of your fellow conspirators as you were safe in the Cockpit. But we had warning of your profusion of letters scattered over London after those taken from the house of William Weston."

"I know not what you mean," said Robin pettishly. "What if I do leave my letters about the city? I have affairs of state to consider. I need secret hiding places."

"You will most particularly remember this letter," said Coke dourly, plucking it from the feeble fingers of the Lord Chancellor. He did not trust Ellesmere to deliver the accusation firmly. " 'But that shall not be,' " read Coke. " 'You and I shall come to public trial before all the friends I have . . .' " Robin looked at that once familiar handwriting as Coke's voice toiled onwards, speaking of his betrayal with " 'that woman' ". " 'Held daily traffic with my enemies, sent me nineteen projects and promises for my liberty, then at the beginning of next week sent me some frivolous account of the miscarriage of them and so slipt out of town.' "

Robin could hear Tom's indignant prating voice, as sardonic and arrogant as his own. Had he read this letter? It seemed unfamiliar and yet he knew why he could not recall it. Sickened by Tom's anger he had thrown it in a box, and consigned it to darkness, then forgotten every word until his prosecutors brought it out like this. Coke's measured voice was like gravel. Robin shook his head; the auburn curls, so often fondled by the king, were disarranged when he ran his fingers through them. He must play his part. He looked up with his old nonchalance, his mouth unnaturally firm.

"Is that all you have against me, my Lord Chief Justice?" he asked.

He had Coke there. All the argument in the world could not make him Overbury's killer because the dead man had sent him abusive letters.

"We might say," said Coke consideringly, "that you had him put down because, as it says here, he would make public your treatment of him."

"Who would care how I treated him?" asked Robin haughtily. "So that I was up and he was down? The world wags that way, my lord. If he were out of the Tower and demeaned, none would listen to his complaints of ill treatment by me."

That was so true that even judicious Ellesmere was nodding.

"We have another letter," said Coke, scurrying through his pile of papers like a squirrel searching for a tasty nut, "from your countess to Elwes."

There was a long silence while he hunted for it. Bacon said nothing. He knew which letter Coke was seeking and he was interested to see if Robin had the wit to refute it. Finally, Coke held it up, scrawled over with Frances's undeniable hand. Had Robin grown pale? How could he know what lies and perversions his wife might have committed in his name? As Coke unfolded it he lost some of his studied disdain, anxious to hear what was to be used against him.

"She speaks of pies, my lord," said Coke heavily. "She says to Elwes that if *he* send tarts to them, the Elwes family must not eat them. Do you deny that you are the 'he' of whom she speaks?"

He sat back satisfied. Robin opened his mouth and closed it again, then said angrily: "By God you are right, I do deny it. *He* might be any man. It might be a pastrycook. It might be her own great-uncle, old Northampton."

"You say it is not you, my lord?"

Robin almost laughed his indignation. "He! He! The mysterious he. It could even be Overbury himself. I have heard he returned pies to the Elwes family if he did not want to eat them. Are you so sure the 'he' of whom she speaks is not Overbury?"

A hit, a hit, thought Bacon. When he had read the letter he had immediately thought she was referring to Overbury as the sender of pies, but Coke, whose head was swimming with conspiracy, had determined it was another male plotter. Why not Robin Carr?

"Have you aught else to plague me with?" asked Robin, flicking casually at his necklace with one well kept thumb.

Coke looked at him sullenly. He had a low esteem of the young man's intelligence and yet it seemed that Carr had been able to refute every accusation. Yet had there been any real accusation? Aye, there was the rub. Nothing could be proved, it was all half questions and sly allusions, and if Robin had the wit to challenge one of them, he might go free. Coke played what he thought was his best card.

"What of the Spanish pension?" he asked abruptly.

Robin looked back at him: "What Spanish pension?"

"Why, all know you are in the pay of Spain to disarm this country and so place it in the hands of Spain by way of your foreign diplomacy."

"My diplomacy! Mine?" cried Robin. "Why, I had as much say in foreign matters as an unweaned pup! Oh, maybe I acted as a go-between, giving Tom Overbury's thoughts to the king or reading letters, but you must know my lord I was not capable of dealing with such weighty matters by myself. If you would have news of Spain, go to Winwood or one of that kind. As to pension—where heard you this?" Unmoved by accusations of murder, the suggestion of treason aroused Robin to temper. He lost his skill as his anger blazed out.

Coke was adept at using one friend against another. "Sir Robert Cotton hath murmured it sometimes."

"Cotton? Never, my lord, a pox on your stories. Why should I line my pockets with puny Spanish pensions when the king gave me the key of the treasury of England?"

That was a potent argument and Coke recoiled a little; he pulled off his spectacles which suggested defeat to Bacon. It did to Robin too. Before another commissioner could question him he turned upon Bacon.

"Ah, you one-time friend," he cried, "go you to Jamie and tell him that if I come to trial I will upset the largest beehive this country has never known and all will be stung—that I will tell the English the truth about their king so that they will throw him off the throne. Aye, the crown will not sustain a fight with me. All will be pulled down. That canting queen who plays diplomacy with yon smooth-faced archbishop; and Winwood, are his coffers not lined with Puritan monies taken to keep the recusants from office? And what of James—who sells every title at a profit? Baronets for £1,600 pounds and lords for little more, that's the price. Aye, Jamie ne'er knows what his hands are about, under the table they move warily, cunningly. He is always at his dirty practices, our king——"

"Hush," said Bacon but it was old Ellesmere who saved Robin from himself.

"Silence," he said sternly and his thin voice carried enough shock to make Somerset pause in his vindictive course. "Say no more. Leave it as it is and none of the commissioners will remember your words against you."

"I warrant," snarled Robin, glaring at Bacon, "I know all my words will be served up to the king like a puddle of dog piss."

"Hush, hush," pleaded Ellesmere, as if he reasoned with a crying child.

Robin stopped, brought up short by his own lack of imagination. "I will bring down king and all," he muttered as he left them, walking out straight between two warders.

"That is a foolish young man," said Ellesmere as the door closed, "and his own worst enemy."

"A murderer," said Coke savagely, "I told you so."

"Oh, not that, not that," replied the Lord Chancellor mildly, and sneezed once more.

XXXV

THE LIGHT SIMPERED down at them, blurred by turning
corners, it stained her violet dress to a deep bruised colour. Frances's
face turned to his, eyes smudged into the shadows. "Do you lead
the way, Sir George."

Moore bounded up ahead of her, turning the corkscrew flight
neatly, and glancing back to see how the countess managed her
skirts. He was rewarded with the sight of leg, valiant in white
stockings with gold embroidery. Her shoes were green kid—fairy
shoes, he thought, then dismissed his own superstition; he would
not believe in a supernatural in his Tower. He gasped.

"I fear the last flight was too hard for you, Sir George," she
said, almost teasing him. Warder Saunders had the door open and
Moore led Frances into the rooms.

"These are the best apartments in the Tower," he confided. "You
will be as comfortable as in your own home, my lady."

"Save for freedom," she suggested allowing her scarf to uncoil
from her head. She wore no cap, and her hair was as pale as Jerez
wine. He bowed while she looked about her. There were two
rooms each with barred windows, he admired the inner room where
the bed had a coverlet embroidered with flowers. Frances looked at
this and then at the desk, a fine piece, thought Moore, carved with a
heron holding a fish in its mouth. Frances began to shiver like a
leaf in a tender wind, at first almost indiscernibly then more wildly,
until her whole body was in motion. Moore thought she was having
a fit. He clasped her by each arm, supporting her towards a chair.
When he tried to lower her body to it Frances resisted him, growing rigid.

"Go you," he shouted at Saunders, "fetch an apothecary, a
doctor, or a woman. Make haste, damn you," as the man fled
precipitously down the stairs.

Clinging on to the countess's determined body, Moore was
terrified lest she was having an attack in which he would be powerless to help her. He wound her white silk scarf about his knuckles,
prepared to push it into her mouth if she showed signs of biting
her own tongue. There was water in the ewer but he could not

leave her to fetch it. In her cataleptic state he did not wish to lower her to the floor, and she had refused to be aided to a chair or the bed. Suddenly, while he held her close, Frances crumpled so that he could rest her on the floor. Her tossed dress illuminated the dark room like a stained glass window. He ran to the water jug and splashed her head and hands, the face she turned up to him was pallid and furrowed like that of an old woman. Her lower lip twitched. He had heard that Frances Howard was like a player, able to persuade men to believe what she disposed to be, so Moore said quite sharply:

"How now, madam?"

"Sir George."

She sat up on her heels. Her shameless slippers were thrown to either side, like fallen leaves. Her hair was beginning to tumble from its net, so that she had to put up one hand to see him, brushing a heavy forelock back without any grace at all.

"Madam," said Sir George more heavily. "If this be some game, leave it. An apothecary has been sent for and will attend you."

"The fault lies not in me," she replied indignantly, "but in this room. I never saw a place I liked less. It whispers terrible things to me. Tells of the dead. I cannot rest here. Give me a cell, a dungeon, any place but this—"

"My lady," he said more gently, for she seemed truly afraid, holding her hands to either shoulder, arms crossed over her breasts like those on a tombstone effigy, while she spoke Frances's eyes darted about the room peering into the darkened corners. "My lady," he essayed again, "this is one of the best places in the Tower. I chose it that your stay might be——" he paused abruptly as Saunders came panting up the stairs.

"I will not remain here," she said firmly, then in a low but determined voice: "I tell you, Sir George, I will kill myself if I stay in this room. You may house me where you will but not in these chambers."

Saunders was looking at her oddly, when he had caught Sir George's attention he made curious beckoning gestures with one finger and nodded at the door. "An apothecary is coming, sir," he said aloud, "who was waiting on Sir Thomas Monson." His eyes continued to signal to Moore urgently.

Moore was aware that he looked incongruous, an elderly bent man comforting a sick girl. He snapped at Saunders: "Is that all? Then begone."

"Sir, I must speak with you," said the man imploringly.

"Then out with it," rapped Sir George glancing at the countess who was still moaning, her teeth clenched round her scarf, her eyes fixed on the desk.

"Not here, sir, not before——" he gulped, "her ladyship."

"Very well. Tell me outside."

Moore stood up and she cried out pitifully: "No, Sir George, dear Sir George, do not leave me alone in this place. Stay with me, Sir George. Do you want me, Sir George? Would you make love with me? Take me. I am yours if you stay with me," her voice rose to a subdued shriek as he went through the door. He did not even blush before Saunders, both men were too shaken by her outcry.

"Is she mad, think you?" asked Moore as they stood behind the door listening to her crying through the crack.

"Sir, I should have thought of it afore. It is our own fault."

"What, man?"

"Know you who rested in these rooms two year agone?"

Moore did not need to ask. "Overbury?"

"The same, sir."

"God's life, how could she know?"

Saunders shook his head. "It is not natural, sir, and yet she must have realized it by its furnishings or some description of it."

"How could she? None visited Overbury except Weston and Elwes and with those she had no meeting, before or after the murder."

Both men were silent, listening to the cries beyond the door which sounded like a bitch locked in a stable, baying at a moon. "She must indeed be a witch," said Saunders, crossing himself.

Moore was too shocked to reprove him for this barbaric act. "Overbury's ghost must haunt the place," he thought aloud.

"And is only seen by her. I swear Sir George, when we got those rooms ready there was no malignant presence there. The sun shone."

"Yet if she does sense something untoward we cannot keep her here," said Moore. "Where else may she go?"

"Sir, there are no rooms prepared for such as she."

"Then she must stay in the lodgings. I will go to Monson's old rooms in the White Tower."

"They are damp, Sir George. They have not been lived in since he was arrested at the tail end of autumn."

"It is all we can do," replied Moore. "Listen to her weeping. She is like a lunatic. I am almost sorry for her. Tell the warders to carry her boxes to my lodgings and I will try and console her." He intercepted a quick slimy grin on Saunders's face. "Go to, you rogue," he said, hitting out at the man. "You see she is demented."

"The trials will be on the 24th and 25th of this month, your grace."

James studied him with a lacklustre eye. He had been drinking deeply and alone, his hand edged towards his cup. "Will ye have a drop, Sir Francis?" he asked.

Bacon's impulse was to refuse but looking at those pleading dark eyes he felt uncouth and asked for a half glass which James himself poured with the careful concentration of a tipsy man. He wore a bedgown covered by a robe embroidered with gold thread in a pattern of lions and unicorns. James's legs dangled until he retrieved a footstool from under his chair, pulling it into position with his stockinged toes.

"So," said the king, "not so long then, a week or so. It is not much."

"The trial will be conducted fairly, your majesty."

"I had nae doot, if ye hae the ruling o' it, Sir Francis."

Bacon stood up, bowed, and sat to his wine again. It was over-sweet.

"If he wud plead guilty a' might be forgot," said James almost to himself.

"Yes, sire."

"I hae a little lucky charm. I passed it to him by way o' Sir George Moore," said James piteously. "I told Rabbie that if he would plead guilty he would be spared his life."

Bacon could not say this was meddling with the law so he said nothing.

"I do not think offering him his life would be enough to make Lord Somerset plead guilty," he said after a short silence.

James spread his hands: "Whut more can I offer? He has mair money from me than the treasury could well afford. Certes, he was lending money to the crown at ae time he made so much frae bribery and monopolies."

Bacon nodded. "Yet he will want more as a bribe if you wish to stop the trial by his pleading guilty."

"What?"

"Clemency for his wife, and an assured future for himself and his child—perhaps exiled to the country."

"I could offer that," agreed James. "I have been using the Lord Lieutenant as an intermediary to Rabbie but they seem to be ill-assorted. Moore is not a sympathetic man."

"He is a servant of the crown."

"Aye, not a soft man."

"Sire," said Bacon, impatient in case James turned against his new Lord Lieutenant of the Tower, "Sir George Moore may lack the craft of a courtier but it is a hard job and he fulfils it well." He ventured: "Elwes was a soft man—pliable—remember what happened to him, your majesty."

"Just so," agreed James slowly nodding, "just so." Bacon was amazed to see tears in the king's eyes. Were they for hanged Elwes?

"I have arranged for Sir George that William James will go to Rabbie. D'you know the man?"

Bacon shook his head.

"He was sometime my lord Somerset's secretary but always in the shade, I know Rabbie ne'er spoke of him. And when Rabbie was imprisoned this lad comes straight out at an audience. He says his master is innocent and unjustly accused, no more. So I had Pembroke look into the case and out it all came—that the young man's master was my Rabbie and he had called out like that so then men would know that at least one thought Rabbie was not guilty. I was moved by it, Sir Francis."

"I would have been also," said Bacon truthfully.

"If some can believe in Rabbie's innocence he may be saved at a trial," suggested James with a little hope in his voice.

Bacon did not wish to hurt the king but could not suggest clemency.

"E'en if he did not try to poison Overbury he has done so much evil that no jury would acquit him."

James looked mournful: "You are very sure o't."

"Positive, your majesty," Bacon sipped his wine, trying not to grimace.

"Ah weel," said James, "if he continues stubborn what hope have I? Rabbie but answers that he will bring me in as one of the plotters, forbye I had Overbury sent to the Tower." He was tearful once more.

"Your majesty," Bacon leaned over and patted the king's shoulder as if he calmed a whimpering dog, "he speaks without thinking. He will not accuse you of anything. I am sure he will not."

"I ha' always loved him. I would have gone on loving him if he were not so set against me. I tell you, Bacon, that last year he made a hell, refusing to see me and acting as if he ruled the land, no' me. He ranted at me in council and jeered at me afore others. What else could I do?"

"I am sure," said Bacon briskly, "you will have no fears of such scorn from young Villiers." He hoped thoughts of his new favourite would drive nightmares of the old one away. He was correct. "Ma Georgie," cried James wonderingly. "Aye, he's the bonny one. A good friend tae both of us, Sir Francis."

"I hope so."

"I hope so too," said James suddenly falling apart again. "I am growing old and need my friends."

"We are here to aid your majesty," said Bacon firmly as he rose to go. He sent the groom in to the king as he let himself out by the backstairs. He had not asked permission to go but he knew his judgement was right as he heard the lad comforting his king with little cries of affection and good humour.

Sir George Moore wrote: "She is so strangely altered in herself, speaks with a modest voice, is ever plucking her hands and oftimes sighs saying 'I would I had never met those persons' or that it was her greed for Lord Rochester made her act so." He considered what he had said and dipped his pen in ink once more. "She is demure in her appearance wearing black or other sober colours. Her time is spent in needlework or saying her prayers. She seems humble beyond the ordinary. I have not seen so great a change in any." He could not find the countess's manner in any part credible, but he did not commit his doubt to his letter to the king.

XXXVI

The crowd had begun to assemble at six o'clock and by the time nine approached and the sun climbed higher and burned warmer, there was a fetid smell of sweat and animal exhalation in the hall. There was a slight disturbance in one of the upper galleries when Essex came in, but he sat in the shadows where few could see his face.

A muffled roar sounded on the river side of the hall, it seemed almost subterranean, as if a cannon were being repeatedly fired underground. After a moment there was a hustle at the entrance to the hall and the public doors were firmly closed so that any late-comers could not enter. At the same time the court was asked to rise and concourse of lawyers and officers swelled into the over-packed hall. They were led by 22 peers, who were packed sweating on to settles which had been placed below the bench. They were subdued, mindful of their responsibility to try the daughter of one of their number. Yet unless she changed her plea from "guilty" they would not act as a jury.

Lord Ellesmere came into the upper seat which was elevated like a throne above the other places on the bench. He moved slowly, edging his way past the seats beneath him which had been added on either side to accommodate the increased number of judges. There were seven, who presently took their places also, with Lord Coke in the centre.

When all the judges were seated the company was allowed to sit which caused several minutes' delay as ladies in wide farthingales, and the men in padded breeches, tried to wedge themselves once more into the narrow space allowed them on the benches. The fatigue, the heat and the smells were forgotten in the excitement of the trial. A humming pervaded the court like the sound of bees swarming in a distant garden, it became subdued at the entry of six sergeants carrying maces. They accompanied other lawyers who could act for the prosecution in the case, among them was Bacon, pale in his black robes, and Yelverton the Solicitor General, who it was supposed was secretly advising the defence. The next few agonized moments passed too slowly, the sound outside the hall had risen to a peak and was sustained there, those in court could tell by the inflexions of noise that the countess was entering by the river gate and had passed over the yard behind the hall, then she moved obliquely, perhaps to some retiring room where she would be able to wipe her face and hands and make ready for her appearance.

There was a hearty thumping at the doors. "Bring the prisoner forward," called the Clerk of the Court, for, owing to Ellesmere's infirmities, many rituals were excused him. First came the headsman. This was drama, he strutted like a black cock through a barnyard, across his shoulder rested a long-handled axe with a decorative cleft blade which was turned away from the Countess of Somerset. She came in immediately behind him, and all rose slightly to see more clearly. When the crowd had sat down, many noticed with some disappointment that she was smaller than they had expected, and she walked slowly, as if her gown were too heavy.

Frances wore black, a dress of some fine soft material which was cut close to her figure and had a short train behind which her maid occasionally raised out of the dust. She had a loose veil through which her pale face could only be seen in outline, her cuffs and high collar were of gauze lace, and now and then she raised a black lace fan to her eyes as if abashed. When she had been guided to her chair by Sir George Moore, who came in behind her, she lifted her veil and held a white kerchief to her eyes, wiping at them. Several ladies in the galleries began to weep in sympathy.

"Frances, Countess of Somerset, hold up thy hand," called Fanshaw, the Clerk of Arraignment, and the murmuring stopped as if the play had begun.

The accusation was long and mumbled so that listeners had to strain to hear that she was accused of intent to kill, and procuration of poison. It was a strange garbled Latinized speech and halfway through she dropped her wrist.

"My lords," said Bacon swiftly, "is there any necessity for the countess to keep her hand up?"

Ellesmere said: "She may lower it," and so she did, using her other hand to elevate her wide fan and cover her face.

Fanshaw lifted his voice a little towards the end when shuffling broke out in the hall. The sergeant called for silence, and into the calm that followed, Fanshaw said crisply "Frances, Countess of Somerset, what sayest thou? Art thou guilty of this felony and murder, or not guilty?"

There was a pause while her fan faltered, then Frances closed it and curtseyed to Ellesmere so that her head dipped almost level with the rails of her pen. Her voice was very low, but, owing to the silence, could be heard all over the hall: "Guilty".

A shivering spread across the crowd like a wind in long grass.

Bacon's voice called above it: "I am glad to hear this lady's so free acknowledgement, for confession is noble."

He was also glad, but he did not say so, that she had not shrieked or blabbed to the court of her husband. He had prepared a speech which he delivered by rote, his eyes all the time on Frances.

The shock of her own plea of "guilty" seemed to have driven out her wits. She had fallen forward and the court was more concerned with her than with the expected fulsome speech from Bacon. While he padded out his oratory he saw how Moore held the countess upright until a chair was found for her and that her maid was pressing some restorative to Frances's face. He carefully went over the main points of the case, omitting nothing which was known to be evidence. This incensed Coke who hauled himself from his seat on the bench before Bacon could finish. Irritated that the justice must overbear him Bacon stood still and silent, determined that Coke should not begin one of his vindictive accusations.

"I wish to tell the court," said the Chief Justice, "that all testimony was taken properly and honestly. Weston did confess his sin and so all came out of that. I have carried out the due observance of the law."

"None doubt that," said Bacon hurriedly for it was obvious from the whisperings among the lords that many did now doubt the validity of Coke's interrogations. Would the foolish old man sit down? Coke, as if Bacon had directed him outright, subsided to his seat and Bacon made a quick signal to Fanshaw to carry out the procedure of the trial.

"My lady," he said directly to the countess, "have you any cause to allege why sentence should not be passed on you?"

Frances looked up exposing a white terrified face. She shook her head and coughed so that Fanshaw stood waiting for her to speak. After clearing her throat again she said: "I could much aggravate but not extenuate my fault. I desire mercy and that the lords will intercede for me with the king."

Ellesmere leaned forward, his hand cupped round his ear, and

Bacon stifled an exclamation of annoyance. "What said she? What said she?" asked the Lord Chancellor.

Bacon walked to the bench and pressed himself between an unwilling Coke, and Dodderidge. "She asks for mercy, and that the lords will intercede for her," he said plainly so that the whole hall heard him.

"It did not sound like that."

"Grief and remorse do not allow her to express herself," Bacon said shortly. "What she hath confusedly said is to this effect: she cannot excuse her deeds and only asks mercy."

Ellesmere looked into his eyes. They were both silent for a moment while the bench and officers of the court waited in suspense. In each man's expression was congratulation for the other. Did Ellesmere seem subdued? Was he, in that long quiet, passing on his office to Bacon and admitting to himself and the Attorney General that his long legal life was at an end? He looked down at the sentence, written out for him in large letters so that he would not have to recourse to spectacles. "Thank you, Sir Francis," he said quietly, and Bacon bobbed out of the way so that the old man might look directly at the black-gowned prisoner.

"Frances, Countess of Somerset," he said, "whereas thou hast been indicated, arraigned, pleaded guilty and that thou hast not a thing to say for thyself, it is now my part to pass judgement. I will only say this much before: since my lords," gazing down at the 22 peers who were all studiously looking at their own hands folded on their laps, "have heard with what humility and grief you have confessed the facts, I do not doubt they will signify so much to the king, and they will mediate for his grace towards you. But in the meantime, acccording to the law, the sentence must be this: "That thou shalt be carried from hence to the Tower of London, and from thence to the place of execution, where you are to be hanged by the neck until you are dead, and the Lord have mercy on your soul."

The confused audience began to gabble. They stretched over the backs of seats conferring with strangers.

In spite of the plea for clemency the countess seemed shocked, she was only apparently alive by a gentle lifting and falling of her black veil in front of her mouth. Otherwise she was immobile. Like the crowd, she must be distressed by condemnation to hanging. Like a common criminal. If she had kept to the misdeeds of her class, high treason or political intrigues, she would have had the block. Frances had not realized that by allying herself with murder she would be doomed to a murderer's end. Although she had been assured that she would not suffer more than imprisonment, she was atrophied by the thought of hanging. Ellesmere had condemned all her tribe with that casual sentence, and now Howards were of no more importance than vagrants who steal purses, or highway robbers.

She heard the voices of passers-by, making their way from the hall: "Ugh, I trow she is sickened by the thought of the rope . . ."; "Why, she will not suffer either. Those 22 lords who came in and went out, they were so many puppets. *They* will not plead for her. 'Tis all worked out on a backstairs in Whitehall, before the trial took place. Playacting, that plea for clemency . . ."; "Aye, but she will be in the Tower for the rest of her life at the very least. A prisoner she is, and must not be let out among honest folk."

A voice cut in from further back in the throng: "Aye, but what of him?" If she is allowed off, her husband's safe enough. They can't hang him when his guilt was so much less than hers."

"But d'ye not see, he will not plead guilty. He is to make a fight of it and that annoys them, he will not confess and ask forgiveness."

"When all is said and done," said a masked lady with finality, "it shows the great ones are not treated like the rest of us."

Frances flickered a glance at her with some surprise, from her elaborate dress she would have thought she ranked among the great, and as the woman came closer, she noticed that her gown was sweat stained and patched, perhaps bought second hand or passed down and worn until the fabric was splitting.

"There she sits, the harlot. No, don't you hush me, Dorothy, she is a whore true-proved. She was the only begetter of these murthers and she used all the others: they, poor wights, are underground, and she's let off. There's no justice in this land."

Moore's hand held her elbow pulling Frances until she was standing upright, supported by his arm and her maid. She swayed down the aisle towards the door, her head at an odd angle as if she had already suffered execution. Her eyes were still shut and her maid directed every step. After her, with a slow ponderous walk, halted on every other foot by the slow progress of the countess, came the executioner. His axe was elevated again but the cruel thin blade was pointing towards Frances's ruff of cobweb lace.

* * *

314

Moore approached his other prisoner with apprehension. Robin had been in an uneasy temper for the past week, and this was heightened by the knowledge that his wife must stand trial. After he had begged the king to allow Frances to creep into a corner to take care of her child for the rest of her days, Robin had been besieged by messages from James, sent by way of Sir George Moore. The lieutenant was like a net between the two balls, forever being buffeted by the king's demands that letters be sealed and kept secret, or else destroyed. James was afraid of what Robin might say in court. It was to the king's benefit if the Earl of Somerset made a very pretty if incredible confession, listened to the sentence and was bowed out. And yet the man still persisted in pleading "not guilty". Moore wondered what so pestered the king that he must send these alarmed messages so often promising full forgiveness if Robin agreed to stay mute during the trial. As he walked across the green towards his prisoner's rooms, Moore considered which fear persecuted James. Was it that the corruption of his court be exposed? Was it that Prince Henry truly had been murdered and his father was a party to it? Had James been one of the unseens who had poison sent to Overbury? Was there a catholic plot, or a secret treaty with Spain known only to James, the Howards, Overbury and Carr? In which case, was the king, with the skill of a gardener, plucking off one grape after another so that he would be left alone on the bunch, to wax fat and profit by his fellow plotters' death or disgrace? All stories seemed equally unlikely to Moore. He had to resort to the notion that James was afraid lest his love for pretty men be made public throughout Europe, if Robin Carr declared all their bedroom behaviour in the trial. Yet the earl could be silenced. And news of their king's sodomy was unlikely to disturb a nation that made it a joke, rather than a scandal. And yet, thought Sir George, his feet blindly stepping out over a familiar track across the grass, the queen would not care to have her husband's love affairs brought into daylight; for all his abuse of her, James had some concern for his fat Danish Anna. He went up the staircase to the closed door of Robin's outer room. Before it stood a dishevelled warder, another knelt inside, inspecting his torn hose.

"The earl sprang at me, sir," he offered.

Moore knocked on the inner door. "My lord," he essayed.

Silence.

"My lord of Somerset, d'ye hear me? I am Sir George Moore."

A snarled sound which might have been an oath came from

within. Moore lowered his voice, pressing his mouth to a crack in the door, "My lord, it is Sir George Moore. I would have speech with you." He knew there was no lock or bolt on the other side of the door but he was reluctant to open it without his prisoner's consent. "I would enter and speak with you," he said again. No sound from Robin. "Come now, my lord," he said cajolingly. "Think on me as a host in whose house you lie. Wouldst refuse me entry?"

He nudged open the door by two inches. As there was no reaction, he cautiously went into the room. Robin was standing by the window, looking out. His hunched shoulders were pitiful, he had been injured in the squabbles with the warder and had lost his shoe and one of his hose was rolling down his leg, exposing white and blue flesh—unhealthy, thought Moore, like the legs of an old man.

"Come now, my lord," he said, advancing gently. He was quite near Carr but dared not touch him, there was a concentrated tenseness in his prisoner, like a clock making ready to strike. "Now, now, my lord," he said as soothing as a doctor. "I have news for you."

"What is that?"

Moore did not wish to tell him. He said: "Shall we sit, my lord?"

Robin looked away from him contemptuously. "I will stand, Sir George."

"Then I will also."

Moore could see a pout beginning to depress Robin's lip which encouraged him, he could manage a sullen lad, not a maniac. Robin did not ask about Frances as Moore had hoped he would, so that he could court him by mention of the plea for clemency. He tapped his fingers once or twice on the glass, it might have been a secret signal to himself.

"I may help you?" suggested Moore.

For the first time, Robin turned round—his puffy face looked in Moore's direction, and away again.

"You have news?"

He had to come out with it then: "Your trial will be tomorrow, at Westminster Hall, at ten o'clock."

It came out pat as an invitation to a masque. Robin looked at him again, his eyes so rimmed with swollen flesh they might have been depressions in a bun. He said: "I will not go."

"My lord?" he asked.

"I said it clear. I will not go."

"My lord. It is your trial. You have to go."

Robin tapped again on the pane. His ring caught the light and broke into a thousand faces of ruby, like the head of a scarlet geranium.

"I will not go," he said definitely.

"My lord, I can take you by force," threatened Moore as quietly as Robin.

"Then that is how you will have to take me. I will not go quietly."

"My lord. Do you not think that in your own interest——"

"I think I will not go." His mouth shut like a rat trap. His fingers went on tap-tap-tapping his private code.

"My lord, you make my duty very hard," pleaded Moore.

"That is your affair as you are Lord Lieutenant of the Tower."

"Would you be carried by force into Westminster Hall?"

"When the king hears of my resolution he will not let you take me so."

Moore decided to assail Robin from another direction: "My lord, why did you attack your warder?"

"I dislike his face."

"My lord, I will send another to you."

The earl's answer was a snarl which lifted his lip to reveal two long blunt front teeth. Like a dog, thought Moore, and he bowed and left the rooms, beckoning the warder out with him. The man looked surly, as well he might.

"Guard the outer door," commanded Moore. "I will send someone to relieve you."

One two, one two, like a good artillery man he paced out across the lawn, aware that he was being watched by that vulpine creature above but determined not to show, by the speed or manner of his going, how alarmed he was by Robin's threat. There was only one man could decide in this matter. He thanked God that in spite of all his wiles and pretensions, the king was easily accessible.

Your majesty,

My Lord Somerset is refusing to come to trial and complains mightily. What should I do in this matter?

Brief and businesslike. He sent it to Whitehall at once.

When James opened Moore's note he was alone, he had sent too many messages to Moore in the past few weeks to expose his feelings by opening the replies before Villiers or the young man's friends. He read the note twice, short though it was. He had almost known this would happen, for Robin was so positive that he would attack the king if he had the chance to give evidence in court that he had expected a complicated blackmail. Robin had said he would plead "not guilty" and had caused such a commotion by it that he now hoped to escape any trial at all. James remembered the other sequences of letters in which the motif was always: "I will reveal all."

He sighed and called his page. "Do you fetch quickly Lord Hay and Sir Robert Carr—you know the one, he that is cousin to the Earl of Somerset?"

Neither could be doubted as friends of the prisoner. Both had been promoted by accident, Hay for his beauty and Carr for his cousin, they still clung to the court like leeches on a wound. James wrote to Moore that these gentlemen had been instructed to visit the Tower to persuade Robin to come to trial, and added; "And when that is done, if he shall still refuse to go, you must do your office, except he be apparently sick or distracted of his wits, in any of which cases, you may acquaint the Lord Chancellor with it, that he may adjourn the day to Monday next." James considered; that gave Robin two days in which to pull himself together. He shook his head and went on writing: "Between which time if his sickness or madness be counterfeited it will manifestly appear." He would tell Mayerne to go to the Tower and see if there were any physical reason why Robin should not appear. All the time he was hoping, hoping secretly that Robin might be so demented he need never appear for trial, or would mouth such foolishness that nothing he could say would be accepted. He thought of those warm close nights—the silk sheets pulled over his head and Robin's, their mouths stuffed with sugared plums, their gossip about the courtiers, their—nay, nay, thought James, returning to his letter: "In the meantime I doubt not but that you have acquainted the chancellor with this strange fit of his, and if on these occasions, you bring him a little later than the hour appointed, the chancellor may in the meantime protract the time as the best he may." James had a picture in his mind of the solemn court scene suspended as the hours passed, awaiting Robin's anguished, forced entry. "If he says anything to Lord Hay, I expect to hear of it with all speed; if otherwise, let me not be troubled with it till the trial be past. Farewell." He looked at the last phrase again, praying he would not be troubled with Robin again.

James considered; the next day was Saturday and he would be receiving Gondomar, the Spanish ambassador, at noon. That would keep him occupied for the afternoon. He hated the thought of the suspense to which he would be subjected, for if Robin told the story of their love affair in court he would hear of it quickly, as he had arranged that light skiffs be tied to Westminster Pier which could bring news to Whitehall in moments. He thought, as he entrusted his last secret letter to a page boy, that however Robin might feel on the morrow his fear and apprehension could not be greater than that of his king.

Robin gave in. After a sleepless night he dozed from four until six and was awakened by the calls of the morning watch taking over duty from the men who had kept the night. Their clear concise cries, as clipped and economical as the sounds sailors make on high seas, cleared his head of bringing down James and his corrupt court.

It would be folly to go to trial and try to shock the English gentlemen. If he spoke of sodomy they would confer on monopolies in the Kent coal trade. If he were to speak of catholic plots they would look down their long English noses and consider the tax on shipping out of the port of Bristol. They would reduce anything he said to figures and dates. "Is this evidence?" he could imagine Ellesmere's quavering old voice now. Robin flung his bedclothes off and decided to keep quiet about the king's secrets. Silence would earn him his life and a pension. It would perhaps save Frances from some lengthy imprisonment, and the child would grow up with them both. He would have smiled six months before at his idyll of 25 May; a country house, a well-set table and such gentry of the countryside about it who chose to eat and drink with him. It was a humble ambition, and in achieving it he would do better than he had ever expected as a raw Scots youth. He put one foot to the cold floor smiling at the thought of Moore's surprise when he found his prisoner biddable.

The lieutenant, James Hay, and his nincompoop cousin, had spent a tortuous evening with Robin, beseeching him to come to Westminster Hall quietly the next day. "Aye," he had said, "and if I go?

Has Jamie thought on the things I might say about him and his like?" He had bragged of the secrets he would unfold. His persuaders had been nonplussed, not knowing what his information might be, and not daring to ask it. They had departed by nine o'clock, walking wearily across the grass. Robin had watched them triumphantly from his eyrie in the Tower. He had felt like an owl watching mice, as their black figures stalked into the shadows of a warm evening. A sky veined with red like a bloodshot eye had warned of the Saturday to come.

At six in the morning he could feel a faint breeze stirring across the floor of his room. He knew it would be the last mercy of a relentless day. By eight the sun was brazen, warders were wilting on the walls of the Tower, their tunics stiff with sweat from the heat of the week before. "Christ save us," he muttered. "If this be May how will we live to June?" Robin had no breakfast, but a mouthful of white bread and a glass of wine and water. He asked if there would be food at Westminster Hall. His warder was so pleased to find the Earl of Somerset tractable that he promised a small basket of cold meats, some sallet herbs, and a flask of wine. Robin thought that the preparations were those for a day in a hayfield, idly lying in the sun while others worked. At nine he watched Moore coming towards his rooms. The lieutenant's pace was slow, he seemed to be making excuses to himself not to collect his prisoner, but looked from side to side, sent one halberdier chasing the paths, picking up dead flower heads, another was given a scroll and hollooed off in another direction. At last he raised his eyes to the window. Robin waved and smiled. Moore frowned, thinking this another flight of madness. He opened the doors unwillingly.

"Sir George," said Robin, "I ha' been waiting on you these three hours."

"The trial begins at ten," replied Moore scowling.

"And I am ready for it."

He had used his three hours to advantage. Robin might have been an ambassador eager to impress an alien court. He wore a plain cut black-satin coat and breeches, their only ornament was a binding of satin ribbon cunningly laid inside the filleted seams. Over it he had cast a gown of uncut velvet, also black, with sleeves puffed out in a stiff silk overlaid with thin lace. His gloves had been made from the same fabric as his suit and had satin cuffs, turned forward and edged with a lace which melted into that on his sleeves so that his hands were invisible, clouded from sight. With a touch of bravado Robin went to his night table and lifted up his George. He smiled as he slipped the decoration round his neck. "I must wear the king's gift," he confided. Sir George Moore was unsure whether Robin was in earnest or sneering so he allowed himself a small unwilling smile which Robin returned with a grimace which exposed once more his brave white teeth. He adjusted the order carefully, ensuring that the chain did not disturb his hair which had been curled and perfumed by a man brought in especially that morning. Moore could not remember permitting it and intended to have a word with the officer of the watch about it when all these distractions were over. Robin fussed about the room like a woman he thought, as his prisoner clouded the air with perfume and chose a phial of violet water from a curious small cabinet. However, he could not criticize, for it was miraculous that the man should come with them so cheerfully after the alarums of the night before. He expected Robin to dart down the jetty into the stinking water as they went towards the river gate, or make a scene upon the river, crying for aid from the watermen. He did neither, but sat quietly in the bows, his velvet gown lapped round him although it was so warm. Moore did not talk to him. He felt tricked by Robin's acquiescence—as if he had unnecessarily warned the king.

When they stood on land once more he deputed two fellows to walk close by the earl's sides. "If he makes any signal, or tries any untoward gesture or cries out, pinion his arms thus," he counselled them while Robin turned about on the privacy of Westminster steps where the crowd could not see the landing. The warders flushed, annoyed by the way in which Sir George had gripped them as if they were felons.

"He seems biddable enough to me," grumbled one, glancing at the strutting earl whose gold and jewelled George made them blink.

"Never you mind how he seems," growled Sir George, "keep close to him. Let no man get betwixt you and the earl, nay not by a penknife blade. He is as cunning as a cat and may cause some commotion during the trial. He is to be overcome at once if he speaks of the king in any unsolicited manner."

He passed them two cloaks which he had secreted on the floor of the boat. They were intended for the night watch, being woollen, with high collars and wide furled skirts. "Do you cover his head from either side with these if he looked to misbehave," he warned them.

The warders were impressed by this extra precaution. They took the cloaks seriously and laid them over their outer arms. Both were in their 40s, grave, stout men who had families to think of, they would not let Robin Carr escape or speak out of turn at his trial.

They all waited in an outer room while the court began its business. Through the imperfectly shut door Robin could hear a man calling out the names of the peers as if they had been little boys attending school.

"Who is he?" he asked Moore. The lieutenant humoured him by putting his head close so that they could both look through the hinge.

"That is Walter Lee, the Sergeant at Arms," he obliged. "Lord Ellesmere you know. Another prosecuting counsel stands there, Sergeant Montague, whom you have met. Sir Frances Bacon will prosecute you on behalf of the crown." He said this hastily knowing no man could argue long or loud against the Attorney General. "Sir Randall Crew sits there. He will develop the argument for the crown."

"Zounds," said Robin wonderingly. "They have a good many set against me."

This was so true that Moore could only shrug his shoulders. There was some confusion over two peers who were sick and had not attended the trial.

"Belike they think I will rise to power again," said Robin sourly, out of the corner of his mouth and then Moore was pushing him towards the door.

XXXVII

IT TOOK A second for Robin to collect himself. The hall was
so much lighter than the room in which he had waited, and the glow
which came through the great window behind the judge's bench
was like looking into the fiery furnace. He heard a swell of sound
at his entrance which died away as he began to walk towards the
bar, as people on either side of the aisle stopped talking to watch
him. He even heard mutters from one side or the other. "God save
us, where's his beauty now?" "Hush." "His eyes are quite sunk in
his head, like stones in sand." "Hush." And as he walked on more
and more hushing spread until he felt as if he passed through a
trough of dried leaves. Behind him at the bar was laid his white
wand of office, now relinquished but being displayed as a reminder
that he was no common man. Lifting his eyes Robin was appalled
to see a face leering from the crowd full at his own. Seeing Robin's
eyes, he lifted one hand, knuckled into a fist, and shook it at him,
and Robin realized that this was the other Robin, the Earl of
Essex: Well, well, thought Robin, he alone would make me fight
for it.

He was told to hold up his hand; Ellesmere coughed occasionally
like an ancient sheep as the accusation came to an end. He shuffled
as he asked "Robin Carr, Earl of Somerset, you have heard the
indictment. How do you plead? Guilty or not guilty?"

"Not guilty," said Robin plainly.

The tension broke in the hall like skin parting on bubbling milk;
until he had pleaded the assembly was not sure whether there would
be an hour's entertainment or a day's; he saw Bacon and his fellows
frown.

Ellesmere cleared his throat, brought his hands together and
began: "Robert, Earl of Somerset, you have been arraigned and
pleaded 'not guilty'. Now I must tell you, whatever you have to say
in your own defence, say it boldly, without fear: and though it be
not the ordinary custom you will have pen and ink to help your
memory. Remember that God is the God of truth. A fault defended
is a double crime. Hide not the verity, nor affirm an untruth, for

to deny that which is true increases the offence. Take heed lest your own wilfulness cause the gates of mercy to be shut upon you."

As Ellesmere paused and wiped his mouth, Robin thanked the clerk for the paper and ink, wondering if his mind and hand would be quick enough to record those points which he might raise in his own defence. For his part, Ellesmere looked upon Robin benignly, realizing that free speech was not truly possible for he knew of orders to shut Robin's mouth at any mention of the king or his part in the story. He gave an instructive talk to the jury, those lords left limp from the previous trial, adding, "free your discourse from all partiality, let truth prevail and endeavour to make it appear".

Upon this, the peers shuffled lower in their seats.

Robin did nothing but dip his pen in the pot. He was frightened now, but rather that he would be too weak-witted than of the panoply of justice.

Sergeant Montague had the dubious task of showing why Somerset should be brought to trial at all after so many others had been tried and hanged for their separate parts in Overbury's death. His notes had been prepared by Bacon and he read them uncertainly and slowly which aided Robin in his writing, "as if I were a pesky clerk," he said to himself, "my right hand'll be seized up for a month". An odd snatch of memory flashed into his mind, of George Villiers' right hand thrusting a poigniard at a pastry stag. Robin smiled grimly. He had fought his fate well and would continue fighting.

"My lords," admitted Montague, "know that the Earl of Somerset stands indicted for little which can be proved with evidence," then he gathered his gown for a final assault on the peers: "And I will conclude with two desires: first, that the lords will not expect visible proof, as this was a work of darkness. Secondly, that whereas in an indictment there be many things charged, you should not expect that there will be proof. Consider only the substance of the matter which is this: Did Lord Somerset procure or cause the poisoning of Sir Thomas Overbury, or did he not?"

Upon this he stepped down, after bowing from one side to the other, like an actor expecting applause. Sergeant Montague had a brief rôle and he wished to receive as much acclaim as possible for it.

The next part of the trial bewildered Robin, for Ellesmere arose and repeated almost word for word the last speech of Montague, and was followed by Coke and several of the judges. It all affirmed, as he wrote for the first time in an ungainly hand on his paper, that the crown had no proof and sought to cover this deficiency by pretending that they did not need any in order to accuse Robin. Bacon made an address composed of fat obscuring bone. There was so little of which he could accuse Somerset. All he could reiterate was that this case was being tried fairly. It sounded deceptive even in his own ears. The crowd shuffled.

Robin looked at his paper, which was empty except for the single line he had written during Montague's preliminary speech, and he felt as if he were being stifled in a soft wool blanket of words. So far he had thought very little in the case had pertained to him, yet it had all insinuated against him in a roundabout way. He scribbled while Bacon was explaining how much more grievous was a crime directed against a prisoner "in the king's protection". He made a plea for the lack of evidence to be ignored, "Poisoning is the most secret of all deeds". His ironic tone suggested that the absence of proof was part of the crime as a whole. Poisoners never left evidence. They were too cunning and worked in the dark. He drew breath and said: "Sir Thomas Overbury".

Several ladies drew out their handkerchiefs and began to weep. The name was like that of a martyr now, calculated to cause sorrow and regret, as the aftermath of those emotional trials conducted by Coke. Others in the court settled to enjoy descriptions of the poor man's sufferings, of his wasted body, and his ravaged spirit. Bacon looked about him with dry eyes. He smiled a little: "Overbury," he said explosively, "was naught and was corrupt". Into the hush of indignation which ensued he added: "The ballad mongers would make him a worthy man, done foully to death by a noble faction. They should be mended and think on the truth."

He glanced at Robin, who was now white faced, half irritated that one who had been his friend was so dishonoured after death, and yet half relieved that a jot of honesty had somehow worked its way into the trial like a real worm into an artificial rose.

"Of Weston's guilt there is no question," Bacon continued, "or that Overbury was poisoned. These are facts which we cannot doubt."

Bacon opened his arms and smiled with sly benevolence. He told Robin to answer clearly without confusion, and gave him a swift lesson in replying to evidence. He added quickly that there would not be too much to answer, hoping none in court would notice that the brevity of the evidence was owing to there being none. "Therefore make your answers in your own good time and I will remind you if you leave out that which might aid you."

The prisoner was confused already. He bit at the end of his quill and screwed up his forehead like a child writing sums on a slate.

"There are four things I will prove," Bacon said looking away from Robin and about the rest of the hall. "First, that there was a root of bitterness, a mortal malice or hatred between the noble prisoner and the dead man." Robin's face creased more. Had there been such a public tangle between Tom and himself? He remembered how they had thrown out insults in the privacy of their rooms, taunting each other, and how often he had flounced from Tom's apartments. "I will treat with each in turn," promised the Attorney General, "so now I will expound on their feelings for each other."

The shuffling stopped when the first witness appeared and was sworn in. Robin was surprised and disconcerted to see that it was Harry Payton, who gave his home as "Bourton-in-the-Water where I am in service to Master Nicholas Overbury". He told the story of his master's quarrel with the prisoner, ending with some satisfaction: "My master shouted 'Seeing you neglect my advice, I desire we should part and that you give me that portion you know is due to me and I will leave you free to stand on your own legs'. At which Lord Rochester says back at once: "My legs are straight enough to bear me up. I will be even with you for this.' "

Into the silence, Ellesmere mildly queried: 'How is't you remember all so well, Master Payton?"

Harry Payton blushed: "As I wrote it all down, my lord, knowing it may be in question one day."

Bacon nudged his memory onwards: "Your next meeting with Lord Rochester was upon a sad occasion, was it not?"

Payton needed no urging; he told of Killigrew's innocent vomit powders; and of the more evil potions sent by the countess.

Bacon held up one hand: "Was he ill upon receipt of the powders from the earl?"

Payton considered a moment. "I know not, sir. Truth to tell, there were so many powders and phials going into his rooms by one way or another, that I know not which made him sick."

"What did you say to Lord Rochester, as he was then?"

"Why, I told him my master was sick and he says: "How sick?'

and I said 'Very sick'. 'Very sick indeed?' he asks, at which I said out: 'Aye with three score purges and vomits in one day'."

Although this testimony had been produced before, at the trial of Weston, the audience relished it.

"What said the earl to this?"

"He said 'Pish' and turned away," reported Payton.

A hissing as pervasive as a wind in dry grass crept over the courtroom. Robin backed from the bar, seeing those antagonistic faces all turned on him. He wanted to cry out: It was not like that. How could I have believed such a story?

"They hanged Elwes on less," muttered Moore to himself.

"One more thing," continued Bacon to Payton. "You had a look at a letter from Overbury to the earl?"

"I did. One sentence escaped from the seal."

There were smiles in the hall. Several remarked on Payton's long thumbnail. He looked about helplessly. Could any say they would not have looked under the seal if they were embroiled in such a tale?

"It matters not how you came to read the letter," remarked Bacon.

"What did that part say?"

"It said: 'If I died, my blood will lie upon you'."

A loud clatter of conversation again broke upon the hall, which only faded when the next witness appeared and word spread through the hall that this was Davies, the other pawn used in the game, they quietened, so that Bacon could ask the first two or three necessary but uninteresting questions in near silence.

"I will keep this witness's testimony to a meagre offering," Bacon promised the lords who were a little irritated by him, for they showed no signs of boredom and had enjoyed the drama of Payton's story.

"Did you hear some comment by Sir Thomas on the proffered embassy, after he had been committed to the Tower?" asked Bacon.

"I did so. He had not been in there a week when I went to carry away his soiled linen and should not have seen him, for Sir William Wade was a strict guardian, but that he saw me through the half shut door and beckoned to me——"

"Overbury?"

"Aye, just so—my master."

"What said he to you?"

"He said there was no need to buy the warm furs and blankets he had asked me to order in the past week. He said that he for one would only have had need of them if he had gone to Muscovy as an ambassador."

"How did he say that?"

Davies paused, putting more emphasis on his answer than Bacon had intended: 'Why, as if he would ne'er have gone anyway without great persuasion."

"Sir Francis, this is hearsay——" interrupted Ellesmere.

"Confine yourself to his words," advised Bacon hastily.

"That he would have gone as ambassador to Russia but had been persuaded not to, by my lord Rochester."

"Thereby incurring the king's righteous wrath," commented Bacon, "and so leading to his own imprisonment." He was silent a moment so that the court would digest the cunning of the plot. "Master Davies," he continued, "like Master Payton you had opportunities beyond the ordinary to read your master's letters."

There was no tittering in court. They were too enthralled.

"Did you not see in one that Overbury said he 'would be even' with Lord Rochester."

Davies looked ashamed: "Aye, it was at the end of a letter I carried."

"Did you observe the reaction of the noble prisoner to the letter?"

Davies looked at Robin for the first time. He seemed awkward and ashamed: "I doubt he ever saw the letter," he explained. "There was a lot of letters taken from me at the gate, some sent on and some not. Sir Jervis Elwes had the right to remove such letters as I carried them on my person, not within pies as was expected."

Robin darted up like a lark from a field of wheat: "You hear that?" he cried. "He says I never saw some letters!"

"It is true," said Bacon, then added ominously, "yet Master Davies found that same letter again, with others, and he recognized that all were in his master's hands."

Robin glared at Davies. What a double-dealing creature he had been, using quotations from these letters that Robin had asked him to retrieve! He doubted if the man had ever seen the letter before he had removed it from the trunk to which Robin had directed him.

As Davies left the witness stand, Robin was sickened to see the Attorney General was drawing out more letters from inside his sleeve. Even across the courtroom he recognized the opulent seal and staccato writing of Overbury.

"I will read now a letter," Bacon confided to the interested lords.

"It will wring the hearts of all honest men for it was sent to the noble prisoner by the unfortunate Sir Thomas Overbury."

Ellesmere was looking affronted at the bias of Bacon's words but before he could remark on them the Attorney General was flourishing his first piece of real evidence before the astonished court. Robin had to look straight ahead, attempting unconcern as those poignant words unfolded.

" 'This paper comes under seal and therefore I will be bold to speak to you as I used to do myself. I understand that you told my brother Lidcote that my unreverent style would make an alienation betwixt you and me hereafter, at least such a one as we should never be again as we had been. With what face could you tell him you would be less to me, to whom you owe more than to any soul living, both for your understanding, fortune and reputation?' " Bacon now and again lifted one eye to see how Robin took it as well as the court. " '. . . You and I shall come to a public trial before all the friends I have. They shall know what words have passed between us heretofore of another nature than these. I upon the rack, you at your ease, negligent of me, and I must speak calmly . . .' "

Fury arose in the well of the hall where the public sat. How rightly had the dead man prophesied? Under the jeers, a deeper darker murmur was arising like the beginning of a storm. Ellesmere heard it as did the sergeant of the guard. They were both experienced in tumultuous trials. At a word the halberdiers who lined the wall began to walk in twos into the hall, standing almost negligently along the aisle; eight of them formed a square about the prisoner. Robin knew that they were preparing to protect him from the fury of the mob. After a moment of dazed shock, Ellesmere realized that he had achieved a furtive silence, and said: "I will have the hall cleared. Sergeant, d'ye hear me?"

"Aye, my lord," his tone suggested he understood very well.

"Clear the court if there is another outcry like that I heard. This trial need not be public."

It had to be, it was important that the law be seen taking effect in this case, but the crowd did not understand that. They simmered like a pot taken off the flame, finally sitting quietly except for odd snatches of comment.

"I will not read further unless there is silence," warned Bacon whose voice would crack if he had to raise it. He glared at Robin and was relieved to see that he did not weep. The prisoner was looking before him, as pale as all in the overhot hall, but composed, controlled. His amber eyes dared Bacon, who continued to read Overbury's letter.

" 'Notwithstanding my misery, you visited your woman, frizzled your hair more curiously, took care for hangings, and daily were solicitous about your clothes, officious in waiting, held daily traffic of letters with my enemies, without any turning of it to my good; sent me nineteen projects for my liberty...' " Overbury's scolding voice seemed to come hot off the paper, " '...and sent me some frivolous account of the miscarriage of them.' "

Robin shook his head. How could he explain how this was all an extension of Tom's quarrel, this upbraiding, nagging tone was one reason the man had been sent to the Tower, and why he had remained there. God's teeth, should they not pity him, receiving such whining threatening epistles, rather than feel sorrow for the writer? He opened his mouth, saw the metallic eyes of Bacon, and was quiet.

" 'By God', said Overbury, 'I have not friends to speak my last words to. I have all this vacation wrote the story betwixt you and me from the first hour to this day...' "

Robin shivered. On one side, Moore looked at him speculatively. He was alarmed for his prisoner. Like Bacon he had observed grimaces, the clenched hands, the starts of surprise. Bacon saw in them guilt or regret. Moore suspected fever. If the man was sickening it might explain that outburst last night, so casually dismissed this morning. And now, God help him, Somerset was shivering when every man there longed to untrusss his breeches and open his shirt to cool air. Excepting that the air was hot, sultry, still; it was the season for a fever——

" 'When I found you first,' " went on Bacon's voice as he turned the close written page, " 'what I found you when I came, how I lost all the great ones of my country for studying your reputation, fortune and understanding; how many hazards I have run for you— what services have passed betwixt you and me.' "

Out with them. Secrets, on which rested all this case. Secrets of Tom's overpowering love. Yet Tom had known how precipitous that path would have been, to rival the king! And then Frances had dared to show the lust of her feelings for Robin. Lust, there was no love in that silver head. So Tom brought all down. With himself.

" 'All these particulars I have set down in a large discourse, and on Tuesday I made an end of writing it fair, and on Friday I have sealed it up under eight seals and sent it by a friend of mine whom

I dare trust (taking on oath not to open it). I send it to him; and then to all my friends, noble gentlemen and women, and then to read it to them and take copies of it; and I vowed I had spoke the truth. This I think you will deny not a word. So thus, if you will deal wickedly with me, I have provided that, whether I live or die, your shame shall never die, but ever remain to the world to make you the most odious man alive.' "

There was no statement. Or else it had been kept too secret to be found. Several sobs could be heard about the hall as ladies lowered their masks, exposing their ravaged faces to public gaze. There was no need to call for quiet. Robin felt that none need ever speak again. He allowed his own face to fall forward into his hands. It looked pathetic but was a gesture dictated by anger. Overbury's threats came to him as the teasing of a sulky child who wanted his own way. And Frances was the same. To what end had he come because of these two clever, sensual, selfish people?

Into the emotional courtroom came a thin cold voice, full of reason. It said: "How do you know Lord Somerset ever received these letters?"

Robin looked through his laced fingers. It was Lord Wentworth, the seeker after truth, the plain dealer, confounding Bacon who stared at him with surprise.

"I can tell my Lord Wentworth," said Coke without rising. Ponderously he began the story of discovering the letters in a box. "We have the testimony of one Simcock," continued Coke. "He with whom Weston lodged those obscene and magical dolls. Weston told him that Lord Somerset had charged him, Weston, to look after Overbury well, for if it all came out, one of those two would die."

Ellesmere might have interposed that this was all hearsay and irrelevant but Robin was on to Coke's mumbled narration like a stoat at a rabbit. "Ha, so said this fellow Simcock, my Lord Chief Justice, but did you ever ask Weston about this tale?"

Coke was affronted and looked back at Robin but did not answer him, at which Wentworth muttered: "What nonsense it all is," then more loudly, "How long were Simcock and Weston acquainted?"

"I know not," said Coke sulkily but Simcock was in the hall and already pushing his way to the front to say that he and Weston had an ancient and familiar friendship.

Bacon began to speak rapidly, guessing by the pulse of the court that if Wentworth or Somerset commenced asking questions they would continue and that the hollow case for the crown could easily be exposed. He said: "Weston had continual access to Lord Somerset and had rewards from him. Lord Somerset charged him to look well to Overbury." He paused so that a sinister connotation could be read into that phrase. "It was not his lordship's marriage to Lady Frances Howard that caused him to fear, but the secret scheming that had caused it, but that is not what I speak of now." He coughed: "A quarrel over a marriage is no cause for murder, but consider my lords how deep these two friends were in with state secrets and the stratagems of the crown. He had devised so many plots and schemes that Lord Somerset was afraid he would be a party to high treason if he went further with them. Their correspondence was conducted in secret and you have heard that Sir Thomas Overbury read the letters of ambassadors before the king's majesty, and that these two men put their heads together to run the affairs of this land. They had a code which I could expound on here but will not for lack of time. It is enough to say that in it the king was named as 'Julius', the Archbishop of Canterbury was 'Unclius'." He frowned at the bench of lords, daring any of them to smile. "The Earl of Suffolk who is unhappily not with us, was called 'Wolfy'. In truth you will see that these two made plays out of all the world excepting themselves. Ha, it was a play then, but hath proved tragical since."

He finished his first consideration by producing that letter from Northampton in which the old man had explained the terms and conditions of divorce. Wentworth made a sly interruption, saying that as Northampton was dead the letter could have been written by any street-corner scribbler seeking to earn a penny. Coke, who felt all queries on evidence he had collected were barbs to torture him, said he would call in an expert in handwriting who would prove this letter had come from the dead earl himself.

Bacon realized Wentworth's deeper motive—that he suspected the prosecution of manufacturing evidence. Would that we had, thought Bacon, and we would not be in this sad state, relying on gossip and hearsay and dishonest servants.

The prisoner looked over Bacon's shoulder to the first row of public benches, a row of turnips laid along a wall, with gouged-out sleepy eyes, slack lips and lolling hams. He hated common men. He wondered if Villiers also despised the crowd. He knew that he would, for such as he and Villiers arose through their detestation of the populace and their desire to escape from it.

"Now to my second consideration," said Bacon and there was a sound of weary subsidence in the hall. The great clock was striking two. Could they bear an afternoon in this glasshouse, attacked by the glowering brilliant sunshine? But none left the hall. They were all overconscious of the occasion. Bacon said softly, "There was a lovers' plot to put Overbury out of the way". Before the earl could reply he continued to read, "I have heard that at one time it was resolved somebody at court should fall out with Overbury and affront him. It is true this plan was not followed. This evidence came," triumphantly, "out of an examination of the noble prisoner, the Earl of Somerset. Note, my lords, he does not say that the plot was disliked. "Now," he added with satisfaction, "we come to the puddle of blood, and the first link—the first drop in the trial we must follow—consider the means by which Sir Thomas Overbury was trapped within the Tower. This was where he would lie, a victim of poison. He was sent there entirely by means of Lord Somerset."

After Sir Dudley Digges had given his testimony a murmur of dissatisfaction emerged from the hall. Only the most credulous had expected that the Archbishop of Canterbury would take the stand, yet Digges was rather like an ancient hobby horse, brought out yet again to regale the public by cavorting through a hoop. Digges's expression suggested that he too felt this, and that he would rather be anywhere but in Westminster Hall on a broiling hot day. He told the story simply as one who was well used to repeating it; that he had summoned Overbury to a consultation with the Archbishop of Canterbury at Lambeth, and he told of the offered embassy to Russia.

As he left the witness stand, he gave a look of sympathy to Robin as he passed him by. "Bear up," he said in an undertone, surprising Somerset who had never cared for Digges, thinking him crude, and obsessed with his voyages.

"Here," said Bacon, shaking out another letter, "is a letter sent to the king by the prisoner."

Robin shivered again. Had James also been untrue? He leaned towards the paper and saw indeed his own careful handwriting which was echoed on the paper. He continued to look sternly before him, only Moore had felt a spasm oppress his prisoner.

" 'In honesty I did not believe I would be arraigned,' " read

Bacon while all stared at Robin, fascinated by the exposure of a man by his own written word, but as Robin heard those phrases he breathed easily again. James had handed over a letter calculated to improve consideration for the prisoner rather than to incriminate him. Ha, so Bacon thought he was clever, producing a document attested by the king? Bacon hesitated over a sentence in which Robin had asked that the king's favour be extended to him. Well, what was unworthy in that? The poorest thief could do as much! " 'Having committed no offence against your person or the state, I hope I may not be brought to public trial, which I wish to avoid for my reputation's sake. If I do come to trial, I know that the strongest presumption against me will be that I consented to and endeavoured the imprisonment of Sir Thomas Overbury.' " And so it was—so it was—the only unjust thing of which he could be accused. Robin continued to look bravely ahead as Bacon read his letter. " 'I designed that for his reformation, not his ruin. I desire your majesty's mercy, and that I may dispose of my goods and land to my wife and child, and that you will pardon her now that she hath confessed her deed. As for myself, not knowing how I may be judged . . .' " He went into a reverie as Bacon's voice dragged on. How could any comment unkindly on his efforts to save something for Frances and the baby he had not yet seen? He fidgeted a little with his hands. Moore leaned forward, anxious. Robin mumbled at him, and both men were allowed to leave the hall "to answer a call of nature".

"Having secured a place for Sir Jervis Elwes, the next condition of the plotters was to bring Weston in as Sir Thomas Overbury's servant," Bacon was saying when the last spectator was seated again. "The Earl of Somerset had a hand in this——"

"That I did not," challenged Robin, "for I never met the man, only heard of him."

"What is that?" asked Bacon disbelievingly. "You say you never knew Weston?"

"Never," asserted Robin.

"Simcock hath declared that Weston said he knew you and that you told him to look well to Overbury," insisted the Attorney General.

Ellesmere interrupted. "Sir Francis, I must uphold my lord

Somerset in this, Weston is dead and what he said to Simcock may not have been the truth."

An old man appeared in the witness stand, gripping with both hands on the bar, his white hair was cut raggedly and his coat was a few years out of fashion. It was old Overbury.

"The king did not aid you?" Bacon asked him.

"He could not, for he was out of London but we saw him, Lord Rochester as we was then—many times, knowing him to be the best friend of our son."

"And what did he say?"

"He said that he would do all in his power to remove our son from that place. And so we believed him. All summer long he promised us with fair words that he would persuade the king to let Tom go, and oftimes said this was not the hour, or that he would wait until the king be in a good humour."

"Did you have any proof that he met with the king on this matter?"

"Alas," said the old man, "I know now that Lord Rochester played with us, and did naught to save our son."

Ellesmere was annoyed by this hearsay opinion, but Bacon had the old man removed and Sir John Lidcote sworn in, who continued the tale of Carr's evasions and dishonesty and who would have accused Robin more forcibly of deceit if Bacon, seeing the expressions of the judges, had not told him to retire.

"My lords, this was the last witness for the prosecution," Bacon told them. "What I will present from now will be parts of the depositions made by sundry persons concerned with the matter."

He began in a low hurried voice to repeat tales from the evidence of Monson and Davies, claiming that Somerset had connived to keep Sir Thomas Overbury in the Tower; adding a few other comments that the earl had not been eager to have his friend released.

Robin said boldly: "I never claimed that I was able to release him or that I wished him from that place. If any confession were needed I would only say that I was industrious in keeping Overbury in the Tower."

"Ha, you admit that?"

"I never refuted it. That was my grievous fault, none other."

"But you knew the plight of your one-time friend?"

"I knew he was sick from taking those powders he had asked of me."

"Did you not send letters on him to Lady Essex, who is now your wife?"

Robin could not remember. The heat was beginning to affect him adversely as all the others in the court; like pale, sweating Ellesmere, he mopped at his face with scented water, looking at Bacon meanwhile.

"Aye," said the Attorney General. "In your own examination you were none too clear my lord, for at the first query you said you had no letters betwixt your lady and yourself on the matter of Overbury. And later you asked that this be altered, thinking that you had written to her of the prisoner." He smiled at Robin. He had managed to suggest that Robin's mind had been changed by the production of those letters he had hoped were undiscovered or destroyed; to support this, Bacon lifted one or two pieces of paper from the table before him. "You also saw the apothecary de Loubell about this time."

"I did," said Robin, "and he will tell you there was no thought of poisoning but that Tom suffered in spirit, being melancholy from imprisonment."

Bacon said swiftly "We are not considering that Overbury died from any cause save that of poison, introduced one way or another."

"Do you call de Loubell as witness," suggested Robin eagerly.

Bacon hardly paused to listen, continuing by reading a letter from Northampton in which he had told Robin that Elwes was their man and that he would ensure that anything sent by Robin would pass unhindered to the prisoner. Robin did not assert that this only proved that his letters (what if they were lying and deceiving?) had reached Overbury.

Bacon was exhausted. There were two more points to prove of his four accusations. He had made copious instructions for the two sergeants at law, Montague and Crew. He begged the court's indulgence and sat down. It was three o'clock or more. He had been speaking since eleven.

As the sergeants rose Ellesmere asked them to hold awhile. "I would have a word with the accused," he explained and said kindly to Robin: "My lord, you have heard what hath been urged against you, and as you may imagine, there is more behind it, therefore you had best confess the truth, or else you will be more and more wound in the matter."

The judges looked sharply at Robin. If he confessed they would have succeeded, for their argument against the earl would have been heard and he would have had no chance to answer it.

But Robin tensed his lips deliberately. "My lord," he said politely to Ellesmere, "I have but one resolution, to defend myself."

The spectators applauded Robin. He had not deprived them of their great experience. He was giving the hounds of the law a run for their money. Many who had groaned at him when old Overbury had presented a picture of a knave who would not aid an aged parent, now encouraged him by crying out: "Go to it, brave Robin!" In this commotion the prisoner looked up and only saw the rock face of Essex, staring at him from the crowd, his eyes as fierce as those of a man in a fever.

"Then, if you will continue, my lord," said Ellesmere, "let us have a few moments' respite from the trial. Sergeant do you ask the guards to open the doors."

He had hoped to allow a flow of air into the stinking hall but when the doors were opened there was no difference. A haze hung over the room. It was stifling. Crew and Montague might prate for the whole afternoon but all knew the real case for the crown had been presented. It remained for Robin to defend himself.

XXXVIII

"I ASK MERCY for one thing, my lords," he said nervously as he rose, "that this case is not dealt with in order, but hindleg first like a driven pig. I have no learning in these matters."

"Take no heed of that" called one lord. "Speak as it comes."

Robin gave a weak smile and began by saying that he had engineered the imprisonment of Overbury, "I had wished to have him in the Tower for my own ends, not for a sinister reason as you have been told today, but as he threatened my marriage with the Countess of Essex by saying he could stop her divorce by telling the commission that we had been lovers some time."

When the shock of this had passed, rather like a wave, Robin saw Essex again, almost in front of the bar. He must have pushed his way there from where he had stood in the main body of the hall. He was tall and wore a brown hat which the guard would have him remove before the officers of law. Essex had ignored them and was advancing on Robin deliberately. Alarmed by his prisoner's hesitation, Moore looked up and recognized Essex.

"My Lord Chancellor," he interrupted, "there is one in the hall who threatens Lord Somerset."

Ellesmere said: "If you retreat not to the back of the hall my Lord Essex, you will be cast from the room. Know you that you cannot advance on a prisoner in such a way."

"I mean no harm," muttered Essex, sullenly eyeing Robin like a dog facing up to his dinner.

"I have no care for what you mean," said Ellesmere, "but knowing your relation to the Earl of Somerset I must ask you to retire if you be not more careful."

Essex shrugged and turned on his heel, reluctantly a way was made for him to disappear into the crowd.

"As for depriving Sir Thomas Overbury of his friends," said Robin hoarsely, "I did fall in with those notions of Lord Northampton to sever the prisoner from his acquaintance so that he would not hear from them that no plans were made to deliver him from the Tower."

"There was a conspiracy against the man," said Bacon heavily.

"There was, and I was part of it. I do not deny it. But the plot was to keep him in prison. I had no access to a plot to kill him, that I swear."

"We have letters showing your desire to conspire against your friend," insisted Bacon, "or else why were your letters to Lord Northampton burned and cut about?"

"My lords," said Robin, rightly addressing the jury, "that cutting and burning was not my doing but Sir Robert Cotton's. I do not know which parts he mutilated, or what was in them. My lords, think of this, if I had known those letters would condemn me, would I not have had them burnt upon Northampton's death, and not left them in a box in another's house?"

There was much nodding at this, all thought Somerset a fool but not as zany as that, why, most men burnt bills as soon as they had them, why keep letters which could have put his neck in a noose?

"Can you say naught of Sir Robert Cotton's work?" asked Bacon "and his attempts to gain you a general pardon?"

"Touching Sir Robert Cotton's testimony," Robert went on, "I did not look to see on what grounds he asked for a general pardon. I had asked for one. I will also admit that; but considering it lawyer's business I did not read the petition, expecting it to be the customary one sent by all high officers when they relinquish their seals." It was a lie, but it passed, who could dispute it? He peered at his notes and went on: "As to Sir Jervis Elwes, I was not part of the plot which put him into the Tower. The first I knew was when Northampton sent me the letter which you have heard today, saying that the Lord Lieutenant was a man who would aid us. At that time I believed that all Elwes intended was to keep Overbury under locks, and make sure that he did not hear that plans for releasing him were not set forward. I have heard that Elwes paid money to secure that position at the Tower. I never saw or heard of the money which was paid to Monson." He shuffled his papers but caught sight of the arm of Sir George Moore on his left side and went off on a rigmarole about being advised to ask the king for mercy by the Lord Lieutenant. "All I submitted to saying in that letter sent by me from the Tower was that I did consent to and endeavour the imprisonment of Sir Thomas Overbury and I say again, that is the truth."

"What of the poisoned tarts sent by you?" asked Bacon.

"What poisoned tarts?" retorted Robin. "I made no secret that I sent food to Sir Thomas, it was the way our letters were carried."

He remembered his wife lying on a bed, admitting to him that she had put Overbury out of the way. He said vindictively: "Frances said in her confession to you that no poisoned food was sent by me or by her. Some tarts were good and some were not. It needs must follow that the good ones were those sent by me and the bad ones came from her." He felt a little regret as he said this, but had Frances not told them that she had sent poison into the Tower, and was able to plead for mercy in spite of that?

Lord Lisle was standing up, and calling out "If you sent Overbury good tarts you might have found a proper messenger. Not that murdering Weston."

And then suddenly the bench of peers was erupting and wrangling, some disputing that accursed letter in which the "he" was so ill-defined, and another in which Frances had written to Elwes that "he bids me bid you send on the poisoned food". Was the mysterious "bidder" not Franklin, as Robin has assumed? Some lords believed it was Robin.

"Why not her husband?" called out Sergeant Montague. "Who better to direct her on the poisoning? The letters between her and him argue that he directed her in all things."

Robin sat appalled. Ellesmere did nothing to stop the arguments, and the quarrelling among the peers was spreading to the rest of the chamber. While Robin stood silent Crew came up close to him and suggested quietly that he might as well admit that the white powders sent to Overbury were arsenic. As the court quietened a little, Crew's voice came determinedly into the room.

"You say the powders were given by you, and made by Sir Robert Killigrew?"

"Aye, and all were vomit powders for his feigned sickness," replied Robin firmly.

"So——" Crew held up his short white fingers and counted off: "There was one carried by Rawlins for which we have his testimony. 'Twas sent in the first week of June."

"I know not the date."

"Suffice it to be so, early June then. The second, on the word of your servants, never reached poor Sir Thomas, for they laid it on the bed and you knocked it down, my lord, and scattered it so that it could not be gathered up."

"I believe I remember that," admitted Robin.

"That was the second powder from Killigrew. There was a third which never came to the Tower for you used it yourself when the court was out of London and you had a desire to sleep and the king wished to see you. On the word of your man, Rawlins."

Robin nodded cautiously.

"Did that not happen?" asked Crew roughly.

"Aye."

"On the word of Sir Robert Killigrew three powders were made up and sent to you. All three are accounted for. Then, my Lord, explain this to us; whence came the fourth powder taken by Davies to the Tower in July?"

The court was silent, all looking at the Earl of Somerset who was licking his dry lips nervously and staring, as did all else, at Crew's fat hands and the way he had counted out powders on them.

"Come, my lord," said Crew. "Shall I add them again? There were three powders sent to you by Killigrew. We have his word on that. And four were used, one way or another. The fourth and last being taken from you by Davies in July. Whence came that final powder?"

Robin shook his head, still sure that he was being deliberately confused, and old Ellesmere decided to play a part, "Come, come," he said. "We know how many may have had access both to Killigrew's signet and his powders and too many witnesses have dates off so pat they are questionable. Let my lord Somerset have a voice in his own defence."

"Thank you, my lord," replied Robin. "I pray you will not take circumstances for evidence——" He said one or two more things which were not pertinent and noticed how the peers looked tired, so he said briskly: "If you should do so, the condition of man's life were nothing. In the meantime you may see the excellence of the king's justice, which makes no distinction, putting me in your hands for a just and equal censure. For my part, I protest before God that I was neither guilty of, nor privy to, any wrong that Overbury suffered." He raised one hand to his hair and considered how to end his defence. "A man must be sensible of his own preservation," he added.

He heard a murmur of approval and realized that he had appealed to the crowd correctly, but what of the lords who were shuffling from the court to the jury room? They had to find him guilty. It was necessary for the crown to condemn him to excuse all those deaths during the past months. Moore touched his arm, a chair had been placed behind him and Robin gratefully sank into it, waving away the flask of wine offered by the lieutenant.

341

After the lords had been absent about ten minutes, Bacon began to frown. They had been out too long. They sent a messenger back asking for Ellesmere and Coke to advise them on points of law and these two tried to slip out unobserved by the crowd although Robin did not fail to see the guard who came for them.

Bacon preserved his usual severe expression but his pulse was beating like a kettledrum. What if the lords decided in Robin's favour? The prosecution case would be dissected by the people like a frog caught in a slimy pond. He closed his eyes briefly realizing that if the law were questioned, the crown would be the next to suffer criticism. He heard a slithering sound and looked up, it was Robert Carr's "George" sliding over his black silk coat as he removed it. He, at least, had no hope of mercy from the lords. He handed the glittering golden order to Moore who held it awkwardly, allowing the chain to dangle from his hand like a dog leash.

"Will you remove Lord Somerset while the verdict is brought in?" asked Ellesmere.

After he had gone the bench of peers sat like mourners outside a tomb, their faces stern and set towards the hall. They were all aware of the gravity of their decision. Fanshaw stepped up to stand before them.

"How do you say, my lord, guilty or not guilty?" he asked the peer at the end of the bench.

"Guilty," was the reply.

Fanshaw passed slowly before the bench of rigid men, who called out "Guilty" 22 times.

Ellesmere sighed. "Ask that the Earl of Somerset and Sir George Moore be brought back in."

As soon as he entered the hall, Robin knew that the verdict had expectedly gone against him. He could see it by the faces turned towards him, excited by his entry, whispering and pointing at his neck where the George had so lately been hanging. He wondered if he would reach the front of the court. The bar loomed up like a rail separating him from a precipice. He saw the 44 curious eyes watching him. They had judged him. Many of those peers had fawned on him when he had been Jamie's darling. He wondered how the king would receive the news of his disgrace. Step by step to the bar. Would James watch the execution? Would there be an execution? Another step. Frances had foiled them it seemed, for all spoke of her plea for mercy as if it had already been allowed. Another step. But she was a Howard, not a son of a Scots squire.

Step up. He had braved Bacon, at least. One more. He would not be remembered as one who ran from a fight. He stopped. His nut-brown eyes looked hard at the peers. Many looked downwards, unable to face his bold, accusing gaze.

Ellesmere said in a low voice: "Robert Carr, Earl of Somerset, you are found guilty——"

He could still fight them, he thought, as Fanshaw said: "Have you anything to say why a verdict of death should not be pronounced upon you?"

"Aye," he said, groping for his paper. They would not be rid of him so easily! He said: "The sentence must be just. I desire a death according to my degree." Not for him a noose about his pretty neck that the king had so often stroked. The Howards had the axe, why should not he? "As to what was said——" he began savagely, remembering how bent and frail the evidence had been.

Ellesmere brought his little hammer down to stop him: "My lord, you can no longer speak in your defence. Is there any reason why judgement of death should not be pronounced?"

"I have nothing more to say," said Robin Carr, blithe Robin, gay Robin, hunting, dancing, laughing and jesting Robin. Behind him, his wand of office was lifted by the Chief of the Court and ceremoniously broken in two.

EPILOGUE

1624

A horse stamps up a hill, its hooves almost soundless on dried grass and mould which shape the path. Beside it runs a garden wall, higher than the rider, and built of bricks burnt apricot by sunlight. Presently the horse is stopped by a door in the wall, it is wooden and well weathered, and as the rider dismounts and slots the reins through an iron ring let into the doorpost, he looks at the coat of arms carved in stone above the lintel. It is the royal emblem but much eroded by age and rain. The rider's face is also carious, rendered soft by time and veined all over by tiny lines, very faintly marked like an old engraving which is rubbed towards the edge. His face and hair are the same colour, that of bread taken from the oven too soon. He struts like a handsome man, decayed.

Opening the door he looks into a garden; it is all grey green for it is filled with moss roses which are hardly out of bud so that a few red knots are the only colour in a woollen shawl of foliage. The rider withdraws swiftly behind the door, allowing it to stand apart a little so that he will know when to enter this enclosed place; he has hidden because two ladies are pacing over the lawn.

When they have made their way on to a formal terrace and away from the wilder rose garden, the horseman returns and walks towards the lawn in the direction they have already taken, flicking his flank with his switch, and looking from side to side under his grim sand-coloured brows until he reaches a shell carved into the inside of the wall where there is a stone seat covered with chamomile. Here he has agreed to wait.

He is an impatient man, and as the minutes pass he stands up once or twice, reducing the garden to the terrain of a battlefield in which he stands in an authoritative position; seeing and hearing nothing but the bushes and the humming of bees, which is like a distant church service imperfectly understood. He sits again, and bites his nails and makes patterns on the dry earth with the end of his switch.

He hears an almost inaudible shuffling, like a sad and heavy beast making its way towards its lair, breaking small twigs and grasses with its passage. Along a tunnel of green leaves comes an old man. His bent back sways from one side to another. His passage is cumbersome and slow. He is encased in a coat which is almost impenetrable, of several layers of fabric, and a fur cloak; and he wears a hat like a hard thimble. From this incarceration his head pokes out, waving from side to side to see the pathway, his body has three legs, all thin and black, but as he comes closer one leg becomes a thick ebony staff, ferruled and topped with gold. When he reaches the sculpted shell, this scuttling beetle halts and breathes deeply while he watches his visitor with suspicion. At long last he speaks, the machinery of his voice groaning a little:

"Ha, Rabbie, is it yourself?"

At which the sandy man comes forward and grips the king's arm as he bows, sure that if this huddled creature moves too fast it will fall. They sit in their stone bower, two ageing gnomes with rattling teeth and powdery knobbled hands.

"I like not the secrecy of this meeting," says Carr at last, and his Scots voice has lost none of its insolent conceit.

"Ah weel 'tis how 't must be," says King James, rocking a little as he sits, and blearily watching a bee trying to penetrate a rosebud, bumbling and kicking like an impetuous lover assailing a virgin.

"Yet am I still disgraced?" asks Carr who will never let well alone.

James looks at him with some contempt. "I wud no have ye back at court," he says finally. "I pardoned you and saved you from death eight years since. I would not have you near me."

"Why not so? Am I worse than any other man about you? The times are past when you could be so nice in your choice of company!"

"What mean you?" asks the old man who had hoped to sit quietly in the sun.

"Why, I have ears and eyes and know what passes at Whitehall. All your nobles cast off for some peccadillo or another, and most by their avarice. Bacon impeached for abusing his office as Lord Chancellor. Suffolk found stealing his master's goods, your own treasury depleted by him like a naughty journeyman making off with the cashbox. And that Steenie! Your lover and your toady. Whoe'er said I was corrupt? I was a lamb compared with that pretty wolf."

"Hush, hush," says James, laying his fragile hand upon Robin's sleeve. "Do not abuse Steenie."

"Ha, when he was young George Villiers he cocked a less dainty leg, did he not?"

"I am not here to quarrel, Rabbie."

Remembering the tenuous position which he holds, Robin allows his invective to spit into silence while the bees murmur and gather, and the sun beats upon their dried indoor faces.

At last James says: "I am like Christ. He had his John, I have my Buckingham."

The mention of Villiers' title inflames Robin but he does not reply, hurt though he is by the king's blasphemy.

"I was gey sorrowed to hear of the queen," he says at last, allowing his finger tips to touch the king's swollen arthritic knee.

"It was sad when she died, and yet not sad. She had suffered long. The body corrupts without we know of it. As with Winwood. Do you remember Winwood?"

Robin could not forget him. "The engineer of my destruction," he says.

"Aye, there was a faction against you, right enough, but he was so small a part of it."

"It was he set those searches in motion, that caused my downfall."

"Rabbie, Rabbie," said the king, "if wrong had not been done and Overbury had not died he would ha' had naught to find. Think on that."

"What of Winwood?"

James had forgotten what he had to say. He sat still for a moment, then he said: "Aye, Winwood that seemed so hearty a man, decayed within three days and died with a withered heart, a spleen as rotten as maggotty wood, no kidneys left and his liver discoloured like a toadstool. What think you of that?"

"How know you this?"

"Mayerne told me," replied James with childish delight. "He brings me reports on all untowards deaths if the bodies be opened." He added slyly, "And your own lady, she is not well?"

"Well enough," answered Robin roughly, then feeling he had been too harsh, said more gently: "You said we must live together, eat our meals together, but after the trials we never brought ourselves to intimacy again."

"It's as well if what I hear be true," said James with some satisfaction; "that she paddles her body with unclean young men and pays them to be with her."

A shudder ran through Robin. He said: "Yet you, sir, are likely rigorous and chaste."

James did not hear his ironic tone or refused to comprehend it.

"My son is long faced, grave as a tomb—ha, ha." His little trickling laughter subdued to a cough. "Aye, and Steenie has altered too. He still loves me," he added hastily. "Both boys love me dearly."

"But they keep you circumspect I hear."

James looked affronted.

"I meant not that," said Robin hastily. "But there are a few blithe nights I understand, and all the jubilation gone."

"I am an old man," said James. "Those two are in the right. I could not bear that riotous way of life we knew, Rabbie. It would kill me in a week."

"You need me by your side, sire. We would make the days bright with hunting and in nights delight in merriment. Remember the times we had? The games, the jests, the tumblers, the dirty tales, the tipsy, wanton pleasure——"

"Aye, I do," mourned James. "But would not have them more. Nor you, Rabbie, nor you. We are older, we are wiser men."

"Perhaps you are afraid of your bear leaders?"

"What?"

"Why, I hear that Prince Charles and your loved Steenie lead their king with a ring through the nose like bearmasters at a country fair, who cry 'Dance' and dance the poor beast must, or 'Sit' and so he does."

James removed Robin's hand from his knee. "Go, you knave," he said. "I loved you once. I would have kept some friendship if I did not still find in you that accursed shrill determination to rule me."

Robin sat silently for a moment then said more gently: "Have you remembrance of the past? Did you not love me once?"

James faced the sharp early summer air while tears gathered behind his eyelids. Slowly the juice oozed out. He could not keep it secret. He wiped his cheek with the back of his hand. "Let me be, Rabbie," he whispered. "There is no place for you about me."

Savagely Robin returned: "Not to show those two young men who is master in your house?"

"I like it well the way it is," replied James, as another tear crept from his eye. It ran quickly down the deeply grooved channel of his cheek and laid its salt upon his lip like a sour kiss.

Robin leaned forward and put his elbows on his knees. He bent his face into his cupped hands. His stifled voice emerged: "So you do not want me?"

"Rabbie. You have pestered me since you left the Tower, asking to return to your old place and then to any position about the court. Have you no pride, man? Can you not see how unwise it would be for you to return? A poisoner——"

"That was never proved."

"Aye, but so close it will never be forgot. You are become a bogey to the court. I could not have you about me, Rabbie, and there's an end to it."

"What should I do then?"

"Live on your land like many others. Bacon has resigned himself to fate. Do you do likewise. You have a daughter, have you not, who lives with you? Is that not a blessing? You are alive, that thought to die."

Robin parted his hands and looked between them at the busy earth where ants were pattering about their business, moving grains of earth and pieces of leaf. "I am but two years short of 40," he said. "What is left for me in this life? Nothing."

"Many men are happy in idleness," replied James. He shut his eyes. His skin suffered in sunlight and he began to lie back in the shade.

"What shall I do?" asked Robin in despair.

The king opened his eyes and looked at him consideringly. "Go," he said. "Leave me in peace."

Doubting his words, Robin stared at that salty mouth, masked by shadow from the cruel sunlight. At last he rose, and bowed with some ceremony but the king's face remained as impassive as the expressions of the royal beasts, carved in the crumbling stone above the gateway. He walked softly away, his spurs jingling very slightly as he passed between the tall arched bushes. The door was open before him. Royston Heath lay like an animal hide pegged out under the blistering sun, yellow and dry in the unnaturally hot May. The hottest spring, men said, for eight years or so. Robin had no energy to mount his horse but walked her away.

After he had heard the thud of the closing door, James continued to sit within the wall, watching the passage of insects with half closed eyes. He could not walk back to the house. The effort of his coming still disturbed him. His heart flickered like a guttering candle. "Oh God," he said to that Supreme Being with whom he had an especial relationship, both being kings, "Do not let me pass away."

He sat very still until he heard light footsteps on the grass and he knew a page had come to support him from the garden.